THE CHESSBOARD QUEEN

THE
CHESSBOARD
QUEEN

SHARAN NEWMAN

TOR®

A TOM DOHERTY ASSOCIATES BOOK

NEW YORK

THE CHESSBOARD QUEEN

Copyright © 1983, 1997 by Sharan Newman

This book is printed on acid-free paper.

A Tor Book
Published by Tom Doherty Associates, Inc.
175 Fifth Avenue
New York, NY 10010

Tor Books on the World Wide Web:
http://www.tor.com

Tor® is a registered trademark of Tom Doherty Associates, Inc.

Library of Congress Cataloging-in-Publication Data
    Newman, Sharan.
    The chessboard queen.
      1. Lancelot—Romances.   2. Guenevere, Queen—Romances.
    I. Title.
    PS3564.E926C4   1983   813'.54   82-16905
    ISBN 0-312-86391-8

First Tor Edition: November 1997

Printed in the United States of America

0   9   8   7   6   5   4   3   2   1

To Cathy, Kimiko, and Bev
who know what friends are for

THE CHESSBOARD QUEEN

Chapter One

The misty, mysterious coast of Britain had been visible for hours, but to the man who peered at it through a blur of nausea, it did not appear to be getting any nearer. He stumbled back amidship, where his horses, even more ill than he, were hobbled and blindfolded so they could not tell what was happening to them. On his way, the man fell against one of the sailors and mumbled his worry that the island was receding constantly before them. The sailor pushed him away with a sneer.

"Don't be an ass! We've been skirting the coastline to land in Cornwall. It may take us as much as another day with the winds running against us. We'll be tacking all the way there."

"But why can't we land *there*?" the poor passenger moaned, pointing to the tantalizing shore.

"Fine with me, if you want your throat cut by the Saxons. They control the whole southeastern part of Britain now and no ships but their own dare come near it. Now, why don't you stop lurching about in our way and take care of those animals you brought? Phew! What a stink! I'd like to know what you paid the captain to let you bring them aboard. Of all the fool ideas!"

The passenger was small, a full foot shorter than the sailor, and had to listen to his harangue for several more minutes before he could get away. At last he escaped and made it to the small shelter on deck that had been set up for the horses. He entered it and immediately slumped against the flank of the nearest one. He breathed deeply of its familiar odor and felt better, strengthened by the musky scent.

Caet Pretani had not been in Britain for almost six years, not since he had run away from Leodegrance, his master, and begged passage on a trading ship bound for Armorica. Then he had been a boy, frightened, lovesick, and driven by a need to become something great. Now he was a man. He had attached himself to one of the grand families there and worked his way into a position of trust and honor. He had proven himself a dozen times in battles against the Franks and other northmen and made many friends among the British exiles, even the lords, who admired his riding skill and knowledge of horses.

His dark good looks and taciturn manner had also intrigued the women of the lord's house. The fact that he never made any advances to them was fascinating and his shy surprise at their interest very touching. Since he was never such a fool as to offend a lady with rejection, he had learned a great deal about life as well as love from the kind and often lonely women.

Certainly his life had been as successful as his most ambitious dreams. So why was he returning to Britain, to a place that offered him nothing, where he had been born only one generation out of slavery? His friends had tried to keep him. His own lord had offered to make him master of the horse, but he had refused. He had never meant to stay away so long.

"They won't know me, anyway," he reassured himself. "I've changed a lot, broadened in the shoulders if I'm no taller, and the beard should disguise me well enough. Who will remember me as I was then? They hardly looked at me. And I must go back. It's my land much more than theirs and I know things that Arthur doesn't. And she . . . she may need me."

He clutched at the small leather bag around his neck. In it was an amulet, made and blessed for him by his great-grandmother, Flora, and around the amulet were woven five long strands that shone pure gold when he allowed them to lie in the sun. But they were softer than metal and finer than any goldsmith could work. He would not admit that these were the real reason for his return. Whatever happened to him, he had to see her again. Someday there might come a time when she would. . . . He thrust the bag back under his robe. There was no point in thinking it. There were some things that Caet Pretani did not even dare to dream.

At last the ship reached land, anchoring in the lee side of a cove on the Cornish coast. There was no town there, not even a villa, but the ship's master knew that there were traders waiting for him not far inland. The goods he had brought were lowered into boats and rowed ashore. One man stayed to guard them while the others returned for the difficult job of getting the horses back to land.

Caet had assured the captain that this would pose no difficulty. "I've made them each a canvas sling with a hook on the top. They can simply be lowered over the side as you do the other cargo."

With the animals standing placidly at the dock, it had seemed logical. As they were hoisted into the air on the long wooden crane, he wasn't so sure. The nostrils of the first one lowered were flared in terror. As it landed in the rowboat, it snorted and reared. The sailors, who were waiting to row them in, leaped overboard out of the way of the hooves, leaving Caet in the boat alone. He managed to quiet it and released the sling.

The second horse was even more frightened than the first and it had to be carefully placed next to the other to keep the balance even. Caet heard the comments from the men hanging on the side. He tried to ignore them. These animals were precious to him and he was not about to take the suggestions seriously.

When the second horse touched the rocking boat, both of them seemed to go mad. They stamped and plunged in terror and one of them leaped into the sea, kicking a large hole in the side of the boat as it did. Caet jumped in beside it as it floundered and removed the blindfold, allowing the animal to see and swim for the shore. Caet then shouted for someone to unseel the eyes of the remaining horse. One man managed to pull the cloth away as the second animal entered the water, capsizing the boat.

The captain stood in the prow of the ship, shaking his fist in fury and telling Caet in no uncertain terms what his fate would be when he was caught. Caet could not make out the words above the wash of the waves, but he knew that it would be well if he and his mounts were far away by the time the sailors managed to land.

They came ashore somewhat west of the place where the trading goods had been left and so avoided the guards. Caet hurried the horses away from the coast, up a narrow rocky trail. A few hundred yards away, the forest began. Even within its shelter, Caet feared discovery. He led the animals farther into the woods, avoiding the traveled paths for several hours, although he knew they were exhausted from the swim and dangerously cold and wet. Finally, he realized that they could go no farther. He had begun to search for some form of shelter when he smelled a campfire nearby. The thought of warmth drove him to risk investigating it.

He saw only one man, sitting on a log near the fire. His dinner of freshly caught rabbit was sizzling on a spit made of his short sword. Caet peered around, looking for evidence of companions, but there seemed to be no one else. The aroma of the meat reminded him that he hadn't been able to eat anything in the whole three days of the channel crossing. He studied the man. He was big, well muscled, and held himself as if he were used to sudden action. But he was whistling merrily and that decided Caet. He stepped into the clearing, faced the man, and raised his hand in the old salute.

"Hail, friend," he called and his voice sounded as waterlogged as his boots. "I am a fellow traveler, in need of company and a warm fire. Will you share yours?"

The stranger looked up at him and smiled broadly. "Surely, friend, you appear to have waded a river up to your neck. Come and dry yourself. I've a spare cloak in my pack. Wrap yourself in that and lay your things by the fire. There is meat enough for two. I shall be glad of company, but I would be grateful if you would give me your word that you will not entertain me with song. I have journeyed for the last month with one who never stops singing and I am willing to do almost anything else to pass the time."

Caet grinned and began settling his horses and himself. "You needn't fear. I have been told that my voice is preferable only to that of a toad; therefore, I take the hint and only play the part of audience to music."

"An important part and highly underrated. We should get on well. Those are fine animals you have with you. Are you planning to sell them? I know where you could get a fair price."

Caet was busily rubbing down the horses and covering them. Their harnesses and the packs he had tied to them had not been lost. The leather bags had protected the blankets and they were wet only in places. His careful attention displayed how much he loved them.

"They are excellently bred. They will look even better when they are rested and combed. But, no, I had not thought to sell them to anyone. This one, Cheo, is mine. I helped him into the world, set him on his legs, trained him. I could not part with him. The other, Nera, I raised as carefully. She is intended for a lady to ride. I had thought to use them both, perhaps to catch the attention of Arthur the King. I would make Nera a gift to him if he would consider hiring me as part of his court."

The man regarded him with interest. "So, are you one of those who hopes to join Arthur's mysterious Knights of the Round Table? He hasn't officially formed it yet, you know, though hundreds of men have come to him in hopes of being selected. It is said that he is waiting until his new city of Camelot is built, at which time Master Merlin will somehow cause the table to appear from its hiding place. I don't know about that part, but I do know that most of those who come to Arthur are not kept on, but told to search for abandoned homes in towns and villas and rebuild them, to reclaim the lands that have been lost. Nera is beautiful, but I don't think she would be accepted as a bribe. Arthur does not even consider them."

Caet finished covering the horses and stood between them, his arms resting upon their necks. He frowned.

" 'Bribe' is a cruel word, and untrue. I would not shame myself with such a deed. But every man needs something which will help him to stand apart from others and, when one is as small as I, it is not a bad idea to be seen astride a horse of great strength and beauty."

The man shrugged. "Perhaps Arthur will agree with you. What name will you give him when you ride up?"

Caet puzzled for a moment. The man seemed to be giving him a chance to hide his identity. Why? He studied his companion: dirty, with torn trews and scuffed boots. Probably a wanderer of no account. Still. . . .

"My name is Briacu," Caet answered. "I am from Armorica."

The other man held out his hand. "Gawain," he said, "of Cornwall."

They shook hands solemnly. Then Gawain yawned.

"This rabbit must be done by now. Would you care to share it with me? The sun is getting low and I am ready for my dinner."

Caet, now Briacu, was more than ready for his and they spoke little as the small animal was split between them. Gawain leaned back on the log, picking his teeth with a bone splinter. He stared curiously at Caet.

"You don't have the look of one from Armorica," he decided. "You seem more like the oldest ones, the Britains who were here before the Romans."

Caet seemed surprised. "Do I?"

Gawain yawned again. "Autumn is coming. Darkness falls earlier every day." He pulled out blankets from his pack and wrapped himself in them.

"If you want to keep watch tonight, it's fine with me, although there isn't much around to bother us," he murmured tiredly. "We'll talk again in the morning. Good night!"

"But the sun has barely set!" Caet exclaimed. "Do you not wish to share the fire and talk?"

There was no answer from the blankets. Caet knelt by him and tried to shake Gawain into a response, but got nothing but a soft snore for his trouble. He moved to the other side of the fire. Whatever was being said about the old ones and their gods dying out, he was sure from the oddness of the man across from him that there were still many strange creatures left in Britain. He began to wonder if his decision to return had been wise, after all.

Caet awoke early the next morning to find Gawain already about and loading his own horse for travel. He scrambled up, annoyed that this vagabond was going to leave him with no word. Gawain heard the movement and turned to him with a wide smile. The look on Caet's face betrayed his suspicions. Gawain laughed.

"I have stolen nothing from you, friend Briacu. As a matter of fact, you seem to have nothing to steal. And, if you don't mind making a meal of cold meat and stale bread, you are more than welcome to share them and to accompany me to Caerleon."

"Caerleon?" Caet echoed, still not fully awake. "What is there? Do you have business there?"

Gawain laughed again. "I may be given some when I arrive. My aunt and uncle live there and I intend to visit them for a while. When the days grow short, I prefer to make my bed by a warm hearth, tended by friends. And if you still mean to submit yourself to Arthur, then that is your direction, too. He keeps winter court at Caerleon."

Caet pulled himself up and realized that his horses had been loaded and were ready to leave. What an irritating fellow this Gawain was! Why should he assume that Caet would go with him? Still, Caet wasn't sure that he remembered the roads in this part of Britain and he had never been as far west as Caerleon. He could look on the man as simply a guide. He had a few coins sewn into the belt of his trews. When they reached Caerleon, he could pay the man off and that way end the relationship. If the man truly had family at Caerleon, he wouldn't need to presume upon the acquaintanceship. Oh, how Caet's body ached! Fortunately, the muscles used in riding were not the ones he had exercised aboard ship. But his legs were still weak and his insides raw from retching. He took the food Gawain held out and ate it quickly, then wrapped up his meager pack and climbed onto his horse. The familiarity of the mount beneath him eased his anxiety, but he longed to reach the court of Arthur, to place his gift before the Queen and, this time, to serve her with honor.

Guinevere loved Caerleon. It was old, Roman, and comfortable. It had been the permanent headquarters of the Second Augusta for two hundred years and the legion had wanted the best when it was home. But all the soldiers had been called away, almost a hundred years before, withdrawn by a terrified emperor to help support his crumbling throne. Or had they gone with one of the British generals who claimed the purple, like Macson Wledig? Guinevere could never remember. But they had gone and the fortress at Caerleon had lain empty, lonely, haunted, perhaps. Until Arthur had remembered it and set to work to restore it as his winter capital, it had been just another enigmatic relic of a greater age. Arthur had seen it with the same military viewpoint the first centurions must have had. The strategic reason for building it had not changed. It lay at the mouth of the Usk river, cloaked by hills and fog. The Usk valley drifted farther west to Brecon, should retreat become necessary. One of the finest of the Romans' roads stretched almost intact to the east and the heart of the Saxons' territory. Caerleon was easily defended and well built.

The last was all that concerned Guinevere. It was a wonderful home. Everything was there: living quarters designed for various ranks, granaries, kitchens, workshops, and bathhouses, two of which were still in working order. The rooms were solid and warm. And in the valley below there was a town which had somehow managed to survive the abandonment of the legion. Guinevere leaned over the edge of the tower to admire it again. Just a few streets lay below, but it was neatly planned, with a forum in the center and a church at the far end of the main road. There were even shops there! Guinevere had never been to a town except for her marriage in London, and shops amazed and delighted her. People living down there made pots and pewterware and wove cloth and baked sweet cakes. She could wander through the shops and choose whatever she wanted. On her father's estate these things had been done to order, often by itinerant craftsmen.

There had been little chance to select. Here whole families worked at their trades and grew in skill from childhood. It was wonderful to go down there and wander through the forum, hearing the sellers' cries, watching a juggler or tumbler. Since Arthur had brought business back again, the old roadhouse had been refurbished, with public baths behind. When emissaries began to come, they would know that they were not dealing with some upstart general, but a real king.

Guinevere sighed. She pushed a lock of hair behind her ear. It was a perfect capital. Why then was Arthur still intent on building another city, where none had ever been before? This was so lovely and so suitable. Why was he obsessed by Camelot? He had tried to explain to her many times. "I must have a place that is mine, that no other lord has set his mark upon. I will not be lost among the hundreds of rulers, names on a list in a saga, nothing more than a row of candles in which, if one be blown out, the light would not diminish. There must be a sign for the ages to come that Arthur ruled here, that my dreams did not simply flow into thousands of others and drown. Camelot will be my city, the symbol of all that I am trying to accomplish in Britain. And it is there that I will set the Round Table."

She could hear him now, even above the wind and the calls of the birds. She couldn't understand it. He was a great king, why should it matter where? Dimly she felt that his need for a visible manifestation of his reign was somehow tied to her and her failure. Five years they had been married and still they had no children. Guinevere did not wish to think of that. It embarrassed her that so many people had such a vital interest in the workings of her body. And it angered her that she had done nothing she knew of to deserve such divine punishment. She knew it was her duty to provide Arthur with children and, though she hadn't cared much for the process, she had obeyed as best she could. But nothing had happened. They had consulted doctors, witches, oracles, and priests, but no one could help them. Although Arthur swore that they were still young and he had not given up hope, he had become more and more determined to build his city as each month passed. He was at Camelot now, checking plans and inspecting the work with Merlin. They were both probably totally happy.

Guinevere shivered and pulled her cloak more tightly about her. Then she threw it open and leaned dangerously over the edge of the tower. Had she seen it? Yes! She was sure. A blaze of yellow and an old checked cloak. Gawain was back! At last, someone to play with. She waved to him, but he was too far away to notice her. He and a companion were picking their way through the vendors, leading another horse behind theirs. Who was that with him? Not Geraldus. Guinevere knew his old nag from any distance and this man rode a horse as strong and elegant as any she had seen. Perhaps he was one of those come to try for a place in Arthur's special cadre. "The Knights of the Round Table" had sounded very silly when she had first heard Arthur explain it. What was a knight, anyway? But she had finally agreed that Arthur had been right. As soon as men heard that it was a select group of the best Britain could offer, they came from all over the island to attempt to gain admittance. Even the sons of some of the lesser kings, who refused to recognize Arthur as overlord, appeared at Caerleon, willing to relinquish their inheritances to become knights. There were even some who came, not from Britain, but from Armorica and even farther east. How they had heard of Arthur, she didn't know, but they swarmed to Caerleon and to London, begging for a chance to see him. Now Gawain was bringing another. Guinevere wondered idly where he had come from. Odd. There was something familiar about the way he sat on his horse. Could he have visited her family before she married? Oh, well. It didn't matter. Why was Gawain taking so long? He could have come up the side road, bypassed the town, and been there by now. The riders finally disappeared into the shadow of the fort. Finally he was coming to the gates. Guinevere picked up her skirts and ran down joyfully to meet him.

Caet was becoming annoyed. This man clearly intended to accompany him all the way to the presence of Arthur. He had been grateful for the company on the road, but had tried to let him know when they came in sight of the fortress that his services were no longer needed. He didn't want to be seen with some craftsman's son, not when he had spent so long in covering the stigma of his birth. Gawain continued to lead the way through the town. Caet kept hoping that he would stop at some shop or other to greet his relatives. But, no, he ambled through the streets, tossing greetings to the tradesmen and receiving enthusiastic welcomes from an amazing number of pretty women. It was increasingly embarrassing. Caet tried once more to rid himself of his guide. He eased his horse forward until they were nearly parallel.

"I am grateful to you for taking me so far. Thank you. But there is no need for you to accompany me any longer. You must be eager to see your aunt and uncle."

Gawain grinned wickedly. "I am. My dear old aunt especially simply dotes on me. You needn't worry. You aren't taking me out of my way at all."

They were almost at the entrance to the fortress. Caet tried to pull back so that it would not appear that they were together.

"Who's at the gate today?" Gawain peered up at the watchtower. "Joelin? Yes, it is. Halloo! Joelin! You should keep better watch than that. We haven't even been challenged!"

They were at the gates. The guard beamed at Gawain and laughed. "If I had missed you, Lord Gawain, I'd be replaced by nightfall. I've been watching you since you started up the main road. Welcome back! The King is at Camelot with Master Merlin, but they are expected home soon. The Queen is somewhere about. I'll have her told you're here."

Gawain laughed back and pointed behind the guard at a gold and blue figure streaking toward them. "No need, Joelin."

Caet looked up sharply. He caught his breath with such suddenness that he nearly choked. Guinevere! She had not aged or changed at all, though her radiance was more intense. And she was running toward him! It was a wonder beyond his dreams. He dismounted and began to move toward her. Then, with an icy shock, he realized that she didn't even see him. It was Gawain she was running toward. He was stabbed by his bitterness, sharper than ever because he thought he had conquered it. Nothing had changed. There he was standing by the horses, invisible to everyone as she was swept into someone else's arms. Gawain was swinging her around as they both laughed and babbled like children. Caet felt as sick now as he had on the ship.

"Gawain," Guinevere was gasping, "put me down now! Show me some respect!"

"Very well." He set her on the ground, went back several paces, and approached again, bowing and fumbling in the manner of so many of the hopeful knights.

She started laughing again. "Oh, Gawain, it is so good to have you back. Will you stay the winter? Will Geraldus be with us, too? When are your brothers coming? Where did you get those wonderful horses?"

"Yes, yes, in the spring or summer and these horses are not mine. They belong to this man, Briacu. I met him on the road. He has come from Armorica to join Arthur, he says."

Guinevere turned her gaze from the horses to the man. Caet was startled at suddenly being noticed and made his best bow to hide a moment before he showed his face. She smiled, but there was no recognition in her glance. He was not sure if he was relieved or sorry.

"Briacu?" she asked. He nodded. "Those are magnificent animals. If they are an example of your skill at breeding and raising horses, I'm sure my husband will be delighted to welcome you to Caerleon and will certainly find a place for you here. Please join us. He will return in a few days' time. I'm sure we can find room for you among the soldiers until he decides your position."

He mumbled something in reply and hoped it was correct. He stood awkwardly, one hand still holding the reins, not certain what to do next.

"Auntie, would you like me to show Briacu where he can stable his excellent horses and leave his belongings?" Gawain asked.

"Yes. I will expect you both at dinner. Oh, and Gawain, stop calling me 'Auntie'!"

She turned her back on them and swept away with mock dignity.

Amidst many confusing impressions, it slowly dawned on Caet that he had been made a fool of by his ragged traveling companion. Even worse, he realized that it was partially his own fault for making assumptions. This on top of everything else made him furious and he stomped after Gawain with a firm idea of rubbing his face in the dirt.

"Why didn't you tell me you knew the Queen?" he whispered savagely.

Gawain grinned and shrugged. "I don't like to flaunt my rich relations before my friends."

Caet refused to be pacified. "Don't tell me she's your aunt. You are almost as old as she is."

"She is my aunt, my irritated friend, because she married my uncle, who is somewhat younger than his sister, my mother. Is that clear enough or must I give you the whole family tree? Look, I'm sorry. I didn't mean to startle you like that. I apologize. All right? You may as well know that I have no intention of fighting you. It's too late in the day for me to win and in the morning I might kill you without meaning to. So why don't we just forget the whole thing and be friends?"

He held out his hand. Grudgingly Caet extended his. He reminded himself that Gawain could not have known how deeply he had been hurt. After all Gawain was not the only one who had been secretive about his past.

Guinevere did not take her dinner in the hall with the rest of the residents, but Gawain took Caet to her rooms. She greeted them eagerly.

"I don't like to eat in the hall when Arthur isn't here," she explained. "It's noisy and rough there and I think that the soldiers and their ladies are uncomfortable with me watching them. It's really much nicer to eat in my room, but lonely."

Gawain sat next to her and squeezed her hand.

"Arthur will be back soon. He can't continue his building much longer unless Master Merlin has found a way to hold back the winter. Geraldus will be with us in a month or two. He had to go visit Mark and Alswytha first. There was a summons from Alswytha, not to Geraldus, he said, but to his 'green lady.' She wanted to borrow her for a while. Does that mean anything to you?"

Guinevere laughed. "Yes, I know the green lady well. I hadn't thought of her as a midwife, but she is probably very comforting. So, Alswytha is having another baby."

Gawain remembered too late that Guinevere would not care to hear about other people's babies. He hastily switched the conversation to stories of his recent travels. Guinevere seemed to enjoy them and asked questions which spun the tales even longer. Things seemed to happen to Gawain, especially when he became involved with women. No one ever seemed to take him seriously enough to get hurt, but his lifelong problem of falling sound asleep from sunset to dawn and then becoming progressively stronger until noon, when he began weakening again, tended to cause confusion among those who did not know him well. Usually stories about him furnished much of the amusement during winter tale-telling.

It was nearly sunset when Gawain rose to leave. Caet had been silent most of the afternoon and thought Guinevere had not even noticed him. He got up to accompany Gawain. But Guinevere held out her hand to him and asked him to stay a minute.

"I did not have a chance to ask you about your horses. Would you mind telling me something about them now?"

Gawain was starting to nod.

"You'll excuse me if I don't wait for you. I can almost hear my bed calling. I hope I have time to get there. If you should trip over me on your way out, Briacu, I would appreciate a pillow and a blanket."

When he had gone, Caet became nervous again. Now that he had had time to study her, he realized that Guinevere had changed. Her body had finished maturing. She had reached her full height and was now taller than he, but she was more beautiful than ever and her eyes held the same innocent joy that had conquered him when they both had been children. She questioned him about the horses: where he had gotten them, how he had fed and trained them. He relaxed as he spoke with assurance on a topic he knew well. It wasn't until he was ready to leave that she shattered all his hard-earned composure.

"Caet. Why did you run away?" she asked.

He stumbled on a crack in the floor.

"My lady, you have made a mistake."

She ignored him. "Father and mother were very worried about you. Father couldn't trace you anywhere and you sent no word for so long."

"I tell you, I don't know what you are saying. I do not know your family!"

She drew a chain from inside her dress. "I still have the pearl you sent me, see? Didn't you get my answer? Arthur made me a chain for it. I am never without it."

The sight of the lustrous pearl did make him pause. It had cost him dearly in pride and honor and, seeing it again, he felt a flush of shame rush through him. He wondered if she would treasure it if she knew what he had done to get it.

"But she has worn it all this time," he thought. "It has lain on her skin, near her heart. She has cleansed and redeemed it. I can regret nothing."

He said only, "It is lovely, my lady, but my name is not Caet and I know nothing of such a gift. May I go now?"

She looked puzzled as she put the jewel back beneath the cloth. "I will call you Briacu if that is what you wish. But I do not understand. Yes. You may go."

Caet walked back to the sleeping area, where he had left his possessions. Snores indicated that Gawain had managed to make his way to bed. It was early, but Caet had no wish to join those in the main hall who were drinking and talking. He unrolled his bedding and lay down. He was awake when the sound of the voices drifted from shouts and laughter to murmurs and then silence. Even when the night was still, he continued to gaze into the darkness, wide-eyed with worry. Guinevere hadn't believed him. What if she told Arthur? Would the king accept a runaway servant as a knight or even a horsemaster? Would he let him stay at all? He gave the bag of odd clothes he used as a pillow one last punch and settled down. He could only wait.

* * *

Arthur was not one for waiting. It was taking all of Merlin's persuasion to keep him from setting out for Caerleon that evening.

"I want to see Guinevere!" Arthur complained. "If I start now, I can be there in two days."

"Only if you kill your horse, Arthur."

"I can change horses on the way, Merlin."

Arthur controlled himself with an effort. After all, he was the king now. He could not indulge in anger. He must put duty before his feelings. But he had had enough.

"Merlin, I have been frustrated at every turning all the time we have been here. 'I'm sorry, Your Majesty, the floors will not lay smoothly. We cannot build the fortifications; we always hit water. We cannot put baths on the top of the tor; the water is too far down.' No one remembers how to work a pump, how to lay tile, how to erect a building of more than two stories. We don't even know how to mix mortar! Merlin, how can we have forgotten how to stick stones together?"

"Arthur. . . ."

"And now you tell me to sit here another night and stare at what cannot be done when all I want to do is go home to my wife! I have been gone a month, Merlin."

Merlin shrugged. "There are many women here, my King. Your father would have made do."

Arthur slammed the plans he had been holding hard upon the ground. The roll tore across. He began fastening his breastplate and then his cloak, his fingers fumbling in his fury.

"My father did not have a wife like mine, Merlin. No man ever has! You can pack our things and follow me in the morning. I'm leaving now!"

"Arthur!" Merlin called. "You can't ride alone. You are the King!"

But Arthur was already mounted.

"Not tonight, Merlin. Tonight I am no man and I am going home. I will be King again at Caerleon! Good-bye, Merlin!"

He was gone.

Merlin pounded his fist into the nearest tree, then cursed himself; it hurt. Camelot would never be finished as long as

Guinevere held Arthur's attention. He could put his mind to work only when she was within reach or when he knew she was safe and away from whatever fighting there might be. And what had he, Merlin, the great wizard, become since Arthur's marriage? A lackey, picking up the scattered belongings of his master. Savagely he stooped for the torn roll of plans. He had waited and worked too long to have it all ruined by one selfish woman. He was so tired. He would be glad when it was over for him and he could at least rest with a calm mind. He studied a bit of the ripped scroll. It would be built. It was going to be a magnificent fortress, a city in the clouds. Guinevere could not stop it for long.

It was an hour before dawn two days later. Guinevere slept soundly. Beside the bed a candle glowed. She always had light by her when she slept alone. In a dream she heard the sound of a horse galloping through the town below and racing to the gates. Then there was a rush of air as if the horse had taken wing and flown through her window. She opened her eyes.

There stood Arthur, muddy, sweaty, too tired to unclasp his cloak. He stared at her as if she were the dream. Guinevere smiled and held out her arms.

"Welcome home," she said. "Let me help you."

Chapter Two

The Lake was calm; only an occasional ripple crossed its surface. It stretched for nearly a mile in the heart of the forest. It was pristine and beautiful. But no bird lit on its surface; no deer drank from its rim; no man tried to pull fish from its waters. The clouds and stars were purely reflected as they gazed down upon it, but the Lake gave nothing of itself to the picture. What lay below the water could not be seen. Travelers, far lost in the woods, told strange stories of dazzling horsemen who galloped across the surface, but caused no splash or spray, and who simply vanished as they approached the center of the lake.

Far beneath the water, in a glittering palace of light and flowers, the Lady waited, and schemed.

The Lady had no name that she knew of, no childhood, no family. She had lived with her retinue within the Lake for thousands of years, so many that she had forgotten the order of the humans and others who had arrived, passed by, and gone on. For the most part, she didn't care. She knew that she and her followers were immortal. Why or what they had once been, whether gods dispossessed or angels gone to seed, concerned her not at all. Eternity had brought only boredom with a few brief interludes of interest. When something happened it was important to the Lady to make it last as long as possible. Now the only important thing was Lancelot.

Twenty-five years before, only a moment it seemed, the Lady had ridden with her men and ladies to hunt an invisible deer, whose skin would have made a most interesting coat. They had ridden far and become separated. The Lady had early lost interest in the chase and had been about to return when she noticed the flutter of some fine cloth on the ground not far away. Curious, she decided to inspect it.

She dismounted and came nearer to examine it. The silk wafted around the base of a tree. It seemed to be attached to something. The Lady circled to the other side, where she stopped. At the root of the tree lay a woman, deeply asleep. Her face was ashen and taut with fear, grief, exhaustion, and starvation. Her clothes were torn and grimy, but finely made of the best materials. Next to her lay a child, the most beautiful creature the Lady had ever seen. He had clearly been kept alive at the woman's expense for he was round and healthy and his sleep was that of a normal infant.

The Lady was enchanted. What a wonderful discovery! He was so new and unmarked, so full of possibilities. Life for her was terribly monotonous, one century almost the same as the last. The only interesting encounter she had had recently was with a man named Merlin. She had engaged him in a duel of wits, which she was delighted to lose. As a prize, she had given him a sword that had been lying around for centuries. He had been a very attractive young man, more alert than most humans, and she had enjoyed other exchanges with him. But still, one could have that any time. She regarded the baby curled trustingly in the woman's arms. This was so much more provocative! Who knew what he might become— and she might have all the fun of teaching him and watching him develop. His present keeper looked at the point of death, anyway.

Without another thought for the haggard, sleeping woman, the Lady snatched the infant from her arms and sped back to her horse.

The woman awoke as the Lady was remounting, the child clasped tightly in her arms. For a moment she was confused and that was all the time the Lady needed. She rode off to the sound of the woman's anguished screams.

"Where are you taking him? My baby! My son! Lancelot! Please, come back! Someone, please, help me!"

She fell on the ground, coughing and gagging on her tears, too spent to follow any further.

The Lady never looked back.

She brought her find to her attendants, who were as delighted as she. They set the child down on the floor and watched it. He was able to sit up, after a fashion, but would fall over if he leaned too far in any direction. He had been crying constantly since the Lady had stolen him, but when he was set down, he stopped. His eyes bulged, his face turned red; he grunted and a pungent smell arose from him. Then he relaxed and lay on the floor, kicking and sucking his thumb.

That was the first of their problems. Once they had cleaned him, they discovered that they didn't know what to feed him. Babies didn't seem to enjoy normal food. He choked on bread, threw up wine and ale, tried to put nutmeats in his nose. He did manage to suck a piece of venison white, but it soon became clear to the Lady and her followers that their new toy would die if they couldn't take better care of it.

It was Adon, one of the retainers, who finally suggested that they break with tradition and go into the nearest town to see if someone there knew about the management of infants. So, he and several men were sent to knock on doors and ask about child care.

Lancelot was howling again, this time with hunger and diaper rash, when they returned. The Lady sent for Adon to report at once.

"Well?" she demanded. "What have you found? Quickly! What must we do?"

Adon shook his head. "You will never believe it, Mistress, the trouble it takes. First of all, we discovered that a child of his age will take only milk."

"Milk? How odd! Nimuë, send for a cow and a flagon."

Adon looked slightly embarrassed, a new sensation for him.

"No, Mistress, that is apparently not the way they do it. It seems that the child's mother must provide the milk, or another woman who has recently given birth."

"Are you sure? How will we ever manage that?"

"I am quite sure. I questioned several people on the matter. All of them were surprised that I did not know this and I could tell they guessed that I was not one of them, for they removed themselves quickly after we had spoken and some barred their doors against me."

He waited a minute while she pondered his information.

"I had no further instructions, but I did not want to return without an answer. I hope I have done the correct thing."

He glanced over his shoulder. From the anteroom behind him terrified screams could be heard, mixed with mewling whines. Adon nodded to two other men. They left and returned dragging a young woman, who continued her howling as she clutched a bundle tightly to her.

"What is this?" The Lady was annoyed. "I didn't ask you to bring me another one."

Adon tried to explain over the din. "We found her on the road. Her family has turned her out because of this."

He pulled at the rags covering the bundle and a tiny hand appeared.

"She can feed Lancelot and her own, too, if she wishes. No one will miss her. Perhaps she can even show us how to keep him from soiling himself so much."

The Lady considered this. The woman was dirty and ragged, but apparently healthy and strong. It was hard to tell through her terror if she had any intelligence, but there would be time to discover that. There seemed no other choice.

"Bring her to me!" The men pulled the woman forward. "Stop shrieking, girl! Listen to me. We have a baby here that needs tending. If you can keep him alive and care for him, we will feed you, clothe you, and let you keep that child of yours with you. If you won't, then we will kill you. Which would you prefer?"

Someone brought Lancelot over to her. He was clearly older than her own child and curious about them both. He held out his arms to her and smiled. She stared at him with dull eyes. Then she reached out timidly and touched him.

"This is a human child?" she stammered, still stroking Lancelot's arm.

"Yes, of course, or we would not need you."

"I may keep my son, Torres?"

"If you must. As long as Lancelot does not suffer for it."

The woman looked from her child to Lancelot and back. She had expected to die, anyway, when her father sent her from home. His anger had terrified her. How could she have known that he had been planning to marry her to a man with wealth enough to support them all? From somewhere, she smelled food.

She nodded to the Lady and took Lancelot with her free arm, balancing him on her hip.

"I will take him," she announced. "I will care for him as I do my Torres. May I have something to eat now? I am very hungry."

"So is he," the Lady replied. "Feed him first and we will bring you food."

The woman was too worn to argue. She sank to the floor, set Torres in the folds of her skirt, and pulled back the opening of her dress, oblivious to the group around her watching closely. Lancelot began at once to paw at her, arching his back and twisting his head to reach her breast. She adjusted him and he latched onto her, sucking noisily. The woman stroked his head.

"When did he last eat?" she demanded. She seemed to have accepted the situation and was asserting her authority as an expert among novices.

"I don't know," Nimuë answered. "A day ago, perhaps, except for the meat juice he sucked."

"He is starving," the woman stated with indignation. "I must have good food if he is to thrive. Where is your nursery?"

"Our what?"

"The place for the babies to sleep and play."

Adon leaped to attention. "We have prepared a place. I will take you there at once." He scooped up the other baby. "No, I will not hurt him. I am inhuman, but not insensitive. Follow me."

As they left, the Lady turned to Nimuë. Her eyes were glowing with excitement. "What do you think, my dear, of this new game of ours?"

Nimuë laughed. "I think it should keep us amused for a long time."

The raising of children was even more enthralling than the Lady had imagined. She was soon glad that they had allowed Meredydd to keep Torres with her. Playing and fighting together, the two boys were far more entertaining than one would have been. As they grew and began to walk and speak, it was clear that they had two very different personalities. Torres seemed to fit in naturally with the relaxed pattern of life beneath the water. Despite the fact that Meredydd became more and more gloomy and forbidding as the years passed, her son never worried. He laughed when he missed the mark with his arrows, cheered Lancelot from the ground when the stronger boy had bested him, and enlivened dinner with his attempts to balance full wine cups on his head or do handsprings over the tables.

Meredydd tried to teach him the hard facts of life, which

were embodied in her own grim and rather garbled version of Christianity. Torres would sit listening patiently to her, smiling until he dozed off. He humored her, but paid no attention. Life was not dangerous and forbidding. Who had hurt him? He saw no disease or suffering. He had never felt either. His mother was very dear to him, but her ideas were sadly mistaken. Adon often thought that if Torres had not been brought to the Lady, he would have come to her himself.

But Lancelot! Adon sighed whenever he thought of him. He could not imagine the kind of man who could sire such a son. Lancelot had taken his first steps as he was to do everything—purposefully. He hadn't wobbled a few feet and then fallen, but pulled himself up and trudged unwaveringly, his eyes glued to the toy he wanted lying on the other side of the room. There was a fierce intensity about him that would not allow for his own failure. Adon remembered the first riding lesson. Torres had laughed and slid on the broad back of his horse and soon demanded to be gotten down. Lancelot had gripped his horse tightly with his short legs, sat painfully erect, and refused to dismount until he had not walked but galloped across the field and back. He had been exhausted and sore for many days, but the next time they allowed him up he had done the same thing, and the next time and the next. Everyone admitted that Lancelot was the best horseman among them now. It would have taken a whirlwind to unseat him. But what was the use of that? When would he ever need to face a whirlwind? It was the same with everything he was taught: archery, swordsmanship, gymnastics, music. He had to know everything about the discipline and he applied himself single-mindedly until he mastered it perfectly. There was no living with him until he did.

And yet, if he gave himself so completely to learning, he also brought the same intensity to caring. Everyone he knew mattered to him. He listened to people and remembered what they cared for most. He worried about them. He inquired after their health, even though no one but he and Meredydd had ever been sick. And perhaps because it was clear to them all that his life would never be easy or perhaps because it was new to them to be loved, they all loved him, too. Emotions of any depth were foreign to them and they were almost ashamed of caring so; but, as he grew older, the decision of what to do with Lancelot was the main concern, not only of the Lady, but of all the inhabitants of the Lake.

Meredydd was concerned about him, too. She had failed in her duty to Torres, but in Lancelot she found a more apt pupil for her convictions. Meredydd was certain that life was simply a series of traps and pitfalls laid for unwary Man to fall into sin and torment. Most of these traps were sprung with no warning and could not be avoided. The only way to counter this was by continual atonement—not only for the wrong one had already done, but for the horrible sin one might commit tomorrow. Cruelty, selfishness, and avarice were not prevalent under the Lake and Meredydd made little of these. But hedonism, voluptuousness, sloth, and carnal behavior were, in her eyes, rampant among the Lake people. Meredydd had been made to suffer so for her one night of pleasure at the wrong time of the moon that she was convinced that sex must be the one unpardonable sin. She drummed this idea into Lancelot from childhood, encouraging him in his physical excesses so that his body would be too worn out to pay attention to the seductiveness of the wanton ladies of the court. She reminded him that it was she who had saved him with her milk when the Lady would have let him die. She continually reviled "those disgusting fiends" who had kidnapped her.

The taunts and slurs amused the people of the Lake. They found Meredydd rather pathetic. But Lancelot trusted her and became terribly bewildered. He could not believe that any of the people who raised him could be evil, but he would not doubt what Meredydd told him.

Gradually Lancelot began to work out his own version of what he had been taught. He knew for certain that the Lady, Adon, Nimuë, Torres, Meredydd—everyone he loved—were good. They could not be otherwise simply because he loved them so. If the Lady and her people sinned, it was only through ignorance. But they seemed so happy in their innocence that he could not bear to destroy it. Yet he could not let them drift to the torments of hell. Meredydd had been vague about the nature of punishments meted out to sinners, but she knew the story of the Crucifixion and was dimly aware that Christ had died to atone for someone's sins, although they did not seem to be hers. Her doctrine was that of personal culpability with no chance of intercession.

Lancelot could not believe that.

"I love them," he reasoned, "and I wish to bear their punishment for them. Why should I not be permitted to give myself for them?"

Lancelot resolved to make atonement in the only ways he knew. He went without eating, slept on the floor, beat himself with sticks, all in secret. The Lady could not understand why he was becoming so weak and pale until one day she was awakened by muffled screams of anguish coming from behind the stables.

Everyone else slept, but the Lady roused Adon to come with her. She rushed in near panic to the source of the noise.

She did not know until that moment how much she adored him. He was crouched in the corner of a stall, trying, with a rock in one hand, to drive a nail into his other palm. He had pushed it nearly through and was conscious only through force of will. For the first time in memory, she completely lost control.

"Lancelot!" she screamed. "Oh, my precious, my dearest, why? How can you do this?"

She wept as she gathered him in her arms, trying to pull the nail out and force him to give up the tightly clenched rock. As blood poured from the wound, she laid her hand over his and called on powers which she rarely dared to touch to stop the flow and numb the pain. Lancelot was hysterical, partly from agony and partly from fear that he would be stopped before he had managed to accomplish his mission.

"Adon! Stop her! Please, my Lady! Let me go! You must let me! I must! I can't let anything happen to you! No, don't! You don't understand!"

"Lancelot, my darling child! Of course I don't understand. How could you do this to yourself? Don't you see how it hurts and frightens us? You must promise never to try anything like this again." The Lady's voice was still shaking and there were tears on her cheeks.

"Please, Lancelot." Adon's voice was also unsteady. "You are mistaken. Nothing will happen to us. Nothing ever has. What did you think you were saving us from?"

Lancelot stared at his palm. The wound was still open, but the blood had stopped flowing. The driving agony was gone, replaced by a dull ache. He searched the face of the Lady. There was no comprehension in it, only concern. He wondered if they would laugh at him. Probably. How could they know that they were on the edge of the abyss and that only he was working to pull them back? He shook his head.

"I can't explain it, Lady. I'm sorry."

"Then we must insist that you never try to harm yourself again, not in any way." Adon's voice was firm.

Lancelot was defeated. "I promise, but I wish. . . . All right, I promise."

Adon carried him to his room and gave him a sleeping draught. Then he returned to the Lady.

"Do you think he is safe?" she asked.

"Have you ever known him to break his word?"

"No, but I am afraid for him. What do you think he was attempting?"

"I am not sure, but I can guess that somehow Meredydd is at the core of it. We should question her tomorrow. I will watch by Lancelot's bed tonight."

"You said he was in no danger," the Lady said in alarm.

"He isn't. But somehow I feel the need to watch. Good night, my Lady."

Lancelot made no more attempts to damage himself, but that incident made it clear to everyone that their toy was turning into something that they did not comprehend and could not control. Some weeks later Adon and the Lady were still trying to decide what to do with him.

"We can't let him out into the world," Adon fretted. "How would he react to the misery of lives out there?"

"I don't know." The Lady paced up and down in her private room. The softness of the furnishings and the gentle waver of candlelight on diamonds did not help to ease her nervousness.

"There is nothing we can do to prevent his going out there. There are rules in these matters. Before he can choose, he must know what the choices are. But how can we teach him about humans? We hardly understand them, ourselves. If we had, we might have realized what Meredydd was doing to him. Oh, how I wish we had killed her the day those boys were weaned!"

Adon sighed and stretched out on the bed. "Well, we didn't. Our ignorance kept us from wanting to take all the responsibility for their welfare. If we cannot make him wise, at least we can be sure he is strong. He must be able to fight his own battles out there. He is sure to find them. It won't be hard to train him. He can already beat any man here in fair competition. For the rest . . . he will have to discover that himself."

"But we can't just take him to the shore of the Lake and abandon him!" Her pacing was becoming staccato. "We must find a place to send him, or someone to care for him."

Adon was starting to get impatient. He enjoyed his turns with the Lady and did not want the evening ruined before it began.

"What about that man who was here, when was it? Not long before you found Lancelot."

She paused to think. "What man? I don't remember. Oh, wait! Yes. Merlin, the one who so wanted that old sword. There was something about him. I think perhaps he was a blend, one of the others as well as human. Do you think he would still be alive?"

"If he used the sword properly, he might be."

"It's an idea." She finally seemed to remember why he was there. She smiled in amusement. "My poor Adon, it's your night, isn't it? And you let me neglect you!"

She bent over him and let him slide her down to the bed. But she had one more request before she waved the lights out.

"Adon?"

"Hmmm?"

"Can you send someone to find out what has become of that Merlin?"

"Certainly, my Lady. In the morning."

But time was inexact under the Lake. If Lancelot and Torres had not continued to mature, the denizens would not have even noticed its passing. It was more than two years before any information came about Merlin and then Adon sent the messengers out again to find out about Arthur. While they were gone, he forgot the matter completely. So Lancelot passed his twentieth birthday and still no decision had been made about his future. He had been amenable to any lessons they gave him and outwardly showed no more inclination for self-torture. He never went above the surface of the Lake except to hunt, and then always accompanied. He seemed content enough most of the time. But the Lady could see that he had now reached his full growth. She knew she could not delay much longer. Every time she was with him she sensed the tension and wild determination that were consuming him. They both puzzled and excited her. If only he did not lose that magnificent fierceness before he returned. It would be such a wonderful change! She shivered at the prospect. It was so pointless to send him to his own kind first. She hated to risk losing him. If only she could remember who had made all those binding rules. No, it was too long ago. Perhaps she had never known. But she certainly knew what would happen if she broke them.

She cursed silently as she watched him stride across the yard below her window, barely reined energy in every step. And so beautiful!

"Where are you going, Lancelot?" she called abruptly.

"To get venison for your dinner, my Lady!" he shouted back. "Torres and Caomh and Riogh are coming with me. We will return before dark."

He waved to her and hurried off to meet the others.

"Well," she thought, "if hunting makes him happy, we must let him hunt. But we must do something soon. I am getting extremely weary of venison every night."

Lancelot had found a horse whose desire to be active

matched his own. It was a fine, tall white stallion with delicate legs. He named it Clades. Today the horse pranced beneath him, eager to be above the water and free to run.

Hunting mattered very little to Lancelot. He knew the larder was full of meat. It was the wind on his face, forcing him back, the speed of the horse beneath him, the near-independence that he craved. He had long ago given up trying to explain himself to anyone or even to understand the thing that was driving him. But he was sure that the Lake was not where he belonged. There was something calling him out there, something he must do or become. Even if Meredydd were wrong about sin and consequences, as Adon insisted, there had to be more to life than banquets and bed. Perhaps the immortals were meant to live that way, but he was human and must have a purpose. He no longer tortured his body for imagined transgressions. Now his mind provided the pain unasked for.

He looked over his shoulder. The others were falling behind. Nothing drove them. They were never hungry. They slowed and Riogh signalled him to stop for a rest. Immediately he pretended to have spotted something just out of their range.

"A deer!" he yelled to them. "A stag, I think! Can't lose him now! Follow my trail!"

He did not wait for an answer, but plunged on, deeper into the forest. A moment later, he thought he did see something. There was a movement, a gleam, from something in the brush. Perhaps it was a young buck or doe tangled in the thicket. Lancelot reined in Clades and turned toward the confusion of undergrowth. As they neared it, Clades became more and more nervous. His eyes rolled and showed the whites and his nostrils flared. About ten feet from the thicket he stopped completely and refused to move.

"What's wrong with you?" Lancelot laughed. "What do you think you smell? A bear? Maybe a dragon? That would be fun for a change."

He dismounted and drew his sword. His heart was thumping erratically. Never before had he been allowed to face danger alone. The brush had accumulated in a small hollow and he had to bend to push it aside. The depression itself was covered by vines which had been torn, perhaps by something which had fallen among them. He heard a sound coming from beneath, a scuffle as of something trying to escape without success. Still holding his sword, Lancelot carefully lifted the vines with his left hand. He gasped as the sudden light blinded him. He threw his arm over his eyes and then steadied himself to look again.

The light was dimmer now, flickering occasionally. He could bear to look at it. Poor beast! Where could it have come from? What must it have endured to arrive at such a state! It was nearly starved and there were scratches and welts all over its body.

Lancelot bent over the dying animal. He had no name for it: horselike but smaller, with tiny cloven hooves and a silky white beard. The radiance about it frightened him, but he also felt drawn to it in pity and wonder. He gave a cry of amazement when he saw what was upon the animal's forehead. An opalescent spiral of lavender and blue arose from the center. It was obviously a natural part of the creature, but now it seemed to be too much for the frail thing to carry.

He stretched his arm toward it slowly, longing to caress it. The animal made a futile attempt to pull away, but it was far too weak. Lancelot waited and began to speak to it soothingly as he would to any hurt thing.

"Easy, all right, don't worry," he hummed. "I won't hurt you. Let me help you, old . . . ." He searched for a word, but none came. Suddenly, as he reached out again, there was a bright flash in his mind and he felt a strong deep voice command him to move away.

"Go!" it thundered. "You can give me no help. You may not touch me! I have broken too many rules, but that one I will not challenge. Kill me, if that is your nature, or let me die in my own way, but touch me not!"

Lancelot dropped his sword with a rush of guilt and fell back, shaking. As he did, the creature lifted its head with a mighty effort and their eyes met. For a minute, Lancelot felt lost in endless darkness and then a flood of relief poured over him and light returned. Startled, he realized that the feeling was not his own, but came from the animal before him.

"You are the one!" the voice sang. "At last! I give to you my place in her heart, but have no fear, for you will find your own way there."

It seemed that the very air about him shimmered joyfully and then the voice died as the glow about the creature faded. Its shape blurred and, for an instant, Lancelot thought he saw something else lying before him. But before he could be sure, it vanished, leaving him alone beneath the trees.

"Lancelot!" Torres' voice was nearby and sounded as if he had been calling for some time. Reluctantly Lancelot turned away from the emptiness where the animal had lain. He pulled himself up and returned to his horse. Clades was calm now and Torres was waiting for him there.

"Are you all right?" he asked. "Did you fall? What's wrong?"

Torres couldn't place the emotion he saw in Lancelot's face and it unsettled him.

"What? Yes, I'm fine. I didn't fall. I never fall. Nothing is wrong. I didn't catch the deer. Let's go home. I'm very tired."

Caomh and Riogh were less easily pacified than Torres. They rode behind as Lancelot and Torres trotted back to the Lake.

"He has encountered some enchantment not of our making," Caomh worried.

"You don't think that the Lady sent something of her own to amuse him?" Riogh was trying to reassure himself.

"After all this time, don't you think I know the feel of the Lady's magic?"

"Well, then. Do you think we should tell her of this?"

Caomh groaned. "You know what that would mean. No one among us would have any peace for the next year while she kept us busy trying to discover what it was. He seems recovered now. Whatever it was doesn't appear to have harmed him. You and I can turn about watching him for a few days to be sure that there are no lingering effects."

"You're right," Riogh agreed with relief. "It's probably

nothing. There are many harmless beings left over from the old days. They have little power now. He may have run into one of them. It would be useless to worry the Lady with it."

"She may notice it, herself, though."

Riogh considered. "No, I don't think so. He's coming back to normal already. Look at him. The traces of the encounter will be gone before we return home."

When they arrived, they soon learned that they had no need to worry about the Lady noticing anything. Adon was hurrying to see her. He was closeted with her in her room all evening. The information on Arthur had come.

"It would be perfect, my Lady. My informant says that he is an amazingly moral young man with an uncanny ability to win battles. It was for him that our Merlin wanted that sword."

"Do you think he has discovered the secret of it yet?"

"It would be odd if he hadn't. Few men can endure many battles without being wounded at least once. But I have heard nothing about it. At any rate, this Arthur has somehow managed to bring a kind of peace to the island and is trying to organize some form of humane government. He would be a perfect leader for someone like Lancelot, full of fiery causes and ideals."

"It sounds too good. Are you sure your informant can be trusted? Whom did you send?"

"A bird I know. A wild goose, but very reliable. He's been migrating here for years."

"I hope you're right. So far, Arthur sounds a perfect human for Lancelot to begin with. One more thing: he's not celibate, is he?"

"No, my Lady. He is married—though quite recently, I understand."

"Well, married is better than nothing. No doubt there will be others to teach our Lancelot the ways of humans in that. If only we could do it ourselves. Who knows what strange practices they have up there!"

"Shall I make arrangements to send him?"

"Don't be foolish, Adon." The Lady spoke sharply. "This will take time. He must think that leaving is his own idea.

And when the time comes, it must be done properly. I may even decide to take him to Arthur myself. The last time I left the Lake, men were wearing animal skins and hitting each other with stones. It would be interesting to see if things have changed at all."

"From what I have seen, my Lady, I don't think you will find much difference today."

"All the same, I think I will allow Lancelot to convince me to take him to join Arthur."

Chapter Three

Geraldus had almost forgotten how much he liked living in the mountains. Somehow, among the sheep and wildflowers where he had first heard them, his invisible voices did not seem so constant or intrusive. It was easier here for him to understand how he could have let his family convince him that his discordant choir could possibly be from heaven, come to prove him a saint on earth. With few trees and fewer people and the clouds often close enough to mist one's hair, it did seem more likely that God would send down some accompaniment for a lonely musician. He laughed to remember it, but tenderly.

Alswytha heard him from her bed and called to him. Her children had come too quickly and the last one had been the hardest. Even a month after the birth, Alswytha was still not strong enough to help Mark care for the others. That was partially why Geraldus had remained, though autumn was fast approaching and he had promised Guinevere that he would winter in Caerleon.

"Can we not convince you to stay with us?" Alswytha pleaded. Her Latin was still slightly stilted despite almost six years away from her Saxon family. "I am already much stronger and soon I will be able to cook for you again. I have been a fine hostess, to invite you to stay and then make you cook."

"I enjoyed it, although I am not so sure your family did."

Geraldus held her hand, thinking how pale it had once been. Now it was a dark ivory tan. She did not have the skin which turned brown in the sun. And a month of rest had not softened the calluses.

"You should have another woman up here to help you, Wytha."

"Someday perhaps we will. There are already Sextus, from Mark's old unit, and Trevelyn, the shepherd that Gawain sent from Cornwall. At first Mark wanted no one but ourselves up here, but now that 'ourselves' are six people instead of two, he is glad of their help. Still I don't think I want to share my children with another woman, not yet. Except your green lady, of course."

Alswytha smiled over Geraldus' shoulder. He didn't bother to turn around. Long and bitter experience had taught him that he would not see her. He sighed and then started and blushed. She had nipped him on the ear. Alswytha laughed.

"You must tell her to be more circumspect on her next visit. I think that Eadwynna and Matthew can see her, too, and I am not ready to start explaining such behavior to them."

Geraldus tried to cover his embarrassment by batting futilely at the air. As far as he knew, he was the only one who could hear his voices and only Alswytha and Guinevere could see them. Why they were so honored was something Geraldus never tried to explain.

"She can hear you," he said in annoyance. "And she is much more likely to pay attention to you than to anything I might tell her. Neither she or any of her friends have listened to anything I've told them since they first started singing to me. If they had. . . ."—he glared around him—"we would be

· 34 ·

doing polyphony and fugues instead of rounds and simple harmony."

There was complete silence, not even a hum. Alswytha laughed again.

"They all just disappeared! I think you insulted them. Oh, Geraldus, it would be so much fun to have you with us this winter. Will you not change your mind?"

"I really can't. I promised Arthur and Guinevere that I would stay with them. And, I admit, I'm curious to know what has been happening to everyone while I've been here. Don't you ever wonder?"

"Sometimes I would like to know how Guinevere is and dear Lady Sidra, but otherwise, no. We never found much joy down there."

They were interrupted by a flurry of small bodies covered with an amazing variety of grime.

"Mama, you're awake now," Eadwynna announced. "Why didn't you call us? We've been waiting for you. Matthew pushed Allard in the mud and pulled my hair and Allard cried, but I didn't. I got mad. And Father won't let us play with the sheep anymore because one stepped on Allard and he cried again and we were supposed to watch him, but I'm tired of watching him. Will you tell us a story?"

They piled onto the bed and over Alswytha, shoving each other to get to the favored spot in the circle of her left arm. Over the commotion, she caught Geraldus' eye and grinned. The new baby woke and began wailing. Soon she had joined the tangle on the bed. All of them were talking, wiggling, crying at once when Mark came in. He surveyed the scene with his hands on his hips and then waded in, tossing Matthew up and catching him until Allard began tugging at his robe to be thrown, too.

Geraldus watched them all: dirty, rumpled, somewhat patched, and indelibly loving. Suddenly he felt that he must be with Arthur and Guinevere. They needed him infinitely more than this so-complete family could.

All the same, it was hard to leave them and the wind had begun to chill and the frost to touch the morning leaves before he actually departed. Once he was on his way, his only desire was to reach Caerleon before he was buried in ice and snow. Although they never seemed to be affected by the weather in his world, the singers with him tended to get little comfort from the cold and to be as happy as he when they were indoors again.

It was early on a gray and biting afternoon when Geraldus rounded the bend in the road and saw the lights of Caerleon above him. He spurred his long-enduring horse, Plotinus, to something resembling a trot. The chorus must have noticed the lights, too, for they suddenly broke into a powerful hymn of thanksgiving. The music, itself, was warming and Geraldus thought with justified annoyance that they might have started sooner, before he was half frozen.

After the cold of the air outside, the warmth of the main hall nearly overwhelmed him. This was the time of year when Caerleon was most populated. Men who had small holdings throughout the west of Britain came there with their harvest to share both food and friendship. They brought their entire households and moved into the old officers' quarters. For these people who spent ten months out of twelve in continual back-breaking work, interrupted only by attacks from Saxon invaders and greedy neighbors, winter was a joyous time. The seas were too stormy to cross and the ground was mire or ice upon which no man, Saxon or Briton, would dare set an army. In the warm conviviality of Caerleon these people were more than ready for a few weeks of stories and singing; of mending harness, armor, and plows; of drinking and dicing at night and teaching, scolding, and spoiling their children by day.

For Caerleon in winter was bursting with children. The prosperity Arthur's victory had brought was so new that there was still a serious shortage of citizens to repopulate his reborn society, but those who were there were trying mightily to make up the deficit. They joked that the best summer crop was that planted in the dark at winter court. It was true that the majority of babies of the last five years had been born at summer's end. In spite of his anguish at having none of his own, Arthur welcomed them with delight, planning a Britain twenty years in the future, when those grubby, cacophonous, beautiful beings would carry on with his dream.

Geraldus had to walk carefully to avoid stepping on Britain's future and facing its mothers' wrath. It took him some time to cross the hall to the corner by the fire, where Guinevere and Arthur were seated. Arthur stood to greet him and cupped his hands, yelling over the din.

"Geraldus! What took you so long to climb down the mountain? And what is the new one, a niece or a nephew?"

"A girl, Arthur, wrinkled, screaming, and bald. They wanted to name her Arthura, but I convinced them that it would be a mistake. She is sure to become better-looking later."

Having reached them, Geraldus lowered his voice.

"However, they really did want to do you some honor. For your friendship and their love of you both, they have decided to name her Igraine, after your mother. Alswytha hoped you would not be offended."

Igraine! Poor sad queen whom Arthur never saw, who was told he had not survived his birth. He realized that Mark had met her several times when he was a child and could have told him about her. How like them it was to remember her, who had no other namesakes.

"Tell Alswytha that I am not offended, but proud. But tell them also, the next time you climb to their aerie, that I am offended that they will never visit us. Can't you make my brother-in-law understand that I need him? Geraldus, of all my lieutenants, Mark was the one who was most my friend. For the love that Guinevere and I have for him, if for nothing else, we would want him with us. No one will shrink from the scars on his face. They were honorably received. We would not ask him about the past. There is too much planning for the future that must be done to care about old sorrows."

Geraldus noticed with a sudden clear vision how much Arthur had aged in the past five years. There was gray in his moustache and his forehead was beginning to be crossed by lines.

"My God!" Geraldus thought. "He's past thirty now. I know men his age who are grandfathers. The task he has taken on will kill him if he doesn't have some help. There is still so much to be done. What could we do without him?"

This passed through his mind so quickly that Arthur didn't notice the brief look of shock that he gave.

"Do you think you can convince him to come down and advise me?" Arthur finished.

Geraldus sat down wearily. "No, Arthur. You know how often I have tried. They will never leave their home again. Each time I visit, I find it harder to leave, too. There is such peace there and they found so little here. But you could come to them, both of you. It would be good for you, Arthur. Don't you agree, Guinevere?"

Guinevere stretched out her arms to him. "First," she said, "I think you should kiss me nicely, because you have been away so long and I have missed you."

As she embraced him, Guinevere whispered, "We can't make him rest. He won't. Don't try to convince him now. Ask him about Camelot."

But Arthur did not wait to be asked. Camelot was all he wanted to talk about. He gestured broadly as he described it, sweeping cups and plates from the table as he tried to make diagrams in the air. And his face had the look of a man who sees visions.

"There are problems. Always. Thousands of problems. No one remembers how things were done in the old days. No one wants to try to find a new way. Sometimes we have been reduced to studying pictures on the walls in the old forts to see if they show how the stones were laid or the land cleared. But it is growing, taking shape at last. We sweat and curse and fall in the mud, dragging the walls with us. I begin to think it will never work, that I must be content with a lesser dream, that I will have to be satisfied with clumsy, unsure work. Just when I despair, something happens. Someone appears who knows how to fire the tile, to make the floors lie even. Someone has an idea for building a hall that will be a fit place for the Round Table. And it's working! Geraldus, as soon as the roads are clear again, you must come with me. The Hall is almost finished—a great open room supported by enormous pillars and beams of wood. I have walked through it, sat on the floor where my chair will one day be, and imagined it all."

Geraldus was aware that Arthur *could* see it all and wished that he himself were not so blind. "When will it be ready?" he asked.

"What? Ready? I don't know. It may never be exactly the way I have planned it. But I do know that I intend to spend the next summer there and properly begin the Round Table. We have waited far too long to set that in motion."

Guinevere's heart sank. She had hoped to spend the summer with her parents again while Arthur went from one place to another, busy with mustering soldiers for defense and recruiting knights for his government. "Perhaps," she thought, brightening, "Arthur will not be able to get that awful table from the cave on my parents' estate. Then he will have to forget the whole idea and settle here in Caerleon."

She rose from the table. "I am going to my rooms, to rest. Geraldus, will you come and dine with us tonight? Constantine, Cador's son, has just returned from Armorica. He has brought back his sister, Lydia. She was fostered for years at the home of Hoel, Arthur's cousin. Constantine is leaving again soon. But she is going to stay with me. Do you remember them?"

"I know Constantine well, but Lydia was gone before I ever visited Cador and Sidra. I will be delighted to meet her."

Geraldus noticed with amusement that Guinevere had directed her explanation of the relationships not at him, but at something apparently hovering over his left shoulder. Being around people who could see what he could only hear was a great comfort to him. They kept him from continually doubting his sanity.

Guinevere was relieved to be away from the noise of the Hall. Though Arthur had set up a school for the older children, the little ones were still enough to cover the floor on a winter afternoon. The babble of their playing was augmented by the gossiping of their mothers, conversations from which Guinevere was excluded, not because of her rank, but because she lacked the vital credential to join them: there was no warm, sticky toddler pulling at her skirts. She returned to the serenity of her private apartment gratefully.

Risa, her maid, was waiting for her. She helped Guinevere into a less formal robe and brought her the codex she had been studying the night before. Guinevere settled down with relief, but Risa continued to move about the room, closing curtains, folding linens, and moving things about on the tables, none of which needed to be done. Guinevere looked up from the book.

"What is it, Risa?"

Risa dropped the jewelry casket back on the table.

"I wanted to let you know that I would like to visit my father again next month, if that is convenient."

"Oh, Risa, not again! Winter has barely begun. Who is it this time?"

Risa crossed the room and sat on the furred rug next to Guinevere's couch. Her dark head rested against it and Guinevere reached down and took her hand to soften the abruptness of her question.

"It's Cheldric, Guinevere."

"Cheldric? I had no idea you. . . . But, Risa, he has only one arm!"

"One is quite enough, my Lady. Perhaps you have forgotten how he lost the other?"

"Of course not. He will want for nothing while I am alive. I simply didn't realize that he attracted you."

"I am very fond of him. He is willing to spend time in talking to me. He tells the most wonderful stories!"

Guinevere sighed. Risa's taste was very strange to her. It was true that Cheldric had lost his arm in trying to protect her, but she hadn't cared for him much before then. He did seem to have become much nicer now that his dreams of military glory were over.

"I don't suppose you'd marry him?" she asked.

"Would it matter if I didn't? I didn't marry the other two."

Guinevere was uncomfortable with the conversation. Risa had always been more of a friend than a maid, but this was one subject that they generally avoided.

"No, it will make no difference to me. I thought you might want to. Cheldric would be a suitable match for you."

Risa smiled. "And the others were either too high or too low?"

"That's not it exactly. I only thought that you might still be interested in Gawain."

Risa's smile became laughter. "Gawain? To marry? My dearest Mistress, Gawain makes love better than any man I've ever known, but no woman in her right mind would marry a man who sleeps from sunset to dawn, and even one who is totally insane wouldn't have a child by him. My Lady Guinevere, no one knows what his father was and everyone knows what his mother is. Would you want your baby to be part witch and part incubus?"

She stopped suddenly. She knew she had gone too far. "Oh, my dear, I'm sorry. I didn't mean to say that. I do like him, anyway, but. . . ."

She scrambled up again and went back to rearranging the bottles and boxes on the table.

Guinevere was very tired. She wanted to lie on her couch, read her *Life of St. Martin,* and forget all about other people's children. She had a wild impulse to let Risa stay at Caerleon and go herself to some quiet little farm away from the clatter and the prying.

"Never mind, Risa," she sighed. "It doesn't matter. Whatever you decide, I will always be happy to have you back or let you go if you wish it. But now I would simply like to be alone."

"Of course, my Lady." Risa was glad to be able to leave.

Guinevere tried to read and then to rest, but she was too tense. She lay rigidly awhile on the couch, trying to make herself relax. She thought of the view from her parents' estate, of summer forests, of almost empty skies, but her nervousness increased. She rose and began to pace the floor. It was not Risa that bothered her, or the chaos in the Hall. Something was wrong or missing in her life, something vital, but she could not discover what. Merlin might have been able to tell her, but she would rather suffer than ask him anything. It could not be that she was bored. She had more than she had ever wanted: friends, comfort, security. She could travel when and where she wished. Arthur gave her clothes and trinkets without her even asking and he still loved her devotedly. So what could it be? She kicked a pillow out of her way. A gust of wind rattled the shutters. She sighed again. Perhaps it was the weather.

Winter was a time of lazy pleasure for almost everyone at Caerleon except the kitchen servants and Arthur. While the cooks and scullery workers slaved to feed and clean up after the increased population, Arthur sweated over plans, reports, strategy, and the settlement of the constant petty feuds which the leaders of the old British tribes still engaged in. The Romans had given them a thin veneer of culture and a semblance of unity, but whenever the fighting against the invaders slowed, they remembered ancient wrongs and set out to avenge them. Only their loyalty to Arthur kept them from open warfare against each other.

"Look at this, Merlin!" Arthur fumed. "Craddoc has sent word that Meleagant has annexed a village that is Craddoc's by tradition. He wants me to give him the extra men so that he can battle to regain it. A village! Two fields, three cows, and fifteen people. By the time they finish fighting for it, the cows will have been eaten, the fields trampled, and the people either starved or forced into slavery."

"You should watch Meleagant, nevertheless. His power is growing and he doesn't like to have his 'private' affairs controlled."

Arthur waved Meleagant aside. "Not now, Merlin. The Round Table will see to him. Here is another. Maelgwn has let it be known that he has no intention of maintaining watchtowers against the Irish unless he is paid in horses and wine. He also mentions that he will accept daughters of a family of good breeding for fostering, if they are no older than fifteen and no younger than twelve. Wonderful. He has three sons that no woman is safe near and his own wife died last fall. The citizens of Chichester inform me that they have not seen any Saxons in the last seven years and therefore don't feel the need to pay taxes to me to protect them any longer. Yesterday a trader from York came to complain that his local priest had raped his wife during confession and it was my duty to see that the church paid for the support of the child. Merlin, will you please tell me again? Why have I spent the last fifteen years fighting?"

Merlin smiled indulgently. Arthur was like this every winter. When spring came and he could travel, seeing what he had done and what was needed, he would regain his spirits. It was having to deal long distance with the whines and protestations of supplicants that discouraged him.

"You should be pleased that they come to you, Arthur. It means that your plans are working. You wanted to re-establish central government and you have. Now before they bash each other's brains out, they appeal to you for a judgment. What we need now is to create an extension of your power. If these children can be taught to look upon a court or an administrator as an arm of your rule, then they will bother you only with a final appeal."

Arthur leafed through the mass of papers and vellum. He shook his head.

"It won't work, at least not yet. The people who do the fighting are the ones who will want control of their jurisdiction. It's all the fault of Macson Wledig. Before he went sailing off to make himself emperor, he handed the cities back to the provincial leaders. They simply realigned themselves back into their old tribes and clans, and we have to deal with that. I need outside people who have no affiliations except to me. They must be able to pass a wise and fair judgment and back it up with strength. They must be respected and maybe a little feared. A long while ago, I considered letting the church handle the matter, but that won't work, either. The bishops and priests are either too wrapped up in God or too venal. All of them are attached to the local kings through birth or friendship. Anyway, they are the seat of as many complaints as the laity. That's why my Round Table is so important. I must have men who are willing to answer to no one but myself. The honor must be so great that they can't be tempted by bribes."

"If you intend them to be administrators, then why bother with military ability?"

"You taught me it yourself, Merlin. Because that is what these kings understand. If I sent them weak-limbed clerks, they'd spit in their faces and laugh. But strong men, armed and mounted and bringing justice instead of tyranny—can't you see them? Men of ability, wisdom, and honor and selected for those qualities alone. It will work."

"I believe you, Arthur." Merlin had been growing in the feeling that Arthur was confident enough to act without him and lately he had felt sure of it. If only his Queen did not try to assert herself and insist that he give up Camelot and the Table! So far she had bowed to his wishes, but . . . it bothered him. From her infancy, he had not been able to think of her without a gnawing dread. If only he knew why.

"I am getting old," he thought. "I shall be fifty soon. Too many years have been spent in following unclear prophecies and signs. Sometimes I forget why I began on this road. Soon, soon there must come a time for me to rest. I would like to be able to rest."

"Merlin?" Arthur brought him back. "Constantine brings word from Cador that several boats crossed to the Saxon Shore before winter set in. Cador thinks that Aelle might be planning to increase his holdings next spring. Apart from a few raiding parties, he hasn't done anything since I made such a fool of him when I rescued Guinevere. I think we should set a more careful watch on him. Whom can we send?"

They spent the rest of the afternoon on matters of state. Arthur pushed the Round Table to the back of his mind. It must wait until spring. He was relieved when Risa came to tell them that the others were waiting to begin dinner.

He stretched his arms and flexed his shoulder muscles.

"Have we finished most of this? God, how I hate the pettiness of it all. There are times, Merlin, when I devoutly wish you had never taught me to read. Hardly anyone else we know is able to and they seem to get along fine."

"Go fill your stomach, Arthur. You've worked hard. I'll get someone to clear this up and take the messages as soon as there is a break in the weather."

"Aren't you coming to eat with us?"

"No, but I'll be along later. Save me some ale."

Guinevere was having a lovely time. She did not have to be careful of her attitude or speech in this company. They were her own sort and did not think it odd that she missed warm rooms or hearing Roman poets. Constantine and Lydia were family to her by that convoluted network of intermarriage that had gone on for the last two centuries. Constantine had been fostered with her family when she was a child and she remembered him as a noisy ten-year-old. He was eighteen now and showed the effects of his training. He lived up to his august name, and his classical profile would have graced a coin impressively. Lydia had spent most of her life in Armorica with still other relatives, and Guinevere had not met her before. She liked her a great deal and hoped they could convince her to live with them permanently.

In appearance, she might have been her mother, Sidra, twenty years younger and unscarred by disease: not beautiful, but appealing, with a promise of comfort in her eyes. She was watching Geraldus tapping time for his choir. He was also trying to listen to an argument among Arthur, Cei, and Constantine about the need for a further military buildup along the shoreline. The scene reminded Guinevere of those of childhood, with her father and brothers wrangling over an idea. She gave a sigh of contentment and leaned against Arthur's shoulder. For a second his body stiffened in surprise and then he shyly put his arm around her. She felt a touch of guilt that he should be so pleased and unused to her touch.

Lydia looked as if she would like to speak to Geraldus, but did not have the courage. Guinevere smiled.

"Have you been introduced to Geraldus, Lydia? You mustn't mind the nonsense people say about him. He is only a little peculiar."

She meant this to be a statement of fact and was puzzled when Geraldus laughed.

"I am honored to meet you, Lydia," he said and stood to bow to her. His arms flailed in the air as though he were shaking something off them.

Lydia gave him her hand. "I have heard about you, indeed. They say you are sung to by the angels."

Her evident awe made Geraldus uncomfortable. He hastened to explain.

"I am accompanied by music of a sort as they say, but I am in no way worthy of notice by the angels. I think that if anyone were to deserve a celestial choir, it would be more likely to be one such as you."

Lydia blushed and hurriedly asked if they thought there would be snow soon. Guinevere was surprised at Geraldus' gallantry. He must have been around Gawain too long. Poor Gawain! The best part of the winter was the evening and he always missed it. It was a shame that no one could find a way to cure him. Oh, well. There was always spring. Everything nice happened in the spring.

Chapter Four

Adon lay asleep in the Lady's arms. He murmured softly as she rolled him away from her onto his back, but did not wake. She patted him with fondness, but absently. She had too much to think of to bother with Adon now.

The time was nearing, she was certain. Lancelot was ready, both in skill and willingness, to be away. They had carefully let drop comments about Arthur and the new society he was creating in Britain. They fostered Lancelot's ambitions by letting Meredydd continue her preaching to him, although it rankled. He was burning now to enter the world and save it from itself. She could feel the fire in him each time she touched his hand and it maddened her to have to wait until he returned to take him. Soon he would suggest that he be permitted to leave. She would have to appear somewhat reluctant, angry, but not too much. It was a nuisance having to go through all these little dramas. But beneath her annoyance, she was delighted to have something to do, to be released from boredom for another few years.

The silver curtains parted and Torres rushed in. He shoved Adon awake as he bounded onto the bed beside him.

"You have to do something about it!" he pleaded. "Lancelot has some crazy idea that he is going to go out there!" He gestured upward, "Not just by the Lake, but off to some place where humans live! He keeps telling me that this Arthur man is just what he's been looking for. What is he talking about? What in blazes is a 'knight'? You've got to stop him. He's been down on the cobblestones praying for the last three hours. He says he needs divine guidance, but I would rather he got some from you. Get up, Adon! This is no time to snore. Put on your pants and come help me!"

The Lady laughed. "You heard him, Adon. See if you can get Lancelot out of the courtyard and I will meet you all in the salon with Nimuë."

Adon grumbled and reached for his clothes. "Yes, my Lady. Do you think this is finally the time?"

"I do," she soothed him. "And for your help you may have an extra night if you like."

He paused to kiss her and caress her breast. "Oddly enough after all these thousands of years, I still do like."

Lancelot had worked himself almost into a trance by the time they arrived and it was with difficulty that they coerced him to come with them. He kept muttering so about signs, portents, and omens that Torres was relieved to see that nothing fluttered after them as they half-dragged him to the salon.

When he saw the Lady, Lancelot threw himself at her feet. He kissed the garnet rings on her toes and begged her to forgive him and let him go. She lifted his face to hers.

"Lancelot, my dear son, why do you wish to leave us and why do you think we would not release you? Our only bonds on you are those of love. Our only desire is for your happiness and tranquillity. Tell me, my dearest, what is it you wish?"

Lancelot blinked slowly, trying to bring the room into focus. His eyes shifted from one to the other—Torres, Adon, Nimuë, the Lady—loving faces touched with concern. Meredydd must be wrong. How could he have let her convince him that they would bar him from his ambition, his destiny? He laid his head in the Lady's lap and let her run her hand along his cheek. Did he imagine that her fingers trembled? His hands fumbled with the thin silk of her dress.

"I must go!" he gulped. "It has been laid on me that I must find Arthur and fight at his side, to help the poor lost humans of this island. He needs me. There are not enough who believe; Meredydd has told me so. You know it is true, don't you? He needs me! Please, my Lady, don't hate me. I must go! It is sinful to live here in luxury while those outside suffer. Please, oh dearest Lady! Let me go to him!"

His tears made the cloth stick to her legs and trickled most disturbingly between her thighs. She tried to ignore the sensation as she answered.

"Of course, you must go to him if that is what your heart commands. If you believe that this is what you must do, we cannot stop you. But let us equip you, prepare you. You have never been more than a few miles from the Lake. Do you know where Arthur is? What will you do when you find him?"

Lancelot tried to compose himself. "I . . . I had thought to take my sword and shield and walk until I found him and then offer them to him. That was all."

"My poor darling! There is much more to it than that. Why, dozens of men come every month to do just that. He can't take them all. You must have an introduction so that he knows who you are and then you still must prove yourself. We will all miss you terribly here, but if you must go, then let us give you the proper gear and instruct you in how to behave once you get there. There is so much you don't know, Lancelot! There is so much you will need to protect yourself."

She had said the wrong thing. Lancelot raised his head proudly and shook the tears from his cheeks.

"God will protect me," he announced, "if it is His will."

"Yes, yes," Adon assured him. "But I'm sure He wouldn't mind if you used the skills He gave you in the defense of others, don't you think?"

Lancelot did not answer. He appeared to be considering the logic of this, but Adon gave him no time to find an argument.

"We will give you our finest sword and shield and have a spear made that cannot be broken. And Clolë will insist you have new clothes, as fine as she can weave. You wouldn't want to embarrass us by appearing in rags?"

Lancelot would not wish to embarrass them if it cost him his life. They knew that and congratulated themselves that they had managed to trick him into doing what they wanted. They could not realize that he perceived them, not as his benefactors, but as errant children who must be pacified and protected for their own good. There was something in his look, though, that made the Lady nervous. Suddenly he smiled at them and her heart turned over. He was more beautiful than the stars! How could she let him go? She stood to dismiss him and felt a chill as the dampness on her dress caught the air.

"Whatever your intention, you cannot ride unheralded into the house of a king. If you insist on setting off for Arthur's court, then I must accompany you as far as the gate."

"Oh, my Lady!"

"It is my duty. You will allow me that, won't you?"

"Of course, I would be honored."

"I should think you would. I have not been to the cities of men for two thousand years. We will see to it that you appear before Arthur with all the trappings of a king's son."

"Thank you, my Lady. But do you think it would be—"

"Yes, Lancelot, I do."

That ended the matter.

Lancelot was so excited that he did not know what to do first. The sight of Torres reminded him.

"Come with me, brother. Wait until we tell your mother the good news."

Torres clapped him on the back. "She won't believe it. Wait until I tell her that I'm going with you."

Lancelot stopped. "What?"

"You will need someone to burnish your armor after you return from your battles, you know. Fighting and praying don't leave much time to clean up."

"But, Torres."

"Don't you want me?"

"Of course." Lancelot paused. He studied Torres closely. He had known him since they suckled together, playing with each other's toes. He took him as much for granted as he took his shadow. But now he really looked at him. They might be brothers, after all, if hair and coloring were all one counted. Both had golden brown curls and hazel eyes in faces that easily tanned. But Torres' face was open and humorous as though he had no thought of deception or fear of guile. He was gentle and kind and if he cared too much for the pleasures of the table and the bed, what else could one expect under the Lake? Yes, he did want Torres, very much. But what would Meredydd say to that?

"Alas!" she shrieked when they told her. "Oh, woe! It's that evil woman, that witch! That serpent! First she lured you away from my arms to the iniquity of her house and now she wants to send you God knows where! How can you do this to me?"

Meredydd was only beginning. Torres knew her too well to let her go on, although Lancelot tried to reason with her until she ran down.

"Now, Mother," he broke in. "Think about it. This is just what you always wanted. We're going back to the world we came from to scourge it of its wickedness."

"Huh! With Torres it'd be more likely to add to the wickedness, you slothful boy!"

"Mother," Lancelot remonstrated while Torres struggled to hide his laughter. "Torres is going to help me, just as you taught us. He had no need of the world or interest in it. He goes only to take care of me. And I promise to watch over him. Is that not the love between brothers you have always wished for us?"

Meredydd eyed Torres skeptically. "Yes, I suppose I have. But I don't believe that one would remember it if he didn't think there was some fun in it for him."

Nevertheless, she supplied them both with amulets, potions, and charms twisted into odd symbols that she vaguely remembered and fondly hoped were Christian.

At last they were ready. Adon privately wondered, from the little he had seen of human society, if sheer silk and cloth of silver were what warriors were expected to wear beneath their armor. And had anyone in Britain ever seen a material like the Lady's gown, shimmering green and gray like the ocean in the wind? She had, after much consideration, decided on aquamarines and diamonds set in gold for jewelry— only rings, necklace, earrings, and a fillet about her hair. "One must have restraint." The metal for Lancelot's armor she had salvaged from the Great Flood, after all mortal life on earth seemed to have perished. It was, as she had promised, the finest ever made and he did not think that anything they had in the world now could dent or splinter it. They had made him a visor the color of silver, in the form of his own face and so light that he hardly noticed it. It fit onto his helm and could be removed for fighting, when peripheral vision was essential. The helm was crested with ostrich feathers. Adon had thought that too much, but it was Meredydd, oddly enough, who had insisted that they remain.

"My Granny told me stories about the soldiers before they all rode off, and she remembered the feathers well. Maybe not that sort, but feathers, certainly, and he should have them, too."

So there were feathers and soft doeskin for his surcoat and riding trews, with heavier leather for his boots. Nothing had been overlooked, down to the trim on the horse's bridle.

Lancelot showed no interest in the physical preparations. He had his own sort to make. It was with great trouble that Torres finally convinced him that fasting and keeping vigil would not fit him for proving his strength on the practice field.

"They say that Arthur wants men who can fight, as well as the pure of spirit," he argued. "How long will you last in the field if you haven't eaten or slept for a week?"

"All right, Torres. Give me the plate of pheasant. Yes, I see it. It's hard to hide a platter behind your back."

Lancelot resented the interruption, but would not hurt Torres by showing it. Torres could not help it if he did not understand. Lancelot sometimes wondered if the true sacrifice he was being asked to make was simply to live with those he loved. Sometimes, in the far reaches of the night, when he felt the weight of the stars on the Lake just before dawn swept them, glittering, from the sky, sometimes he knew that he could almost touch what he sought. If only he could escape just a little bit further. He would reach out until the pain in his muscles recalled him. Another moment . . . but it never happened and he wept for his unworthiness and resolved to be kinder and more considerate to those around him.

So he ate what Torres brought and slept when they told him to and allowed the Lady to arrange things as she thought best.

The day they were to depart, Adon's bird brought the message that Arthur was no longer in Caerleon, but had moved his entire household to a new fortress-city he was building at Cadbury, which he had named Camelot.

"Where is that?" the Lady asked. "Has he already settled there? I don't want us lost in a chaos of wagons and furniture."

"He has been there about a month now, the goose says. He also tells me that it is an old place of magic, but I cannot put too much weight on that. He is a good enough spy, but not at all versed in history."

"Very well, show us the way and we will go there. Torres! To Camelot!"

Camelot! Guinevere heard nothing magic in the name. And when she arrived, she saw only mud and buildings of raw wood unpainted and courtyards half tiled. She saw at once that the traditional heating system, with hypocausts sending warm air under the floor, would be impossible with all that timber. Arthur assured her that the construction was solid and sturdy, but she did not like her upstairs rooms any better because of that. Her distaste and despair showed so in her face that Geraldus felt obligated to pull her aside and point out to her that Arthur would never be truly happy there unless she was, even though his heart was set on the place.

"I've known you most of your life, Guinevere, and I know how much you hate change of any kind. But try to see it as Arthur does. It is fresh and new, untainted by the past. When it is finished, I think it will be startlingly beautiful because there will not be another place like it on earth."

Guinevere grimaced, but acknowledged that he was right. "I know. I have heard it many times. I try to remember how important it is to Arthur, but I feel uneasy away from what I know. He asks only that we summer here, thank goodness. We would freeze in the winter, even if the roofs don't leak, and I suspect that they do."

"Is it Arthur's fault that so much lore has been forgotten? He has accomplished a miracle here. The planning is brilliant and the craftsmanship painstaking. Have you seen the carving on the pillars in the Hall where the Table is to be set?"

"No, not yet."

"It is incredible, a miniature forest on each one and painted so that each branch and leaf has its own color as well as shape. And there is a glass window at the pinnacle of the roof so the sunlight will pour down upon the table, leaving all else in shadow. There is not a villa in Britain that can boast of such splendor."

"Yes, my dear Geraldus, I know." She enjoyed his enthusiasm. Arthur needed people like that around him and she had not done her part. "I admit that I am an old hedonist for wanting every home to be as comfortable and familiar as that of my parents. You are right. I will try to see the beauty of Camelot as you do and encourage Arthur all I can in his dreams, if only you will grant me a warm corner for the winter."

"Now you are teasing, Guinevere." Geraldus smiled at her. "You know very well that you would be perfectly happy in a dripping cave if Arthur were there."

She did not know that, but allowed him to think so. She was very fond of Arthur. She would go wherever he wished and try not to complain, but as for being happy? That had not occurred to her. Content was the most she had ever been. Except once, long ago. She tried to remember where and why. Sometimes it almost came back to her. A dream? No, but not quite reality, either. She recalled something silver and lavender, something both cold and warm, a touch, and within the halo of its love she had indeed been very happy, with that piercing joy which is almost pain. Some nights she woke without cause, thinking it still called to her, but the sensation faded before her mind grasped it and there was only her room around her and Arthur sleeping by her side. Then she would remember who and where she was and settle down again among the pillows, with a sense of loss which she could not explain.

She and Geraldus climbed to her rooms. The maids were busy there, hanging the arras and arranging the bedclothes, so they retreated to the balcony.

"Arthur knows how I love to stand high above and watch what is happening, and since there are no towers at Camelot, he made this for me. Look! You can see the gate from here and, on the other side, the practice field. I can sit here with my cup of wine and not only watch all the warriors trying to best each other, but also see who is coming to visit us." Her laugh was genuine now. "When we are sure that this will hold more than a few people, I can bring the other ladies here with me and we can observe and comment on the knights without our talk disturbing them."

"It seems strong enough," Geraldus commented, "and very practical. Arthur may like to use it himself. Up so high, we can not only see everything, but also be seen by anyone across the courtyard."

He pointed across the yard to the Hall. Merlin was standing in front of the doors, beckoning to them. When he had caught their attention, he cupped his hands and called to them. "Can you see Gawain from up there? We need him!"

Geraldus yelled back, but he was not sure he could be heard. The breeze seemed to blow the sound back at him.

"He had word that his brothers are coming! His brothers! He rode out to meet them!"

With broad gestures and pointing, he finally made himself understood. Merlin disappeared into the building.

"Guinevere, have you any wine handy?" Geraldus croaked. "I hate to shout like that; it spoils my voice for singing."

She poured cups for them both.

"What do you think Merlin wants Gawain for?" he asked.

Guinevere shrugged. Merlin never confided in her.

"It is rumored that tonight he is going to bring the Round Table here," Geraldus prodded.

"He and Arthur were closeted together for several hours yesterday," she admitted. "But they didn't tell me why. Arthur has been so excited since we came here that I can't tell if something new is being planned."

"If you don't mind, I will go down there to see what I can find out." Geraldus drained the wine. The cup tipped itself away from him and then back.

"Sorry," he said to the air. "Next time you may have some."

He returned to his conversation with Guinevere. "I wasn't born when that Table was put in the cave under Leodegrance's villa, and I have never seen it. I have heard that it is enormous, though, and would dearly love to see how he intends to move it."

"Father never spoke of it at all, other than to tell us that it was not ours to touch. The cave was too dark to see it well, but I remember that it seemed to go on forever into the blackness. Yes, go and see what they are doing. Let me know what is happening. If Cousin Merlin is ready to place the Round Table at Camelot, then it would appear that Arthur plans to start enlisting his brotherhood of knights. That might be worth seeing."

Geraldus considered that an understatement. The men of Britain had dreamed of nothing else for the past five years. Some had been training themselves or their sons all that time. When word got out that the Table was in place, they would arrive from every corner of the country to vie for a seat.

Arthur was wise to wait so long. Not only was interest at the straining point, but the men were that much readier. The selection would be greater and the standards tougher. Once the Table. . . .

His mind returned to his first question. How was Merlin ever going to be able to move it?

Merlin was even more closemouthed than usual, though, and Geraldus could get no answers from him. Arthur looked worried.

"He sent word to my father-in-law not to be surprised or concerned if the ground shook a bit at his villa tonight. He keeps telling me he has no doubts, that what he did once, he can do again. But I don't like the way he looks. He's withdrawn into himself more than I've ever seen him and he won't tell me what his plans are. He just says that everyone must stay indoors tonight and no one must light a fire of any kind. In the morning the Table will be in the Hall."

"But how will he get it in? The doors are in place and the glass in the roof. And even if they weren't, the Table is supposed to almost fill one end of the building. Any entry will be much too narrow."

"Do you want to tell him that?"

Geraldus shook his head. He noticed that his singers were nowhere around him or, if they were, they were silent. Even they seemed disinclined to meddle with wizards.

Merlin sat on the ground some distance from them. He paid them no attention. He didn't like the looks of the sky. Too many clouds tonight could ruin everything. It had been almost thirty years since he had done this sort of thing. He had been a boy then, eager and without respect for the forces he was dealing with. Now he felt his age. He had lived enough to learn fear and he tried to avoid trafficking in magic. But it had to be done. One last great foray between the worlds, into and, he hoped, out of sorcery and ice. He felt a touch of excitement. The boy he had been was not dead yet. He stroked his beard, mindful of the gray rimming the brown. Yes, it would be worth it, not only for Arthur and his dreams. Britain would remember him for this and maybe credit it against the deceptions he had been forced into in Uther's time. He studied the sky again. It would be hours yet until night and there was a wind coming up which might blow away the clouds. That would help. For now, he would rest.

There were still clouds scudding across the sky by the time it was full night. But they were few and fleeting. Merlin gazed around at the sleeping Camelot. His orders had been obeyed. Not so much as a candle glowed from the buildings and the Great Hall was hollow and waiting. Merlin let himself in and barred the doors behind him. A clear circle of moonlight shone through the thick glass above the spot ordained for the Table. As he studied it, the glow flickered as the clouds raced over. It steadied again. Whatever might happen, it must be done now. The moon was full and close to the earth. He couldn't wait another year for the chance.

He removed his robe and tunic and, wearing only his woolen trews, stood bathed in the light. The bronze bands on his wrists, normally so tarnished that they went unnoticed, were burnished to a red-gold brilliance. He held himself motionless, not even breathing, and slowly tensed every muscle, like a lion preparing to pounce. With a sudden motion, he leaped into the air and vanished.

There was a gasp from the corner deepest in shadow. Caet's hand thrust out quickly as if to grasp what wasn't there. He alone had disobeyed the order. The lure of the old magic was too strong. He had been born to it. His family had given the old religion its priests and scholars, *drui* and *fili* for generations. But he had believed the old gods dead and that he himself had been the last to speak with them. Even though the memory of his encounter with the goddess still terrified him, he had hoped that it was not true that she had gone, that Merlin had come tonight to make sacrifice and to beg for divine intercession and help. He should have known Merlin better than to think he was merely a passive medium for the gods. Merlin had been a part of Caet's life as long as he could remember. He was kin to his mistress Guenlian and her daughter, Guinevere. Caet had often seen him, talked with him, even caught his horse once after it had thrown him. He had believed, unlike many others, that Merlin was only a man, not the demon that some called him. But he was not merely a crusty magician or teller of tales. He was a man of action. He did not rely on anything to create his magic for him. Caet felt no supernatural fear of him, only intense admiration that this human, whatever his connections, would dare to cross the abyss between worlds.

Merlin did not dare to look around, to examine the place where he now walked, so cold that his breath froze on his beard and ice crystals formed on the hair of his chest and arms. He felt the cold to his marrow, but ignored it. He had to keep the image of the Table before him, first as a picture and then as reality. He knew that the most difficult part was yet to come, in the deep cave where no light pierced. The darkness about him grew. He felt the Table take shape beneath his hands and knew it was real. His eyes closed and he imaged the circle of light back at Camelot. The Table rose.

The cold increased so that the metal on his wrists contracted and froze. His hands and fingers grew numb and his forearms were shot through with pain. He faltered. Was it from his weakness or was a cloud across the face of the moon? He could not let his mind wander enough to speculate. He must only take each step carefully, knowing that the Table floated before him, but totally concentrating on the circle of light waiting empty for him to return.

Caet waited, ten minutes, twenty. He had never thought to know someone who would attempt this. His grandmother had told him stories of those who had peered through the passageway when they were looking through the eyes of the gods. It was said that the sight erased all color from the eyes until they were as gray as old ice and that those who had seen could never again bear the light of day. How long did it take? Caet began to fear that his presence had taken some power from Merlin. What if he came back too late? How long could a man live where only gods should tread?

※　　※　　※

Merlin could feel his strength evaporating with the heat from his body. He had no idea of how close or far he was from his goal. Only at the last second would the image fade and reality appear again. He had no way of judging time, but he thought he was slowing. His left foot skidded on something and he lurched to that side. He caught his breath in fear, but the image didn't fade. The Table was heavier, though, than last time, harder to guide. It might have been easier to bring from light into darkness than the other way around. His side was beginning to ache and his throat to burn when he thought he felt the burden lighten a fraction, as if there were someone on the other side of the Table, pulling. His pace steadied and quickened, eight steps, ten, thirteen, and then a sensation of choking on thick fog—those damn clouds again! But it meant he was almost through. Another push. Yes, something was tugging him from the other side. With one huge effort, Merlin shoved the table before him and fell on top of it with a thud, slightly askew in the Hall at Camelot.

He lay panting on the Table as the ice encrusting him melted in the summer heat. His lungs felt as if splinters had been driven into them. It was some time before he was aware that someone else was in the room. A face appeared above him. His back was to the light and his features were blurry. Merlin tried to rise.

"No, don't move yet, Master Merlin." The voice was familiar. "I'll get your robe and some water. Just rest. I won't be long."

Merlin's eyes closed. Lord, he was tired. The solid wood beneath him was reassuring. He had done it. The Table was in place, Arthur was in place. He had fulfilled his part of it. There would be no more need for magic. At last he could rest without worry. The weight was gone. Whatever happened now, for good or evil, was not his responsibility.

"I think I may go visit Guenlian now," he thought sleepily. "It would be nice to retreat for a while, to go back to the old world, with no threats of dire prophecy looming."

The man had returned. He forced a cup to Merlin's mouth. The water had been mixed with wine and herbs. He knew the blend. It was an old remedy for frostbite. The thought amused him so that he laughed and splattered the liquid down his chest.

"Careful, Master. It was all I could think of," the voice warned. "Does it help?"

Who was this man? Merlin squinted to bring him into focus. How could he know about the cold? Of course, there had been the ice. His hair was still wet and his skin clammy, but. . .

He sat up. "Let me look at you. Weren't you told to stay away from here?"

The cup shook. "Yes, Master Merlin."

"Well, have you no explanation? Wait, you seem familiar. Who are you?"

"I'm Briacu. King Arthur has made me his horsemaster."

There was some bitterness in his voice, as though that had not been the post he had hoped for. Merlin studied him.

"Briacu? No. You had another name. I can't remember now. But I know you. You were the boy at Leodegrance's. Your great-grandmother was the high priestess of Epona. A remarkable woman. Did she teach you? Were you the one who guided me here?"

"I . . . I don't know. You were gone so long. I thought of a charm, a spell my family used to use. But it wasn't magic, just a blessing for travelers. It was all I could think of."

"A blessing?" Merlin laughed again. "Well, the gods may be gone, but there's life in the old spells yet! Thank you, friend Briacu. You must have come here to remind me that even an old wizard can learn humility. But listen to me! There are those who would be horrified at what we did here tonight. I have some immunity because of my position and power, but there are still those who have complained about my trafficking with the old ways. They also fear me. You are young, Briacu, and will have to spend more time in this world with its growing fear of what it cannot touch. I advise you never to speak of what has happened here. Never think of it, if you can help it. If the horses which Arthur brought with us are an example of your skill, then you will never need magic to aid you, nor will you end your life on a pyre, with the flames licking your feet."

Caet nodded. He did not need to be told. He glanced up. The texture of the light was changing. It would be dawn soon. Merlin followed his look.

"I agree," he said. "The Table is now where it should be. They will discover it soon and we can examine it further then. Now all I wish is to find my way to bed. Can you help me? My joints are a bit stiff."

They hobbled out together, shutting the door without a backward glance. In the growing sunlight, the carving on the Table began to show and, in a clearing a day's journey away, Lancelot prepared to ride.

Chapter Five

The first thing everyone did upon seeing the Table for the first time was to reach out and touch it. All that day people filed past, running their hands over the ancient, silken wood. They spoke in whispers, as if in the presence of a sacred relic. Arthur stood nearby, watching. His excitement was too great for him even to sit down.

He had awakened that morning at first light and hurried out to the balcony. It was not high enough for him to look down into the main Hall and see if anything were there. The sun rose higher and caught the glass in the roof so that it was reflected. It seemed to him that the glow was a good omen, like a huge golden chalice. Arthur couldn't wait any longer. He returned to the room and began throwing on his clothes.

He was glad that it was summer; a tunic and a belt and quickly-laced sandals were all he needed. He started to run out, then stopped and looked back at the bed. Guinevere had burrowed down into the sheet until only a truant braid could be seen. He hesitated, went over, and folded down the linen to find her face. She winced and mumbled something as the light hit her eyes. Arthur laughed.

"Wake up, my love. Don't you want to see the Table? You must come with me. It's your dowry, after all."

She mumbled something more and tried to turn her face back into the sheet, but Arthur lifted her by the shoulders, propping her head against his chest as he continued to exhort her.

"The Table, Guinevere! Merlin said it would be in the Hall by morning. I want you with me when I see it for the first time and I will not wait another minute. Wake up, dearest, please! What did you say?"

"I said," she spluttered, pulling a loose strand of hair from her mouth, "I said, I will come with you." She yawned. "Only couldn't it wait? I need my hair done and a clean robe."

"You look beautiful, Guinevere," Arthur assured her and meant it. "This robe is clean enough. No one will see us. Just run over there with me and then we can come back and get properly dressed."

"All right," she said as she stretched and yawned again. "I hope we don't awaken the rest of Camelot. Hand me the robe, please."

Arthur watched patiently as she tossed off her nightdress and pulled on the robe. Even after five years her body was still so beautiful to him that he felt something close to awe every time he saw her undressed. Perhaps that was why he still felt so clumsy making love to her. It was more like the violation of a shrine than the tender union of two people. He blamed himself that Guinevere had never learned to enjoy it.

She caught his intense stare and felt unsure. Her fingers twisted her braids, disheveled after the night. She undid them and her hair fell loose, almost to her knees. From the protection of that cloak, she smiled at her husband.

"Do you really believe the Table will be there?"

The robe slipped over her head. She pulled her hair out from under it.

Arthur grabbed her hand. "Yes, I do and I want to be the first one to see it. Let's go."

They ran across the courtyard like guilty children, laughing in whispers, and arrived breathless at the doors. Arthur stared at the grain of the wood. At the moment of truth, he almost doubted. Then he raised his arms and, with a dramatic sweep, pushed the doors inward.

The Great Hall was still dark except for the ring of golden light pouring down on the Table. Carving could now be made out on the legs and around the rim. It was enormous, practically brushing against the pillars supporting the roof. Guinevere had never seen it before in the light. Her memories of it were of a hulking shape lurking in the dark. Her brothers had taken her with them to see it and had dared her to touch it. The sight of it then had terrified her into weeks of nightmares and they had all been forbidden to enter the cave without an adult. Now it stood before her, solid and with form. It was her dowry. Arthur had asked nothing else of her father. In a sense, it was hers. But she wanted no part of it. It still unnerved her. The wood was almost black with age. Where had it come from? Who could have built it and why? Could any tree have been so huge as to be sliced to make the top of it? Against her will, she was drawn to it. She started to walk around it, feeling the top with her fingers. Suddenly she stopped and traced the grooves she had felt.

"Arthur, look at this! Merlin has put your name here!"

"What? That shouldn't be. There was to be no sign of rank."

"I don't know anything about that, but here it is."

His hand covered hers as again they felt the carving. They needed touch as well as sight before they could believe what was written there.

"ARTURUS REX"

Despite his protest, Arthur stared at it in delight. "Merlin couldn't have carved this here. The edges of the letters are smooth and as worn as the table itself. Could it be that it was always here, that it was meant for me from the beginning?"

Guinevere shrugged. She never speculated on the impossible.

She continued wandering around the Table, suppressing a strong temptation to see if she could slide across its smooth surface. She wanted to do something that would reduce its mystery.

Arthur could not move from the spot that bore his name and title. His throat constricted as he tried to force back the tears. It had been here waiting for him all along. There was a purpose, a destiny for him to follow. His knees buckled and he knelt on the rough new floor, his cheek against one of the Table's legs. A great surge of relief and hope swept over him. He was not alone! In spite of Merlin, Guinevere, Gawain, and Cei; in spite of all the tenets of religion he had been taught; in spite of his long-ago vision of the Virgin, he had doubted and feared. Too many nights it had seemed to him that the fate of all civilization in Britain lay with him and the weight was suffocating. Here at last was proof that somehow things had been ordained, that someone somewhere had known he would exist and had cared enough to leave him a message. Perhaps even now someone was watching, helping in secret. Thank God, at last he could believe that he did not dream alone.

Guinevere had reached the other side of the Table. She stopped and again ran her fingers over the surface.

"So that's what it was!" she said in excitement. "Arthur, come and see. I felt this once before, when Father and I were down in the cave, getting wine. There was no light then, but I am sure it is the same. I tried to spell it out. S-I-E-G-E-P-E-R-I-L-L-I-E-U-X. Siegeperillieux? What does that mean? Is it someone's name?"

Arthur roused himself and went to stand beside her. He regarded the letters. "It doesn't look like any language I've ever seen. It's not Brythonic and it's not Latin. That last part, could someone have been trying to spell 'perillustris'? Maybe 'siege' means 'guest.' It could be a place for a distinguished guest. What do you think?"

"It sounds reasonable. I wonder why they carved places only for you and a guest?"

Arthur circled the Table quickly, his hand skimming the top to catch any hint of further engraving. There was none. He wondered how many could be seated . . . fifty, at least, maybe more. And a guest? There was no sense in puzzling over it now. He could ask Merlin. He took Guinevere's arm.

"Come, my love. We had better get ourselves properly dressed. Wear something special. Something for a coronation. This day is the true beginning of my reign. Now there can be no doubt that there is but one High King in Britain. The best of them will come to me and from Camelot will issue forth order and justice and a reawakening of the kind of society our ancestors knew. It will be a rebirth. And you will be its Queen, Guinevere."

He held her tightly and swung her around, kissing her over and over in his joy. At last he set her down. Both of them had become entangled in her unbound hair. With gentle, trembling fingers, he parted the snarls and kissed her again, whispering, "But even more, you will be *my* Queen, Guinevere."

After everyone had seen and been awed by the Table, Arthur declared a day of celebration. It was a week to Midsummer's Day and the afternoons were hot and humid. It was only sensible to build the roasting fires for the meats out of doors and to take the amphorae of wine and ale down to the stream to chill. The elders, the children, the farming landholders who lived at Caerleon in winter were now back on their lands. That left the most active, the strongest, the most restless to inhabit Camelot. There were fosterlings, sons and daughters of all the great families, there to be trained according to their station. Some brought their own servants; others fended for themselves or recruited cheap service from the household staff. Strangers also appeared at Camelot, people with no family connections at all. They were traders often, traveling jugglers, or peripatetic monks. Some young men arrived, each—as Lancelot had planned—with only a sword and a shield, hoping to win honor and loot in the fighting. Later, when Arthur's fame had spread beyond his realm, there would be more exotic visitors, with dark skin and rich and bizarre clothing, who spoke Latin with musical accents and knew no Celtic language at all. But that day was far in the future. Today Camelot was still a tight family, young, brave, and sure of its destiny.

Gawain heard the music and laughter as he guided his brothers through the barricades that wound, mazelike, up the hill to the gates. He urged his horse on.

"Agravaine! Gaheris! Hurry! It sounds like there's a festival at Camelot today and I don't imagine that it's in honor of your coming. Let's get up there and get our duty introductions over before the best wine is gone!"

"Festival? What for?" Agravaine worried. "Damn! Mother never would let us learn about the old days. It's probably some Roman holiday that everyone else knows all about."

He chewed the corner of his moustache. Agravaine was shorter than Gawain, but broader in the shoulders. His dark hair, gray eyes, and square chin marked him as a true son of King Lot, probably the only one of the five who was. Lot was partial to him for this reason, but allowed himself to show no overt favoritism, reasoning that the boys were not to blame for their mother's behavior. Agravaine had always felt cheated by knowing his own father, for all his kindness. The others had spun wild tales of their possible parentage and each of them had some trait, some hint of mystery, that he had always longed for, even if it meant living only half a life, as Gawain must. His certainty about himself had made him determined to be certain about everything else. He wanted to know his proper place at all times, to be aware of what was occurring and, most of all, to be in control. He spent a great deal of time being nervous.

"I'll drink to any holiday they like," Gawain answered. "But if we don't get out of these blasted earthworks soon, everyone will be too drunk to tell us what to toast. I know this is supposed to make the place impregnable, but I wish there were a back door for friends to use."

Gaheris made no comment. He rarely did. He may not

have been listening. He noticed the fresh dirt dislodged to create the barricades. Where the sun hit the top of it, wildflowers had begun to sprout.

Gawain was greeted with loud cheers and catcalls. He and his brothers left their horses and gear with one of the stableboys and hurried back to the wine table. Geraldus was there, happily tapping a beat on the wood with an empty cup. As they neared, he stopped and yelled into the air.

"I said, you come in at the third measure. One . . . two . . . three. . . ! And all together. This isn't a stroll in the woods. Think of a march! Together! Now, try it again. Baom . . . da . . . da, da, da . . . ! Listen to me!"

Gawain reached around him for full wine cups for himself, Agravaine, and Gaheris. He pointed to Geraldus.

"You know our resident saint? He and his whatever-they-are came with me to Tintagel about three years ago."

They nodded and reached for their cups. The movement caught Geraldus' eye and he grinned at them.

"I'm having some trouble with a triumphal march. Arthur has his Table at last, you know!" he shouted while waving his arms. "It's in the Great Hall. Go see it before you get started here. Cei! Gawain brought his brothers—two of them, anyway. Go show them the Table. No! No! Can't I stop to talk a minute? You've gotten it totally scrambled. Do you want to go back to monotones?"

Cei, Arthur's milk-brother and seneschal, greeted the new arrivals in Arthur's name.

"If you wait to see him you'll never eat. He's off with Master Merlin, trying to figure out how many the Table will seat. They've put circles and lines and some sort of symbols all over an old scroll. I don't know why they don't just call us all in and see how many fit. But I'm neither a wizard nor a king, I'm glad to say, and I don't try to understand their ways. Come have a look at the thing. You won't believe its size, and Arthur's name, they say, carved right on it, all this time."

As they entered the Hall, they received the same impression as the other visitors had. There was no light but that from the window overhead. Sunlight streamed palpably upon the table, the rays alive with dancing flecks of dust. They had the sense of entering a sacred place and their voices were muted as they approached it.

Cei felt that his role as host meant that he must keep a conversation going. "It makes the whole thing more real now, doesn't it? You know, Gawain, right now you and I are the only official Knights of the Table. I've sometimes thought we would be the only ones ever. But this thing, well, you can imagine it filled, can't you? Only for Arthur could all of this have come about. It's been so long since he planned it. He's worked and fought and worried himself gray over it. But here is his city and now his Table. I believe him when he says that soon there won't be another court to rival it for learning and honor in all of Christendom."

His voice was soft with awe and devotion. Gawain put his arm on Cei's shoulder.

"I know. I haven't always paid attention when he tried to pull me into his plans. I couldn't understand him half the time. It was enough for me to do what he asked and not consider the reason. But now, with something I can see and touch, there seems some sense to it. He told me once that his court would be like the sun; his justice would fall evenly upon all in the land. Equally. How could that be? Yet look at this table. Where is the high seat? It always seemed impossible, but now I think I begin to believe."

Gaheris had been watching the slow descent of the motes to the wood's surface. As they landed, he raised his hand to brush them away. The hard wood depressed as his fingers touched it. He jerked his hand up and looked around quickly to see if anyone had noticed what he had done. Then he saw the marks that had been made. His jaw dropped.

"Gluuk!"

Agravaine was on the other side of the Table, trying to puzzle out the "siege" engraving.

"What is it, Gaheris?"

"G . . . G . . . Look!"

They all rushed to him, but the writing was complete by the time they got there. They stared when he pointed. Gawain felt a jab of terror. He had grown used to unseen, unheard singers; he didn't mind if tables fifty feet across wandered into locked rooms; he accepted his own odd inability to stay awake at night—but this was too much. His own name, carved in the Table and outlined in gold, just to the left of Arthur's, where ten minutes before there had been only bare wood: SIR GAWAIN.

He glanced nervously at his brothers on either side and backed away, a step at a time. Perhaps the words would be gone when he came back. Where had he left his wine cup?

He was stopped by a cry from Cei. It was truly a cry. The man could hardly speak through his tears.

"See what they did? Right there. C-E-I and some other thing before it. I'm at his right hand. He always said he would, but I thought Merlin or Cador or you, Gawain. He didn't have to, I wouldn't have minded. I've got to go thank him!"

He wiped his face on his sleeve and stumbled out.

"I don't understand this at all." Agravaine was affronted. Gaheris took his arm.

"It's all right, old fellow," he soothed. "No one else does, either."

They went back to the celebration to blanket their shock with food and drink.

Merlin had no desire to join in the festivities. He did not care for juvenile orgies. After he had tolerated Arthur's enthusiasm and assured him that he could count on seating at least fifty knights and perhaps even a hundred, he closed his eyes and refused to open them. To the news that more names were being supernaturally engraved on the Table he only grunted. It was time for them to start finding their own explanations.

Guinevere and Lydia were on the balcony. Lydia's brother had sent her up when the dancing had not stopped with the music. Guinevere knew well that her presence inhibited the pleasure of others and had returned to her rooms quite early. Lydia had managed to consume more than her share of wine, however, before Constantine had decided to be protective and she was piqued at having to miss the fun.

"I love to dance!" She hopped a bit across the balcony,

which started it creaking. She sat down. "Don't you ever want to just dance and dance until the moon rises and then float away into the night air?"

Her arms fluttered and she stared at them as if puzzled that she did not levitate. Guinevere helped her up.

"I never learned to dance," she said. "I never really wanted to," she added quickly as Lydia showed signs of weeping at such deprivation.

"I think we should go back in now, Lydia. The day is cooling as the sun gets lower."

"Certainly, Guinevere." Lydia leaned against her and started to obey when she happened to glance down at the field.

"Oh my!" She clapped both hands to her mouth. "Guinevere! Look at those amazing people!"

Guinevere followed her gaze. "What . . . ?"

Standing motionless on the practice field were three horses, two brown and one an ivory white. Upon them, just as still, were two men and a woman. The woman's hair was unbound and kept in place only by a gold and jeweled fillet which glittered in the last rays of the sun. Her clothing was of silky fabric that shimmered and changed color in the breeze. The men were even more incredible, apparently armed in silver and bronze. The one in silver wore a mask covering the top half of his face. They seemed to be waiting for someone or something. Guinevere wondered how long they had been there. It didn't appear that they intended to enter Camelot uninvited. Perhaps she should send someone. Her eyes swept the revelers. No one down there looked alert. The laughter was beginning to sound hysterical, and the singing more slow and slurred. Oh, good! There was Caet—Briacu, rather. He didn't look as if he had been celebrating with the others. She called to him.

"Briacu! There are some strange people standing out in the practice field. Can you send someone to find out who they are and what they want?"

Caet nodded and bowed. He looked around. The revelers looked as if they couldn't crawl to their own beds, much less negotiate the twisting embankments to reach the field. He did not mind going himself, but not on foot. He went to the stables and slipped a bridle on Cheo. At least he would not be the one who had to look up.

Guinevere and Lydia continued to watch the three strangers below them. They still had made no movement at all. Guinevere wondered if they had any idea that they were being watched. Lydia was fascinated. She had sat on the floor again and was peering at them through the rails.

"Where do you think they come from? They certainly don't look like anyone I ever met in Armorica. Ireland, do you think?"

Caet had reached the people. He made some greeting, but Guinevere and Lydia could not hear it. In answer, the man in bronze moved forward and handed him a scroll. Then, without a word, the three turned and rode into the forest. Caet watched them go and then, with a shrug, turned his horse back to the gate.

He brought the scroll to Guinevere.

"What in the world?" She unrolled it and read. " 'To Arthur, King of Britain, Greetings from the Lady of the Lake.' Briacu, can you find Arthur? I think he should see this at once."

Arthur had just gotten his dinner. He had forgotten to eat all day and was starving. He wasn't interested in mysterious visitors. There had been enough sorcery and strangeness already today. He only cared about the reality of the meat and bread on his plate. But Caet was waiting for an answer. Arthur sighed and decided to bring the plate with him to Guinevere's rooms.

"Look, Briacu, I know it's not your job, but could you search out a wine jar and bring it up to me? Bring a cup for yourself, too."

He found Guinevere tucking Lydia into a blanket on the couch. The wine had overcome her. Guinevere shook her head at his anxious expression.

"No, you won't bother her. I don't think that her foster parents ever allowed her all the wine she wanted before. Oh, Arthur, haven't you eaten yet? Sit down at once. Let me call someone for wine."

"Briacu is bringing some. Why don't you read me the message while I eat?" he suggested as he started in on the meat. The juice ran down his fingers and he wiped them on the bread.

"Briacu told you about the people, what they looked like, didn't he?"

He nodded, still chewing.

She began reading. " 'To Arthur, King of Britain, Greetings from the Lady of the Lake.' Who is that?"

"I think Merlin told me something about her once. He won Excalibur from her. I don't remember the rest. Go on."

" 'I come before you to present to the court of Camelot my Protégé, Lancelot of the Lake. Tomorrow morning Lancelot will prove in combat with any knight you so choose that he is a worthy and gallant man of great prowess, more than fitted to be a member of your company and to be a true and valiant Knight of the Round Table. He will await you then on the spot where we stood today. Be it also known that Lancelot and his squire, Torres, are under my protection and any ill treatment of them will not go unmarked.' "

"But that's wonderful!" Arthur exclaimed. "Read that part again about a 'true and valiant Knight.' The very thing I want. What was he like? Do you think he can fight?"

"Arthur, I have no idea. You won't believe the costume he had on. I think there were ostrich feathers in his helmet. He sat his horse well, though. What will you do?"

"What else? Send someone down to fight him in the morning. This will be exciting. How about Gawain?"

"Do you think that would be fair? It's almost midsummer."

"That's true. Cei then. He'd like that and right now, he's the only other knight we have. Oh, Briacu, the wine. Thank you. Do you know where Sir Cei is? Down there somewhere? Oh, well. I'd better go find him myself. All right, my dear. I'll be back as soon as I find him. Do you think Lydia will have to sleep there *all* night?"

Not far away from Camelot, the Lady had set up camp in her own way and with her own elegance. She saw no reason to be uncomfortable, even in the middle of a wilderness. She had finished her meal and reclined gracefully upon her divan, waiting for Lancelot and Torres to complete dinner.

"Now, you both understand what you will do tomorrow? I have brought you to your Arthur, but it is up to you to earn your place with him. I'm sure you will have no trouble, but you will find that life may be very different up here. Not everyone lives the way we do and, I confess, I have never cared enough to find out much about the customs of these humans. But if you live among them, you must learn to adapt to their ways. And of course, my dears, whenever you want to return to us, you will always be most joyfully received."

She was surprised at herself. There was a catch in her voice which was totally uncontrived. She must be careful. It wouldn't do for Lancelot to know how very much she wanted them to return.

Torres laughed. "I imagine I will miss you all very much. But I'll stay as long as Lancelot needs me. Someone has to remember to feed his horse.

"After all," he added in a lower voice, "the poor beast has done nothing to repent of."

Lancelot wasn't listening. He was seeing himself defeating one opponent after another, disarming them and then politely returning their weapons with such grace and skill that all who saw him wondered and admired. Suddenly he stopped himself in shame. The sin of pride! How often Meredydd had cautioned him against it. He pushed his plate away and left the table, retreating into the woods to pray for forgiveness and humility. Torres frowned as he watched him go.

"Oh Lord, I wonder what dreadful thing he managed to do while simply eating his bread. Do you think there will be others like him at Camelot?"

"I hope not," the Lady replied fervently. "This compulsion of his has to be cured. If I could stay and help you, I would, but I have already been too long away from my Lake. Take care of him, Torres. This whole enterprise frightens me. For the first time in centuries, I have no idea of how it will end."

Chapter Six

Cei was astounded to hear that he had been made champion for Arthur. He immediately stopped drinking and retired to his corner to rest and prepare for the morning's encounter. He worried a little, though. He was confident that he could hold his own against any man he had ever met, except Gawain at noon. But what if this Lancelot had some magic? Was he human? They said he came from a lake. He had heard a tale once when he was a boy about a forbidden lake in the woods that lured travelers to their deaths. What if Lancelot were the ghost of such a wayfarer? Could ghosts be seen in the daylight? He wasn't sure. He decided to double-check his gear. If the man *was* a man, he must be prepared to defeat him.

As Lancelot approached the field the next morning, his only thought was to be permitted to win and yet be spared from hurting anyone or inflicting humiliation upon them. In spite of his night-long penance for pride and overconfidence, Lancelot could not deny that he had never been beaten in practice combat. Torres rode behind him, feeling like a child sent out for the first time without his mother. The Lady had been gone when they awoke, along with all her paraphernalia. Lancelot had not been surprised or concerned, but Torres did not have his serene confidence. His armor did not feel grand today, only clanking and silly.

Lancelot was relieved that the Lady was no longer with them. She did not exactly represent the goals he had set himself. He also feared that anything he won in her presence might be because of her help and not of his own doing. He was eager to stand before the crowd and face his opponent as a man alone.

When they reached the field, he was surprised and crushed. There was no crowd. Hardly anyone was there. Nine-tenths of Camelot was still abed, sleeping off the effects of the celebration. Lancelot thought it was another punishment for his pride. He tried to accept it meekly, telling himself that the only reason for an audience was to pander to his own ignoble desire for glory. But the deflated feeling remained.

Cei, waiting at the other end of the field, knew who was there and, far from being disappointed, was honored and therefore far too nervous. As he compared Lancelot's gear and build with his own, he began to feel terrified that he would make a fool of himself. Gawain and both his brothers were watching. He saw Constantine, wrapped in a brown and yellow striped cloak, lead his sister to one of the seats. And Arthur was there, hunched down in an old blanket to keep warm.

"Please," Cei whispered. "Don't let me look an ass in front of them all."

Despite his lack of education, his prayer was just as fervent as any Lancelot had ever made.

Torres was reassured by the lack of people. He trotted over to Cei.

"Good morning!" he beamed. "I suppose you are the champion Lancelot will fight today?"

Cei nodded.

"Fine. If it's all right with you, I'll give the signal for you both to begin. We don't know your rules, but we always count points if you stay on your horse, keep your shield, or manage to nick the armor of your opponent. We allow no blows to the face. We end the contest when one man is down or disarmed."

"That matches our rules well enough." Cei's voice was stern.

"And also," Torres smiled again, "we want to join you and someday fight at your side. So do your best, but remember that he isn't an enemy and his weapon someday might be needed to protect you. Do you understand me? Why are you looking so fierce? All I mean to say is, he doesn't want to hurt you and I would rather that you didn't hurt him. It's just a formality, this match, you see?"

He held out his hand. Cei stared at it for a second, then clasped it. He did not trust himself to make a speech. He just wanted the whole thing done.

"Begin it," was all he could say.

Torres returned to the center of the field. When the two men signalled that they were ready, he raised his arm and then dropped it. The contest was begun.

The hardest part of fighting from horseback was keeping one's seat. To do that, the rider had to be able to remain almost motionless below the waist, with his knees and thighs gripping the sides of his mount tightly. In battle against warriors on foot, the main idea was either to throw a javelin from a safe spot or to thrust into the unit with a lance or sword, jabbing quickly and accurately, so that the man attacked had no chance to grab at the weapon and pull down both lance and rider.

When facing an enemy on horseback, the strategy was even more complex. Each man would be armed with lance, shield, sword, and perhaps a short dagger for emergencies. The shield, on the left arm, was kept up at all times. As the other rider neared, one had to throw the javelin with such force as to hit the shield and break the other rider's arm. This was almost impossible. The lack of stirrups meant that any attempt to throw a javelin with force might result in overbalancing and being left in the dirt. So the most one hoped for was to hit the other rider hard enough to knock him off his horse, leaving him to the ground troops to handle. If the lance did neither of these things, then the sword must be drawn quickly and another attempt made to throw the opponent to the ground.

It was generally agreed that, in this sort of one-to-one combat, a man who could keep his shield and his horse was nearly invulnerable. All he needed to do was block sword thrusts. Even if he had lost both his own weapons, it might still be possible, through careful maneuvering, to unseat an armed challenger.

In a practice meet, strategy was more complicated, as one did not want to kill the other man. Therefore, the aim of the lance had to be nearly perfect, throwing the other rider from his horse through swift, skillful action to unbalance him, instead of violent hacking to maim and kill.

In any case, everyone tried to avoid hurting the horse, as it was a highly valued prize of combat.

Lancelot studied Cei as they neared each other. He was holding his shield too far to the right to give him room to throw. He was a good horseman, though, guiding his mount by varying the pressure with his knees. Even if he caught the shield and jerked it away from the man's body, he didn't think it would unseat him. Lancelot raised his own shield as Cei aimed to throw. Just before the lance left Cei's hand, Lancelot threw his. Without waiting to see where it had hit, he drew his sword. He felt a thud as Cei's lance struck his shield straight on and was embedded. He had to waste precious time snapping it off. It was a fine throw, utilizing the speed of Lancelot's charge to add to the force. But in making it, Cei had let his shield swing wide and Lancelot's lance had struck him in the side. It had not penetrated the chain mail, but it was clear that Cei was bruised and winded by the shock. He had not drawn his sword.

Lancelot reined in his horse and waited.

Arthur nudged Constantine. "What's he doing? He can't think he's won already?"

"I'm not sure," Constantine muttered. "You don't think he could be waiting for Cei to draw, do you?"

Arthur considered. "I think he is! Now, if he can still win after giving Cei that edge. . . ."

He did not finish. Cei's sword was out and they were circling each other, waiting for a miscalculation.

Lydia grabbed Gawain's arm. "Why didn't he end it when he hit Cei?" she wanted to know. "He may be hurt!"

Gawain paid little attention to her. He was fascinated by the action. He didn't notice the concern in her voice.

"He's not hurt much. He shouldn't have let his shield out like that. I hope they remember to swing wide of the horses. Wait . . . he's down! Damn! I missed it! Lancelot was between us. What happened?"

Arthur was standing and applauding. "It was classic! He let Cei see an opening and then pulled back so that he reached too far and went right over! He almost kept his grip, but he was putting too much force behind the thrust and off he went! Magnificent! Gawain, go tell him we'd be happy to have him here. Send him to me at the Hall. If he speaks as well as he fights, he shall be made a knight today!"

Rubbing his hands in delight, Arthur returned to his rooms.

"Did you see it, Guinevere? He not only beat Cei, but gave him an advantage, too."

"It was too windy out to watch, Arthur, but I heard the shouts. I don't like to see those things. No one was hurt, were they?"

"No, dear. Cei may have a bruise on his side, but he'll be fine. Lancelot wasn't even dented."

"That's good. It seems a very silly way to judge people's ability, anyway."

Arthur gave her a kiss and left. He was not going to try to explain the principle to Guinevere. Every time he got into similar discussions with her he ended up wondering if they were speaking the same language.

He waited in the Hall for several minutes. Sounds from the various other buildings indicated that Camelot was beginning to rise. A head poked through the opening of the door. It was not Lancelot, but Lydia.

"Gawain says to tell you that the stranger won't come in."

"He won't come! Why not? I thought that was why he came to Camelot in the first place!"

She entered a little way. "I don't know, Arthur. Gawain told him that he would welcome him as a knight. But then he and this Lancelot and Constantine started arguing and waving their arms about and I was told to tell you that he felt it was too easy a test and he won't enter the gates until he has proved himself. What do you want me to do?"

Arthur was not sure. The more he heard of Lancelot, the better he liked him. This man certainly had the right idea. After all, the whole point was that the knights should be a select few of proven ability. Perhaps Lancelot feared that Cei had not been the best man or that he had not been feeling well this morning. He chewed the corner of his lip, a sure sign of perturbation. There was simply too much to do today to waste time sending out one man after another until Lancelot decided that he had shown them what he was worth. Unless.... Arthur's eyes lit up. Why not?

"Lydia, run and tell Constantine that I will send out another man to challenge this stubborn applicant. Then why don't you go back to bed? You seem a bit pale."

Lydia went out. When the door closed, she furtively pinched her cheeks. She was a little tired—the aftereffect of the wine—but that was not the reason for her paleness. Cei had been limping when he left the field on Briacu's arm and no one had as yet bothered to find out if he were all right. If Lancelot had not been so skillful, Cei might have been killed and yet those *men* just sat there commenting idly on the finer points of lance-throwing. As soon as she delivered her message, she was going to put her pride in her pocket and search out someone who could tell her how he was.

Guinevere heard Arthur again, rummaging around in his old-clothes chest. He looked up when he heard her enter, a guilty, mischievous grin on his face. Then he went back into the huge oaken coffer, tossing cloaks and boots out over his shoulder.

"Arthur, what are you looking for?" She sounded very prim. "You are making a terrible mess."

"Fidelo can clean it up; he won't care." Arthur continued burrowing. "Aha! I knew it hadn't been discarded!"

He drew out a battered sheath from which emerged an old sword. The hilt was a bit rusty, but the blade was still clean and shining. Arthur cradled it gently with loving remembrance.

"This was my sword before Excalibur. I won it by beating old Ector in a training bout. I don't know which of us was the more proud."

"What do you want it for?" Guinevere had seen Lancelot still waiting out on the practice field and she was becoming suspicious.

·79·

"Because it has no magic and no fame. Its only power comes from the arm of the man who wields it. I have waited so long to be able to use it again."

Guinevere felt a chill. "You are not going to meet him yourself!" she exclaimed.

He stared at her, prepared to fight. "Why not? It's the perfect answer. I can't risk having my men invalided with broken limbs or shattered lances until Sir-Lancelot-that-will-be decides that he has done enough to finally be worthy of us. However, if he defeats me, he certainly can't call for a more worthy opponent. At least, I hope not."

"If he defeats you? Why should he? And what do you think will happen to Britain if you should spend the next six months waiting for a broken leg or a broken head to heal?"

"Thank you, my love. I appreciate your concern. It's very flattering. Even if I let him knock me down, why should I be hurt? After all, I am a famous warrior. How many men was I supposed to have killed at Mons Badon . . . a hundred? Five hundred? That was eight years ago. Even if I struck down only ten or twelve then, I should be able to hold my own against one man today."

Guinevere saw that it would be no more use to argue.

"I wasn't there at Mons Badon. Mark was and he refuses to fight ever again. I will not watch you now. But I will go and be sure there will be a hot bath for you when you return with your muscles sore and your pride bruised. In this humid weather it seems that only the frigidarium has been maintained. And, Arthur, I wish you would talk to someone about the separate facilities for men and women. There has not been much work done on the wall between the rooms."

When she was gone, Arthur started whistling. She was upset. Maybe she cared for him more than he suspected. He dug out an old helmet with a visor that would cover his face, not that Lancelot would know it. His hair also had to be concealed. He ran his hands through it. Often men had rallied to him at the sight of his red mane above the fray, but now the gray was dulling it. Even more reason to keep it out of sight. It wouldn't do to have Lancelot think he was being insulted with an old, retired warrior to challenge him. He put the helmet and visor on and wrapped himself in an old brown cloak. He could feel sweat pouring down his face. He remembered the first time he had put it on, full of excitement, to ride with Cei and Ector. They had gone to a muster meant to choose a leader for Britain. He had found Excalibur that day. They had watched in awe as he pulled that sword out of the stone and then replaced it, over and over, until his arm ached and his scalp itched from perspiration. From then on, he was as much a symbol as the sword. He had accepted it, even reached for it, but now, just once more, he wanted to be that boy again, unknown.

He took Briacu's mare, Nera. She was not as tall as her brother, but more agile. He did not want Lancelot to think he was winning too easily. He grimaced as he mounted. He hoped he could make it look as though Lancelot were not winning too easily.

On the field Torres was growing impatient. He didn't see why Lancelot could not be satisfied with his win. Sir Cei had fought as well as any man.

"Lancelot," he complained, "we don't want to embarrass them. You don't have to be perfect. Why don't you go on in and take the oath or whatever they require and then I can get out of this hot, sticky, uncomfortable costume."

Lancelot smiled at Torres. "Go ahead, you don't have to stay in that. It is awfully hot, isn't it? I would have thought the Lady would come up with something cooler. This silk underwear has plastered itself to my skin. I may never peel it off."

"Let's both go then. No one is keeping us."

Just then Lancelot saw the new man riding toward them. This looked interesting: patched cloak, tarnished helmet, a shield with no markings. But the man was tall and powerful and rode with the air of one who led.

"I think, Torres, that our waiting has been worthwhile. Could you go ask him his name?"

Arthur had forgotten that part of the ritual. He stammered. "Name? Of course, I am . . . I am Ector, of Northumbria."

Torres seemed not to notice the stammering. He went to

the center of the field and again gave the signal. The two men advanced.

Lydia was furious. No one knew anything about Cei, except that he had bathed and gone out again, presumably to his bed. How was she to find that? Her own rooms were in the same building as Guinevere's and she had never been in anyone else's quarters. How could they be so thoughtless? He might be seriously injured. Lydia had never given much thought to Cei, except to note that his eyes followed her wherever she went. But when she saw him this morning sent out like a sacrifice to test a new knight, as if his life were of no consequence, all of a sudden he took on new importance. The unmarried soldiers were all supposed to be in this building. She peered in.

It wasn't much more than one long room, with a hearth at one end. Lining the walls were tables which converted to beds. There were clothes chests underneath. Swords, shields, and other gear were hung on the walls. She did not see anyone, but sensed that the room was occupied. Nervously she entered. A voice from the hearth end of the room made her jump.

"What are you doing here? Arthur allows no women . . . oh, Lydia!"

It was Cei. He had gone to his corner by the fire, a traditional place of rank, although Lydia did not know that. He thought he would be left alone to lick his wounds. His side ached terribly and he hoped he was not bleeding internally. He had seen a man die that way once, from nothing more than a bruise, it seemed. But, of all people, he didn't want Lydia to see him this way. He tried to rise and gave a quick gasp as his muscles failed to respond.

"No, you mustn't get up." Lydia's voice was soft and caring. "They've left you here all alone after you were so brave and strong today, all for their silly entertainment. Please, let me get you something cool to drink. Do you think someone should tend to your side?"

Cei was flustered by her attention and understood little of

what she was saying. He had had no experience of the type of woman who cares most about the injured and helpless. He would much rather have seen her when he was a victor. How could he know that she would probably not have noticed him as a winner? Champions needed no one. Hawks could find their own meals. Lydia cared for the sparrows.

She brought him a cup of cool water laced with mint. He forced himself to drink it. She sat by his bed and watched him and then began talking, telling him about her days in Armorica, the family there. Before he knew it, he was sharing his childhood with her, talking about his parents and foster brother, Arthur. By the afternoon they knew each other as if they had been friends all their lives.

Guinevere had said that she would not watch, but she found that she couldn't bear to hear the crashes of sword and shield and not know what was going on. She stood at the balcony door, where she was in shadow, and bit her fingernails as the match progressed.

It seemed to her that it would go on forever. Both the men had lost their lances in the first encounter. Now they circled and feinted and swung their swords over and over. She saw no variation in the pattern. She wondered if Arthur had remembered his mail shirt or at least a leather jerkin. Constantine and Agravaine were watching intently. Gawain seemed to be explaining something to Gaheris. Geraldus had joined them and was talking and waving his arms around, too. But whether he was commenting on the match or directing his singers, she couldn't tell.

She was starting on her thumbnail when, with no warning, Arthur lunged at Lancelot with his sword. His shield dropped by the merest fraction, but Lancelot was there and caught him with the flat of his sword. Arthur tumbled over.

There were cheers from those watching. They raced over to the two men. Arthur was apparently not hurt, for he was standing now and pulling off his helmet. He wiped his brow and grinned up at Lancelot. Guinevere spit out her thumbnail and cursed the lot of them for the worry they caused.

Arthur was glad it was over. Lancelot had missed one opening he had given him and he did not think he could have lasted long enough to give him another. He rubbed the sweat off his neck. This was insane. Autumn was the only sensible time to fight anyone. All other seasons were either too hot, too cold, or too slippery. No wonder the Saxons almost always mounted their major offensives in late September.

"Well, Sir Lancelot. Will you come with me now and have a cold bath and a good meal, or do you insist on carrying this on until we all die of sunstroke?"

Torres dismounted and gratefully removed his helmet. He greeted Arthur.

"Thank you, sir, for saving me. Lancelot and I thought you might be someone important when you first arrived, but we never thought it would be the King. You have my respect, both for your brilliant swordplay and for your diplomatic and unselfish ability in stopping the thing before I was boiled alive."

"You are more than welcome, Torres. Have you come to be made a knight, too?" Arthur asked.

"No, indeed. I will let Lancelot do that. I just came with him to look around and be of service whenever I might be needed. I have no ambitions."

"That is a refreshing change," Gawain said. "Do you think we can get your friend off his horse in time for dinner? I fear we have already missed breakfast."

"I will talk with him," Arthur said. "You all go on up. We will follow soon."

The others went willingly. The day was indeed already too warm for exercise. Arthur walked over to where Lancelot still sat. He lifted his visor as the King neared.

"Well, Lancelot of the Lake, how much of an invitation do you need? I have said that I think you will be a fine knight and have proved it with my body." He rubbed his hip, where he had landed. "What more do you want?"

Lancelot climbed down. He made a contrast to Arthur, slim and tidy, even after a morning of battle. He was slightly the shorter, but Arthur was not trying to hold himself in military bearing, and they seemed of a height.

"I wonder how old he is," Arthur thought. "He reminds me of the way I was when I first met Guinevere, so damned unsure of myself that I tried too hard to be correct. Is that his problem?"

Lancelot dropped his gear on the grass.

"Why did you let me win?" he demanded.

"I?" Arthur was shocked. "Why should I let you win? I am the King. Haven't you been told that I never lose?"

They stood glaring at each other for a full minute and then Arthur's mouth began to twitch. Lancelot realized that he was being foolish. Here he was face to face with the great King Arthur at last, and he was behaving like a child. He started to grin, too, and all at once they were both laughing and pounding each other on the back as they strolled together up the hill to Camelot.

"Before you do anything, Lancelot, you must meet my wife. She is the greatest treasure in the entire realm. Come up with me. Guinevere!"

He bounded into the room with such exuberance that she knew he was unhurt. He hugged her tightly and she didn't mind the sweat and dirt he got on her dress. She sighed and whispered to him, "Why must you worry me so? Isn't it enough that you must fight real battles?"

He didn't answer, but held her hand and extended it to their visitor.

"Guinevere, this is the man who has worried you so. He will be staying with us for a long while, I hope. Lancelot, this is my wife."

Lancelot had been staring at her since he entered the room. He had not been prepared for this. Who would have thought that this man had married a goddess? He touched the hand offered to him and bowed over it. He raised his eyes to hers.

Guinevere caught her breath. She nearly cried out. His eyes! Something about them was familiar. But that was nonsense. She had never seen him before. She controlled herself and greeted him civilly. He only stared at her the more.

Arthur laughed. He was used to Guinevere having that effect on people the first time they saw her. He guided

Lancelot out of the room. At the door he turned and winked at her.

"He'll be worth it, Guinevere, wait and see. Come along, Lancelot, your destiny waits!"

Chapter Seven

"But, Mother, everyone else is at Camelot!" Gareth pleaded. "Modred and I are missing all the excitement. Why can't we go, too?"

Morgan Le Fay did not look at her son. She was having her hair arranged for the day, carefully layered in tiers of curls gently touched with a saffron compound to enhance the shine. It was a laborious process and one sudden twist of the neck would ruin it. Gareth knew that very well, which was why he had chosen this time to beg her once again to let him go. When dealing with Mother, it was always better if one could avoid her eyes.

She sniffed and delicately touched her nose with a scented cloth. "Would you leave me here all alone, bereft of my children, my only joy in life?"

Gareth was perfectly aware that her children were only a by-product of her only joy in life, but he did love her and hated to have to quarrel.

"You could come visit us," he coaxed. "After all, Arthur is your brother. You took all of us to see his wedding and you haven't been to see him since. They say that his courts are the most splendid this side of Constantinople! Just think how you would shine there! There is nothing here at Tintagel. I can't understand why you stay here."

The tower of curls trembled dangerously as Morgan fought with her anger.

"I stay here because it is my home as it was my father's and his before and on as far back as our line reaches. And . . . there are other reasons not of your concern. Perhaps I will visit Arthur one day, although we hardly have any happy childhood memories to share."

She laughed. The memory Arthur had of her was not one he would like recalled. He had been such an easy conquest, a boy left for the summer in the care of a group of dour monks. It was all the more amusing that he had turned out to be her brother. Even better, Arthur was ashamed of the whole episode and frightened of what she could say if she wished. She would attend to him one day. But she was not going to let him get control of all her sons.

"I will not listen to your whining any longer, Gareth," she continued. "I have sent my three eldest sons to Camelot. Arthur has bought them away from me. I will give him no more. You and Modred are staying here. Now leave me!"

She picked up her hand mirror, ostensibly to study the effect of the maid's work, but really to be able to watch as Gareth stomped out.

"Stupid child!" she cursed him to herself. "No wonder I have to dye my hair. Any woman would go gray, having to deal with that."

She examined her face closely in the polished silver. Another wrinkle? She made herself relax until the skin was smooth and her expression vacuous. No, it was gone. But it would be back. No matter how she fought them, the tiny lines always snaked back. She sighed. Perhaps she would send all the boys away. They made her feel old. Well, older, anyway. She glanced in the mirror again. Certainly she was still as beautiful as ever. But, she admitted sourly, time was passing. Morgause had hinted on her last visit that there were potions one could take. She had not aged at all in the last twenty years, it seemed. But Morgan did not care for the kind of dealings one had to go into to purchase those potions. She preferred her enchantments to be more subtle and less dangerous. Damn! There it was again! Wrinkles! She slammed

the mirror down on the table and dismissed the maid. Gareth
had upset her more than he intended. Not about going to
Camelot; that was natural in a young man, if annoying. But
how could he be so insensitive to Tintagel! He must have
gotten that from his father. She tried to remember which one
he had been. There had been a great many insensitive men in
her life. She hoped the other boys didn't feel that way. Not
Modred, at least. Modred must understand what Tintagel
was.

Morgan had been born at the castle on Tintagel. She had
been left behind there when Uther Pendragon had taken her
mother, Igraine, away with him. He had wanted no part of
the daughters of Gorlois. She and her older sister, Morgause,
had played and explored unsupervised throughout the dank
corridors and tunnels; had watched from the towers as the
small community of eremitic monks below went about their
silent business. The men had asked leave to suffer in the tiny
caves along the coast beneath the castle and Gorlois had
agreed, whether from piety or sadistic pleasure, no one was
sure.

It was at Tintagel that Morgan had first learned about men
and their uses. Her husband, Lot, had married her to get the
castle and for the right to control that strip of Cornwall. He
had proved a better husband than she had expected, willing to
ignore her constant affairs and to accept all her children as his
own. He never expected her to accompany him if it meant she
must leave the castle for more than a few weeks. It was here,
also, that she and Morgause had discovered the possibilities
of magic and deception. Tintagel was where her sons had
been born and raised; where she had bound them to her
before they were old enough to judge her. Tintagel, jutting
out into the ocean like a hand upraised against the storm, was
woven into their bones and souls. Even Arthur was part of it.
He had been conceived and born there, although he might
not yet know it. Morgan had felt that in him when she had
first seen him in his sixteenth summer. Even before she knew
who he was, she had sensed the common cords linking them
and Tintagel.

She smiled at the thought of what she had in store for

Arthur. His touted high ideals and sense of justice would help her to her revenge. In the last few months he seemed to have made quite a start toward this new world he wanted to create. Perhaps it was time that she began work, too. She had to compose a message to Morgause, who would be furious if she missed the fun.

Gareth found his younger brother, Modred, in the main hall, polishing his sword. He was sitting close to the fire, even though it was high summer. At Tintagel, warmth never penetrated the stones. Fire glinted on the metal and the red of Modred's hair, making him appear to be wreathed in flames. He was, as always, performing the job with a minimum of effort and a maximum of grace and skill. His long, elegant fingers swept the blade as if it were an instrument.

Gareth did not care about creating an effect. He slumped down into the pillowed chair next to his brother and stuck his chilled feet as close to the hearth as he dared.

"I presume she said no," Modred commented lazily.

Gareth muttered something under his breath.

"Well, what did you expect?" his brother asked. "After the fuss she made when Agravaine and Gaheris wanted to go, it isn't likely she'd give you her blessing to follow them."

"It's not right, Modred," Gareth argued. "I'm almost twenty now and I've done nothing with my life but sit here at Tintagel. Don't you ever worry about what will happen to us? We're the youngest sons. Agravaine will get Tintagel. None of this will ever be ours. Mother won't even consider marrying us to families with property and only daughters to get it. What is she holding us for?"

"Mother has plans, Gareth. She won't let us rot here forever."

"It looks uncommonly like it to me. There are days when I can almost feel the mold creeping across my skin, sticking me to this castle like the hangings stick to the walls."

He lifted his hands from the arms of the chair as if surprised that they would come away.

"Look," he continued, "I know she hated Arthur's father for what he did to our grandparents. But what has that to do with us? It was over thirty years ago. Arthur had nothing to do with it and he welcomes us to join him. Why shouldn't we?"

"I don't care if we do or not, Gareth. I'm content to stay. You know, Arthur has no sons of his own and it isn't likely that he will. Nephews have been known to inherit whole empires. Mother has never been a fool. Leave it to her to know when the time is right."

"While I do nothing!" Gareth suddenly stood. "I won't. Whomever she is planning her tricks to help, it isn't me. You know very well that you're the one she'll make a king, if any of us. Gaheris will be your archbishop and I . . . what minor post do you think I will step into? I won't have it. I don't want some office with no meaning tossed to me. I don't even want to be king. I want to be a knight, like Gawain. That's all; nothing more. And I want to do it on my own, not because Arthur feels the need to find jobs for all his nephews."

Modred gave his sword one last wipe and sheathed it. He regarded Gareth with fond pity.

"That is very noble and grand of you, my brother, but unrealistic and unnecessary. We are glutted with family and neither of us can do anything without their knowing and commenting. Since we must put up with the foibles of our relatives, I think we should also enjoy the preference we are due from them, too."

A noise by the doorway caught their attention. There was a woman waiting. Gareth could not see her face, but he guessed she was not waiting for him.

Modred hung the sword again in its niche in the wall.

"I had almost forgotten that I promised to teach the Lady Avena the finer points of chess. You will excuse me?"

Gareth waved him away.

Yes. Modred could wait. Why not? He was sure to get what he wanted in the end. He always did. No one could resist him. Gareth tried to ignore his jealousy. He liked Modred, too. But sometimes it seemed unfair that he should have so much with no effort. He was handsome, strong, skillful, and had a talent for making friends of both sexes.

From babyhood, Modred naturally reached out for whatever he desired and it always came to him. Gareth thought ruefully that between the charm and flamboyance of Modred and Gawain he was the one who was always overlooked.

He was not tall, his build was slight, and his hair, eyes, and skin were all the same dark tan. He was easy to miss in a group, blending in with the background.

He never asked for preference, never dreamed of immortality, but he longed horribly for some sort of accomplishment, anything to stand against the unusual qualities of his brothers. Even Gaheris had an air of mysticism about him that made others listen on the rare occasions when he chose to speak.

No! He would not sit here impotently any longer. He was going to Arthur, too. If Mother would not equip him properly, he would do without. He would walk there if he had to.

Filled with certainty as to the rightness of his decision, Gareth hurried to his quarters and thrust a few extra tunics and trews into a bag. A comb, a knife, a cup, and an amulet from his Aunt Morgause—he didn't really own much. He slipped out a door cut in the main gate and raced along the narrow spit of land that attached Tintagel to Britain. There were no guards to see him. Lot wasn't home and Morgan never bothered to set a watch. He wondered if he dared take a horse. No, they would surely go after him. Anyway, it pleased him to walk. As he rounded the tumble of rocks which marked the line between shore and land, he felt compelled to break into a run. With a shock of delight, he realized that he was not running from anything but to it. The whole world lay before him, literally. One foot before the other could take him to Camelot, London, Marseilles, Rome, Jerusalem itself! Gareth was not in a mood to think of obstacles: mountains, rivers, oceans would part before him. He was free. And the most wonderful thing about it was that, until this moment, he had not known himself captive.

At Camelot the autumn muster had begun. Arthur intended to take his men on a circuit of the kingdom, stopping only now and then to let the people know that there were strength and order in Britain at last. He meant to pay special attention to those places near the Saxon settlements and, in the west, to the tribal kings, like Meleagant, who had no intention of relinquishing their power. It was at this time of year that Guinevere usually stayed at her parents' old Roman villa. Because of the settling at Camelot, Arthur was later than usual at starting out and Guinevere was more than ready to go.

"When can Geraldus take me?" she asked Arthur one afternoon when she was able to catch him alone for a change.

"I'm sorry, my dear. Geraldus has to take Lydia to Cador. I thought you could have Lancelot escort you home."

"Lancelot! But why, Arthur? Couldn't someone else go? Agravaine would, I know, or Cei, if you can spare him."

"I can't spare either one of them. Cei already asked to escort Lydia and I told him I needed him here."

"But why must it be Lancelot? I thought you wanted to take him with you especially, to show him off."

Guinevere's voice twisted as she spoke. Arthur looked at her sharply.

"What do you mean?"

"Well, he is your perfect knight, isn't he? Strong, just, honorable, owing allegiance to no one but you."

"Yes, he is. He is all I dreamed of. But he is not being accepted as completely as I had hoped, even by those here. You, for instance. You don't like him. Why not?"

Guinevere had wondered when he would notice it. It was true. She didn't like Lancelot. She had tried to hide it, but not successfully. It was a new sensation for her. Normally she either enjoyed someone or ignored him. But Lancelot wasn't enjoyable and he couldn't be ignored. Those haunting, lonesome eyes of his seemed to follow her everywhere. But what could she tell Arthur? He was waiting for her to answer. His look was patient, loving, but mildly disappointed. She took his hand.

"I don't really know why, Arthur. Maybe it's because he is so conspicuously perfect. He doesn't play games or tell stories. He drinks only water. And the way he is always going off to pray at the chapel site! It's as if he's reproaching you for finishing the living quarters first. Why should he pray there? It's not even consecrated yet. And, Arthur, he's always staring at me!"

Arthur laughed at her exasperation. "But everyone stares at you, my love. You are radiantly beautiful. Aren't you used to it yet?"

Guinevere flushed. She knew she was beautiful; she had heard it all her life. She accepted the gapes and gasps as natural and hardly noticed them. However. . . .

"Lancelot is hard to ignore, Arthur. I try to talk with him, but he has such strange ideas of conversation. What do I care about the true nature of the Trinity? Geraldus is a saint and he doesn't worry about such things. Please send someone else with me."

"I can't, Guinevere," he replied. "I'm sorry. I must take everyone else with me. It is important that we appear in force on this journey. Also, I can't bring Lancelot with me this time. I am learning that from his reception here. He is the perfect knight, the one I want all the others to become. But I am still hunting for more recruits. The very sort I want, those who are capable but modest about their talents, would hesitate to measure themselves against Lancelot. I want them with me at Caerleon or Camelot when they meet him, after they have committed themselves to my cause. Do you understand?"

Guinevere did, but she was still not happy about it. "I will allow him to accompany me if it will make you happy, husband. But only to please you. It will certainly be the most boring trip I have ever taken."

"Thank you, my dearest." Arthur kissed her and held her a moment. He wondered for the hundredth time if it would ever become easier for him to part with her and if it would ever matter to her if he were there or not.

Guinevere wandered back across the courtyard, still full of rebellion. Four days with Lancelot would seem like years. He was pompous and pious and generally impossible. How could Arthur be so taken in by him? All he ever did was strut around in that outrageous costume. Why, since the day he arrived, he had not fought at all, not even for practice. Perhaps he had just been lucky in unhorsing Cei and Arthur. Guinevere smiled as a plan came to her. What if Lancelot could be beaten? But whom could she get to challenge him? Most of the men were so taken in by his posturing, they might lose through lack of confidence. Whom could she get who would be sure to win?

Most of the men were working or training in one way or another and gave her no more than a glance as she passed them. She tried to study their techniques and concluded that they all looked clumsy next to Lancelot. They were panting and sweating in the hot sun, often stopping to mop their brows. No. It must be someone who could appear elegant also. Guinevere shook her head. This was becoming more difficult than she had first thought.

She paused at the sound of her name and footsteps behind her. Gawain caught her up from behind and swung her through the air as if she were a child.

"Stop it!" she laughed. "Gawain, I'm getting dizzy! Stop! What's gotten into you?"

He put her down reluctantly. "It's the summer. On a day like this I could race to Land's End and back or topple a giant. But there is nothing for me to do."

"Why don't you practice your swordsmanship with the others?"

"What good would that do?" Gawain grumbled. "I spend most of my time trying not to hurt anyone. I broke a man's arm once. I wasn't even fighting with him, just playing."

"You know, Gawain"— Guinevere's eyes lit wickedly— "what you need is someone of your own ability to spar with. That Lancelot, for instance. I understand he has the same problem you do."

"Lancelot?" Gawain considered. "He's not that good. I saw his match with Arthur and I'm sure Arthur let him win."

"Really? Lancelot doesn't seem to think so. He says he won't practice with anyone here for the same reason you won't; he is afraid of the damage he can do."

Guinevere waited. She was not sure it would work. Gawain was so easygoing, he might just laugh. But, oh, if he would do it! He was a fine one to put Lancelot in his place. Gawain was at his best in the summer: golden, vibrant, strong. He could look the part as well as play it.

Gawain was thinking it over. Guinevere could see the idea appealed to him. But. . . .

"If he's that good, Guin, I might forget myself and kill him. Damn! Just once I'd like to face a real opponent."

"You could ask him to meet you in the afternoon, when you're not quite as strong. That would be fair, wouldn't it?"

"I don't know. This time of year I do very well until almost sundown. Still . . . you say he believes he is the greatest fighter at Camelot? A man like that should be knocked down for his own good."

Guinevere nearly clapped her hands for joy. That would take care of him. Once Arthur saw that Lancelot was no better than any of the others, surely he would not insist that she endure his company on her trip home. Lancelot could ride along with Arthur and the other knights without intimidating anyone.

Lancelot wasn't aware that Guinevere disliked him. When he was around her, he wasn't aware of much of anything. There was something about her, something beyond her obvious beauty, that drew him against his judgment. When Arthur told him that he was to be her companion and guard, alone on a four-day journey, he was both honored and frightened.

"You would trust me with your wife?" he blurted.

"Of course. You won't let anything harm her. And between here and there I don't expect you to have any trouble. If I did, I wouldn't send her there at all. You won't have any problems. And you'll enjoy meeting her parents. They can tell you a lot more of what has happened in Britain in the last thirty years than anyone here can. They were at the center of it all. Apart from Merlin and them, I don't know of a soul who really knows what life was like in the old days."

Lancelot wondered if Arthur had purposely misunderstood him. Meredydd had often told him that no sane man would allow his wife to be left alone with another, even for an hour. Arthur, however, seemed not to consider proximity a matter of concern. Lancelot was deeply moved by this evidence of Arthur's faith in him.

"I will be greatly honored to escort the Queen," he said, then bowed deeply and hurried out of the room.

Arthur gazed after him. What an odd man he was. Of course, his background must make it hard for him to feel normal anywhere. But of all the knights, Lancelot was the only one who had come simply because he understood and believed in what Arthur was trying to do. At last, here was a man who could share the vision, who could be a partner in it. This winter they would take all the younger sons and adventure-seekers, and, together, they would shape them into knights. By next spring they would be ready. His eyes glowed. It was coming nearer. He could almost grasp it. The fulfillment of his dream—why was it always so close and yet unreachable? This time it would be true: a city of God and a city of man, a benevolent and strong rule for Britain. Soon there would be no more need for him to dream.

"And then what?"

He swung around. Who had thrown those hard words at him? The air hung motionless about him. He was alone. He shook himself. It must have been his imagination.

Gawain had found it easier than he had supposed to convince Lancelot to join him in a little sword practice. As a matter of fact, Lancelot had seemed delighted to be asked. Gawain could not decide if the man was that confident or if Guinevere had been mistaken about his attitude. No matter. Gawain whistled as he wrapped cloth around his sword to blunt it. It would feel good to do more than watch for a change.

Word had gotten out about the match by the time Gawain reached the practice field a few hours after the midday meal. The sun was still high enough for him to feel its strength. It would be several hours yet before he needed to worry; he had plenty of time and energy left to defeat Lancelot. He noticed quite a crowd out. That was good. He had been the butt of too many jokes in his weak state for him not to enjoy the knowledge that they would now see him at his best. The afternoon promised to be very pleasant.

Lancelot was waiting for him. He, too, had wrapped his sword. He had also discarded his plumed helmet and wore for protection only the common type of mail shirt, leather with pierced metal plates sewn across it.

They bowed to each other without speaking and raised their swords. Gawain studied Lancelot's stance as they circled, wondering how to make the fight last a few minutes without causing permanent harm. As he made up his mind, Lancelot lunged. The blow to Gawain's shield almost knocked him backwards. His eyes lit up with incredulous joy. He stood straight and almost laughed in his delight. Any man who could start with a blow like that needed no pampering. He regarded Lancelot with new respect and set out to enjoy himself.

Lancelot was astonished at Gawain's reaction to his opening strike. That blow would have flattened most men. The fellow only looked from the dented shield to Lancelot and back again and grinned at him. A trickle of something that was not so much fear as confusion entered Lancelot's mind. Had the man asked him to practice only to make a fool of him? Was that why everyone was there? Even Arthur silently watched. Lancelot set his teeth. They could not know that he was bound to win because God protected him. He would have to show them.

As the fight continued, Gawain became more and more happy. Every blow he gave, Lancelot parried. Each time Lancelot attacked, Gawain turned the sword away. At noon, perhaps, he would have had the edge, but now they were matched so evenly that the betting that had started died out with the conversation as the crowd watched in breathless excitement.

Agravaine nudged Gaheris. "Did you ever think you'd see that? They've been at it for almost three hours and Gawain hasn't even winded him. Do you think Lancelot is human?"

Gaheris answered without taking his eyes from them. "If he is, he's the most remarkable swordsman in Britain."

Lancelot was growing angrier as the afternoon wore on.

His arms ached from shield and sword, and his whole body was rattled from the force of the blows he had taken, but this Gawain simply stood there, seemingly impervious to anything he could do. It wouldn't have been so bad if the man didn't seem happy about the whole thing. The sun was so low that its rays caught the polished surface of Gawain's shield and blinded Lancelot.

Without looking, Gawain knew the sun was setting. He could feel exhaustion creeping into him and knew he would not last much longer. He wanted to get out of this gracefully but saw no way to. He would rather be run through than fall asleep at Lancelot's feet, but he knew there was no chance of beating him now.

"He's tiring at last!" Lancelot thought and pressed forward. But he, too, was so tired that it was a feeble lunge. He forced his muscles to stiffen. He would not give up.

Gaheris was too intent on the fight to notice the passage of time, but a slip of Gawain's foot caused him to look up in alarm at the darkening sky. He edged over to Arthur and whispered in his ear.

Arthur nodded. He stepped forward between the two men. "Lancelot! Gawain! Hold!" he cried. "Never in my life have I seen such a duel! But it is nearly dark and the dinner hour long past. Let us stop now and call it a draw."

Lancelot and Gawain dropped their weapons. Lancelot tried to open his fingers without attracting attention. Gawain made no such pretense. He held his hand out to Lancelot only after massaging it ruefully.

"No man has ever stood against me under the sun and lasted long enough to parry. I ask your pardon for any doubts I may have had about your ability. I would consider myself honored to have you as my friend."

Everyone waited. Arthur stood smiling proudly at him. Slowly Lancelot extended his arm and shook Gawain's hand. As if on cue, they both winced and then laughed. The crowd surged forward, surrounding them and slapping them on the back enthusiastically.

From her balcony, Guinevere surveyed the scene with dismay. She slipped back into her room and allowed herself the pleasure of kicking the pillows across it. It was clear that she would be traveling with Lancelot, after all.

Guinevere and Lydia were folding their clothes and choosing which ones to pack and which ones to send on to Caerleon. Apart from the annoyance of having to spend time with Lancelot, Guinevere felt happier than she had at any time since she had first seen Camelot.

"Arthur will expect me to be at Caerleon when he returns, so I can only be home six weeks or so. But, oh, how lovely it will be!"

Lydia was more subdued as she looked over her wardrobe, wondering in passing how Guinevere's clothes could look so like her own in the clothes press and so very different when she put them on. She pulled out a yellow and green checked woolen dress. She might as well take the winter things. It was always cold by the ocean. At least, that was what she remembered. She had forgotten much of her childhood home.

"Tell me again, Guinevere. What does my mother look like now?"

"Lydia, stop being so worried. You know very well that you won't mistake her for anyone else."

"But it's been so long since I've seen her!"

"All right, I'll tell you how you will know her. She'll be the little gray-haired woman with her arms around you and tears spilling down her face. Don't you know how she has longed to see you?"

"She has always sent me letters and presents, but if she loves me so, why couldn't I have gone to her at once? I'm sorry. I have loved being here with you and I hope to be back at Caerleon by winter. But I had so hoped she would insist that I come to her as soon as I left Armorica."

"I don't think she was allowed to. Your father wanted you to come here. Sidra hasn't been well, you know. I always forget that she is not strong, she would never let anyone see a weakness in her. Perhaps he thought you should wait until she was feeling better."

The excuse sounded weak. What was the real reason?

Guinevere knew how dreadfully Sidra missed her only daughter. All the fosterlings in Britain couldn't make up for the one child she had been coerced to send to safety. Lydia was still looking at her questioningly. Guinevere shrugged.

"I don't really know, Lydia. I suppose the only thing you can do is ask her."

Footsteps clattered up the wooden stairs. Gawain burst into the room.

"You'll never believe this. With everything almost packed and ready to leave, who do you think should ride up with ten of his hangers-on? Meleagant! Who does he think he is? Says he's decided to see this famous city of Arthur's. Seems he's never heard of an invitation. Arthur needs you two to come down and be gracious or something. He's furious, of course, but doesn't want Meleagant to know it. He's having the kitchens set up again. Cei is seeing that the hangings are put back on the walls in the Great Hall and the dining hall. Merlin is down at the gates now, holding Meleagant off until we can get things looking regal again."

Guinevere looked wildly around the room. Her best robes were already boxed. The maid had just finished wrapping her jewelry in leather and silk. Each parcel was carefully tied and stowed with the clothes.

"But, Gawain," she gasped. "I'm leaving tomorrow morning!"

"I know. Arthur would love to send you now, if he could. It's just like that bastard Meleagant to pull something like this. Anything to put Arthur at a disadvantage. He's boasted to half the kings that it's all nonsense to try to reunite Britain and that even if it weren't, Arthur isn't the man to do it."

The room could barely hold Gawain's anger. Even his vibrant curls seemed to shiver with wrath. Guinevere felt the emotion more easily than she understood the reason for it. No one must put Arthur in a bad light! She wrenched open the box which held her summer dresses.

"Lydia, help me find that midnight-blue silk with the silver trim. Gawain, on your way out, send one of the maids up to do my hair. Lydia, which box do you think she put my gold earrings in, the ones with the lapis in the center? Don't bother to open your things. One mess is enough. We don't want to repack everything. Take one of my robes. There, the red silk one. That will be fine for you; it will bring out the auburn in your hair. Gawain, why are you still here?"

Gawain jumped. "Sorry. I'll tell Arthur you'll be right down." He grinned at them.

"That's the way! You two will knock them out! We'll show that imitation, upstart, so-called king what a real court looks like! He has nothing that can compare with Camelot!"

Guinevere waved him off. She frantically pulled material out of boxes, rummaging through them for ointments and perfume vials. Lydia stood with the silk gown in her arms, staring at it as if it might fly away.

"You want me to wear this?" she breathed.

"Yes, if you would. I know you don't like ostentation, but I think we ought to overdo a bit for this. Make Meleagant think we dress this way all the time. I know I have a necklace to match that gown, gold and rubies. Where could it be? These packages all look alike. Come help me, please. We have to hurry."

Meleagant's party was given a very thorough tour of the earthworks that wound around and around the hill up to Camelot. Merlin made sure that they noticed every detail of the defenses, especially how people in the mazelike paths could neither see out nor up to the city, but men in the watchtowers could spot and aim at them perfectly. It took half an hour to arrive at the main gates at the top. Arthur had stationed guards there with horns, which they blew loudly if with little skill. These were both to salute Meleagant and to warn everyone that he had appeared. Cei greeted Meleagant's party formally and led them to the Hall of the Table, where Arthur awaited them.

The room was brilliant with torches. The Table shone in the glow. Arthur was seated at one end of the room in a great, carved throne. He did not intend to ask Meleagant to seat himself at the Round Table and there were no chairs anywhere else. As they entered, he rose and came forward to greet them, arms outstretched, as if their visit had been long awaited and desired.

"Meleagant!" he cried. "We are honored that you have taken the trouble to travel so far to see our new capital. Did my messenger not reach you? Your neighbor, Lord Craddoc, has invited us to stay with him in only a few weeks. We certainly planned on visiting with you, also. There was a matter of a village that Craddoc wished us to mention."

Meleagant was taken off guard. "That village is mine. It always has been. Craddoc only wants it because there is a pond there that is supposed to make all animals which drink from it produce twin offspring."

Merlin laid a hand on his arm. "You haven't greeted the King yet," he said calmly.

Meleagant felt the warning beneath his words, the slight emphasis on the title. He shuffled his feet a bit and finally made a perfunctory bow.

"We beg your hospitality, King Arthur." The bile rose in his throat at the words. This so-called son of Uther! What gave him the right to be Overlord?

"We plan to stay only a night or two and then return to our own lands. If you intend to honor our dear neighbor, Craddoc, with your company, we hope you will also spend an evening at our castle. I am sure you will find my defenses as interesting as your own."

Arthur smiled graciously. "My knights and I will be delighted to inspect your castle. Your secure defense system there is well-known. Now, fortunately, you have arrived here in time for our evening meal. Will you give us the honor of sharing it with you?"

Meleagant had not considered doing anything else.

Lydia and Guinevere were waiting at the door of the dining hall as they approached. Arthur could tell from the quick intake of breath from the man beside him that Meleagant truly had no one at his court to compare with his Guinevere. He allowed himself a smirk of complacence. Whatever awe he might still feel toward her, it was nothing to the wonder of those who saw her for the first time. But what had happened to Lydia? Good Lord! The mouse was beautiful! The red silk gleamed against her pale skin, accenting the fragility of it. Her hair had been looped and curled and was bound with a red-gold cord. The curls suited her far better than the simple braids she usually wore. Well. That was unexpected, but certainly a bonus. Arthur began to feel more comfortable about the prospect of an evening with this uninvited guest.

The wine was not the best. That had already been sent ahead to Caerleon. But it made no difference to Meleagant. He only knew that the wine was wet and potent and that was all that mattered. Arthur had planted him firmly between Merlin and Guinevere, where his determination to cause trouble could be checked. His men were also well spaced among the tables. Cei had taken one look at Lydia and seated himself next to her, regardless of his duty as seneschal.

Even before the meal arrived, Meleagant was boasting about his impregnable castle. No army could broach its walls or besiege it with success.

"We have our own water inside and are well-stocked with fish and fowl. We trade only for bread and ale and, in time of war, we could make the sacrifice and do without. Great as your Camelot is, I don't think you could do as well."

"Perhaps Arthur will never need to withstand a siege," Merlin said smoothly, reaching for a slab of bread. The bracelets gleamed on his wrists.

Meleagant was reminded that Arthur had access to powers which were other than human. He changed the subject.

"What about these 'knight' fellows of yours? I see that you have Lot's oldest boys here or, I should say, his wife's." He broke into a loud guffaw, which turned into a belch.

Agravaine, quick to feel a family insult, reached for his knife. As his hand went to the dagger, it was covered by that of Geraldus, who shook his head.

"A knight, Agravaine, must learn not to fall into such simple traps. Ignore him. He is baiting us all."

Meleagant appeared not to have noticed how nearly he had come to being spitted as he ate. He continued, "What is so special about these men of yours? They don't look like anything to me. Faugh! Most of them are still boys. The men who fought with you before, such as myself, have all re-

· 103 ·

turned to manage their lands. Do you propose that these unweaned calves are to tell us what to do? I'll bet that not one of them could manage to penetrate my castle. Not one!"

He glared around the room, waiting for the uproar. All was polite silence. Arthur smiled.

"I think you might be wrong, sir. I have chosen my men for their intelligence. I assume that they will be able to employ it as well as their military prowess should they ever need to enter without your invitation. But, naturally, it will never be necessary to test them on you. We are allies, are we not?"

His voice was so silken that even Merlin could not be sure the threat was intended. Meleagant set down his cup with a clatter.

"Of course we are!" he boomed, and everyone released their breath. "But let's just say, for a wager, an amusement, that my men and I can take something of yours and keep it hostage at my castle. I'll bet that not one of your so-called 'knights' or all of them together can get it back. Come on, Arthur! If I can do it, I get to keep whatever it is until, say, Easter. If you can retrieve it, then I'll acknowledge your overlordship and back you against the other kings. I'll even send you my second son for fostering. How would that be?"

He lolled back in his chair, the picture of a drunken lout. Arthur knew better. His father-in-law had told him once that Meleagant was known for being able to drink steadily all night while never missing a target at stick-knife or needing to leave the table. An hour of wine would hardly have dented his capacity. There was no doubt that he had come all the way to Camelot for the purpose of making this "wager." Arthur tried to catch Merlin's eye. Damn! He wouldn't turn. Merlin had told him that the time had come when he would have to make his own decisions, but a little advice was not so much to ask for. Arthur took a sip of wine and leaned back on his cushions. Torchlight flickered on the walls and on the faces of all those waiting—waiting for him to act. Gently he set down the cup. Foolish as it might seem, this was the sort of test that would be understood by all the kings and lords in their various holds and kingdoms. The native Celtic lore was filled with many such contests. He could only hope that he had not overestimated his knights.

"Very well, Meleagant." He spoke softly, drawing out the name until it sounded like a pagan curse. "It is heard and witnessed by all here that if you are able to steal something from me and hold it in your castle until Easter, you are free to be independent of my laws. But if any of my men can enter your castle and recapture the thing, you will henceforth consider yourself my loyal subject."

He emphasized the last word. Meleagant squirmed, but it was pretense. He was totally confident, as he proved at once.

"Right," he said. "I agree. Remember that the man must enter the castle and then find the object. I will even allow him to leave without hindrance if he can but lay hands on the thing. That's fair, don't you think? No sense in getting him killed trying to fight his way out. Right?"

Arthur inclined his head. "Certainly. But first, Meleagant, you must be able to take something of mine. I will not insult you by asking your men to be searched before they leave. I know you will not bother with anything as trivial as a spoon or a wine cup."

Meleagant grinned and Guinevere realized in horror that he was totally sober. She wondered if Arthur knew. Yes, she could tell he did. She shivered. What an odious man! Thank goodness she was leaving tomorrow. With luck, she might never have to see him again. He looked at her. She smiled sweetly at him and rose.

"Please excuse us, gentlemen," she said. "The Lady Lydia and I have to finish packing for our journey. Please continue to enjoy yourselves in our absence."

Cei stood when Lydia got up to leave and so, belatedly, did the rest of the men. They waited in respectful silence as the women left.

Outside, Guinevere took Lydia's arm.

"What dreadful people Arthur has to mollify. I didn't understand half of what they were talking about. It sounded to me like silly games for boys to play. What did you think?"

"I'm sorry, Guinevere. I wasn't paying attention. Cei was telling me about his father's lands and the things he and

Arthur used to do before he became King. I didn't notice what else was happening."

Guinevere gave her a sharp glance. "Lydia, are you in love with Cei?"

Lydia blushed, but the night hid her face. "I don't know. I only find that I am very happy when I am with him and long to see him again when he is gone."

Guinevere did not know if that was love or not. Did Arthur make her feel happy? She was not sure. She missed him when he went away, but did it really matter that he was with her? No, she could not pretend that.

"How interesting, Lydia. You must tell your mother about him," was all she said.

It was late when Arthur came in. The noise from the Hall had awakened Guinevere once or twice, but she was asleep when he carefully climbed into bed. Dimly she felt his arm go around her and she tried to pull herself awake. Maybe if she snuggled in closer, he would go to sleep. No, he wanted her to wake. He was murmuring in her ear. She did not need to make it out. She knew that he loved her and would miss her terribly. Of course he would. She wanted so much just to roll over and stay asleep, but she could not do that to him on their last night together. Why couldn't she love him the way he did her? She knew it was her job, but . . . if only he would be quick tonight! She forced herself to wake and kissed his cheek.

"I will miss you, too, my dear." She spoke her lines. "But it will only be for a few weeks. I will be waiting for you at Caerleon. You will be much too busy to think of me."

He held her more tightly. "I will always think of you and yearn for you. I will send word wherever I am. You will write me?"

"Of course I will. Don't I always? Tell me everything you are doing and I will praise you." She did not have to pretend that. It was amazing how much she enjoyed hearing from him when they were apart. It was only when he was this close to her that she was nervous.

"Guinevere?" he breathed.

"Of course, Arthur," she sighed.

Chapter Eight

After the evening with Meleagant, even the prospect of four days with the self-centered Sir Lancelot did not seem so awful to Guinevere. It was such a treat for her to get away from Camelot and home to her parents that she felt a bit guilty for leaving Arthur. Why should he have to stay and tend to all the problems? When she had married him, it had not occurred to her that being a king meant that you could no longer do whatever you wanted. That was not the way Uther was supposed to have behaved.

They said good-bye in the early morning. The mist of night still hung in the air and wove around the trees and buildings, making mundane Camelot look magical. After waiting as Arthur kissed his wife, Lancelot assisted her to mount her horse. Normally women rode pillion, but both Lydia and Guinevere had insisted on having their own horses for the long trip. Sitting sideways for so many hours was too uncomfortable, they explained. But Guinevere had an ulterior reason: she had no intention of spending four days with her arms wrapped around Arthur's new protégé.

Arthur walked with them all the way down the hill, to the end of the earthworks. He smiled and waved as they set out. A few minutes later, Guinevere looked back and saw that he was still there, waving shakily, as though he had forgotten to stop. Against the wall of earth he looked so small and frail that she ached with pity for him. She thought with a flash of surprise, "He should have had a different sort of wife. I'm not what he needs."

The path went down an incline and she could no longer see

him. Her moment of introspection passed and was forgotten.

Although Lydia and Geraldus were going farther south, to the coast, they would not leave Guinevere and Lancelot until the next day. The ride was beautiful. The woods were cool and fragrant and the road smooth. Guinevere chatted happily with Lydia and Geraldus as Lancelot rode stiffly behind them. Sometimes Geraldus would suddenly break into fragments of song and the two women would join him. Finally he complained that it was too confusing hearing voices from two worlds. They laughed and stopped. But even the quiet was companionable.

From behind, Lancelot watched them and longed to be like them. They had that ease of long friendship which allows periods of silence. When they spoke, there was no need for them to explain themselves, to justify anything they might say. He felt that way only with Torres, who had chosen to stay at Camelot and help with the moving. He doubted that he could ever feel so at ease around Guinevere.

He tried not to stare at her, but everywhere he looked it seemed that she was there. As he watched her riding before him, he felt that the very air sparkled in her presence. She radiated a sense, not only of beauty and position, but certainty. She had never doubted her faith or the rightness of her actions. In all the people Lancelot had met in his weeks at Camelot there had been at least a trace of self-doubt. Even the most bombastic old soldier had a slight undercurrent of uncertainty.

But not Guinevere. If she had been old, ugly, and poor, Lancelot would still have been fascinated by the sublime solidity of her self-assurance. But she was young, beautiful, and a queen. Lancelot's fascination was soon complicated by other feelings. He was not stupid; he knew quite well how she attracted him. He could only add this torment to his other penances and pray that his soul would overcome it, too.

They were all too tired for talk when they camped that night. Lancelot and Geraldus took alternate watches and the two women slept in a lean-to hung with curtains which they had brought on the pack horse.

The next morning was foggy and chilly, but Geraldus insisted on getting an early start.

"We're heading for the coast, anyway, Lydia," he teased. "We won't see the sun again there until next April. We might as well become used to it now."

Guinevere hugged Lydia with affection as she said good-bye. "You must promise to come to Caerleon this winter," she begged. "Make Sidra come, too. It will be lonely until you get there."

"I'll try, Guinevere," Lydia sniffled. "If I can't, you will send word to me of . . . what is happening to everyone?"

"Don't worry. If you don't come, I'll see that Cei brings the messages himself."

She and Lancelot watched them until they disappeared around the bend. Guinevere sighed and steeled herself to be pleasant, as she had promised Arthur. Lancelot had loaded the packs and was waiting to help her. Guinevere faced him and placed her hand on his shoulder, to be boosted onto the horse. He was not wearing armor now, but soft leather riding gear. She felt him flinch as she touched him and deliberately increased the weight, all the while avoiding looking at him directly. He cupped his hands and she stepped up. When she had seated herself, she glanced down at him. He was gazing up at her with such naked adoration that she felt a little sick. Quickly she turned away.

She set a steady pace, keeping him always behind. She had the idea of making it home by the evening of the third day. They ate a quick lunch with no conversation and continued. It was nearly dusk when Guinevere realized that her horse could go no further and she signalled a stop.

Still without speaking, Lancelot set up the lean-to and put Guinevere's bags and bedding inside. Then he set about finding wood and striking a spark for fire. Guinevere busied herself in organizing the lean-to so that she would have room to sleep and no roots in her back. When she came out, Lancelot was struggling with the fire.

"May I help you?" she asked. "I often have good luck with campfires."

He handed her the stones. She looked at them and then back at him.

"But these are ordinary rocks!"

"What do you mean?"

"You can't get just any stone to strike a spark. Didn't you know that?"

Before he could answer, she returned to her tent and searched the pack for her tinderbox. Using the flint, she had a small fire going in about five minutes. She smiled at Lancelot.

"Would you mind fetching some water so that I might wash my hands?" she asked.

He went at once.

As he poured water over her outstretched hands, he tried to explain. "I never had to do that before. Under the Lake, there are always torches lit. I saw the men at Camelot hitting stones and thought that was what one did to light a fire here. I'm sorry you had to dirty your hands."

"And even more sorry that I look such a fool in front of you," he added to himself.

Guinevere dried her hands. "It doesn't matter; I would not have learned, either, if I had not once spent a summer with some friends of my family. They felt that everyone should know how to do many tasks and so they taught me. Would you like me to cook, also?"

She knew that they had only dried meat, bread, and fruit to eat and so there would be no test.

"No, of course not!" He rushed about, getting food and wine for her. He set her plate and cup on a thick piece of bark and presented them to her. He was very clumsy about it. With Gawain or Geraldus, she would have been touched, but, for some reason, Lancelot annoyed her. Perhaps it was the sense she had that he was disparaging her right to have fine silver dishes and silken bedding even while he arranged them for her.

She ate quickly and then announced that she was going to bed. It took some time in the dark to tie up her braids and change into a warm nightdress. Then she realized that she would have to leave the lean-to again, after all. She wrapped a cloak over her nightclothes and crawled out. As she stood, she hit her toe on something sharp which was lying directly before the curtain.

"Ow! What is this thing?" She stooped down and found Lancelot's short sword, unsheathed, on the ground.

"Lancelot!" she called. "You dropped your sword here. You should be more careful. I nearly cut myself."

He jumped to his feet and bowed jerkily. "I left it there on purpose, my Lady."

"What?"

He gulped. "Isn't it the custom? I put it there to show you that I have no dishonorable intentions. It was for your protection."

"My protection!" She tried not to shout in the still night. "What do you think *you* are here for?"

"I meant, in case I had any intention of . . . bothering you."

"You leave a sword outside my tent, to rust in the dew, because I might need it to protect myself from you?"

He nodded.

"But what would prevent you from stepping over the sword while I slept? And, if it were lying here, how would you be able to defend me from an intruder who might decide to 'bother' me?"

"I didn't think about that. Something Agravaine said, a story he told, gave me the idea that it was the right thing to do."

"You don't mean that old Cornish tale about Tristan and Iseult? If you had paid attention, you would have known that there was no honor in either of them."

Guinevere picked up the sword and wiped it on her cloak. She handed it back to him.

"Please keep this to battle Saxons and wolves with. You needn't worry about my being safe from you. If you should feel like attacking me in the middle of the night, please remember that, like every other woman in Britain, I am well supplied with brooches, hairpins, and, of course, a small bodkin, for carving meat and unwelcome suitors. Good night."

She went about her business and returned to her lean-to.

Lancelot slunk back to his seat by the fire.

Guinevere shook her head sadly as she settled down among her blankets. "And Arthur is planning to present this idiot as the perfect knight!" she mused. "Poor Arthur!"

Lancelot sat all night watching the fire, occasionally adding another log. The Lady had been right in warning him that he would make mistakes. He seemed to do nothing else. How did Torres manage to fit in so comfortably?

His thoughts tumbled and cascaded as he watched the flames. He slept eventually, his head on his knees. He had a sharp and painful dream of himself standing, naked and bleeding, in the middle of a room full of people, with Guinevere facing him and laughing.

He awoke with a shiver. It was growing light out, but the sky was still gray. He could not have been sleeping long, for the coals were still glowing. He fanned up the flames and went to get water to heat for morning washing. His dream was becoming blurred, but it had left him shaken and nauseated. The icy water of the stream splashed him as he filled the bucket. On an impulse, he stripped off his clothes and waded in. He swam upstream a few yards and then let himself be carried back. His skin fairly crackled with the cold. An hour of this would be penance enough for anything. But he had to hurry back.

He pulled his shirt and trews back on over his wet skin. He felt clearheaded again and free of the taste of his nightmare.

Guinevere did not wake until he purposely rattled a spoon and pot near the lean-to. She had said she wanted to start early. He left a clay jug of hot water outside the curtain and called to her. A hand slipped out and pulled it in.

She put a few drops of perfume in the water and bathed her face and arms. Arthur must have given Lancelot very clear instructions. She put on clean clothes and wound her braids about her head. Tonight her mother's maid would comb them out for her. She wrapped up her mirror and nightclothes and stepped out of her lean-to.

Lancelot was standing by the remains of the fire. He turned when he heard her, and then he smiled.

Guinevere's heart turned over. She grasped the curtain behind her for balance. Resolutely she looked away from him. She was not going to let the strange reactions she felt from him affect her common sense.

"Good morning," she muttered as she stretched her arms. "Is there anything warm for breakfast? No? Never mind. I'll get it myself while you pack our things. If we hurry, we can at least eat a hot dinner tonight with my parents."

While she ate, Lancelot loaded her lean-to and bedclothes on the pack horse. She avoided meeting his glance this time as he assisted her into the saddle.

As they rode, Lancelot wondered if this day, too, would pass in silence. Why could he not speak to her easily? He had never stumbled over his words with the women of the Lake. Every time he tried to start a conversation with her, she replied politely but with a minimum of words. It was almost as if she didn't like him. Lancelot blinked mentally. Could that be it? He reviewed his meetings with her and her behavior on this trip. She certainly was distant. That must be the reason. But why? What could he have done to offend her? He had to know.

He reined Clades in near her. She glanced at him quickly and then looked straight ahead as if the road were too treacherous to watch anything else. Actually, it was one of the better Roman thoroughfares, still in good repair and as smooth as one could wish. Lancelot would not be put off. He continued to ride even with her. Finally his presence at her elbow was too much to ignore. She faced him.

"You wish to say something, Sir Lancelot?" All her superior haughtiness was in her voice.

Lancelot suddenly discovered that he had a temper, too. It surprised him.

"Yes, my Queen." He emphasized the title. "Why are you treating me this way? What have I done that you should so dislike me?"

Guinevere started. She could not remember anyone ever taking that tone with her before. He was not supplicating; he was demanding.

"When have I said that I disliked you?"

"You have never needed to. You treat the potboys and scullery maids with more courtesy than you do me. What horrible sin could I have committed that you should act so? Tell me what it is and I will atone."

"And to whom would you atone, me or God?" she snapped. "Never mind. It doesn't matter. You have done nothing evil as far as I know."

She tried to pull ahead, but he grabbed the reins of her horse and forced it to stop.

"Then what is it?" he insisted. "I cannot go on living so near you and enduring your disdain."

She stopped herself from suggesting that he move somewhere else. Arthur wanted him and needed him, even if she didn't understand why. But what could she say, that she found his piety offensive? That his striving for perfection was an insult to others who felt no such need? Those things would sound idiotic and make her seem either irreligious or a prig. What right did he have to upset her like this? What difference did it make if she liked him or not? What was she to him? He was Arthur's man, not hers. She could feel him staring at her again with those haunting eyes. She felt trapped by his eyes when she met them, forced into an intimacy that frightened her. She glared back at him, concentrating her gaze on his slightly cleft chin rather than meeting those dangerous eyes.

"I would prefer that you not stare at me," she announced. "It makes me uncomfortable to be so scrutinized."

That took him aback. He blushed with guilt. He had not realized that she had been aware of him.

"I'm sorry. I did not mean to disconcert you. Under the Lake there are no women like you. When you are in the hall, there is nothing else worth looking at. Please forgive my boldness. I will try not to turn my glance in your direction so much.

"It will be," he added in wonder, "a more difficult atonement than many I have undertaken."

Now she felt a fool. It seemed overbearing to deny him the pleasure of watching her. But there was something about being caught in his gaze that made her feel dizzy, compelled somehow to be aware of him. He must not be allowed to do this to her or to know what effect he had on her. She forced herself to smile.

"It would be even odder if you constantly turned away from me, Lancelot." She laughed shakily. "Can't you do as the others? No one else has any trouble looking away from me."

Without thinking, she met his eyes again. Her lip trembled. "You see? When you are looking at me, I feel as if you see no one else, that I can never escape you."

She had not meant to say that.

He let go of her reins. Gratefully, she moved ahead, pulling up the hood of her cloak.

Lancelot went white. He could feel the blood draining from his face. "This can't be!" he thought in terror. "My God! What have I done? I cannot be in love with her. Not like this. My life is dedicated to mankind. No one person should ever mean this much to me!"

But he knew that she did.

Meredydd had assured him that all men had wicked sexual longings and he had promised to overcome them. It had not occurred to him that he could feel something more. He had never met a woman before who could not be ignored with a little self-discipline.

The rest of the journey was made in polite silence. Lancelot rode behind Guinevere, totally enmeshed in the ramifications of his discovery. His first impulse was to run, not back to the Lady, but farther away—across the sea, if necessary. He had to get away from her before she became an obsession. Perhaps it was already too late. Almost bitterly he watched her riding before him. She was tranquilly unaware, he assumed, of what she had unleashed. She did not even like him. What right had she to shatter him so?

But his martyr's soul would not allow him to flee. He knew he would stay, do for Arthur what he had meant to do, and fight his spiritual battle until he won. It did not occur to his pride that the decision was not certain.

Both of them were relieved when they rounded the bend and the villa of Leodegrance appeared, softly lit in the twilight, waiting for them.

They crossed the stream. It was low this time of year and

did not even wet the horses' legs. As they approached the gate, it swung open. Guinevere's parents were there to greet her, their arms open.

Gratefully she fell into them. Lancelot sat at attention, waiting to be introduced.

Guenlian held her daughter close. She had been proud to give her to King Arthur and had never doubted that he would love and care for her. But it was such a comfort to hold her again and be sure that she was well.

Guinevere was astonished to find herself weeping as she embraced her parents.

"My darling!" Guenlian asked, "What is the matter?"

"I don't know," Guinevere sniffed from her father's arms. "I'm happy to be home again, I suppose. And I'm very tired."

"There isn't any news, is there, dear?" Guenlian hinted. In her parlance, the question meant only one thing.

Guinevere shook her head. "No, Mother, I'm only tired. I'll be fine as soon as I've washed and changed." She wished they would stop hoping. It would be so much better if they gave up their dreams of a grandson of theirs ruling Britain.

Hastily she wiped her eyes. She realized that Lancelot had not been introduced.

"Mother, Father, this gentleman is Sir Lancelot. He has been kind enough to escort me here. Lancelot, the Lord Leodegrance and the Lady Guenlian."

Guenlian smiled. When Guinevere used formal titles, one knew that she did not approve of someone. This Lancelot seemed all right. In the growing darkness, she could not see his face well. He was quiet. Guinevere usually became annoyed by the more brash of her escorts. Well, there would be time to find out at dinner.

"Welcome to our home, Sir Lancelot. You will want to wash and change for dinner. Rogan will show you to your room and the baths. He will be happy to attend you there. We ring a bell at the dinner hour and he will show you the way. Don't worry about your horse. He will be taken care of."

Lancelot bowed and followed the servant, who had already unstrapped his belongings and was carrying them to the villa.

"Not very conversational, is he?" Leodegrance put his arm around Guinevere as they walked to her old room, always ready for her return. "Who is he?"

"One of Arthur's new acquisitions," Guinevere answered. "If you mean his family, no one knows. He was raised by some enchantress who resides under a lake, I gather. They say he is human, though." Her tone indicated that she had some doubt of this. "Certainly his companion, Torres, is. I really don't know much about it. You could ask Cousin Merlin. They say he recognized the Lady when she brought Lancelot and Torres to Camelot."

"And they say there is no magic left in Britain!" Guenlian said in amusement. "I always thought the Lady of the Lake was simply a nursery tale to keep children from straying too far into the forest. How very interesting! Do you think Lancelot will tell us about her?"

"He's rather shy, I think." Guinevere searched for the right phrase. "I don't know if he would like to. But tell me about things here. Your letters never say enough. Where are Rhianna and my niece? Why wasn't Pincerna waiting for me outside? Is he ill?"

"Hardly," Leodegrance assured her. "He has been terrorizing the kitchen servants since dawn to make sure that your welcome-home dinner was perfect. As for Rhianna and Letitia, I believe they are waiting for you in your room."

Guinevere opened the door and felt for a second that she had been delivered back into her childhood. It was just as she had left it: the narrow bed, the dressing table, the clothes press with the chipped corner, and the woodland mosaic covering the floor. But now her sister-in-law and niece were there, too, eager to hug her and tell her all the vital things that had happened in the year since she had last seen them. They never asked about Guinevere's life away from them and for this she was grateful. It was then even easier to imagine she had never left.

"Letitia has already been fed," Rhianna was explaining.

"But she wanted to see you so badly that we thought she might be allowed to attend dinner for a while. Do you mind?"

Rhianna was still shy and beautiful, with an added serenity which came from knowing that she was safe and loved. Letitia was a delicate child of nine who showed that love and total devotion need not produce a spoiled brat. She was bright and curious and more aware of those around her than Guinevere had ever been. She resembled her mother, but she had something of the fighting spirit of Matthew, Guinevere's dead brother. She seemed content to live in this tranquil haven, but she also seemed to have no fear of what lay beyond. Guinevere loved her dearly.

"I would be happy to have Letitia at dinner with us," she assured Rhianna. "At her age all of us were at the table with the adults except on the most formal occasions. I have heard that Mother was criticized by her friends for being so lax, but I was glad she paid them no attention. You two can observe the escort Arthur sent with me this time and tell me what you think of him."

"If we are to do that, we had better leave you to bathe and dress," Rhianna said. "Come, darling, I'll let you wear your new yellow gown."

"I told you Aunt Guinevere wouldn't mind." Letitia kissed Guinevere again. "Please hurry, Aunt. We have heard so many stories about this Lancelot. Is it true that he wears armor made out of silver and diamonds?"

"I haven't noticed the diamonds," Guinevere told her, "but I think that part of the armor is silver. How did you hear about that?"

Rhianna grinned. "You should know your father well enough to realize that he gets all the news from wherever you are. Now do hurry! I'm starving!"

Lancelot, meanwhile, had left his clothes in the small apodyterium, the dressing room for the baths, and had plunged directly into the frigidarium, despite the fact that the night outside was already growing cool. The water was almost as cold as the stream that morning had been. He emerged blue and chattering to find Rogan waiting for him with a clean towel. Although he protested, he was led to the tepidarium, where he was given the strigil to scrape himself clean and then coerced into getting a massage with fragrant oil. Rogan viewed his fuming with amusement.

"If you think I am making you too comfortable, I could pour some salt into those scratches on your back. Whoever gave you those must have been a real hellion!"

This comment shocked Lancelot into silence. He submitted to enjoying the rubdown and finished off with another cold swim to nullify the pleasure.

His host and hostess were waiting in the courtyard to see him to the dining hall. Lancelot bowed and thanked them for their kindness.

As they passed into the lighted room, Guenlian gasped, "Leodegrance! Look at him!"

Lancelot stopped and put his hand to his face, wondering if there were a mark of Cain branding him. Both of them were staring at him, their faces puzzled.

"My word!" Leodegrance said at last. "You could be right. The boy is his image."

"But what was his wife's name? It's been so long. The summer before Guinevere was born, wasn't it?" She broke off, realizing that Lancelot did not understand.

"Sir Lancelot, forgive us." She laid a hand on his arm. "We were surprised. You bear an amazing likeness to someone we once knew. You wouldn't happen to know the name of your father, would you?"

Lancelot shook his head, his eyes flickering from one to the other. "The Lady who raised me told me that I was a foundling. I was abandoned alone in the woods and she rescued me."

"Ah, yes, well. That wasn't exactly the story we heard, but it happened a long time ago and it may not have been completely true. The poor woman was half mad by then. It may not even have been you. But, wait a minute—wasn't one of the child's names Lancelot?" Leodegrance turned to his wife.

"Yes, I remember now, Galahad Lancelot he was named, for both his grandfathers. I don't know why the mother's name escapes me. I see her face so clearly. We spent almost a month with them that summer."

"What are we doing!" Leodegrance reached an arm to steady Lancelot. "Look at the poor boy. We've forgotten that this is unknown to him. Come, sit down. Have some wine. While we wait for Guinevere, we will try to explain."

Lancelot took the cup and drained it, forgetting that he never touched wine. "You are trying to tell me that you know who I am?"

He stared at his hands, almost expecting them to have changed.

Leodegrance began again. "It must have been about twenty-six years ago. We were in exile again, this time at the court of King Ban of Benoit. We thought it was safe, tucked away in the Western mountains. But word came one day that Ban's old rival, Claudas, had raised an army and was coming to attack Benoit. The reason lay in an ancient feud known only to the genealogists. Ban knew that he did not have enough men to do battle and his castle was circled by only a wood and mud wall. An invader would smash it in no time. We sent Guenlian and the children away for safety at once—to Geraldus' family, wasn't it? But King Ban's wife would not leave him or allow their infant son to be sheltered with them.

"Claudas had over a hundred men to our twenty or so. They broke through the wall almost at once. It was stupid, mindless carnage. At the last moment, I and a few others who were still strong enough to ride took the woman and child and escaped through the broken defenses. She berated us for our cowardice and pleaded to be left to die with her husband. He was dead already. We had the choice of remaining to die or fleeing in the hope of life. We did save the baby."

His eyes closed. Guenlian took his hand. "You were right, my love. You could have done no more for him than to save his family and no more for me than to save yourself for your family."

He did not look at her, but squeezed her hand. One could sense the love and strength that bound them.

Leodegrance continued. "We rode hard all that day and far

into the night. We finally found refuge at an abandoned villa. Although we posted a guard, he must have dozed, for the next morning, Ban's wife and son were gone. We thought she had tried to return to Benoit, and searched for her in that direction. It was several days before we found her. She was wandering alone in the woods, lost and starving. She was half-mad with grief and deprivation. Finally we were able to understand some of what had happened. She had apparently lain down a moment to rest. As she slept, the child, Galahad Lancelot, was stolen from her arms by a glittering woman on horseback. To humor her, we searched for a trace of the child or his kidnapper, but none was ever found. We assumed that he had died and the woman, in her madness, had invented the tale of abduction. Now, seeing you and hearing where you have come from, I am forced to believe that it was true."

He waited for Lancelot to make some response but he was too bewildered. So he was a king's son. That was nice, he supposed. The Lady always said he must have come from a good home. But how much more did she know? All this time she had lied to him! How could she? How could she have ripped him from his poor mother's arms? No! The Lady could not do such a thing! There must be a mistake. Perhaps the woman was mistaken. He could have crawled away while she slept so that when the Lady discovered him, she had assumed he was lost and alone. . . . That must be it. He had to have an explanation that would exonerate his dear Lady. At his left, someone was pouring him another cup of wine. He took it gratefully.

"Mother? Father? What is wrong with Sir Lancelot?" Guinevere had entered unnoticed and was poised at the door. "Is he ill? Shall I call Tenuantius to see to him?"

Leodegrance rose and beckoned her to him. "No, my dear. Come in. He should be all right soon. We have been rather clumsy in telling Lancelot what we know of his family. I'm afraid we have upset him."

Lancelot put down his cup and gazed at Leodegrance, a slow smile of wonder appearing on his face.

"Upset . . . no, only amazed," he assured him. "You have

given me a wondrous present. I only need a few moments to understand it properly. You say that I look like my . . . my father?"

"Remarkably!" Guenlian said and Leodegrance nodded in agreement.

"How strange!" Lancelot itched to find a mirror and see himself in this new light. He put aside his worries about the Lady. He had never considered it before: somewhere back in the dim reaches of history, a man had lived and died and passed his visage on to his son. What else had he given him? And his mother, how determined she must have been to prefer death to life without her husband!

"My mother, Lord Leodegrance, what happened to her?"

"I went on to find Guenlian and the boys, but I heard that your mother was taken to the home of friends and lived there for a time. Then she joined a group of women and formed a religious community near the western coast. That was many years ago and she was very worn and ill. I'm afraid there is little chance of your finding her now."

"But certainly I must try to let her know that I survived!"

Leodegrance seemed not to know how to answer this. Finally he said, "Your mother was always very delicately balanced. What she endured would have unhinged any mind, but in her family there were rumors of madness. If she still lives, she has made her peace and found her solace in God. For you to appear alive, grown and looking so much like Ban, might be too much for her to comprehend."

"You have a duty to Arthur now, too, you know," Guinevere added, surprised that she should make any suggestion that would keep him about.

"Yes, of course," Lancelot's smile was gone. "But I would like to know what happened to her, and, if she has died, be able to say a prayer by her grave."

Pincerna, the family steward, entered to ask if he might allow the food to be served. Rhianna and Letitia had been sitting quietly in a corner listening to the revelations, but Rhianna sighed audibly with relief at the news that dinner had arrived. Lancelot was astonished to discover that he, too, was starving. He had always assumed that momentous news took away one's appetite.

The dinner was superb and they somehow managed to move the conversation to more general matters, although Lancelot barely heard what was being said. Finally he rose and begged to be excused.

"I must leave tomorrow morning. Arthur has requested that I meet him in Caerleon in six weeks' time. I would like to spend the weeks in searching for some word of my mother. May I ask, by the way, what happened to King Claudas?"

"He is still alive, I believe, though not well. He leaves the governing of his lands entirely to his son, Meleagant."

Meleagant. The man who had visited Arthur. Lancelot knew he was arrogant and powerful. And his power was drawn from the death of Ban, the robbing of Lancelot's birthright. He clenched his fists until the nails cut his palms. Then he took a deep breath.

"Revenge is not the duty of man," he reminded himself. "We are allowed only to forgive."

But he longed bitterly to taste revenge just this once. The strength of that desire told him why it was a pleasure that God reserved to Himself. The violence in his heart terrified him.

"I will need a month alone to come to terms with this," he mourned to himself. "I vowed that I would never be tainted by earthly love or hate and now I am consumed by both. I have been in the world of men such a short time. What am I becoming?"

He avoided looking at Guinevere as he bade them good night. He went at once to his room.

Guenlian hesitantly put a hand to her hair. The air in the room was so charged, she half expected it to be in disarray.

"My dear," she commented to Guinevere, "you do bring us such interesting guests."

Chapter Nine

Lancelot did not sleep that night. Whenever he closed his eyes, he felt himself pursued by flaming demons slavering in their eagerness to destroy him. He tried to sort out his feelings logically, to put them in tight, narrow boxes from which they could not escape to trick him into denying his mission. In the darkness it was the Lady he kept seeing. Had she lied to him?

"It is not your place to question the deeds of the Lady," he told himself sternly. "Wasn't she always good to you? Did you ever want for comfort or love?"

"But why did she leave my mother to die?" a voice within him demanded.

"How do you know she did? Perhaps she didn't see her or perhaps she didn't realize the woman meant anything to you. She is not human. There are many things about us that she doesn't understand."

"Things that you understand?"

"Yes, I am human."

"Are you? There are many at Arthur's court who would deny that."

"I have heard them. I forgive them. They don't know. . . ."

"Just how human you are," the voice persisted. "Would you like them to know? Shall we tell them that you want to cut the heart out of your enemy? That's a human impulse. Or perhaps they should learn how you lust after another man's wife, and that man your leader and friend? Why don't we tell them the things you dream about Guinevere? Nothing could be more human than that."

"Stop it!" Clutching his aching head, he sat straight up in bed.

The linen was cool and clean and smelled vaguely of rosemary. The bed was soft, a feather mattress. Lancelot could bear the comfort no more. The sky had turned that morning gray when all objects are one color and the edges blend together. He could not remain here. In this place of ease and grace he might forget all he had committed himself to. Here, much more than in the opulence under the Lake, Lancelot felt at home. This was a place where he might belong if he gave in and rested; if he relaxed. He stood up and was surprised to find that the floor was warm beneath his bare feet. This was too much! He mustn't give in! What an insane idea. What would happen to all those poor suffering souls that he had sworn to save?

He pulled on his clothes and gathered his equipment. He knew it was rude to leave without thanking his hostess, but the social sin seemed far less than the mortal one that was tempting him. He tiptoed through the sleeping house and out to the stables. Clades had been well cared for and greeted him with a loving whinny. Lancelot put his arms about the horse's neck and stood a moment drawing strength from the safety of the animal's loyalty.

The watchman at the gate showed no surprise at the haste of his early departure and so he was spared the added burden of manufacturing an excuse. He plunged across the creek and headed for the welcome loneliness of the forest.

When Guinevere heard that Lancelot had left, she shrugged.

"He is a very odd man, Mother. I don't understand him at all. But he is Arthur's friend and, they say, an excellent soldier. I try to be nice to him."

Guenlian was relieved to hear no trace of interest in her daughter's voice. For all the revelations they had given Lancelot last night, he had given them one which was equally disturbing. They had noticed the way he looked at Guinevere and how he strove to conceal it. The only question had been if Guinevere noticed it, too.

"She seems to have no interest in him," Leodegrance considered cautiously. "She does not seem aware of his attention."

"She has been the wife of a king for more than five years now. The first thing she must have learned was to dissemble."

"To us?" Leodegrance blurted. "No, I know, to everyone. It becomes a second nature after a while. But you are sure she cares nothing for him?"

"She seemed more embarrassed by him than anything. But she must be used to some of these men becoming infatuated with her."

"Was that what it was?" Leodegrance was still worried. "There was something more in his eyes last night. He's running from her now, even more than from what we told him. But he is Arthur's man. How long do you think he will stay away? How long can he hide from her and from the way he feels? You didn't know his father as well as I did. The way he loved his wife was almost idolatrous. No wonder she wanted to join him in death. Her family wasn't sure they wanted him to marry her; thought they might find someone with more land. She was willing enough, though. He came and carried her off by night, then sent word to her family that they could burn her dowry for all he cared, but if they wanted her back, they would have to kill him first."

"Really?" Guenlian was impressed. "Would you have done that for me, my dear?"

Leodegrance laughed. "The way your parents kept you locked up, I never could have captured you at all. But you know very well that it was not your dowry that enticed me."

Guenlian did, but it was worth hearing again.

"Still," she sighed, "I wish I felt as sure about Guinevere's marriage as I do ours."

"Nonsense, Arthur adores her. He would have married her with no dowry at all."

"Of course, he is a fine man. But perhaps we should have given her more opportunity to have wanted to marry him."

Leodegrance felt a shade of worry. He had felt it many

times in the years since Guinevere's marriage and each time he told himself it was the natural paternal dislike of giving up one's only daughter to another man, however kind and well-off he might be. He quelled it again.

"If we had left Guinevere alone, she would still be living with us, wafting about in the woods half the time, with no future at all. We didn't force her to choose Arthur. We only gave her the chance and let her know we would not be unhappy with him. She was getting far too dreamy. And think how romantic their meeting was, a midnight rescue from the Saxons! What girl could want more? She is perfectly happy now and infinitely more mature."

Guenlian argued no more, but she was not certain. Guinevere had been a fey child, not like any other she had known, beautiful and effervescent and always too elusive to be sure of. It seemed sometimes that she did not entirely live with them, that she was claimed briefly by another world. But she had been theirs and no one else's and it was to them that she always returned. Now, she wondered, did Guinevere still occasionally drift back into that other world? If so, was Arthur able to hold her to him when she came home? And, if she never left the order and rules of the courts, how much longer could she bear being earthbound?

Guinevere reflected that she was glad to be back. It was lovely to be home again, to slide back into the irresponsibility of childhood. Let someone else plan the meals and count the linen! She gratefully forgot that she was a queen and settled down to enjoy the pampering she had always known and expected.

Lancelot had always cringed when pampered, so the following few weeks were not at all unpleasant to him. Sleeping on the ground, wrapped in a cloak; waking with the rain on his face; eating stale, sodden bread—all were his idea of serious life: facing reality. He remembered Meredydd's strictures that life was a constant climb against the wind, naked and alone. The only reward would come at death, when the good fighters would finally be given rest eternal. On days like these, he had no doubt of his reward.

Everywhere he went, he asked for information on the wife of King Ban. But no one he spoke with had any idea of where she might have gone or if she were still alive. As he went farther west, he was surprised to find that some of the elderly he asked actually remembered her and his father. They looked at him curiously and some commented that things were better in those days, they were. But they knew nothing.

From traders and wandering monks he found that there were hundreds of small religious communities along the western coast. No one knew all of them.

"Have you tried Docca's school?" one asked. "St. Docca takes in boys from all over the island and teaches them their letters. Never heard of women there. But he might know about them. Only there's no sense in your trying to get there this year. Winter's coming early. There'll be snow in the mountains by now. You could never find the trail."

The trader pulled his cloak more securely over his face and urged his men and horses on to a villa or a town, perhaps, with an inn and a chance of a warm bed. It was altogether too cold for September. It might not hurt to leave a coin for the goddess. This looked like the kind of year to take no chances.

Lancelot made his gloomy way to Caerleon, hunched under his guilt, confusion, and frustration. He went there because he had promised to and because he could think of nothing else to do. He was not in the best of moods.

The Lady of the Lake was growing impatient again. "Where is that bird of yours?" she demanded of Adon.

"I'm sorry, my Lady. He migrates, you know. He can spy for me only when he is in Britain."

"Have you no other spies?"

"Yes, but they are not nearly as reliable. They don't get the information firsthand, you see, and tend to send everything on to me with no verification."

"Well, what do they say?"

"It's very general. There are rumors that Lancelot has become good friends with King Arthur, but there is no mention of him on the King's recent journey. Torres, however, was there. There is some tale that he was seen at the home of the Queen's family, but I doubt this. Also, one report said that he had been overheard asking for the wife of King Ban of Benoit. He seems to believe that she is his mother."

"His mother!" The Lady sat bolt upright upon her couch. "She died. She must have. She was almost dead when I found him."

She sat for a while, chewing on her knuckle. Her attendants stood warily, wondering what she would demand of them next.

Finally she noticed them. Her eyes raked the room, looking for a likely "volunteer."

"Do you know where Lancelot is now?" she asked Adon.

He jumped. "Not exactly. I know where he is going—to Caerleon for the winter court."

"Still obsessed, I suppose, with his messianic nonsense?"

Adon shrugged.

"He needs to be distracted," the Lady announced. "It won't make any difference to the rules if one of you seduces him. He still has to discover his own kind. But one of you might at least comfort him, offer him some solace in his misery. Yes, I know you couldn't interest him while he was here, men or women. But now, after a few weeks out there, he may be more susceptible. But to whom? . . . Nimuë!"

"Yes, my Lady?" Nimuë came forward. She had been busy flirting with Riogh, to whom she had promised the night. She hoped she hadn't missed anything essential.

"I want you to find Lancelot and bring him our love. Show him how he is missed. As soon as possible. Do you understand?"

"Find him? But how?"

"Ask Adon. I want you to leave at once. Take a horse and some trappings. You need not be uncomfortable just because everyone else out there is. But be sure he receives as much affection as you can give."

Nimuë was crushed. What an assignment! "Yes, my Lady," she mumbled.

"Good." The Lady left the chamber, followed by most of her retinue. Riogh gave Nimuë a sorrowful wave as he went. She turned to Adon.

"What am I to do?" she moaned. "You know I love Lancelot dearly, but *making* love to him? How can she ask it? It would be easier to have sex with a dead fish."

Adon patted her shoulder. What could he say? Nimuë was right. But the Lady had made her orders clear.

"Perhaps he has changed since he's been living with humans. Maybe he is lonely and would appreciate your comfort."

"Of course, and diamonds grow on daffodils."

He abandoned solace. "Nimuë, you have no choice. You have been ordered. Who knows? You may be surprised."

She sighed. "Lilith showed me a different make-up. I'll try that on him. Perhaps Ori will lend me that diaphanous dress of hers with all the glitter."

"There. You see? I could not resist you in that. Lancelot won't be able to, either."

Two nights later, Lancelot had made camp a day's ride away from Caerleon. The weather had broken and the night was mild for a change. He sat by the fire and listened to the sounds of the forest. He felt oddly peaceful. He had tried. He had failed. Soon there would be another job to do, but for now he would rest body and spirit.

A sound like the tinkle of a thousand tiny bells mingled with the rustle of night creatures and the sleepy calls of the birds. Lancelot stood. It was coming nearer. He listened, apprehension growing. A soft blue light was glowing through the trees. He had seen that shimmer in only one other place.

"Who is it?" he called out, half-pleased and half-angry.

"Only me," a timid voice replied. "Nimuë. The Lady sent me to you, to see if you were all right."

"Nimuë!" Lancelot relaxed. "You shouldn't be traveling alone!"

She was near him, both she and the horse enveloped in the

gentle light. She smiled at him. "Who would dare hurt me?" she asked.

He helped her down and waited while she untied the knots that bound her bed and pavilion. She closed her eyes and chanted a few words. When she opened them, the pavilion stood nearby, the covers on the bed turned down.

"Oh dear," she said. "I wanted the bed to face the moonrise. Well, never mind. I'm much too tired to change it."

"Nimuë," Lancelot expostulated, "there was no need for you to come looking for me. I want to take care of myself. I don't need anyone to watch over me. I'm not a child!"

"But, Lancelot," she pouted and swirled closer to him. "We all miss you so. We worry about you. Are you eating properly, dressing warmly? Are you sleeping well?"

She was almost touching him now and he noticed for the first time that he could see through her gown and that she was naked underneath. He felt a tinge of suspicion.

"Nimuë," he said fiercely, "why are you here?"

She smiled and put her arms around him. "To ease your sojourn in this ugly land, Lancelot. Come, lie with me tonight, just for a respite."

Horrified, Lancelot pushed her away. "How can you? I have never done any wrong or evil to any woman or girl and I shall not begin with you!"

"Done wrong?" Nimuë was fascinated. "You can do me wrong only by refusing my request. It is lonely here, so far from our home, and you are a dear reminder of it. Here is our bed; share it with me as you did when you were a child."

"I have told you, I am a child no longer!" he huffed. "And I know you would not be content to tell me a story and rock me to sleep as you did then."

"Of course I would; I can tell you some wonderful stories." She took his hand and tried to guide it under her gown.

He yanked it back as if burnt. "It is a sinful thing you ask of me. Would you have me contribute to the damnation of your soul?"

"Lancelot, you keep forgetting! I am immortal. I have no

· 131 ·

soul. There is no heaven or hell for me; there is only the Lake. When it vanishes, so shall I. Until then I may do whatever I wish. Tonight I wish to make you happy."

"Then leave at once!" He folded his arms and turned his back on her.

"Lancelot, how can you be so cruel?" She put her arms around him and tried to draw him to the bed. Harshly, he pulled away from her. She hurried around to face him again and held her hand to his chin to force him to look as she opened her gown.

"My dear," she crooned, "no man of any make has yet refused this. There is no sin. I am not human. Enjoy yourself for one night of your life."

He looked at her body, taut and ready, and his gorge rose. He threw her from him so hard that she landed on the earth.

"How can you reject me?" she sobbed. "Is there nothing in your code about kindness to women?"

"No, Nimuë, only to ladies," he stated.

"I see." She got up and dusted herself off. "Well, if you will have nothing to do with me despite my honest offers, then I will go. Will you at least give me a kiss good-bye?"

"All right, for our friendship." He bent down to her and she raised her lips to his. As they touched, she grabbed him again and held him until she cried out sharply and fell back.

"You bit me!" she screamed, holding her lip. "You monster! How dare you?"

Lancelot was equally angry. "You stuck your tongue in my mouth! You are disgusting! I don't believe the Lady knows you're here! Get out of my sight!"

"That is all! No one but the Lady could have forced me to attempt to give you a little pleasure." She glared at him as she snapped the bed and pavilion back on the horse. "I hope, Lancelot du Lac, that someday you get a mistress as cold and cruel as yourself! It's a pity you are not like Torres. He knows how to respect a woman's wishes!"

A moment later she was gone. Lancelot sank down to the earth, his sense of peace shattered. He felt sick. How could anyone want a woman like that, one who simply appeared and offered herself? He had known Nimuë all his life, but he could not remember ever seeing her body before. It was revolting. Then a thought hit him. Guinevere was a woman. She must look something like that, too, under her garments. He tried to recall Nimuë, to see her with Guinevere's face. His breath came more quickly. Somehow he knew that Guinevere's body would not disgust him.

He tried to blot out the image, but it lured him on. He beat his hands upon the earth, crying. Finally, he sat there rocking, his face buried in his arms.

Furious and afraid, Nimuë trotted down the road. What would the Lady say when she reported her failure? Did she have to go back at once? A few days, she could be absent that long. Maybe by then something would happen to distract the Lady from Lancelot.

Dawn was stretching her fingers across the sky when she rounded a bend and came upon a man sitting beneath a tree. He seemed quite at home there and did not bother to look up as she jingled nearer. He was doing something. She got off the horse and came closer. He had several thin rods of glass in his hands and, one by one, he was holding them up to catch the morning light. As he did, rainbows were cast upon the leaves and rocks. Nimuë was entranced.

"How do you do that?" she said, forgetting everything but the beauty of it.

The man looked up, startled. He was not used to meeting exotic women in transparent gowns on the road at dawn.

"Hello," he greeted her. "I didn't catch that. What did you say?"

She pointed. "Those rainbows. How do you make them without water?"

"Ah, yes," he considered. "There is something in the property of the glass. I haven't figured it out exactly, but somehow the curve of the glass causes the rainbow to appear. I am beginning to learn how to shape it properly, but I am still not sure why it works."

She smiled at him. "May I stay with you and watch?"

"Of course. Is there no one with you?"

"No. Just the horse."

He nodded politely at the horse, since that seemed indicated. Then he returned to the woman.

"I do not know your name," he said. "But it seems to me that I have seen someone very like you, long ago, in a place of light and flowers."

She clapped her hands. "I remember you now! Merlin! The man who could answer all the Lady's questions. You stayed with her awhile. But then you left. No man before had ever asked to leave her. She was amazed."

"Was she angry?"

"No, just surprised. She has other amusements."

"That is reassuring. I had hoped she wasn't vengeful."

"Oh, no. She has watched you with interest now and then. You are with that Arthur-man now aren't you? The one she sent Lancelot to."

"Yes, I am. Was that why she sent Lancelot to him, because of me?"

"You led her to him. That was all."

"I should have expected that it would be my fault. I have always held a double-edged sword."

He seemed so discouraged that Nimuë ventured to place a hand on his arm. "Lancelot is rather unusual, even under the Lake, but for some reason we are still very fond of him. Is he causing you trouble, too?"

He shook his head. "Not now, but I sense it coming. There is a dark scent when he and the Queen are in the same room. I can't explain it, but some calamity is associated with them. Whether they will cause it or be destroyed by it, I don't know. But you said, 'too.' Do you have a complaint against him?"

"Yes." Nimuë still felt grievously wronged. "I came out here, left the Lake and all its pleasures to bring Lancelot a bit of sympathy and cosseting, and do you know what he did?"

"No," he answered, amused.

"He bit me."

"What!"

"Right on the lip. See!" She puckered for him to notice. "Tell me truly. If I had come to you and offered you this"—

she opened her gown—"would you throw me on the ground and yell at me?"

He studied her body seriously and finally smiled. "Not at all," he said flatly. "I would have been honored."

She let the robe fall back into place and gazed at him with a half-puzzled, half-delighted expression. "The Lady said there was something different about you. I don't have any swords to offer, but I can give you a goose-feather bed with silken sheets on a silver pavilion. And," she added as an after-thought, "myself."

Merlin smiled again. How long had it been since he had known anything from others but fear or respect? He thought he remembered her better now. Thirty years ago it had been and she was still young and beautiful. Nimuë her name was. He wondered how many millennia she had existed and then dismissed it as irrelevant. She was soft and warm and lovely and inviting him to share her bed. And, he remembered, she had just been callously rejected. What else could he do but agree?

"Really?" she asked and her eyes shone. "Oh, thank you! And later can you show me some more rainbows?"

She set up the pavilion a few yards into the woods, away from the road, and she led him in. Hours later they didn't hear Lancelot pass by at a gallop, hell-bent for Caerleon.

Chapter Ten

Until he left Tintagel, Gareth had never walked more than a mile or so in his life. He was prepared for tired and aching feet, but how could he have known that every muscle in his legs and hips would also hurt terribly? On the morning of his second day away from home he found that he could barely hobble. So much for his plan of reaching Caerleon in a two- or three-day walk.

A farmer on his way to the fields found him collapsed by the side of the road and took him home with him. Neither he nor his wife believed a word of Gareth's story that he was a poor itinerant laborer hunting for work. But because they liked his looks, they fed him and taught him a few simple tasks to earn his keep: cutting rushes to spread on the dirt floor, weeding the kitchen garden, scrubbing the pots. He paid them for their kindness by trading his fur and leather boots for clogs of wood and lamb's wool made by the farmer. He did not realize until later that he had gotten the better deal.

He spent the summer traveling and doing menial work for his dinner and bed. After the quiet, cool gloom of Tintagel, Gareth found the rough and jovial contacts he made with the farmers and artisans he met along the way stimulating. Those that peddled their skill in metal or leather also carried news, moderately fresh, to all those who gave them shelter. Much of it was about King Arthur. In this way Gareth soon discovered that there was no need for him to hurry; it would be weeks before Arthur returned to Caerleon. As that time passed, Gareth became less an insecure princeling from Cornwall and more a solid, hard-working citizen of Britain.

Consequently, when he finally did arrive at Caerleon, he appeared a great deal different from the young man who had set out in haste from Tintagel some months before. His clothes had been traded, piece by piece, for some which were roughly made, but more substantial. His hair was longer and bleached from the sun. In the last few places he had stopped, he had been taken, without comment, for what he claimed to be and he had learned to perform his tasks well.

As luck would have it, he arrived at Caerleon at just the time when a man who had a strong back was needed more than an elegantly mounted soldier. The guard at the gate pointed Cei out to him and told him to apply there for work.

"No doubt you'll have more than you want of it," he chuckled. "But if you can stick with it, you'll see first-hand more soldiers, warriors, scholars, saints, and just plain addle brains come through here in a winter than you'd expect to meet in your whole life. Winter at Caerleon is too good a show to miss."

Gareth thanked him, wondering which category his brother, Gawain, came under in the man's mind. He presented himself to Cei and asked if there were any job he could do.

"I haven't anything left but a few odd-jobbers and pot-scrubbers. Will you take that? You get your fill of food, no scraps, a place to sleep and, at winter's end, your choice of livestock to take back to your farm. And don't think it will be fun. There will be a flock of highborn knights here this year as well as the usual crowd and most of them have never so much as washed their own faces in their lives—or, if they did, they'll think they're too good for it now. Some of 'em might also think you're here to fetch and polish for them. Don't let them do it. Tell me, instead. Arthur doesn't want that sort here. Do you still want to stay?"

"Yes, sir," Gareth insisted.

"All right, then. Put your gear in that hall over there, farthest from the fire. You're the new man. Then get over to those buildings where everyone else is working. We've got to clean out a hundred years of dust to get them ready for the new recruits. What did you say your name was? Gareth? Old Cornish name, isn't it? Never mind. Just get to work. For now, do anything the foreman, Struthair, tells you to. He's the big, bald man with the wart on his chin. Once the hordes arrive, you'll probably spend most of your time in the kitchens. Wait until you see what it takes to feed them all. But if you can keep awake in the evenings, you'll have leave to come to the dining hall and listen to the tales, if you like. Is that all clear?"

"Yes, sir," Gareth said again.

Cei had already started yelling at someone who was arriving with bags of grain piled high in a cart. Soon Gareth was surrounded by a cloud of dust and silt as he joined the others trying to clear out the old barracks for the new models of the centurions. He did not seem any closer to knighthood than he had been at Tintagel, but he had made it to Caerleon and here anything might happen.

A day or two later, he was told to report to the stables. After the hours of filling his lungs with century-old dirt and mold, the thought of scooping up horse manure sounded positively refreshing. Gareth reflected on how one's viewpoint could alter with the situation and wondered what his mother would say if she could see him. He was beginning to feel a sense of pride in making his own way.

He found the horsemaster, Briacu, currying an elegant white stallion. Gareth whistled in admiration. He had not seen anything so fine before. Most of the horses in Britain were hillbred ones, small, sturdy but not overly graceful of line. He commented on it as he started in on the opposite stall with his shovel.

"Yes, he is an amazing specimen," Briacu agreed. "He's Sir Lancelot's horse, Clades. There may be a touch of magic in his siring. I never saw his like in Armorica, either. I'd like to try and crossbreed him with my Nera, here, but he's so much bigger than she is, I'm afraid that he would hurt her or that the foal might kill her. If I can find an old brood mare to test him on, Lancelot has given me permission to try."

"Which one is Lancelot?" Gareth asked. "I haven't been here very long."

The horsemaster grew more expansive. "Don't worry. This fall almost everyone is new. You'll soon recognize Lancelot, though. He's the one with all the gold-lined cloaks and jewels in his clothes. He arrived yesterday. The guard says he roared up the side of the hill as if demons were chasing him, but Clades wasn't even panting when he was brought in." He gave the stallion an admiring pat.

"Within the week," he continued, "they'll all be here. Then this place will be full of lords and farmers and we'll have no more time to lean on shovels and listen to gossip."

There was a bitterness in his voice that Gareth felt was not directed at him. But he took the hint and went on with his work.

Caet hid his face against the horse's flank. He had found that under any name there would be no knighthood for him.

To be so near Guinevere and still be nothing but a servant increased the bitterness of his fate.

Merlin stirred softly in the warmth. He was not awake enough to remember where he was. He felt so peaceful and free that he resisted facing the morning, which always brought him tension and worry. A gentle hand slid across his hip and Nimuë's body pressed against him. With a gasp of joy, Merlin opened his eyes. It was not yet mandatory to re-enter the world.

Nimuë lay nestled in the circle of his arm. She felt the steady beat of his heart beneath her cheek with a kind of awe. The Lady was right. This man was different—rare and wonderful—and she could not let him depart from her life. She clutched him more tightly.

He tilted his face down to meet hers. "What is wrong, Nimuë?"

"My power is fading, Merlin," she whispered sadly. "I cannot stay so long away from the Lake. But I do not want to leave you."

He wrapped both arms around her, as if to keep her from escaping. But his voice held little hope.

"My life has always been so. Whatever I have loved has slipped away from me. I should thank you for staying this long."

Her eyes opened wide in amazement. "You love me?"

His mouth twisted in a self-mocking smile. "In all my human arrogance, I do."

"Oh, Merlin. No one has ever loved me before. Please, please, let me stay with you!"

"But the Lake . . . Nimuë, my dearest naiad, how long could you survive in the human world?"

"Long enough to love you in return."

There were tears in her eyes. They astounded him. He had believed her kind were incapable of caring enough to cry.

"That would not be long enough for me," he said, choking. "There must be some world, some other place, where the two of us can exist as we were meant to."

She caught his defiance. "There are other places of magic. I do not know how to reach them, but the Lake is full of amulets and spells. I will search them all to find a way. If I do, will you go there with me?"

"Forever," he answered.

It took them many hours before they were able to say good-bye. Merlin had no idea what day it was as he watched her slow departure into the morning mist. They might have been there for weeks. He hoped that the Lady would not scold her much for her long absence. He worried about it. Without her by him, he would always worry now.

It was not until she was irrevocably out of sight that he realized that he had no way of sending word to her. They had not discussed it. "Who is the dullard now?" he thought. He knew that the Lady guarded the Lake with paths that went nowhere and trees that moved by night. Only those who weren't looking for it ever found it. He started to run after Nimuë, but then realized that she traveled by magic and was now far beyond his reach.

Merlin arrived at Caerleon in a terrible mood. Cei, who had braved his rancor before, could tell at a distance that this was not a good time to approach him with plans for the winter, but he steeled himself. It had to be done. But Merlin would not listen. He waved Cei away.

"Tell Arthur about it when he comes. It is his problem now and yours. My job is almost finished. Only a few loose threads are left. Don't bother me with trivial nonsense."

"But, Master Merlin, I don't know. . . ."

It was no use. Merlin had spotted Lancelot and, with a cry of delight, was advancing on him, leaving Cei and his problems behind.

"Sir Lancelot."

Lancelot bowed. "Master Merlin."

"Do you still communicate with the Lady of the Lake?"

"Oh, no, sir!" Lancelot was shocked. "I have joined King Arthur!"

"You mean there is no way for you to contact them? Don't you care anything for the people who raised you?"

Lancelot drew himself up proudly. "I care very much, sir. But I made it clear to them that I didn't wish to rely on their influence for my position here. Torres sends word of how we are, every so often, I believe."

Merlin sighed in relief. "Why didn't you say so at once? Where is he?"

"Traveling with Arthur, sir."

"Damn! All right, all right. Never mind."

And Merlin strode off again, oblivious to Lancelot's quick movement of the fingers to ward off evil spells. He had learned something from the others at Camelot.

Cei came over to him.

"What's wrong with Merlin?" he asked. "I've known him all my life and I've never seen him this bad."

Lancelot shrugged. "He wants to contact the Lady for some reason. I told him I couldn't help."

"You told him that to his face?" Cei stared. "You must be awfully powerful or an awful fool. No matter. I don't meddle. Look, Lancelot, I need your help. Guinevere should be along in a day or two. She promised she'd be back before Arthur, and I have word he's at King Dubric's and should be back within the week with who knows how many people. He's been picking them up like maggots in meat all summer long. The old-timers are already arriving for the winter. I rank here, but I'm too busy to see to them all. Can you act as the official host here for a bit, just until Guinevere comes? You only need to be here at the gate, greet them, and tell them you're glad to see them. If they were here before, they'll go to their old quarters. If they weren't, get Cheldric to assign them some. All right?"

"I . . . I suppose. I've never done anything like that before."

"Doesn't matter. You look the part. Find Cheldric or Risa. They'll know what to do. Hey, you!" he yelled to a passing workman. "Where are you going with that ladder? Thanks, Lancelot. Arthur likes to have everything in order when Guinevere arrives and we're not nearly ready yet. I hope she's delayed a few days more."

Guinevere would not have minded a delay. She felt set free when she was home again. It was an idyll from another era and she had now seen enough of the rest of Britain to know it. The colors were brighter here and the days softer than anywhere else. She sat high in the watchtower as she had as a child, but now her niece sat with her. They watched the peasants working in the fields below, reaping the grain that would sustain them all in the coming year.

"Do you know, Letitia," Guinevere reminisced, "I would sit here for days on end when I was your age, watching the road in the hope that your father and uncles would come galloping down it."

"What was he like, my father?" Letitia asked nervously. "I don't like to bother Mama; she starts crying and Grandmother only says what a lovely baby he was."

"I don't know if I can tell you what you need to know," Guinevere answered. "He was ten years older than I and my memories are mostly of riding on his back and running away when he teased. He loved to tease me. He was the one who dragged me down into the cave to touch the Table and he called me a coward because it scared me. Oh, but I loved him! He was strong and brave and he protected me from everyone else. He could be very thoughtful. He once spent a night alone in the forest hunting for an herb Flora wanted that would bloom only on a moonless night. He thought it was exciting. I think that's why he loved being a soldier—not for killing, but for setting himself against another, testing himself. That was life to him. You see, I can't bring back what he really was. So much of his being was in the way he lived. He was wonderfully alive, Letitia. I'm glad you are part of him. I hope, of all the qualities he might have left you, that you have his joy in living. He was never afraid. He must have seen even death as a new adventure."

Guinevere trailed off. She was crying. She hadn't wept for her brother since the day he died. Then it had been for what she had lost. Now it was for him.

Letitia put an arm around her.

"Thank you, Aunt Guinevere." She kissed her damp cheek.

Guinevere gave her niece an absent hug. She had already

lost interest in maudlin grief. A rider had appeared in the road. A middle-aged man on an elderly horse was picking his way across the stream.

"Geraldus!" she screamed, forgetting her queenly dignity and acting as she had ten years before.

He waved up at them as the gate was opened swiftly for him. "I've come as I said I would," he shouted. "We haven't much time, Guinevere. We promised to be back at Caerleon to greet Arthur."

Guinevere and Letitia rushed down to embrace him.

"My dear Geraldus!" Guinevere gushed. "I'm so glad to see you back. But where is Lydia?"

Geraldus smiled broadly. "Lydia was shaking with nerves when I brought her to Cador, but now you couldn't pry her away from her mother. She sent her apologies and promised to see you again next spring. Now, don't be hurt. She has spent most of her life without her mother and they owe themselves the chance to enjoy being together again."

Guinevere sighed. "Of course. I do understand. You always let me know when I'm being selfish, don't you?"

Geraldus kissed her. "Yes, I do and I always will. But I love you all the same. When shall we set out for Caerleon? My tribe here wants a bath before they will set out once more. I don't understand it. You would think they could go where they wish and manufacture their own baths, but they never do. I think it's pure laziness—ow!"

"You mustn't criticize them, Geraldus," Guinevere laughed as they strolled to the villa. "Come!" she called to them all. "Don't mind your singing master. He would be desolate without you. There is hot water and wine for you tonight. But I am firm: we must go tomorrow!"

"That will settle them," Geraldus said with pleasure.

He was surprised to see how ready Guinevere was to leave. Her clothes were packed and her gear was ready. She smiled at him in a sort of apology.

"I don't understand it myself, but this time I feel that I must get back, no matter how much I love to be here. It will always be the place I think of as home, but somehow I find myself thinking more and more of Caerleon and wondering what is happening there and if everything is being done properly. Could it be that I have two homes now?"

"It is very likely, Guinevere. I am only surprised that it didn't happen sooner."

But it was a hard farewell, as always, and Guinevere's neck ached from turning to see if her family were all still there at the gate, waving good-bye. When they could be seen no more, she sat disconsolate upon her horse for an hour or two until, creeping insidiously into her mind, came images of Caerleon, of Arthur and Gawain, of Caet watching her with silent adoration, and of Lancelot. She began to be more interested in her arrival there.

They were but a few hours away, in the last stretch of forest before the town, when it happened.

Geraldus and his choir had drifted farther ahead than usual, working out a rondelet. Guinevere followed at her own pace, enjoying the stillness of the day. Suddenly they were jolted by a wild shriek as a troop of men leaped out of the surrounding trees. Meleagant rode out from his hiding place as the foot brigades surrounded them. He grabbed the furious Guinevere from her horse.

For a moment she was so astonished and outraged that there was nothing she could say. Finally she found her breath. She beat against Meleagant's armored chest, bruising her hands.

"How dare you!" she screamed. "You barbarian boor! Put me down at once!"

Meleagant laughed. "I told Arthur I could steal something from him and you are mine until Easter unless he and his lisping 'knights' can retrieve you! I hope that pack horse has warm clothing in its bags."

This made Guinevere angrier. She kicked so suddenly that he almost dropped her. "Arthur will punish you for this! My father will! If you dare lay a hand on me. . . ."

"Don't worry about that, my dear," he purred. "Not but what you might be fun to tame. Leodegrance is an old adversary of my family, but I respect him. I just want your upstart husband to know that I could have you if it pleased me and there would be nothing he could do to stop me. Now, quit that kicking or you'll injure my horse. Who taught you such unladylike behavior?"

He looked over his shoulder and Guinevere followed his glance. With no weapons, Geraldus was doing his best to fight off Meleagant's men. He was being easily defeated. She was more afraid for him than herself. She yelled at the attackers.

"Don't you dare hurt him! He's a saint! Angels flying all around him. You'll fry in Hell!"

Her warning, however, was not needed. Those who slashed their swords at him were startled to see them bend in the air before they ever reached him. A man who tried to pull him from his horse was flipped upon his back without ever being touched. He picked himself up in an instant, however, and was away and down the road without a backward glance. The others soon followed him. They weren't sure about angels, but there was something protecting the man and they wanted no part of it.

"Thank you!" Geraldus called. "Can't you help Guinevere, too?"

The voice of his alto was so close to his ear that he jumped. She sounded out of breath.

"There was very little we could do for you. We aren't used to this sort of work. Anyway, we're bound to you and she's far away already. You'll have to ride for help."

"It's all right," he reassured her. "Don't worry, Arthur will rescue her."

Geraldus spurred Plotinus to a gallop for the first time since he had owned the horse. His only hope was to reach Caerleon soon. The poor steed had not been pressured to do more than walk for the last twenty years, but he tried to respond, dimly remembering his days in battle. They managed to reach the gates of Caerleon before sunset.

Geraldus leaped from the almost prostrate horse and straight onto the first person he saw: Lancelot.

"Guinevere!" he gasped. "Meleagant. He's kidnapped her!"

Lancelot caught Geraldus as he fainted. He heard only one

word clearly, "Meleagant." The son of the man who had killed his father. He gripped Geraldus' arms painfully as he came to.

"Meleagant! What has he done?" he shouted.

"Ow, stop that! Guinevere," Geraldus panted. "On our way here he ambushed us. He captured her. There was nothing I could do. Arthur back yet?"

"No, not for a day or more, they say. Do you know where Meleagant is taking her?"

"To his fortress. I must tell Arthur!"

"But there is no time. Which way is this fortress?"

"Northwest, through the mountains. But. . . ."

He was talking to the air. Lancelot was halfway to the stables. Geraldus called after him.

"This is for Arthur to decide, Lancelot! He'll know how to deal with Meleagant!"

Lancelot did not appear to have heard. Geraldus grabbed one of the guards who had come running at the shouts.

"Where is Sir Cei?"

The guard pointed to a figure coming toward them, and Geraldus, having caught his breath, hurried to meet him. He gave his news as quickly as possible. Cei's face hardened as he listened.

"That scum!" he spat. "He thinks it's all a great joke, 'stealing' something of Arthur's. Arthur is going to be furious. I'll send a messenger to him at once. This is going to be tricky."

Meanwhile, Lancelot had saddled Clades and was halfway mounted before it occurred to him that he might need a cloak, or at least his sword and shield to confront that monster with. There was a young man shoveling out the adjoining stall.

"You there! Go to my quarters at once and fetch my gear. Hurry!"

The man stared at him stupidly. "Why?" he asked.

"What?" Lancelot glared at him.

"Why should I go? My job is cleaning the stables."

"Because I ordered it. Because your Queen has been kidnapped and I am going to rescue her . . . if I get my weapons!"

At that the man's face changed. He looked almost intelligent. "I'll get them for you, Lancelot, but only if you saddle another horse for me."

It was Lancelot's turn to stare stupidly. The man laughed.

"I want to go with you."

"You must be insane!" Lancelot yelled.

The man shrugged, but did not move.

"Very well. You may come with me. But hurry!"

Gareth shook the straw out of his hair as he obeyed. He snatched up his own bag as he grabbed Lancelot's and was back by the time Lancelot had readied another horse.

"You won't regret taking me," Gareth promised as he handed over the sword. "I will stay by your side whatever happens."

"Just keep up with me," Lancelot muttered grimly.

Ignoring the cries from the guard and the frantic waves of Geraldus and Cei as they realized what he was doing, Lancelot du Lac, greatest Knight of the Round Table, galloped off to rescue his beloved.

Chapter Eleven

Arthur lolled against the pillows in his tent, relishing the chance to relax unwatched. It had been a good trip, worthwhile. Craddoc had been more than eager to swear allegiance to Arthur, especially if he received protection from Meleagant in return. It had not surprised Arthur to learn that Meleagant had decided to go on an extended hunting trip just at the time that Arthur was to have visited. He considered it a compliment. The man was more wary of him than he had hoped.

It had been a good recruiting trip, too. The new men were fresh and enthusiastic, as were some old men. Ector, Cei's father, had gotten quite carried away and promised to come down in the spring and help with the training. This journey had shown the mettle of some of Arthur's fosterlings, too. He had not previously noticed Bedevere much, but the boy had blossomed into a diplomat of rare persuasion. All in all, Arthur was satisfied and more at ease than he had felt for years. Now, as soon as he could get home to Guinevere. . . .

He set down his wine cup and drifted off into a semiconscious dream, familiar and never quite fulfilled.

Someone was making an outrageous racket outside. Arthur started awake, knocking over the cup. He stuck his head outside the tent. The guard hurried over.

"What is all that noise?" Arthur demanded.

"I'm not sure, sir. I believe that a messenger has arrived and insists on seeing you at once. The watch told him you had retired, but he refuses to wait until morning."

"If the man wants to see me that badly, send him in! Who told the watch that it was their decision to make?"

The guard did not answer. He was already gone.

Arthur stretched and mumbled as he wrapped himself in a proper cloak instead of his fur blanket. The watch should have been able to figure out for themselves that any man who wanted to see him in the middle of the night must have a good reason. Those men would have to be switched to some duty less mentally taxing.

He had hardly sat down again when the tent flaps were pulled open and Cheldric burst in. He was breathing heavily and trying to slip his cloak off with his one arm as he bowed to the King.

"Sir Cei has sent me to you with evil news, my Lord. The Queen, on her way to Caerleon, was kidnapped by King Meleagant."

"What!" Arthur leaped to his feet. "This is no subject for humor."

Cheldric backed a pace. "I would not have come all this

way for a joke, sir. The roads are treacherous. All the able-bodied men are preparing to set out at once, upon your arrival."

"When did this happen?" Arthur snapped. He no longer doubted. This was just the sort of trick which would appeal to a mind like Meleagant's. He ground his teeth. Just the sort, too, that would amuse the other powerful kings like Maelgwn. He knew that unless Guinevere were retrieved soon, versions of the story would be all over Britain, most of them implying that Arthur couldn't keep his own wife at home.

"It was almost three days ago, sir," Cheldric replied. "Saint Geraldus was slightly wounded and took some time getting to Caerleon. I was sent out at once. We think they may have already arrived at the fortress."

Arthur stiffened, his fists clenched against his thighs. Three days. If that unspeakable bastard of a baboon and a village idiot had so much as mussed her hair, he would have the man's ribs out and laid one by one upon a table. If the man had done anything more, he would do the job with his own knife.

He moved so quickly that he almost knocked Cheldric over and did ram into the guard on duty outside.

"Agravaine!" he hollered. "Bedevere! Torres! Get up! Get out here! We're leaving at once for Caerleon. Pack your weapons and a change of clothes. Everything else stays behind. Cheldric, you remain and see that the tents and kitchens are brought later. Well, hurry! Where are you all?"

He strode over to the nearest tent and pulled the occupant from it. Torres struggled groggily to stand. The woman next to him snatched the blankets and hid beneath them. Torres was torn between anger and embarrassment.

"What . . . what are you? How dare you. . . . Oh! King Arthur! What's wrong?"

"We're heading for Caerleon tonight and then north, to teach Meleagant the folly of flouting a king! Get your sword and tell your friend there good-bye."

He pushed Torres back. There was a muffled squeal as he tripped over the mound of blankets.

Agravaine emerged from another tent, Gaheris peering out from behind him.

"We're almost ready, Uncle, but what about Gawain? We can't wake him!"

"Dress him and tie him to his horse. He's coming with us."

They pounded into the night with little regard for the safety of men or horses. Arthur led the way. Those who saw his face as he passed by them barely recognized him, and some of the younger men, who had known him only in peace, realized now why he had been able to defeat the Saxons at Mons Badon, despite the odds. Gaheris got a glimpse of him as he sped by. The look in his eyes frightened his nephew. There was something about it that reminded him of his dreaded Aunt Morgause. But he and Agravaine had no time to compare impressions. They were too busy trying to keep up with the others while leading the sleeping Gawain on his horse. His wrists were tied about its neck and a rope from ankle to ankle held him to its back. But he tended to twist about as if attempting to lie on his side and this caused him to slide over until he was hanging against the horse's flank like a parcel.

"This will never work!" Agravaine exploded as he dismounted for the third time to right his brother. "One of us will have to ride behind him and hold him."

"All right." Gaheris clambered up behind Gawain and wrapped his arms about Gawain's waist. "This won't be easy. He's a lot bigger than I am. You'll have to lead both the horses. I can't hold on and guide, too."

Agravaine could barely hear the riders ahead of him. Swearing freely, he grabbed the dangling reins and yanked the party along. It was not the first time he wished he had been born into a less interesting family.

The morning was still gray when they arrived at Caerleon. Cei was at the gate to meet them.

"A messenger came from Meleagant last night," he told Arthur as soon as he was close enough to hear. "He said that the Queen would be his guest until Easter and requested that more robes and a lady's maid be sent to her, as she had only the things on her pack horse with her."

Arthur clenched his fists. It was a full minute before he could trust himself to speak.

"Send the man back at once. Have him tell Meleagant that my wife shall dine with me at Caerleon before the week is out, and I will use his beard to wipe my hands. She will not need any more clothes."

"Yes, Arthur," Cei replied. He was startled by the sudden fierceness in Arthur. Even as a boy, he had never given way to anger. Cei had not suspected it was possible. "What do you want me to do then?"

"Food for everyone and fresh horses. Send Lancelot to me—and Merlin. We leave again as soon as we can be fed and armed. I intend to see just how well Meleagant can withstand an attack upon his fortress."

Cei gulped. "Arthur!" he called as the King strode onward. "Lancelot, he isn't here!"

Arthur did not seem to hear him. "Oh, well," Cei thought, "Merlin will tell him. Why should I bring all the bad news?"

Food was hastily being thrown on the tables in the dining hall. Hollering for Merlin, Arthur grabbed a goose leg as he passed them. Finally the adviser appeared.

"Didn't take you long to get here, did it?" he stated. He was not in a good mood. Nimuë was gone and he couldn't reach her and now Guinevere was missing again. The last time it had been the Saxons who took her and the whole thing had resulted in her marrying Arthur. Why couldn't that woman stay in one place instead of traipsing all over the country with no guard but a haunted saint? He knew by the look on Arthur's face that she would have to be retrieved. If it weren't for the insult Meleagant intended for Arthur, Merlin would have been glad to let her stay at the fortress forever.

"Merlin, how do we get past Meleagant's defenses?" Arthur demanded. He tossed the half-finished drumstick to the dogs under the table and drained a cup of wine.

"Don't do that, Arthur." Merlin felt chilled. "You look exactly like your father."

Arthur threw the cup down with a clatter. "Damn it! Half of me *is* my father! Why should we keep avoiding it? He was a strong king, whatever else he did. He wouldn't have been somewhere else when his wife was being kidnapped! He would have had Meleagant's home uprooted and smashed by any means he could find. And you were never above giving him those means, were you, Merlin?"

He glared at the wizard, his jaw working, his lips tight and drawn. "It never bothered you when you were with him to conjure up a fog or an earthquake to help him pillage. But for me it's always, 'Do it the hard way, Arthur, such power is evil. You must rule by reason.' Right now I don't care about reason or even mercy. I want power *and I will get my revenge!*"

He was screaming. The doorway was crowded with men coming to get their food and their orders. They stopped in amazement at the sight of the King ranting out of control. The servants cowered against the walls. No one spoke or moved.

Arthur felt the quiet. He turned from Merlin and saw them all staring at him with hurt or awed disbelief. He felt sick.

"Then look!" he yelled at them. He picked up another piece of meat and ripped off a chunk with his teeth. "I'm Arthur! You made me King, whether I willed or not. You come to me for every answer any time, as if I were an oracle. Well, I'm not a god, like the old emperors were. I can't raise my hand and make the oceans part. Isn't that what you expect of me? Miracles? Divine justice? And all imparted with celestial calm and detachment. Look at me!" He threw down the meat, to the joy of the dogs. "I'm human! I'm hungry and tired. I'm growing old. My teeth are beginning to crumble. I have been robbed and insulted and I'm angry. Just how do you expect me to act?" His glare beat upon them as their disbelief turned to sorrow and embarrassment. Arthur's shoulders sagged; he took a deep breath. Just as he was about to speak again, an outraged voice echoed from outside the hall.

"Who the hell tied me to this horse?"

A burst of laughter released the tension as Gawain was remembered. Everyone hurried out to set him loose. Only Merlin remained. He watched Arthur with an indecipherable expression.

All the energy seemed to drain from Arthur's body. He collapsed onto the nearest bench.

"I'm tired," he whispered from the reaches of his soul. He wiped his face with his forearm. Merlin laid a hand on his shoulder.

"I am sorry, Arthur, truly. All the years I have been scheming for you, it has been too easy to forget what I was also doing to you. I cannot help you the way I did your father. Uther was only a soldier. His dreams went no further than his own pleasure. He wasn't worried by the sins he carried. Do you want me to make an earthquake for you? Will having Meleagant destroyed in such a way bring you any closer to what you seek?"

Arthur stared at the floor. When he spoke, his voice was distant and wrenching.

"I am in a cage, Merlin. There are no doors. I cannot smash it or bend the bars. Only when I look up can I see clear sky with no barrier. So I must climb the bars, hand over hand. I have been climbing for so long. Every time I think I am almost there, I discover there are a few more feet to go, only a few more, on and on. What happens, Merlin, if I should simply let go?"

Merlin's eyes filled. He thought of Nimuë and how he yearned for her and the peace and joy she brought him. He struggled to find the right words. But there were none.

After a long pause, Arthur spoke again, in a different tone. "Meleagant would not hurt her, would he?"

"Of course not, Arthur. If Aelle couldn't harm her, I don't see how Meleagant would dare." He sighed. "I will help you get her back—at least with advice. Don't worry. Call your people in and get them fed. I will come with you."

Nimuë was immortal. She could wait. But how long could he? Merlin resigned himself to one more mission. But no more, please, no more.

Meleagant did not quite know what to do with his "guest." She intimidated him and that made him angry. She puzzled him, too. His main knowledge of women of her class came from his wife, Gilli. Gilli had been acquired as part of a peace treaty his father had made with a neighbor. She had been nice enough to look at then, but clearly not delighted with her fate. She gave Meleagant his due as a husband but little insight into the female mind. After fifteen years of marriage Meleagant often wished they had risked war with her father, after all. Guinevere was a new prospect for him. She was beautiful—her looks were already legendary in Britain—but she was not only ornamental. In some way he could not exactly follow, she seemed to exert an influence on those about her.

He had installed her in a small room in one of the towers. It was not a prison, but a bare place with no amenities. She had made no comment on it, but by the end of the first day there were hangings on the walls, clean rushes on the floor, furs on the bed, and even an ancient copper brazier to warm the air. The last had been donated by old Claudas, who had never bothered himself about any of his son's household before. Meleagant scratched his head. Even his brood of slovenly, half-grown offspring showed vague signs of intelligence when they were around her.

A fear began to grow in Meleagant that perhaps he had not been so clever when he stole Arthur's Queen. Even his retainers were drawn to her. They might decide not to help at all if this should lead to warfare. There was only one logical reason for it. The woman must be a witch, a sorceress, enchanting all who came within her sphere of influence. Meleagant crossed himself automatically at the thought. He had forgotten that aunt of Arthur's, Morgause. What if Guinevere were another like her? And it was he who had brought her within his walls. . . . He called to his seneschal.

"Is the Lady Guinevere securely locked in her room?"

The seneschal came to attention. "No, my Lord. Your father wanted to talk with her and complained of the stairs being too much for him. So she was escorted down to the hall."

"She is there now?" Meleagant said in alarm.

"Yes, sir."

"Then I will speak with her there."

Meleagant strode angrily to the common hall. What business had his father to concern himself with the prisoner? The woman was dangerous and the sooner he could be honorably rid of her, the better.

Guinevere, when she had gained control of her anger, reflected that, for all its military value, the fortress was a dreary place to live. It was even worse than the dank halls of Cador, where she had been fostered. At least there had been some interesting people there. Guinevere wasn't impressed with the inhabitants she had met here so far. With the exception of Meleagant, they were very kind to her and eager to please, but they were dirty and they sniffed into their sleeves a great deal, even the adults. She had taken to handing out handkerchiefs as gifts, but no one seemed to take the hint. Guinevere hoped that Arthur would waste no time in rescuing her. She sipped from the cup she had been given upon her arrival in the hall. It was mulled ale and much too bitter. She stifled a sigh and regarded the old man across the table from her.

Claudas was so old that his memory often became confused with myth. It was popularly believed among his grandchildren that he would never die since neither God nor the devil had any use for him. *They* certainly had none. He had long ago lost all of his teeth and survived on a diet of grain boiled and mashed with milk and ale. The stench of it smothered those who came close to him.

He raised his decrepit hand and pointed at the game pieces on the table before them.

"Do y' know this, girl?" he asked sharply. "The soldiers used t' play it when I was a boy. Have y' seen one before?"

She nodded. "It's a chessboard. My father taught me to play."

"You're Leodegrance's girl, I heard. Don't remember him. Your mother, now, she was something to look at. Y' don't take after her much."

Guinevere smiled. He peered through the rheum in his eyes.

"I remember your grandmother, too. You've got her name. Don't take after her, either. Her eyes were brown and her

· 155 ·

hair curled all around her face and neck. They don't do it that way anymore. Too lazy."

He leaned forward, trying to take her in. The chess pieces were knocked over and rolled across the floor. Claudas ignored them.

"Well, girl, who *do* y' take after? Never saw anything like y' before. And in my time I saw most of the world. Nah, you're not even Saxon."

Guinevere let him run down, but gave no answer. While a servant chased after the chess pieces, she examined the hall. It was old, she guessed, maybe from before the Romans. The upper walls were thick with soot and the stone steps were worn into soft curves by thousands of feet. Claudas watched her. He bent closer to whisper to her. His breath came in acrid waves.

"They say my seventh great-grandfather was one of the dark gods. He built this place as his sanctuary and to last. Even with water on three sides, in all these centuries, the land has never eroded an inch. Know why? He had the mortar mixed with dragon's blood and a prince of Gwynedd buried at each corner. Their ghosts are doomed to guard it for eternity. Only those the lord permits may enter by land and the only way across the water is by bridges over and under. No man has yet trod upon them and lived."

His breath was making Guinevere queasy. Under the pretext of gathering up the stone pieces the servant had replaced, she ducked for a gasp of fresh air. She hurriedly set up the game. Claudas slumped back into his chair. She smiled at him.

"Shall we begin the game, sir?" she asked demurely.

Gareth and Lancelot were camped for the night by a swift, cold mountain stream. Neither one of them had the slightest idea of where they were. They had traveled north and west as far as the road allowed, passed through some small villages and a few farmholds. But no one knew where Meleagant lived. Gareth tried to appear unconcerned as he prepared their evening meal, but he wondered what, if anything,

Lancelot would do next. In the few days they had been together, Gareth had come to almost worship the knight of the Lake as his image of the perfect man. This was what the traveling storytellers meant when they spoke of the ideal that Arthur sought. Already Gareth feared the possible defeat of the man beside him as one dreads a flood or plague or some other such disaster beyond the control of man. It could happen, but it was unthinkable.

Lancelot abruptly got up and walked into the woods. Gareth relaxed. Certainly he had gone to be alone and pray for divine guidance. Gareth had no doubt that the information would be given.

In a few moments Lancelot returned and silently took the offered plate. Gareth respected this. One could not commune with God and immediately chat with mere mortals. Lancelot paid him no attention. He was wrestling with himself again. His devotions had not helped him tonight. He had mouthed the words, but his mind had not been on them. What filled his thoughts were terrible visions of Guinevere being pawed and tortured by some faceless monster. He was not at all aware of what he was eating and had almost finished before he remembered that he had not prepared the food himself. He looked up. There was that stableboy sitting motionless across from him. Lancelot regarded him curiously.

"Did you tell me your name?" he asked.

"Gareth."

"Have you eaten?"

"While you were in the woods."

Lancelot put the plate down. "Why did you come with me?"

Gareth blushed. "I want to help you. No, I mean I want you to teach me to be like you. I want to be a knight, like you."

"Me?" Lancelot felt uneasy. "I cannot teach you anything. Only Arthur creates knights. Cei is the man you should ask about it, or Gawain. They have been his friends for many years and know what is expected."

Gareth shook his head. "No, you are the one I want to be like. They may know what is wanted, but you *are* that. I want to be what you are, strong and brave and sure of yourself! Like a hero from the old stories!"

Despite himself, Lancelot gave a little smile of pleasure. "Beware of pride!" his conscience warned him.

"Well," he conceded, "if you prefer to assist me, I will do what I can for you. But you must understand, I do not live as the others do, although I do not fault them. I believe that, to be what King Arthur dreams, we must be pure and chaste of body and spirit. That is the most I would ask of another. I have other duties laid on me, but that is my affair and a matter in which I answer only to God."

His voice failed. How much he had to answer for! Gareth assumed he was overcome by the awesomeness of his proximity to Heaven. He felt unworthy to eat even the crusts left by such a man.

Lancelot wafted back into his inner debate, forgetting again that Gareth was there. Gareth tiptoed about the campsite, afraid of disturbing him. When it appeared that Lancelot was fixed upon his log for the night, Gareth reluctantly rolled up in his cloak and blanket and fell asleep.

The next day was much as the last had been: riding up and down narrow mountain paths, always trying to stay pointed somewhat toward the northwest. Deep into country that the Roman forces had never penetrated, they discovered that the few people they met spoke a dialect of Brythonic which was hard for even Gareth to understand. The farmers and shepherds they met had been too long isolated to give them any help. Lancelot was getting desperate.

Late in the afternoon the road widened a bit. It seemed to be turning downward again when they overtook the cart.

It was a simple, rough, mule-drawn cart, with two crude wheels and three sides and an open back. It was empty. Lancelot wondered why it was there at all. Most of the local goods were transported by pack animals. Although they carried less, they were far safer in these mountains than a clumsy cart that could fall apart before a few rocks in the road. He wondered at its being there as he waited for the trail to widen enough for them to pass. His shouts to the driver were ignored.

"Do you think there is a driver?" he asked Gareth.

"There's nothing on the seat but a bundle of rags."

"I think, sir, that is the driver," Gareth answered. "I think we should get away from him as quickly as we can."

Lancelot did not answer. The path had broadened enough for him to come abreast of the cart. He saw at once that Gareth was right. Out of the front of the bundle, two strong hands emerged, holding the reins. They seemed far too large and powerful to belong to the body beneath all the wrapping. To Lancelot's eyes the body seemed to have no shape at all. He shouted again.

"Driver! Sir! Can you help us? We have been traveling several days and are lost. We urgently need directions to the castle of King Meleagant."

The mule walked on until they rounded a bend where they were sheltered from the wind. Then the hands pulled the cart to a halt and one of them unwound the cloth at the top part of the rags. A pair of bright eyes appeared and then a nose and mouth. Lancelot stifled a gasp. The man had a head and hands but hardly any body, just a twisted shape. How could this be? Gareth reined in beside him.

"He's a dwarf, Sir Lancelot. Haven't you ever seen one?"

Lancelot shook his head. This seemed to amuse the man.

"I'm a rare creature," he wailed in glee. "One of a kind, I am. Right? Where does your fancy-dressed friend come from, boy, that he's never seen anyone like me? No matter. He can stop staring now."

The cloth was again drawn over the face.

"Wait!" Lancelot stopped him. "I beg your pardon for staring. But can you help us? Meleagant—do you know how we can find him?"

The eyes reappeared. "Yes, I do."

"And how are we to get there? We are in a great hurry."

"Oh, are you? Invited you to supper, has he?"

Gareth intervened. "He has kidnapped the wife of our King. We must rescue her immediately. We have no time to spare."

The man uncovered his mouth again. He considered Lancelot, poised straight and tall upon Clades, plumes waving in the breeze. Quite a noble picture.

"I suppose this woman is beautiful."

Lancelot's eyes misted. "You have never seen anything to match her."

"No doubt. I haven't been to court lately." The dwarf spat into the dirt. "What makes you think you can get her out of the fortress? I've heard the front gate is guarded by ghosts. Do you believe that sword of yours will frighten them?"

"One of the farmers we met told us that there were bridges leading to the rear entrance," Lancelot told him. "Do you know about those?"

The dwarf laughed. "Bridges? If that's what they are, then no man has ever crossed them. One is a bridge of planks held by ropes tied to the shore."

"That doesn't sound difficult," Lancelot commented.

"Oh? The bridge itself lies five feet under the water, which rushes so viciously that no one has ever been able to swim across it. All who have tried have been drowned and washed out to sea. Could you keep your footing on such a path, with your sword and lance and shield?"

Gareth thought Lancelot could do anything. Lancelot was not so sure.

"And the other bridge?"

"That one is even better. There are two oak trees, one on either side of the river. Embedded in them and reaching across is a giant sword. It is barely a finger's breadth wide and as sharp as the day it was forged. It's been there as long as the bards can remember and there's not a trace of rust upon it. No man has ever attempted to cross it."

"Why is it there, then?"

"Who knows? Some joke of the gods, perhaps, like me. What difference does it make?"

Lancelot's jaw tightened. "I must enter that fortress. If there is no other way, I will cross on the sword. Will you tell me how to get there?"

The dwarf shifted in his seat and then grimaced, as if in pain. He looked again at Lancelot, perfect, arrogant. Then he announced, "It's not often that I have company worth talking to in my rounds. You get in the cart and ride with me, and I will show you the way."

Gareth grabbed Lancelot's arm. "Sir! You can't! He wants to disgrace you!"

"What? How?"

"The cart! Don't you know what it is for? No man would ride in a cart, not if he were dying! It is used only to convey criminals to be executed or branded. Only murderers, cattle thieves, and adulterers are put in carts."

Lancelot hesitated. "Do you know how to find Meleagant?"

Gareth shook his head.

"Then either I ride with him or we continue wandering lost in these mountains.

"Besides," he added, "there is no one around to see. Will you lead Clades for me?"

Lancelot dismounted and leaped into the cart. There was no room next to the dwarf, so he was forced to stand in the rear.

"That's right." The dwarf nodded fiercely. "Can't be too proud when we want something, can we? This wife of your king, what is she to you?"

Lancelot glared his reply, but the man was satisfied. "I thought so. No one tries something like the sword bridge for the sake of another man's property. I never did meet a man whose soul was as straight as his legs."

He settled back into a contented silence. Gareth followed behind them, his heart bleeding for the shame he presumed Lancelot was feeling. Then he saw where the dwarf was taking them.

"Sir Lancelot, quickly, get out! There's a town ahead of us. He's going to drive you right through it!"

"Stay where you are," the dwarf commanded. "If you want to reach your dear lady before Meleagant woos her away from you."

Lancelot did not move. He called back to Gareth, "Stay there! No one need know you are with us."

"No, I can't leave you! There must be someone else who can show us the way. Please, get out before someone sees you!"

It was already too late. A man working in a field had spotted them and given the cry. The whole population of the town was running from all quarters to get a sight of the criminal.

"My, he's a pretty one," one woman simpered. "What do you think *he* might of done?"

"Don't know, dear, but I wouldn't mind if he did a bit to me before he goes," another leered.

"Look at them clothes! Pearls and rubies, oh my!"

"What'er them things on the top of him? Bet I can knock one off!"

One of the boys took aim at the ostrich plumes with a divot. He missed, but the next boy was luckier. The feathers waved and broke, one falling across Lancelot's face. He remained immovable. Gareth, watching, wanted to gallop in and flatten all of the taunting crowd, but dared not say or do anything. They continued to mock Lancelot and threw things at him all the way through the town. Some people even followed behind them for a mile or so, shouting curses and jeers. Lancelot never seemed to notice them. Gareth was in tears. What if someone from Arthur's court should hear of this? The torment continued as they passed farms and groups of traders. Soon Arthur's name was heard. Gareth's worst fear was coming true.

"Must be one of Arthur's new knights," a man laughed. "Who else would dress like that? He doesn't look like much to me, though, underneath that fine cloak. And if old Pumpilio has him, he can't be any better than that last bunch we had ruling us, and not as smart. They never got caught."

Another trader agreed. "I been saying that all along. What do we know of Arthur except they say he drove the Saxons back? He's just a warrior fancied up, like this one. What did any of them ever do but burn the fields, steal the pigs, and carry off our daughters?"

More comments like these pursued Lancelot and accompanied the clods and rotten fruit thrown at him. Without realizing it, Gareth allowed himself to fall back several horse lengths behind the cart. He could not bear it. Lancelot never moved or answered the catcalls and sneers. He had not lifted a finger even to wipe the slime of rotten carrot greens off his face. Gareth choked back tears of fury and shame. What must Lancelot feel?

After the first shouts, Lancelot heard and felt almost nothing. His mental wrangling absorbed him immediately. When he realized what was happening, the Christian analogy occurred to him almost at once, and he basked in the sacrifice of it until his conscience began jabbing at him again, far more painfully than the blows of the divots.

"Suffering again? Bearing it all without a murmur. How grand of you! To which of your sinful friends can you dedicate this abuse? Whose soul is most in danger now? Why are you doing this, Lancelot? I know, if you don't. It's nothing more than vanity turned inside out. How glorious we are in our abjectness. How near divine!"

Thus battered by his own doubts, Lancelot had no interest in the actions of the crowd. The voice within hammered at him until he was forced to admit to his motives.

"It is for myself that I must suffer now! That's what she has done to me. I can no longer reach outside myself to others. No! No! You are right. She has done nothing. It is all my own folly. I am to blame. But I cannot stop now. If I rescue her and then depart, go back to the Lady and never return, will you leave me in peace then?"

"I will never leave you," the voice within him mocked.

With a sharp cry, Lancelot threw his hands over his face.

The dwarf turned around. "I wondered when you would finally break," he stated. "But it doesn't matter now. We haven't passed anyone for a mile or so. You may as well get down."

Gareth had caught up with them. He was ashamed that he had not had the strength to stay closer. He covered his guilt with admiration.

"Sir Lancelot! Let me help you down. You were wonderful! You never once lowered yourself by answering those filthy scum! I . . . I couldn't have done it. Now, please, let's get our directions and go!"

Lancelot shook himself, trying to bring things into focus. He saw Gareth—what was his name?—yes, Gareth, standing before him, his face twisted in emotion. Lancelot rubbed his eyes and removed some of the slime.

"What was that? Thank you. I'm fine," he mumbled. He faced Pumpilio. "Now, I demand that you fulfill your side of the bargain," he insisted, his voice gaining strength. "Tell us at once the way to the fortress of Meleagant."

Pumpilio raised his head and tried to straighten his back. He flinched at the pain, but he spoke bravely.

"The sun is almost down. In the morning I can show you the way. You can be there by mid-afternoon. Now, help me down."

Gareth exploded. "I'll twist your body even more, old man. You can't treat Sir Lancelot in this way and survive!"

Lancelot held Gareth back. "No, do not touch him. It would be wicked to force him to speak. Anyway, I am very tired. We would have to start in the morning in any case." He helped the man down.

Pumpilio looked at Lancelot's face for the first time. He studied it, pursing his lips. "I may have been mistaken. Perhaps you do notice the feelings of those around you a bit." He shook his finger at Gareth. "But don't *you* ever forget, young man, what he endured today is no more than what I have lived with all my life and for even less reason."

They camped not far from the road, but no one bothered them that night.

Guinevere was discussing fashion with Gilli in her room when Meleagant entered, looking pleased. Gilli had learned to detest that expression, but hoped that this time it meant that someone had already been caught trying to rescue Guinevere. It was not often that they had any civilized company and Gilli had no interest in letting Guinevere go before Easter, either.

"Your husband has some strange servants," he smirked. "One of my men just arrived saying that only today some fool with white feathers in his helmet was conveyed in a cart through the village and farmlands nearby, like a common thief. The rumor is that he has come here from Caerleon. Maybe to rescue you from my clutches, Lady Queen? If this is the best Arthur can pick, a fool or a brigand, I wonder whom he expects to employ to arbitrate among the clans? This is one wager it will be easy to win. I hope your warm clothes arrive soon, my dear. This will be a cold winter, they say."

He had no intention of letting her stay long enough to need more clothes. One look at them and Gilli would be nagging for some like them. But this cart episode was just what he needed to get out of the thing gracefully. He could give the Queen back and still refuse to join Arthur.

He went out again, laughing. Guinevere felt sick. Lancelot. Why had Arthur sent him, of all people? And why, how could he do such a shameful thing? She reddened thinking about it. Gilli patted her arm, misunderstanding.

"Guinevere, please, don't pay any attention to him. I can lend you some clothes if you tell the seamstress how to alter them to the latest styles. I'd like you to stay the winter as a guest. I'm sure that Meleagant won't hurt the man Arthur sent. Do you know who he is?"

Guinevere nodded. "Sir Lancelot of the Lake. Silly name, isn't it?"

Gilli glanced at her sharply. The mysterious Lancelot! That was exciting. And Guinevere was sitting next to her, blushing. He was said to be very handsome. Gilli gave a wistful sigh. It didn't seem fair that some women should have so much and she should have nothing but Meleagant and a haunted castle.

Pumpilio kept his word and at dawn showed Lancelot and Gareth the way to the fortress. Lancelot thanked him gravely and gave him a jeweled pin from his cloak.

"What is this for?" the man asked angrily.

"For your trouble," Lancelot answered.

Pumpilio threw the jewel on the ground. "For your pity, you mean. I want none of it. If you really intend to cross the knife bridge, you will be dead by sunset. In that case, all I ask of you is to search the next world for the god responsible for my creation and give him my curse."

He gave the reins a pull and the mule started off. Lancelot never saw him again.

They reached the fortress late in the afternoon, just as the dwarf had directed. Long before they saw it, they could hear the river roaring around the walls. The sword bridge was just as they had been told: a great, narrow, shining span stretching high above the water, each end of it embedded in the trunk of a mighty tree. The fortress wall beyond it was thick, bare stone, with the exception of one small window near the end of the sword.

Gareth broke the silence. "Somehow, I didn't think it would be so narrow. They were right, no one could cross this. There is a wind along there, too. See how the leaves are blown skittering over the river. Why don't we look for the water bridge?"

Lancelot did not answer at first. He stared in fascination at the length of steel. It had been there all those centuries and it was still gleaming and sharp, pure and clean and smooth. Without taking his eyes from it, he leaned over and began to remove his boots.

"Didn't you hear me?" Gareth shouted. "No one can do it, not even you. You'll kill yourself!"

"I can do it," Lancelot said calmly. "If Guinevere is in there, I can cross on a strand of silk. Hold these for me."

"I won't let you. You are sure to die!"

Lancelot smiled. "You won't let me? What does it matter to you? You are just a stableboy. It is of no concern to you."

"I never told you I was a stableboy and, even if I were, it would be my concern. What am I to tell Arthur?"

"Tell him I was not afraid of the cutting edge. If I do not return, Clades is yours. Good-bye, Gareth!"

He cast his armor on the ground, slung his belt and scabbard about his neck, and placed his foot upon the sword.

Chapter Twelve

Guinevere was enduring another game of chess and rambling reminiscence with Claudas when the commotion broke out. People hurried from all corners of the hall, pushing and pulling at each other for a turn to look out the small window in the far wall. At first she ignored them with well-bred disdain, but then she remembered that the only reason the window was there was to see the sword bridge. Her heart froze. She dropped her queen with a thump on the board, leaving it open to capture by both a rook and a knight. Claudas pounced upon the piece before she had a chance to finish the move.

"I've got you now!" he chortled. "Can't let your mind wander when you play with me!'

He drooled as he spoke and wiped the moisture off on his sleeve, already stained by the dregs of his last three meals. Guinevere winced. She had to get away and find out what was happening. She picked up a pawn and rolled it across the room. The voices from the window were increasing in excitement.

"Look at him! He's walking on the sword like a *funambulus*," the priest shouted, proud that he knew the correct word. "He doesn't even have his boots on!"

"I'll lay you odds, five to one, he doesn't make it," a guard declared.

"You're on!" another answered.

"I'll make that ten to one," the guard added. "Look, he's cut himself!"

Lancelot was not aware of the people at the window. He barely felt the lacerations in his feet as he slid along the blade. His chief problem was the fierce wind. It wasn't steady enough to brace against, but came in gusts, now from one side, now another. If it continued this way, he knew he could not keep his feet for long. The belt and scabbard around his neck swung wide, helping to throw him off balance.

"He's down!" someone cried.

Guinevere stooped to pick up the pawn and found she could not make her fingers grasp it.

"No," another voice announced. "He's caught himself; he's on his hands and knees now. God! Look at all the blood!"

Guinevere's stomach seemed to fall and lurch upward again. She swayed and would have fallen if Gilli had not suddenly appeared and wrapped an arm about her.

"Meleagant has commanded that, if he manages to cross alive, no one from here is to attack him. He'll be all right, Guinevere," she whispered. "Do you think he's the one from the cart, that Lancelot?"

Guinevere did not answer. Meleagant had arrived and was tossing the spectators aside as he made for the window.

Lancelot was vaguely aware of the commotion. Part of his mind tried to prepare for battle. He unhooked the scabbard from the belt and held it in two hands to steady himself. When he touched the opposite bank, his sword could be drawn in an instant. As he drew closer, he saw the man awaiting him at the window. Meleagant! It had to be. This was the man who had stolen his Guinevere; the son of the man who had killed his father! He faltered no more.

Inside, Claudas was yelling for one of his grandsons to help him to the window. "No one ever tells me what is happening!" he shrieked. "Do y' all think m' brains fell out along with m' teeth?"

As he shambled forward, Meleagant stood aside. "There, old goat." He pointed. "The impassable bridge is being crossed. I have sworn that if he makes it, I will give my allegiance to Arthur. And I intend to do it. What do you think of that?"

"What's that? What are you saying, boy?" Claudas stormed. "Get an archer, lock the girl up, do something! You could knock him off now with one arrow. A child could do it. *I* could do it! Give me a bow!"

Meleagant laid a firm hand on his father's shoulder. "No, your day is past. I am tired of spending all my energy trying to hold on to the worthless land you conquered. I have my own plans. It may not be such a bad thing to be on the side of such a powerful ruler—for a while, at least."

He looked out the window. "By Lugh's thunder! The man has made it across!"

Claudas tried to focus on the man approaching the window. They were almost face to face when the old man's eyes opened wide. He screamed in stark terror and fell back, tripping on his robes.

"Get away from me! Don't come any nearer!" he babbled as Lancelot began to climb through the window. "I killed you. I know I did. I ran you through on your own hearthstone twenty-five years ago and more! You can't come in here! You're dead!"

He climbed to his feet and tried to take a sword from the belt of the man nearest him. The soldier shrank back in disgust.

"The old dotard is mad!" Meleagant sneered. "Someone take him away and put him to bed."

Quickly Claudas was removed, still whining for someone to put that Ban of Benoit back in his grave.

Once he was gone, silence gripped the room. Meleagant stepped back as Lancelot entered the hall. He was bareheaded, clad only in his tunic. Blood was running down his shins and dripping from his hands. His face was dead pale and his eyes burned like those of a man staring at Hell. More than Claudas wondered if he were not a wraith.

Lancelot looked about him in confusion. Why did no one challenge him? Where was Meleagant? How could he find Guinevere in all these people? He was growing dizzy from loss of blood. No one moved. Why were they all staring at him? What was the matter with them? He stumbled forward as in a nightmare and then he saw her.

The others had moved away from her, some in fear, some out of pity. To Lancelot it was as if a shadow lay upon everything but her as he dragged himself toward her. Mesmerized by the sight of her, he had forgotten even why he had come there. With a broken cry, he dropped to his knees at her feet, catching at her skirts to support himself.

Guinevere could not move. She thought she had conquered the feeling that invaded her when she was caught in his sight, but she was held now, worse than ever. As he clutched her, his face showed such naked, wild passion that she was terrified.

"I can't live with this!" she sobbed to herself. "I won't! He mustn't do this to me. I won't let him! No!"

She panicked. She ripped his hands from her skirts, flinging him back onto his heels.

"Get away!" she screamed hysterically. "Look at you! What have you done? Blood all over me!" She brushed at it jerkily. "It will never come out. Why are you here? Arthur didn't send you, did he? I know he didn't. Your damned pride! You've made a fool of yourself. Whose sins did you dedicate this to? Mine? Arthur's? You know so much more about that than the rest of us, don't you? Everyone is laughing at the brave knight of Arthur's who was driven through the country in a cart, like a common thief. What was the purpose in that? To save me? Save me from what? If you had bothered to ask, you might have been told that I was in no danger. But the gallant Sir Lancelot listens to no one. You've embarrassed us all and half killed yourself for a game! A stupid wager! That's all it was. Now what do you think of yourself?"

She was raging, unable to stop, frightened by the violence of her reaction. Lancelot stared at her in horror. A fool? Only a game? Hide-and-find, like they played under the Lake? His eyes flickered around the room. Dozens of people were watching him. Their faces seemed to shift and grow, coming closer to him, ready to mock him and laugh. It was all a joke and he had made himself the butt of it. Arrogance and pride. They lurked in him like ravenous monsters. He could hear their roaring in his ears.

Someone started toward him, to hold him up, but Lancelot

did not understand. He backed away, dropping his sword with a clatter. He thrust his hands, palms out, before him. Blood ran down his wrists. Then, so quickly that no one realized what he intended, he leaped back through the window and dived into the water, giving a cry like that of a wild animal as the hunter's arrow sinks into its heart.

A woman screamed and everyone tried to rush to the tiny window. Meleagant swept them back with a command and in an instant had the view all to himself.

"My God!" he called to the anxious room. "He's actually swimming the river. He's across now, on the bank. What is he doing? He must be . . . he's gone insane! He's stripped off his tunic and is making for the woods. Naked as a baby, he is. Kinel! Daibidh! Follow him and bring him back here! Hurry! He won't survive on his own."

Guinevere was standing in the center of the room, still brushing at the stains upon her skirts. Gilli shook her roughly.

"Guinevere! What have you done? That poor man has gone mad because of you! How could you say such things to him? Good Lord, if any man in the world had ever looked that way at me, I would have gone to Egypt and back slung across his saddle. Guinevere! Listen!"

But Guinevere continued rubbing at the blood. "Blood always," she keened. "There was blood the other time, too. Flora held the knife to my heart as he did, but then my own love saved me. There was blood, but I felt no pain. Blood hot on the cold stone. Mother washed it off and they told me it was but a dream. Lancelot! Don't make me look! Mother! I want my mother!"

Gilli was frightened. She had dealt thousands of times with ranting drunks and senile bletherers, but she didn't understand what was happening before her. All she could think of was to try to get Guinevere to bed and hope she would come to her senses by the morning. They would take her to Arthur if they had to. She couldn't stand any more of this.

But the day was not quite over yet. As Guinevere was being led away, a hollow pounding was heard at the front gate.

"By the blood of Epona's mare!" Meleagant cried. "Now

what? Have the ghosts at the gate gone mad, too?"

The huge wooden doors were quickly opened and there on the doorstep stood Gawain.

"I come in the name of Arthur the King!" he bellowed. "To fight any man here in fair combat for the release of the Queen!"

But his challenge was met by silence.

Chapter Thirteen

Arthur was furious. What the hell had been happening? From the beginning, it had seemed simple. Gawain had been chosen to rescue Guinevere and he had been delighted. This was his opportunity to prove his worth. The water bridge had posed no problem to his strength. The current could not topple him; the ghosts merely bewildered him, as he had never felt the terrors of the night. Their gibbering and howling roused his pity. He was feeling smug as he banged upon Meleagant's gate. But instead of a gentlemanly duel and a polite surrender, he found the place in turmoil. When Arthur entered soon after, he was greeted by a mass of hysterical people, a blood-spattered floor, and the news that his finest knight had gone mad and vanished and that his wife had collapsed and been led away, crying for her mother.

It was not the first time Arthur had reflected that there must be someone else who would like to be King. As he started toward Meleagant, Gilli intercepted him.

"Come over here, please. My husband will only roar and argue. I was near her. I can tell you what happened, though I don't understand it."

She led him through the chaos to an alcove, dark and sooty, but private. Gilli draped her cape across the filthy bench before motioning him to sit. She wrung her hands nervously. Arthur must hear the story from her first, before gossip made it something worse. She told him what happened as if giving a field report—clearly, but without detail.

"It was the blood that seemed to upset Guinevere most. I don't think she realized what she was saying to Lancelot. Has she always had this fear? Lord knows, we've all seen more than enough blood in our lives."

She closed her eyes a moment and Arthur noticed the deep lines the years of harsh weariness had cut upon her face. He put his mind to the question.

"I'm trying to remember," he said slowly. "Geraldus told me a story once, something that happened years ago. They had a servant—a nurse, I think—who went insane and tried to sacrifice Guinevere to her goddess. The story was never clear, but it seems the woman killed herself instead. Geraldus said Guinevere was soaked in the woman's blood, but that she had been drugged and never realized what had happened."

"If she did remember, that would certainly explain her behavior."

"Perhaps." Arthur clenched his jaw. "But it is not enough to excuse what she has done to Lancelot."

He stood abruptly, knocking soot off the wall. Gilli vainly tried to brush it off him.

"Guinevere must be ready to leave within the hour," Arthur announced. "I am taking her home with me tonight."

"But it is almost sundown. We would be happy to lodge all of you here. My husband is embarrassed and ashamed of his part in this. He would be honored if you would forgive him and stay, your . . . sir. . . . I'm sorry. I don't know how to address you."

"Arthur is my name," he said tiredly. "You have the right to use it. You are a queen."

She swept her hand across her hair. On her wedding day they had placed a crown upon her.

"How odd," she said. "So I am. In this place I had almost forgotten."

When Gilli entered, Guinevere was sitting up. She seemed calmer, her hands folded tightly in her lap.

"Has Arthur come for me?" she whispered.

Gilli nodded. "He wants you to dress for travel and come with him at once."

Guinevere smiled. "Of course. Arthur will take care of me. Does he know what Lancelot did to me? He must realize now how unsuited the man was to be a knight."

Gilli said nothing more, but her face was worried as she helped Guinevere change her robe and pack her belongings to take home.

Guinevere ran down the steps and straight to Arthur. She flung her arms about him.

"Oh, my dear! I'm so glad you've come for me. I knew you would. Oh, Arthur. It was so awful!"

She stopped. Arthur had not moved to embrace her. His face was turned away.

"Arthur," she quavered. "Arthur? Is something wrong?"

She turned one by one to the others watching. "Gawain? Agravaine? Bedevere? Cei? . . . Merlin?"

No one would answer her. Their expressions ranged from pity to disgust. A chill alit upon her heart. "Arthur, you aren't . . . angry with me, are you?"

His lips were stiff. "This is not the place for a discussion, Guinevere. We will talk about the matter when we reach Caerleon. Now, come at once. We have been inconvenienced enough because of you."

Merlin gave a grim smile of appreciation. That was better. He had not needed to interfere. Arthur was beginning to see through her. Soon he would be free from her spell completely. Then the last danger Merlin feared would be gone and he could leave with a clear conscience.

Guinevere gave Arthur a numb stare that wrung his heart. But he could not relent before everyone, so he turned on his heel and marched out, trusting that she was well-bred enough to follow without making a scene. He gave Meleagant no farewell.

They were mounting their horses when someone shouted, "Isn't that Lancelot's horse? Where did he come from and who is that with him?"

Clades was being led to them by a scruffy young man. His clothes were torn and greasy, his face streaked with dirt and tears.

Agravaine gaped at him and then moaned. "Oh, God, not Gareth. What in hell are you doing here, boy?"

Gareth stopped, still holding the reins. They all stared at him. Gawain tried to clear away his tiredness enough to focus. Gareth. Why not? During this day he had kept his feet against a malevolent river, walked through ghosts and been left looking like a fool in front of a roomful of strangers. Why shouldn't his brother pop up out of nowhere, dressed like a kitchen drudge and leading a horse? It rounded out the whole experience nicely. He let his head fall against his horse's neck and closed his eyes.

Agravaine dismounted and stomped over to his brother. "Why aren't you at Tintagel? Where did you get that horse and why are you wearing those disgusting clothes?"

"Agravaine!" Gareth pleaded, looking at Arthur.

"What is it? Oh, yes. Sorry, Uncle. I didn't mean to overstep myself. I just always . . . I mean, well . . . this is my brother, Gareth."

"I gathered that." Arthur was relieved for any diversion from attention to Guinevere. "You are doing fine. Now let him answer your questions."

Gareth wiped his nose with the back of his hand. "I was waiting for you to come back to Caerleon. Lancelot said I could come with him to rescue the Queen. I want to be a knight, too! But I did everything wrong. I was no help to him at all. And now he's gone away. He left me his horse, but I don't want it! I want him to come back! This isn't what I thought it would be like. Agravaine, I think I'd rather go back home to Mother."

Arthur sighed. Was he the only one here who could not

run home? He almost felt like laughing at himself and at Agravaine, so clearly torn between wanting to cuff his brother to make him shape up and keeping his own dignity before his peers.

"You needn't take him back now, Agravaine. I imagine that this brother will end up staying with us, too. Find out tomorrow if he has any other clothes. For now, put him up behind Gawain. Can we expect any more of my nephews to appear soon?"

Gareth rubbed his eyes and shook his head. "No, sir," he sniffed. "There's only Modred left and he wants to stay with Mother."

"Then I trust we can go? Gawain, Gawain! Your brother will be responsible for seeing that you arrive safely tonight at our camp. We will rest on Lord Craddoc's land tonight and set out again at dawn. Guinevere? Are you ready?"

She was standing next to his horse, shivering in her woolens and furs. Her face was bleached by the twilight. Arthur steeled himself against his love for her as he lifted her up behind him. Her arms crept timidly about him, but she did not speak. She held her body away from his back, fearing rejection. When she had settled herself, he made a curt gesture to the rest of the party and they started off.

The group plodded along the narrow pathways. There was no conversation, no song. The growing darkness served to complement their depression. Guinevere felt the animosity surging about her and cringed further into her hood. She was confused and adrift. What had she done? How could they not realize that what had happened to Lancelot was his own fault? He was an idiot, self-righteous, priggish. . . . She had only told him the truth about himself.

The image came back to her of Lancelot's face as he stared up into hers, of his hands pulling at her, climbing up her skirts, demanding. She closed her eyes. She had almost carried the scene further, finished it in another way. What might have happened next if she hadn't found the strength to push him from her? She bowed her head with a soft whimper and brushed against Arthur's shoulder. Her arms tightened about him and she felt him exhale and relax his muscles a fraction. Briefly he let go of the reins to cover her right hand with his. Gratefully she laid her cheek against his back. No, that was one explanation she could never use. It would hurt Arthur. And anyway, there was no danger now. Lancelot was gone, perhaps forever. Even if by some chance he should regain his senses and return, by then she was sure she would have learned to protect herself from the sorcery in his eyes.

The shepherd, Cloten, hurried through the dank wood, anxious to be home. His winter traps had garnered three foxes and a stoat so far, which was not bad. The fifth trap had caught what might have been a rabbit, by the traces left, but the gate had been pried open and the animal removed. Cloten did not like that. It was not the work of a beast. The few people who lived this deep in the mountains respected his territory. That left only thieves and cutthroats. Cloten had no illusions about his ability to deal with them.

He occupied his mind on the way by totting up what he could expect to have by spring to trade at the market in Clynnog. With the pelts and the wool and perhaps a few piglets, he could make a good deal with the metalworker and maybe even have enough left over to bring something frivolous home to Edra. That would delight her. A brooch, perhaps, from Ireland. She would enjoy that; it would make her feel like a grand lady.

With a start, Cloten realized that while he had been daydreaming, someone or something had emerged from the dark woods and was following him on the path. He had only his short knife with him and that had been notched near the tip. He wished that the skins on his back were already traded for a new knife. He could feel whatever it was gaining on him, could hear it panting. There was nothing else for it but to turn and fight. Snatching the knife from his belt, Cloten whirled around to face his pursuer. He froze in amazement, his knife hand still raised to strike.

There on the pathway was what looked to be a man. He had no weapon. His body was covered with cuts and scratches, and his hair and beard were so tangled and matted that only his nose could be seen. Only his nakedness assured Cloten of his humanity.

"What do you want?" Cloten demanded gruffly. "Where did you come from?"

The creature grunted and held out his right hand. In it was a piece of raw meat with rabbit skin still clinging to it. The man quickly switched the meat to the other hand and continued to extend the right.

"What is it? Can't you speak?" Cloten backed away. It occurred to him that this might be a spirit or demon native to the mountains. Everyone had heard stories of the slaves carried far underground to serve the dark gods. Or could this man be one of those slaves, somehow escaped? Either way, it would not be safe to be around him for long. Cloten brandished the knife.

"Get away from me! Back! Back to your hole! I've cold iron here. You cannot touch me."

The man stepped back a pace, his head tilted quizzically. He held out his hand again, palm up.

Cloten was more angry than frightened now. It was getting dark. He was hungry and he wasn't getting any closer to his home. He tried appeasement.

"Look, fellow, tell me what you want or leave. You still won't talk? Good enough, then don't. I'm going on."

Without sheathing his knife, Cloten carefully turned and started on his way again. The hairs on the back of his neck were curling, but he fought the impulse to look back. He reminded himself that the fellow clearly carried nothing to throw at him. If he were inhuman, then he could use his magic any time, whether Cloten ran or not. He continued walking. There was a rush of steps after him and he quickened his pace. The sound continued behind him, but did not catch up. He could bear it no longer. He looked. A few feet away the shaggy man was still trotting along. When he saw Cloten look at him, the untamed growth on his face parted to reveal a hopeful smile.

"For all the world like a stray dog following me home!" the

shepherd thought. He shrugged. Perhaps the poor thing was harmless. He might be nothing more than a madman seeking shelter from the cold. They said it was good luck to have a fool living under one's roof; the gods protected fools. Perhaps he could be trained to carry wood and water and watch the sheep. But what would Edra say?

Edra had been watching for him for the last hour. She worried when he went to the woods alone. She wouldn't have him know it for anything. Alternately she feared that he would be eaten by wolves or seduced by some farm girl sent to gather wood. Both terrors were equal in her mind. When she saw him enter the gate with another figure close behind, she did not know whether to be relieved or angry. Where had he been—to meet someone else? Had he gone into a village on his way home to drink and whore? He had never done so, but who knew what a man might suddenly decide upon? Once out of your sight, you could never be sure.

"Edra!" She pretended to be busy mending. He called again and she came to the door.

"You must have gone far," she began as she lifted the bar to let him in. "And you have brought a guest?"

Her mouth dropped open. "Cloten!" she screamed. "What is it?"

"Hush, dear one." He guided her back into the house. "I found him in the woods. He's cut and starving and stark mad, but not dangerous, I think. I didn't know what else to do with him."

"Cloten!" she whispered fiercely. "He's also stark naked!"

The madman drew closer to the fire and she watched him as he lifted his hands to the warmth. A half-smile passed across her face. She composed herself quickly and returned to her husband.

"Are you suggesting that we keep him?"

"I could teach him to help you, to do the heavy work. The birthing woman said you worked too hard. That was why we lost the baby. With him to help you, next time it would be better."

"Yes," she agreed slowly. "It is hard for me when you are away tending the sheep or at the markets. But I do not know if I would like to be left alone with him."

"I will go nowhere this winter. Let us keep him with us that long. By spring we should know if there is any harm in him."

"Well," she considered, staring at the man, "if it is what you wish, husband, I—oh, no! Cloten! Stop him! Look at what he is doing on my clean floor!"

Cloten darted forward, but could think of no way to effectively stop the course of nature.

"He's not even trained, Cloten. Just a disgusting wild beast! Put him on the animals' side of the house. He can sleep with the pig. She won't mind. Get him there at once and then get a shovel and clean this up!"

She held her nose and retreated to a corner until her orders were carried out. "You'll have more to teach him than how to fill a water bucket!"

The house was a simple stone rectangle divided in half by a partition about four feet high. On one side the people lived; on the other, when the weather was cold or wet, the animals. In the winter this arrangement provided heat and shelter, which was beneficial to all. Cloten pushed the man to the animal side of the gate and shut it firmly behind him.

"You haven't started out well for a guest," he informed the uncomprehending face. "I'll bring you some food in a minute. Don't be eating the grass, now. We need it for the sheep."

Edra was scrubbing the floor with sand and water. Her energy indicated her feelings and Cloten let her work awhile before he sat down at the table.

"He's really no more than an innocent, overgrown babe, you know," he suggested. "Maybe no one ever tried to teach him better."

"You will have to be the one to do it, then. I want no part of him."

But he noticed that she didn't mention sending him away. "You're a kind woman, Edra. The gods won't let us stay childless. Do I smell meat in that pot?"

He handed a bowl of meat and a slab of bread to their guest. The man ate sloppily, but seemed to know that the bread was to wipe the juice from the bowl. Cloten watched him curiously.

"You know, Edra, I don't think he was always like this. He may have had a fever or a fall. Recently, I mean. Some of those cuts are too deep to be from brambles. Perhaps he was a trader set upon by thieves. If we care for him, someday we may be rewarded."

Edra smiled. "You always have such grand dreams, Cloten. I love to listen to them. But, if this poor fool were a rich man, why would he have been traveling alone? No, I will be content if the gods give us our reward. But," she added significantly, "we must give them some help. Are you very tired from your journey today?"

For answer, he grabbed her about the waist and lifted her high as she laughed. Then he banked the fire and washed his feet while she braided her hair. Before he went to join her in bed, he checked on their guest.

Curled warmly between two ewes, Lancelot was sound asleep.

Far away, in the southeastern corner of Britain, Aelle, the Saxon king, was not sleeping well at all. It was not the snoring from the others which kept him awake, although a stranger would have been deafened by it. He was deprived of his rest by news he had gotten that day about Arthur. Aelle had counted on the natural animosity among the British tribes to pull Arthur's conquests apart with no help from the Saxons, but it was not working. Somehow the man was bringing them together. Aelle pounded his sleeping furs in anger and then sneezed at the dust rising from them. There must be a way to stop this so-called King of the Britons before he gathered the strength to attack Saxon land.

Twice before, Arthur had defeated and humiliated Aelle. The first time was at Mons Badon. Then, by all rights, the Saxons should have won easily. Their position was by far the stronger. That was bad enough, but the next time, Arthur had played upon the superstition of the Saxon soldiers and frightened them into giving up that Whynhevere woman they had kidnapped. Then he had married her!

"She would have made a fine hostage, too," he muttered to himself. "Even a useful alliance. Something must be done about this soon."

He ruminated for so long about it that it was deep into the night before he finally rested and far into the day before he awoke. But, even as dawn was blossoming, Aelle's nephew, Cissa, was up and outside.

To those who were native to Britain, it was an old land, familiar and unchanging. But to Cissa, newly arrived from crowded Saxony, it was a raw, unknown, wild expanse, to be tamed or conquered. The forests were rich with game and there were rumors of gold and silver mines in the west. But the Britons had allowed themselves to be sapped and weakened. The slaves here were small and spiritless, fit to be nothing more than chattel. The few free Britons he had met were not much better. They seemed unable to see or use the treasures around them. They had even stopped breeding, it seemed, if the empty farms and towns around were any indication.

"They are nothing. We could wipe out the whole population with one hand," he said aloud.

"Not quite," a voice behind him answered.

Cissa jumped. He had not heard his cousin, Ecgfrith, approach. He did not think much of Aelle's son. Ecgfrith had been part of that night rout when Arthur's men had made a fool of Aelle. No one paid Ecgfrith much attention these days.

He sidled up to Cissa. "I said, 'Not quite the whole population,' but there is a way we could do some serious damage to it. Remember how, back in our first days here, Vortigern called our grandfathers to Britain to fight for him? We gave a dinner then, a council, and invited the lords of Britain to it. Do you know what the last course was?"

"Certainly, a knife in the throat. Over four hundred of them were killed that day. We should have conquered the whole island then."

"Perhaps, but our grandfathers made one mistake. They

thought only in the present. It was the old ones who died. They were the war leaders, it is true, but they left young sons and sister-sons to carry out their revenge. That is why we lost at Mons Badon. Why should we bother with the old men? What good are they without their progeny, what threat? Leave them to wither and destroy their young!"

Cissa moved away in disgust. "You are expecting Saxon warriors to slaughter children? You do not deserve to live in your father's hall."

Ecgfrith swallowed, but let the insult pass. "Not children, but soldiers, being trained now to one day lead the Britons against us. And now is the time to stop them. I know how we can do it."

Cissa turned away. The glory of the morning was spoiled for him. Ecgfrith's plans always had a smear of dishonor about them.

"If you have such grand ideas, cousin, then Aelle is the one you should speak with. He is still our lord."

"You know he will not listen to me!" Ecgfrith snapped. It had been his idea to steal Guinevere, and Aelle did not forgive failure. "But he will pay attention if you and your brothers join with me in proposing a raid. My plan is perfect. We will not only destroy those who would one day raise armies against us, but we will also capture one of their watch stations that keep us from bringing the men and supplies we need from the homeland."

Against his will, Cissa was becoming interested. "You mean Cador, don't you, the place where you were held? They say it is impregnable, all stone and sand with no cover. How would you take it?"

"I know every stone of it. The way I escaped is the way we will enter. It cannot fail. You have heard that only the greatest families send their children there. Our revenge would be greater for the hostage price the women will bring."

That was a thought. Gold was the measure of a man here. And Cissa was intrigued by the few British women he had seen, so small and dark, totally unlike the proud Saxon women who stood of a height with the men and looked them in the eye when they spoke. One always knew what they thought. Perhaps a hostage might be convinced to stay. But Ecgfrith must not be given the satisfaction of knowing that he had finally gotten Cissa's attention.

"I have other things to do today. Talk to my brothers, if you like, and to your father. I will not argue against it if it is mentioned in the moot this winter."

He strolled away, affecting boredom, but Ecgfrith was content. He was caught. The others would be easy. By spring they would do it and at last Ecgfrith would have his revenge.

Chapter Fourteen

Arthur leaned forward in his chair at the council table at Caerleon. He searched the faces before him: Merlin, Cei, Cador, and Cador's son, Constantine. They stared gravely back, waiting for him to begin. He cleared his throat.

"I have called you all here today to get your advice. I've been hearing over and over this winter that Aelle and his family are traveling from one Saxon stronghold to another. They've been seen in almost every one of the villages. There is something going on. Normally they don't set foot out of doors until the end of March. I have a list here of the places they were known to have been. Even Ecgfrith seems to be taking part in this. I thought he was out of favor."

Cador studied the list for a few minutes. It was written on thin, many-times-scraped vellum and at some places the old writing showed through and made it hard to decipher. He squinted at the scratched lines.

"It could be merely an internal problem, some sort of power challenge," he suggested. "Aelle never really regained the strength he had before you tricked him so well six years ago."

Arthur shook his head. "It might be, but I suspect something more. They've been much too docile these past few years. . . . What is all that noise out there!"

In the courtyard outside the King's quarters a wild fistfight had erupted. Two men were floundering in the mud, trying to get a clear shot at each other, while the rest of the knights circled them, shouting encouragement or personal insults. Arthur pulled aside the leather curtain and leaned out the window.

"Gawain!"

Gawain had been leaning against the opposite wall, watching in amusement.

"Yes, Uncle?"

"Stop that fight and bring those men up to me—after they've been washed."

A broad smile filled Gawain's face. "I'd be happy to, sir!"

The winter sun was watery and weak, but it was enough to make Gawain the equal in strength of any ten men at Caerleon. Happily he waded into the melee and bodily lifted the two combatants out. He held them dangling at the ends of his arms as they glared and struggled.

"The King wants to see you, such sterling examples of knighthood that you are," he told them. "But since he wants to recognize who has been disturbing him so, a trip to the baths is first in order. I myself will escort you there and see that you receive full benefit of the water."

As the group laughed and shouted advice to Gawain, he dragged the two discomfitted men to the huge antique baths, where they were helped out of their clothes and into the water by several of their companions.

Arthur watched as they made their way across the yard. What a mess! He wasn't thinking of the mud.

"That's the third fight this week. Can't we find anything else for them to do?"

The four men at the table were silent. Arthur turned back to them. "Well, what is it? You obviously have an opinion. Tell me."

Constantine looked to his father, who cleared his throat. "Master Merlin?" he asked, hoping he would take the initiative.

Merlin seemed to have been paying no attention. He started up as if he had been sleeping. "Eh, what now? Fighting? That's your business, not mine. Solve it yourselves."

Abruptly he got up and left. Arthur sighed.

"He's been like that more and more lately. I can't get out of him what the problem is, only that it has nothing to do with me. But you don't need him to tell me what you think. What is this continual friction among the knights?"

Cador rubbed his fingers in his palms nervously. "Arthur, that is not my business, either. I'm no good off a battlefield. But I have heard things, hints. I could be completely mistaken."

"Constantine, will you tell me what your father is too diplomatic to say?"

Constantine coughed and then swallowed. "You see, sir, as he said, we might be wrong, but the feeling is that some of the men are upset about what happened to Sir Lancelot."

"Of course they are! Don't you think I am? It's been three months and no one can find a trace of him!"

"I know, but it's more than that. Some of them—not all, of course—seem inclined to blame the Queen. I know that's a lie," he added quickly, "but it has caused bad blood among some. They say that she should have been reprimanded."

"What! Who dares to tell me what I should do with my own wife?"

Cei intervened. Constantine was too young to stay firm in an argument like this.

"No one tells you what to do in private, Arthur, but you have forgotten that this is not a family matter. Lancelot is an officer of Britain. If you had sent him away, no one would have spoken, but Guinevere had no authority, no right, to speak to him in such a way. The younger men, especially, looked up to Lancelot. Some of them are very bitter."

"What do they say?"

"It doesn't matter, Arthur. They are angry and don't truly

mean their words. I suspect that there may be only one or two people who start the others off, who whisper lies until the truth is forgotten. They take advantage of the winter and the men's resentment. I will discover who they are soon. But something must be done now."

"What do you suggest? I can't very well announce to the world that my wife has the power to drive men mad, but she is very sorry and will not let it happen again. Is that what they want? If they suggested that I burn her for a traitor would you agree to that, too? Who is ruler here?"

Cador began rubbing his hands again. "You were planning to move to Camelot at the beginning of April, weren't you?"

"Yes. This summer I will stay in one place. I had planned to send some of the more experienced knights out to deal with the complaints and demands. I thought they might each take one of the new men as a sort of apprentice. It's time we began. What has that to do with Guinevere?"

Cador's fingers were warm with the ferocity of his nervousness. "It might be a good idea, just for the summer, to send Guinevere somewhere else."

Arthur exploded. "What are you saying! The first time I've managed to plan a year with her, you want me to send her away. I thought you were one of those so eager for the two of us to have children. It won't be easy with me at Camelot and her—where?"

Cador shied away from the subject of children. There was no point in it. "She might be seized with a longing to see her parents. She is very attached to them. Hear me out, Arthur! We might mention Lancelot, not that she is to be blamed for what happened, but that she is grieved for your loss of such a friend. She can go on a retreat to pray for his recovery. That would quiet those who slander her and give her defenders something to point to. It might work."

"This is ridiculous!" Arthur muttered.

"Wait, Arthur, let me finish. With her gone, there would be no reason for most of the other women to stay. We need some time for intensive training and discipline. You can see how unruly the men are now. How can a man be at his best when he's got a woman pampering him or after listening all night to a baby screaming? That's what I think. You asked me and there it is."

Arthur had to laugh, even through his anger. Ten years ago, Cador had been his leader, had given all the orders. Now he hesitated to give a simple difference of opinion. Nothing brought home more strongly Arthur's position in Britain.

"And what would *your* wife say to a suggestion like that, Cador?"

Constantine chuckled. "I'm sorry, Father. But I can just hear her, agreeing with you and then ignoring everything you had said. She always has followed her own mind, you know."

Cador smiled sheepishly. "Yes, but Sidra is different. Don't laugh. You know it. She keeps everyone on their toes doing what she wants and they never know how it happened. There isn't a wiser manager in the whole of Britain." He stopped, again aware that he had implied insult to Guinevere.

Arthur ignored it. Guinevere had her own ways of dealing with people. But was Cador's suggestion reasonable? Arthur tried to consider it without counting his own desire to have her stay with him. He dreaded broaching the subject to her, partially because she might not mind being away from him all summer. What would he do if he saw relief on her face when he told her?

"Yes," he said at last. "There may be some sense in what you say. If I can get Merlin to attend to what is happening around him, I will discuss it with him. Then I'll take it up with Guinevere. She must agree also. Now, what are we going to do about Aelle?"

In her rooms, Guinevere was happily sorting some new cloth that had been sent to her by Alswytha and Mark. The tightly woven wool shone with bright and cheerful patterns.

"I don't know where Alswytha finds these colors!" she exclaimed to Risa. "Look at that red! The patterns are a new design, too. How does she manage!"

"They are beautiful," Risa agreed. "Does she have anyone to help with the dyeing and weaving?"

"I don't see how. I can't imagine my brother steaming over a dye pot and the children are still too young. What can we send her in return? They are so contemptuous of most of our possessions."

Risa thought. She hadn't seen them since the day Alswytha and Guinevere's brother had eloped. They had taken little more with them than their clothes and showed no apparent interest in acquiring anything more. They made their own food and shelter.

"Perhaps some wine?" she guessed. "And something for the children—toys or baubles. That could not offend."

"How smart you are, Risa. You know what children like. Find some things for them in town. Here are some silver pieces. Will that be enough?"

Risa looked at the old coins, remnants of the vanished empire.

"The wine merchant will take these. They still use them in Gaul. But the toymaker would rather trade. He would take a chicken or a strip of this cloth for his wife."

Guinevere was losing interest. "Well, I know you can see to it. When you get everything, bring it here and I'll write them a note to go with it."

Risa could tell when she was being dismissed. "Certainly, my Lady." She curtsied and left.

Arthur had not gotten much help when he consulted Merlin. The gist of Merlin's advice was to forget the matter and try to get along without Lancelot. He seemed to think that it was just as well that the man had vanished. After sounding out some of the older knights, including his foster father, Ector, just down from the north, Arthur had climbed the narrow steps to Guinevere's room with sad determination. Everyone had agreed that a summer without her would be less decorative but more productive.

"For everyone but me," he thought ruefully. "I should be like Merlin and announce that I'm resigning. Then let them all do as they like."

But he knew he would never do that—too proud, too stubborn, maybe too stupid. He was left with the task of trying to convince Guinevere to do the one thing he wanted her not to do. Only a fool would want to be a king.

Guinevere was warming her hands over the coals in the brazier when he entered. She greeted him with a wistful smile.

"I'm glad you've come. I was lonely here."

"Were you? I'm sorry." He sat on the mat next to her, leaning against her legs. Automatically, she began to massage his neck.

"You're very tense," she said. "Was it a bad morning? Everyone comes to you with problems. I heard you tell Gawain to break up a fight. He must have enjoyed that. They laugh at him, you know, because of his affliction. It's good for the men to be reminded of how powerful he can be."

"Mmmm . . . that feels good. You always know just where it hurts the most. No, it wasn't worse than any other morning, but I have come especially to talk with you. How would you feel about spending the summer away from Camelot? I know you don't care for the place much. There is a group of women, religious, living near the coast. Would that interest you?"

He had looked away from her as he spoke, afraid of the response, but he was completely dumbfounded by her reaction.

She threw herself on the floor beside him, wrapping her arms about him, her nails cutting into his tunic in her panic.

"No, Arthur, please!" she cried. "Don't put me away. I'm sorry about Lancelot. I'm sorry I haven't given you children. I'll do anything you ask, but don't send me to a place like that! Please, Arthur, forgive me! I didn't mean to destroy your plans. I will say nothing if you take a mistress; I will love her children as your heirs! Only don't, don't send me away!"

"Guinevere! What are you talking about? I've never seen you this way. Who has been frightening you so?" He tried to pry her loose, to smooth her hair and calm her down. She was so terrified that she was gasping, unable to catch her breath.

"I promise you," he insisted. "I will never send you from me. I don't blame you for Lancelot anymore and I don't want a mistress. Good God, woman, don't you know yet what you are to me?"

"Oh, Arthur," she sniffled, which made him laugh through his fears.

"Here," he said, handing her a handkerchief. "Wipe your nose and tell me why you could ever imagine that I would let you go."

She sniffed some more and blew her nose. When she spoke, her voice was still wobbly.

"I hear all the rumors, the troubles you are having. It's my fault, they think. Some of the women say I'm cursed and . . . barren. That I'm not really a woman at all. Meleagant thought I was a witch. No, he didn't say so, but I found out. No one can keep a secret when everyone lives almost in the same room. One of the boys had a wart on his rear and even the scullery maids knew of it and offered cures."

That did make Arthur laugh. Then he gently cupped his hand under her chin and tilted her face up to him. Her eyes shone like emeralds beneath her tears.

"Would it make you so sad to live without me?" He had never dared to ask it before. "Do you love me that much?"

She kissed his palm. "There is no one on earth whom I love more than you. If there is some reason that you want me absent this summer, I will do as you wish. But not to those women, not even for a small number of days. They are too rigid there and grave. On fast days, they not only abstain from meat, but also bread, wine, and cheese. I will not survive on onion tops. And it is very far away. Which one of your advisers wants me to go apart from you to redeem my soul?"

"You are right. There are no secrets." He held her tightly. "But it is more that you might appear to be praying for the recovery of Lancelot's soul. I shouldn't have said that. Do you think anyone can hear us?"

She considered this. "No, I think our room is a good place to talk. We can hear if someone comes up the stairs. The wood creaks no matter how quietly one walks. I can hear voices clearly, though, from outside and the rooms below us. People say many things there, forgetting that I am above them."

"And is that how you found out about this?"

"I wish I had. I would like to be warned before getting news like that. I had heard only rumors. You frightened me terribly, Arthur. If I must go, I would rather go home. If I must do penance, it is a more comfortable place to do it."

"No one said anything about penance, my love. You have nothing to atone for. I've already told you that. However, it might be well for you to still the clucking tongues of Britain. But if I let you go there, would you come back in the fall?"

"Of course! I would run all the way!"

At the end of such a dreary day, Arthur could not believe how happy he felt. It never occurred to him that Guinevere's answer about her love for him had been completely equivocal.

Edra set down her carding comb to stretch her arms. She smiled in contentment at the scene before her. Cloten was busy repairing his traps and the madman sat watching him, his eyes following the deft movements as the shepherd knotted and strung the cords. One of the sheep dogs lay nearby and the stranger would now and then absently scratch its ears. It seemed odd to her now that she could have ever been afraid of him. He was gentle and sad, like a newly weaned puppy. And he had brought the luck that Cloten had foretold. She patted her stomach. The child had quickened last night, she was sure of it. Cloten was so happy and so careful with her. This one, she knew, would live.

The dog's ears pricked up and he ran to the door, growling. Cloten put down his work.

"Who could be out in all this snow?" he wondered. "Anyone with sense is under shelter."

"It may be some traveler who has lost the trail," Edra answered. "But before you unbar the door, ask who it is."

As if in answer a sharp rap hit the wood and echoed through the small house.

"What do you want?" Cloten called over the wind.

"A warm fire and rest, good sir!" a voice answered. "I am a messenger of King Arthur. Let me in, I am near frozen!"

"Open the door," Edra counseled. "We cannot let him

freeze on our doorstep. If he is dangerous, we have you and the dogs to protect us."

Cloten opened the door, letting in the messenger and a blast of icy wind and snow. The shivering man stumbled to the fire as Cloten replaced the bar.

"Thank you, good man, and my thanks also to your wife. I am Sir Bedevere, a knight of King Arthur, on a mission to find another knight of my group, Sir Lancelot. He suffered an . . . accident some months ago and disappeared. We think he may be ill or may have lost his memory and be unable to find his way back to us. I have been hunting him since fall. Will you allow me to break my journey for the night here by your fire? I can pay you in coin."

"My Lord," Cloten spoke shyly, for the man's manner awed him and his language was almost incomprehensible. "I do not understand much of what you are asking. We are poor people and know nothing of kings or coins. But you would honor our house with your presence and we would be pleased to offer you a share of what we have."

"Thank you," Bedevere replied as he shook the snow from his cloak. "Is your weather always like this? It is nearly spring in the valleys."

Edra hastened to help him with his wraps and to fetch a bowl of soup. In the commotion, Lancelot had at first retreated to the sheepfold, but now his shaggy face appeared over the partition. Bedevere, glancing idly about, noticed him with a start.

"By the saints!" he cried. "What is that?"

Cloten was about to answer when Edra spoke up. "Only my brother, sir. Don't be afraid of him. He's quite simple and understands no more than a child, but he would not hurt anyone."

"Oh, your brother. Excuse me. For a moment I thought . . . but that is ludicrous." Bedevere checked himself, hoping he had not offended his hosts. "I have a horse outside. Is there any place I could stable him tonight, away from the wind?"

"Yes, certainly." Cloten bustled into the fold as Lancelot's face disappeared. "Bring him through the gate here and we can put him in with the other animals, if you would not mind."

"Mind? It looks perfect. Warm and dry, very fine. This is much superior to many places we have been forced to lie since I began this quest."

Worn out from his journey, Bedevere ate and slept almost immediately. The storm had abated by morning and he went on his way again with many thanks. When he was safely gone, Cloten turned on Edra.

"What made you say that the madman was your brother? What was wrong with telling him the truth?"

"Didn't you hear him? He was looking for a nobleman, like himself, who was hurt. I was afraid."

"Why? Do you think this is a nobleman? We've spent all winter just getting him to wear a tunic and relieve himself outside."

"That's right. We found him and trained him and he's ours now. But remember how he looked when he first came to us? You said it yourself: like a man who had been in a battle. 'Lancelot,' he said. Lancelot!" she called. There was no answer from the sheepfold. She went to the madman and stared straight into his eyes.

"Is your name Lancelot?" she asked.

He smiled without comprehension and went on playing with the wooden top Cloten had carved for him. Edra was relieved but still uncertain.

"He would know his own name, don't you think?"

"I don't see why he should. Look what else he has forgotten."

"If that Sir Bedevere were a friend of his, they would have known each other."

Edra said no more, but watched her madman more intently after that, looking for some sign of nobility. It was true that he ate more neatly than they, but his other habits! She could not decide.

She was not entirely surprised, though, when spring reached the mountains and Cloten took the stranger with him to the passes with the sheep, that her husband returned alone.

"You mustn't grieve, dearest. He will be all right. I woke up one morning and he had gone, but there was no sign of wild animals or of thieves. He must have simply decided that it was time to go. Perhaps he'll come back."

Edra shook her head. "No, we have been given what we wanted most. It is a healthy child I carry. The gods have sent him on, to bring good fortune to someone else. That is their way. We have been truly honored and we must sacrifice one of the lambs this year in thanks. But I do not think we shall see him again."

Lancelot did not know what compelled him to leave his friends and the warmth of the sheep that morning. Something in the darkness of his mind stirred and ordered him to go and he obeyed. He left his top next to Cloten and set off down the mountain, with nothing but his wool tunic. Sometimes people gave him food and a place to rest and sometimes they set dogs on him, but he paid neither much mind and never stayed anywhere more than a night. He moved eastward, facing the sun each dawn and, in the strength of his madness, traveled far and quickly. He passed within a few miles of Caerleon, but it drew him not at all. At last, one silver evening, he emerged from the forest. A road led across tilled fields and up a hill, where a gleaming white wall surrounded red-roofed buildings. With the wariness of a wild thing, he avoided the road, slipping from one spot of cover to the next, until he came to the stream. There he paused to drink and rest. He lay back against a stone and closed his eyes.

The child's cry of discovery awakened him. He shrank back as the little girl knelt beside him and put her hand on his shoulder.

"Don't be afraid." She patted him reassuringly. "I have called Pincerna. He will get someone to help you to the villa. You must have come a long way."

He relaxed under her gentle voice, but made no response.

"Letitia, dear, I don't think he can talk." Her mother's arm went around her. "Poor man. Someone must have hurt him terribly. Look at the scars on his arms and legs. I don't think he understands us. I wish we could tell him that it will be all right now. Guenlian will not turn him away."

Lancelot was too exhausted to fight the men who took him gently and led him up the hill. He did not know where he was or who had found him, but the next morning he awoke content. The call which had driven him had finally ceased.

Chapter Fifteen

"Lydia?" Sidra asked her daughter softly. "Is anything wrong?"

Lydia was up in the watchtower, staring at the ocean. It was too foggy to see very far. Even if the day had been clear, there was nothing to see but water. Sidra wrapped an arm around her. She tried not to act like a protective mother when she felt the chill through the girl's dress. It wouldn't work, she knew. They loved each other dearly, but not as mother and child. Lydia's devotion rested with her foster mother, across the channel. Sidra knew she would have to learn to accept this as she had counseled other women to.

"Lydia?" she asked again.

Lydia shook herself, awakening from her thoughts. "Mother, you shouldn't be up here; it's freezing!" she scolded. "You must take care of yourself."

"Just what I was going to suggest to you, my dear," Sidra rejoined. "What were you thinking of? You seemed so far away from me."

She hadn't meant it to sound pathetic, but it did. Lydia smiled at her.

"I wasn't very far at all. My thoughts were not following my eyes. I was wondering if Arthur was getting ready to move to Camelot yet.

"You know," she added quickly to forestall the hurt she feared Sidra would feel, "you should come, too, this year. There are hardly any fosterlings left now. This place is more for the soldiers on watch than anything else. And I don't believe that you've been a hundred feet from Cador since I was born."

"That is true," Sidra conceded as they entered the stairway back down to the hall. "There was always so much to be done here. And this is where I belong. I don't think I would make a good guest in another woman's domain. It was a kind thought, my dear, and I know the reason behind it. I wonder if it would have been so dull for you here if your Cei had come for the winter."

"Mother!" Lydia blushed. "I did not say it was dull—"

"But it is," Sidra interrupted dryly.

Lydia ignored this. "It is true that I am very fond of Sir Cei and he seemed to reciprocate my feelings. But he can't leave Arthur whenever he wishes. He has many duties."

"He might let you know that he 'reciprocates your feelings' in a letter, don't you think?" Sidra asked.

Lydia's chin took a stubborn tilt and Sidra feared that she had bungled again.

"He would write, I know, but I'm not sure that he can."

"What?" Sidra tried to check her reaction. "I have too many old-time prejudices," she berated herself. "Why can't I be as unjudgmental about him as I am with the fosterlings? Goodness knows, half of them have never seen soap for washing before they come here, much less a stylus and parchment."

But she thought that Cei could read and write after a fashion. She remembered careful, painfully correct letters on a provisions list he had made for her to fill. The spelling was uncertain and the grammar nonexistent. One could almost smell the dried beads of sweat that had dripped from him as he composed it. She wondered if he had seen the letters sent by Lydia to Guinevere, the easy, flowing classical script, the allusions to the ancient authors. He must have. She felt a rush of pity for him. Better to be virile and illiterate than laughably ill-educated.

They entered the hall. Only a few people were there, although it was mid-afternoon and most fosterlings had completed their duties. Echoes followed their footsteps as they crossed to the fire. One person was next to it, lying on an old couch, languidly munching pickled vegetables.

"I should have known that Geraldus, at least, would know enough to stay inside in this gloomy weather," Lydia laughed.

"You look quite like the old times!" Sidra exclaimed. "I remember my grandmother bewailing the modern generation. She had been invited once to a home where people actually sat on benches to eat. She left at once, insisting that only peasants and slaves had so little concern for the proprieties. She reclined at every meal and never spent less than an hour, even at breakfast. How nice to see someone keeping up the old customs!"

"Only now," Geraldus said, as he swallowed the last turnip, "it's a sign of laziness."

He stretched his arms, but did not rise.

"I must be growing old," he complained. "I find the quiet here very soothing. Even my chorus has been less abrasive since we've been here. But I suppose it's far too peaceful to Lydia, eh?"

"No, not at all," she lied. "But I did promise Guinevere that I would meet her at Camelot this year. Of course, that was before her . . . um. . . ."

"That's all right, child." Geraldus grimaced. "The whole story is gossip all the way to Armorica and my part is usually forgotten. The truth is, Guinevere was thinking of not going to Camelot this summer, so you don't really need to be there at all."

"Oh?" The one syllable covered an octave as she tried not to show her disappointment.

"Don't tease her, Geraldus," Sidra interposed. "Your brother will be there and your father. There is no reason why you couldn't visit them for a time. Say a month? Could you stand that?"

"Oh yes!" Lydia nearly clapped her hands and leaped into the air, but was restrained by her new sense of maturity. "Oh, thank you, Mother. When can we go, Geraldus? It's almost spring, isn't it?"

"There was no rime on my drinking cup this morning," he conceded. "In a few days, when the weather clears, we can start. But we may have to go to Caerleon first. The mud may not be solid enough at Camelot yet."

"I don't care. It doesn't matter. I'll start packing."

She rushed to her room, not to pack but to dance across the floor, imagining all her friends swirling around her—and then only one. And the dancing stopped as she put out her hands to him.

Ecgfrith waited in the cold outside his father's hall. His flaxen hair was dulled gray by the water. He had stood there so long that his braids were sodden and heavy and his leather vest smelled strongly of the animal it came from. He was icy to the marrow, but still he waited, unwilling either to enter or to leave. Finally the door opened and his cousin, Cissa, appeared.

"Well?" Ecgfrith demanded. "What did he say?"

Cissa pulled his cloak more tightly about himself. "Can't we discuss it somewhere dry? What have you been doing out here? You smell like a drowned dog."

"Never mind that. Tell me what happened. Will he do it?" Ecgfrith snapped, but he followed Cissa as he headed for his hut.

"He still wants revenge. You needn't worry about that. He wants to know just how sure you are about the people there: few guards and many hostages. He won't be sympathetic to another disaster."

Ecgfrith winced. "I have it planned exactly. I can get us in behind the guards and take them before they realize we are there. But it must be soon. They're not so watchful this time of year. They think we all hide in burrows until the sun comes out."

"Aelle knows that. He'll let us go and take any man willing to share the risk and the reward. My brothers, Cymen and Wlencing, will come. They are bored with hunting. But Aelle won't do it himself. He said that it would not be a dignified way for a war leader to behave."

"More likely, he thinks he's too old to row and climb rocks. He's right. It's not important, as long as he won't oppose us. He has preferred to forget that I carried out my part in the taking of Guinevere without a flaw. I got that girl to him. It was those devoted idiots of his who panicked and lost her."

The other man shrugged. "I don't care about the past. I will do my part in this and expect an equal share in the ransom. It is time my household expanded and that cannot be done if I have no rewards for those who would serve me."

Ecgfrith did not deign to answer that. He would make sure that no part of the credit for this fell to his ambitious cousin. Aelle was already far too fond of him.

"Then it is settled," he said. "We can leave tomorrow at dawn and be at Cador in a week's time."

"Agreed." Cissa gave his hand to it. "My men and I will be ready."

But he had an uneasy feeling about the whole endeavor. The day before he had seen two crows battling in the air for a piece of bread. In their fury, the crust had fallen, to be caught by a sea gull which had swooped from nowhere to retrieve it. One shouldn't ignore such obvious signs.

The rain and sleet finally abated. At the first sign of clearing, Lydia reminded Geraldus of his promise. He had not forgotten, but he gathered his gear together with great reluctance.

"It may turn rotten again," he warned her. "There have been storms in April before."

"No, Geraldus, it's spring inland," she pleaded. "It will be invigorating."

"Are you sure you don't want to wait for a larger group to

travel with?" he cautioned. "You know what happened the last time I escorted a lady through the forests."

"Oh, Geraldus! No one wants to steal me away. I'm not at all important. We'll be fine. Please! Can't we go soon?"

Every ounce of her body was thrown into her plea. Geraldus gave in and nodded. She immediately leaped upon him, hugging and kissing him, and he tried vainly to calm her down.

"Yes, thank you, that's enough. It's fine, Lydia. You can save all that for Cei. You waste it on an old man like me. Lydia, my dear, you're embarrassing me."

Lydia backed off, still grinning. "I'm sorry. Do you think he'll be glad to see me? I'll go and get ready. Can we leave tomorrow?"

She hurried off without waiting for an answer. Geraldus sank down on the couch, worn out with her enthusiasm. The air seemed darker now that she had left the room, and he felt suddenly lost and sad.

"Tell me," he said to the emptiness. "When *did* I begin to grow old?"

He sensed her nearness before the warm, soft arm crept around his neck. Her breath was also warm as his alto whispered in his ear.

"I do not think you changed, musician. Does the life you have now seem tiresome?

There was a note in her voice he had not heard before. He could not tell if it was hope or fear.

"Of course not!" he answered with false heartiness. "Only a moment of self pity. Humans have them. It's nothing at all. I presume you know that we are going traveling again. Are you all prepared to work on the new piece I set you while we ride? We have too much to do on it to waste time sulking because it's a little dreary and wet out."

There was no answer. Geraldus raised his voice. "I know that all of you are here. Now, either you work or you will never see the baths at Caerleon again."

Another stretch of silence. Then the tenor section began a hesitant tuning and the basses and sopranos discordantly hummed the opening bars of the song.

Geraldus sighed. Twenty years and more he had trained them and they still could sound like this! He wished for the millionth time that he could see them. He was sure some of the voices were different this trip and he hated breaking in new singers. He put his hands over his ears.

"All right! I take it you want to come with me. We start tomorrow as soon as the fog lifts. It will probably be afternoon by then so you may spend the morning finding your notes. There is no excuse for such cacophony!"

His voice was pitched forcefully by then and a servant girl entering the hall jumped and dropped the bowl she carried, thinking he was yelling at her. Geraldus sighed again as he apologized, realizing that the mulled ale in the bowl had been for him. He would never completely be reconciled to the life that fate had given him.

Ecgfrith, Cissa, and their company made camp in the woods along the shore and spent the evening cutting green wood to bend over the stretched, oiled leather each man had brought. They would be crude boats, each large enough for one man only, but they would be enough to carry the men out beyond the rocks, a mile down the shore, and still keep the knives and spears dry. Cissa was impressed with that part of the plan; it was the actual invasion that worried him.

"Tell me again," he ordered Ecgfrith. "Where are the guard towers? How many to a watch? Where will the others be? You make it sound too open. People could be wandering about anywhere. I don't trust it."

Ecgfrith repeated the plan. By now it was a rote lesson for him. Then he explained why he knew it would work.

"I tell you, they are so arrogant that they don't even think of attack. Their only purpose is to watch for our boats and light a signal fire to alert the armies inland. They feel so invulnerable that they let a woman run the entire place."

"Yes, perhaps." Cissa's worry was becoming more mystic and less rational. "You are sure that your men know that we are going for hostages only? I have no wish to be a part of the murder of women and striplings."

Ecgfrith made an effort not to shout. How could his father so favor this indecisive coward?

"It will be simple. We come in under cover of the fog. We wait until they have all gone in to eat. They will all then be in one place. We take care of the guards with little noise. Last, we simply surround them and announce that they will return with us. There will be nothing they can do. They will have no weapons."

Cissa did not answer. It seemed to him that the gods were not in favor of this. The man-price of these hostages would have to be as great as Ecgfrith insisted for this to be worthwhile. He regarded the ocean roaring below. He had not seen it since his arrival in Britain in autumn. He had not remembered the sound of it as so loud, so angry. Were even the beasts of the waters trying to warn him?

"You're sure, darling, that you'll be warm enough?" Sidra asked. "I have a fleece-lined blanket I can give you, too."

"Mother, I will be fine. It's quite warm today and the sun has almost cleared the fog. We'll stop tomorrow night at Guinevere's parents and you know they will see to it that I'm clean and presentable and very healthy before I leave. Please, don't worry."

"Who said I was worried?" Sidra retorted. "I'm only concerned a little."

She was angry with herself. "Too late!" she kept thinking. "I can't make her go through each stage of childhood again, just because I missed the first times. Oh, how I want to hold her and rock her and make her my baby again."

She was careful not to let the young woman beside her know she had such designs on her. Yet she wanted so much to bind her daughter just a little to her. There must be something Lydia could take that would remind her of her mother.

"Wait just one more minute, dear," Sidra said as they were preparing to go. "I won't be long."

She hurried to her room and threw open one of the chests, searching among the good linens. Finally her hand struck something hard and she drew it out. Her eyes clouded as she rested her hands upon the polished surface of the box. Then she shook herself and hurried back out to the waiting group.

"I'm sorry, my love," she panted slightly. "I wanted to find this for you."

She handed Lydia the box. It was of a rich auburn wood inlaid with oak, upon which was painted the likeness of a man and a woman. They seemed familiar to Lydia, but she couldn't place them.

"Your grandfather had it made for me when your father and I were married. The artist was a Greek. My mother's jewels and a few other things are in it. I was saving it for your wedding, but take it with you, in case I can't get away to see it. Please, dear, to remember me?"

Lydia dismounted and carefully stowed the box among her clothes. She wavered a minute and then flung herself into Sidra's arms.

"I won't forget you, Mother," she wept. "I love you terribly. I'll stay if you want. I wouldn't be unhappy here with you."

Sidra soothed her back, content with the reception of the gift. "Maybe not, my dearest, but you will be happier where you are going. If your father approves, I will be glad to see you next fall with this Cei of yours. It's about time one of you gave a thought to marriage. Constantine . . . well, never mind. I know you're eager to be off. Take care of her, Geraldus."

Sidra watched them as they slowly picked their way among the rocks up to the road. They would be out of sight soon—a turn, a bend, and the stones obscured them. She sighed and put her mind to the day's work.

"Cornelius! Lamden! Isn't it your turn to curry the horses? John, get a crew to bring some water from the well. What are you girls doing? Standing? Take advantage of the sunlight, bring your work out here!"

She bustled back into the castle. She was glad that they had eaten early today to give Geraldus and Lydia a good meal before they left. It kept her from having to oversee the fosterlings now while she still ached from the parting. A few hours alone, struggling with accounts and reports, would do her good. She gave the sky one look before she went inside. Perhaps it would be a nice day. The fog had almost gone; there was just a strip left clinging to the shoreline. The sun would burn it off soon. Spring might have reached the coast, after all.

She had not reached the first staircase when she heard the strangled screams from the guard tower. She froze only long enough to catch the startled cries and the sudden clink of metal.

The children! She raced back outside. The girls were still gossiping in the courtyard. Thank God, they hadn't obeyed her!

"Cornelius!" she cried. "Get all the horses out and put the girls on them at once. Take them into the forest . . . far! No, Merith, you can't go back for your shawl!" She pushed the girl toward the stables.

"We're being invaded! Hurry! Go! Get help!"

They seemed paralyzed. She shoved at them and screeched again for the boys with the horses. They came loping out, each holding two sets of reins. Sidra fairly threw the girls on, two to a horse, and sent them off as the boys went back for more mounts.

"Go on! Faster! This is no time to cry, child. You're a soldier's daughter. Now you boys, both on one horse. I need some for the others inside. Stay with the girls and don't any of you come back for any reason. Do you understand?"

She slapped the rump of the final horse as it went off. The screams were becoming louder. Who else was still inside? Some of the boys were working there, she knew, and a few servants. They must have heard the noise by now. If only someone had the sense to grab a torch and head for the signal pyre, always dry and ready. She smelled smoke. Good. But she had no illusion that help would come in time. Her only hope was to get everyone but the guards safely away.

Odd. The smell of smoke was stronger as she entered the interior of Cador castle. She started coughing, her eyes watering. In the great hall it was impossible to see or breathe and she had to feel her way around the wall to the far door, the one leading out to the ocean and the pyre. She was choking by now and crawling, pulling air from the crevices in the stone. She bumped into something. She recoiled from it and then reached out her hand again.

"Oh, no! My poor boy! Whatever am I going to tell your father?"

One brave child had kept his head and run to give the signal. But he had been seen as he raced down the corridors, flaming torch in hand. He had traveled only a few yards after the spear struck him. The torch flew from his grasp as he staggered and fell and the oily straw on the floor had picked up the flame and carried it across the room to the wooden tables and chairs and the cloth hangings.

Sidra dragged herself out into the air. In her horror and near suffocation, she had not noticed that the sounds of battle had ceased. In the open air, she heard the crackle of the growing conflagration behind her. Then she saw them. Her smoke-scorched eyes were almost blinded as the sun struck their silver hair and golden trappings. She reached for the knife at her belt. She also was a soldier's daughter—and a soldier's wife and a soldier's mother. Sidra had no intention of giving the Saxons a hostage.

Her last comfort was the knowledge that Lydia was safely away.

Lydia and Geraldus had not hurried after they left. There was no need to rush. Geraldus was deep in a recital of the new piece and Lydia deep in her dreams when the first of the girls caught up with them.

She was sobbing violently as she fell from her horse. The girl behind her tried to push out a few words between gasps.

"Saxons . . . guards . . . attack. . . ! Sidra . . . sent us. We can't stop. Hurry, hurry!" she panted as she tried to pull the other girl back on.

The other girls and the two boys were just behind them. Lydia gaped at them a moment and then her face went blank.

"Mother!" she screamed and turned her horse back toward the ocean.

Geraldus was bewildered by the cries and garbled noise

around him, which was mixed with the continued singing of his chorus. But he knew at once that Lydia had to be stopped. He nudged old Plotinus to a trot, but the ancient beast could manage nothing faster. Geraldus strained forward. She was getting too far ahead. With a rush of panic, he dug his heels hard into Plotinus' flanks. The horse was so shocked that he actually broke into a run.

They would not have caught up with her, though, if she had not stopped at the top of the path when she saw the thick brown smoke rising from the castle and the two Saxon men near the wall.

"Mother!" she screamed again. They looked up and spotted her.

Geraldus called out to her. But she did not heed him. She was intent on reaching the castle. Plotinus made one last effort and cut her off. Geraldus grabbed the reins and turned Lydia's horse around.

"There is nothing you can do!" he yelled at her. "We must go back to safety!"

He felt the thump against his cloak as a hard shock and thought someone must have thrown a rock at him. He prayed that the horses would give them the advantage and that the Saxons would not try to follow. It was not until they reached the comparative haven of the forest that the pain began to grow, sharp and hot across his back and his left side. Lydia twisted around on her horse to berate him for pulling her back. When she saw him, her face went white.

The spear must not have entered up to the barb. If he had been wearing leather mail, it might not have penetrated at all. At any rate, it must have struck him as he fled and then clattered back onto the stones. Blood was running freely down his side, staining Plotinus' flank and dripping to the earth.

Lydia eased him to the ground and tried to staunch the flow with a gown from her bag, but the bright red seeped through and onto her hands. She wrapped him in all the bedding and pillowed his head in her lap. The sunshine receded from beneath the trees as she sat there, her hands pressed tightly over the wound, trying to keep his life within him. She spoke to him, but he only cried out or murmured words she could not understand.

To Geraldus it seemed that the fog had returned, accompanied by an occasional stab of light, which was his pain. Sounds around him were muffled and his music had ceased altogether. As the day lengthened, he thought he saw hands reaching to him through the mist, but he could not tell if they meant to rescue him or snatch him away. Once he opened his eyes and saw Lydia's face inverted above him. It wavered and then vanished.

"I must help her," he thought. But his body would not respond.

The light was getting brighter, a fire burning into his heart. He tried to breathe, but could not feel the rush of air.

"What is wrong?" He made an effort to form the words. The fog was growing thicker and cold. "I am dying!" He heard a voice, not angelic, but alto.

"Geraldus, Geraldus, please. We haven't much time. In another few moments there will be no choice. We don't know what happens to humans when you leave your bodies. We can promise you nothing. But now, and only now, you may decide to stay with us. We are not immortal. Our lives will reach only to the end of this world. After that, we have no clue. We offer you a place of honor among us for that time. We want you so much, Geraldus—*I* want you so. But you must choose. It has been said that man has been promised eternal rest and bliss. We can offer you only ourselves as you know us. Geraldus?"

Odd how the agony had faded. He felt nothing. He could see nothing. But he had the feeling that somewhere in front of him there was a door and that on the other side of it he would be welcome. She was asking him to turn aside from it and go with her. He thought of all the nights she had shared his bed. He had never seen her, but he never doubted that she was as she felt and sounded. He had not tired of her voice in over twenty years. And the others! The chorus was just beginning to take form. There was so much more to do. It might be the end of the world before they sang the way he wanted them to.

Yet he wanted desperately to see the other side of the door. If only he could have one glimpse of her. It would make it easier to decide. Geraldus felt the beat of his life slowing and stopping.

All at once he was sure. "I have not finished my work. I won't leave you until it is done. If my soul is lost for this, then so be it."

The fog vanished. There she was, standing before him, beautiful and radiant, with tears of joy blotching her face. She gave him a shy smile.

"Can you bear a millennium with me, do you think?"

His last thread of human existence broke and fluttered away. The pain was gone, the loneliness, the sense of belonging nowhere. Geraldus found himself surrounded by people shaking his hands, clapping him on the back, all overjoyed to see him.

"Thank you, Master, thank you!" they exclaimed, and they all tried to speak at once, making promises, offering shelter and tribute, trying to tell him about their place on the earth. Over it all, he caught the eyes of his alto.

"We're not what you expected, are we?" she asked.

He shook his head. They were not all beautiful or young. They were not of the same race, but mixtures of many. They were so different and the possibilities of life with them so far beyond what he had imagined that he was suffused with delight and eagerness.

They were all standing together in the clearing. A little way from them, a drab shadow compared to the vividness of the chorus, sat Lydia, alone, in despair, sobbing over the body that had once been his, crying for him, for her mother, and for the fear of being left alone in the dark. Geraldus took a step toward her, but the alto stopped him.

"There is nothing you can do. We can only watch. She is not one of those who can see us. It is hard sometimes. But I can tell you that someone is coming soon who can give her some comfort."

"Can we stay until then? I can't bear to leave her yet."

"It would be better to go, I think. It is hard to watch such suffering. They will mourn you, you know. I first discovered

I could touch you on a night of such sadness. In all my life, I was never before able to give a human my solace."

He drew her close to him. "But in all this time, you never gave me your name!"

She laughed. "I'm afraid it would sound ugly to your ears. Let us find a new one for me. In a hundred years or so, there may be one we like."

A hundred years! He kissed her. And that would only be the beginning!

In the darkening clearing, Lydia shivered and cried until she could cry no more.

Chapter Sixteen

Guinevere hung over the watchtower wall, the guard stiffly on duty behind her. He wished violently that she would stop her mooning and go find something to do. His back was killing him.

She paid him no attention. All her life she had found that the only solution to a troubled mind was to look at the world from the highest place possible. The guard's discomfort was his own problem.

She couldn't put a name to her sense of unease. Everything was well enough. Arthur was kinder than ever. The women had stopped glaring at her as she passed. Merlin was too wrapped up in whatever was bothering him to worry her. The knights were back to being funny and entertaining for her benefit. Even Torres seemed not to be angry with her after it was announced that she was going to spend the summer in religious retreat. Sir Ector had assured her that God would take notice of such piety and not only restore Lancelot but also give Arthur an heir. How nice. Spring was definitely making itself known. The sky was buoyant with sunlight and high clouds, and small flowers were creeping over the rocks and up the walls of Caerleon.

But there was something missing, something not in tune. Could it be in herself? She ought to be relieved that the tragedy of Lancelot's disappearance had been pushed to the back of life here. It *was* his own fault; it was. A pity, of course, but he would turn up. The Lady of the Lake protected him, didn't she? Perhaps he was with her now. No point in dwelling on it. There was much to do to build the new Britain.

Perhaps that was it. There was an effervescence about people at Caerleon, a joyous pride in being part of a dream fulfilled. Guinevere did not share it, though she wanted to. Some nights when Arthur held her and his voice went on and on in the darkness, full of hope and promise, she almost got a glimpse of what it meant, almost touched what was so real to him. But in the morning he went away, taking his vision with him. And Guinevere was left behind, puzzled once more.

If Lancelot returned, could she then put her mind to Camelot? Would it be easier to forget what had happened to him if he were there and whole again? Guinevere was unused to mental wrangling and it irritated her. It seemed that Lancelot was destined to annoy her in any case.

All at once she realized that she had been staring for some minutes at Geraldus and his troupe. How wonderful! They weren't supposed to be at Caerleon this spring! The air must have been exceptional; the singers had never seemed so clear. She waved frantically to them and Geraldus grinned from ear to ear as he waved back. His green lady was standing with him, her arm about his waist. She said something and he looked at her and laughed.

Guinevere turned to the guard. "Go down and open the gate quickly. Saint Geraldus has come!"

The guard started to obey and then glanced at the path. "Where, my Lady? I see no one."

·211·

"He's right there, almost at. . . ."

But he wasn't. The guard raised his eyebrows and resumed his post.

"That's odd," she wondered. "Where could they have gone?"

Just then, Cei called to her that she was needed in the hall. She hurried down and the guard gratefully relaxed and took a pull off the wineskin under his cloak. That woman should stop sitting about and start producing children. It was unnatural, that's what it was.

It wasn't until dinner that night that the boy, Cornelius, arrived with his story. He was muddy and exhausted. He had lost a boot somewhere on his journey and limped as he walked to face the King. But he stood straight at attention as he told of the Saxon attack.

"Lamden and I took the girls to the home of my brother and then we returned with all the men we had." He faltered as he realized that Cador was there.

"It was too late. A fire had started. There was nothing left but blackened stone."

His eyes begged forgiveness. "Sidra ordered us to leave. We didn't know it was so bad. She stayed behind."

His lip trembled and he screwed up his eyelids. Constantine covered his face with his hands. Cador showed no emotion as he carefully moved his wine cup farther from the edge of the table.

"And my daughter?"

Cornelius took a deep breath. "She is with the other girls. She should have been well away, but she went back. Saint Geraldus was with her." He crossed himself. "We didn't know what to do, so we put him on the old horse and brought it back with us. My brother is perplexed. He thinks we should build him a shrine, but will not take it upon himself to do so without orders from the bishop."

"What are you trying to say?" Arthur commanded.

"I thought I told you. He was dead when we arrived. Lydia wouldn't let go of him. She sat there, making an awful noise." Cornelius shivered. "They sent me to ask you. Please, sir, what should we do?"

Everyone began exclaiming, crying, expostulating at once. Guinevere tried to make herself heard.

"But he can't be dead. I just. . . ."

Arthur patted her hand. "I know. It seems impossible. Please go help Cador, Guinevere. He is much more upset than he appears."

"But, Arthur. . . ."

He had already left the table. Cei ran after him.

"Arthur, what will you do?" he asked.

"Raise an army and drive Aelle back into the ocean with the rest of the slime. Every man who owes me allegiance must be here—no, at Camelot—in two weeks' time. Send out riders at once."

"No, Arthur. I won't have time. I'm leaving now. I must go to Lydia."

Arthur stopped. "Don't be foolish. We have work to do. This is no time for romantic nonsense."

Cei stood firm, blocking the way. "Arthur, since you became King, I have never questioned an order of yours. I have done whatever job you set me. But now I must go to Lydia and I will do it, no matter what you say. If you still want me, I will meet you at Camelot. Otherwise I will challenge Aelle alone."

"But I need you here!" Arthur began. Then he stopped. He had not seen that look on Cei's face since they were boys. "All right, go to her. I'll find someone else. But be at Camelot or I'll have you. . . ." He couldn't think of a punishment. "Be off, then. Bedevere! Agravaine! Gawain! Come here! And where is that horsemaster? Briacu! You'll have to come with us. Prepare the horses. We are leaving at dawn!"

Guinevere had made a sleeping draught of hot wine and herbs for Cador who refused it scornfully. She gave it to Constantine, whose grief for his mother broke through all his training in self-control. She put him in bed in the anteroom next to Arthur's. As she tucked in the blanket, she realized that her hands were shaking. She couldn't stop them. Something, a scent, the sound of feet upon the rush-strewn floor, brought back to her vividly her years at Cador castle, the smell of the sea and mold, the dogs, the people, the chaos, and Sidra, drab, plain with her pock-marked face. She had been everywhere, soothing, chiding, chivvying, smoothing over the transition the young Guinevere had had to make between her home and the reality of life in Britain. Sidra, left alone to face the invaders.

Trembling, Guinevere sank to the floor and cried as she never had before. She wept out her sorrow, her guilt, and her forgetfulness. She had never told Sidra how she felt, had never thanked her, never apologized for all the thoughtless, snobbish things she had done, for her total selfish absorption in her own very special person. Now she never could.

It was only a flash of insight, a moment of humility in the midst of sadness, but it was the first. Guinevere had never before doubted her own wondrous worth. She shrank from the idea, but the question now existed and would hide within her until it was faced.

Arthur did not come to bed until the early hours of the morning. He found Guinevere asleep in a chair, her face drawn and stained, a scroll of devotional essays on her lap. He was filled with pity and remembered his past sharp words to her. He wondered if Cador was regretting his last words to Sidra or all those which had been left unsaid. He woke her gently and guided her to bed.

"I think you should go to your family as we planned. You can set out tomorrow, when the rest of us leave. In the morning . . . Guinevere, are you awake?"

"Mm-hmm," she grunted. "I will go home in the morning with Geraldus."

"Yes, I'll tell him . . . tell Geraldus . . . oh God!" he choked. "I feel so cold, Guinevere. Come closer to me. You are all the warmth I have."

In the raw dawn Arthur woke her and bade her good-bye. Before the rest of Caerleon was stirring, she and Cei departed. He had promised to escort her on his way to find Lydia. For the first time, when Guinevere looked back, Arthur was not there. Today there was no time for a lingering farewell. Arthur was not working on a leisurely creation of an ideal world, but embarking on an ugly, necessary war. Once he had seen her safely off, Guinevere and her worries could have no place in his thoughts.

Cei had little to say during the trip. It rained the first night, but they were able to take shelter with a farmer and his family. The next night they reached Cirencester, which had an inn most honored to accommodate the Queen.

The innkeeper and his family fluttered about them the next morning as they prepared to leave. Did they have everything they needed? Would they like some fresh bread, meat pie, ale to take with them?

The obsequious service made Cei uncomfortable, but Guinevere accepted it without question. It was tiresome, but to be expected. She would be glad when she reached home and could dispense with such ceremony.

After the cataclysms that had been roiling about her for the past few months, Guinevere expected that her home might be somehow changed, too. It was with some hesitation that she crossed the stream and waited for the gate to open.

As the first crack appeared in the gate, Guinevere heard a shout and then started laughing. Letitia was racing down the hill to meet her, barefoot and scruffy, just as she herself had run so many times to meet Geraldus. Relief flowed through her. It was wonderful to be home.

Cei rode to the courtyard with her, but refused to take a meal with them.

"A cup of water is all I need, Lady Guenlian," he assured her. If he hurried, he could be with Lydia by nightfall.

Guenlian understood and did not press him. "Give our love to Lydia and tell her how much we share her grief. Go on! You needn't worry about protocol here."

"Thank you, I will tell her." And Cei leaped back on his horse and was gone.

"He has certainly changed since I saw him last," Guenlian said in amusement. "Do you think Lydia will marry him?"

"Of course," Guinevere answered. "She loves him too much to say no."

Guenlian gave her a sharp glance. The tone was light, but there was an undercurrent that unsettled her. She sighed.

"Are you happy to be back, darling?"

"Oh, yes! It's so comforting to be here with you all again, away from the pettiness and troubles of court. Poor Arthur! I wish he could take the time to come here and hide!"

"So do I, darling. It has been so long since we have seen him. But your father has gone to the muster. At least Arthur will have his support."

"Father! But he's too . . . I mean. . . ."

"He took forty men with him. I did not try to stop him. Geraldus was our dear friend and Cador is kin. Your father is not too old to fight for those he loves."

Guinevere could see that her mother did not want to pursue the discussion.

"It has been a long ride, Mother. I need to change and wash before dinner. It will be nice to eat in peace and quiet again!" She kissed Guenlian and hurried to her room.

She entered the dining hall relaxed, clean, and ready for a simple evening at home. How lovely not to be always on display! As she took her place at the table, she noticed a man seated in the corner. He was playing a children's game, rolling balls across the floor, making them hit each other. Guinevere turned to her mother with a puzzled expression.

"Who is this?" she asked. "Why is he hiding in the corner?"

"I forgot to tell you, dear," Guenlian answered. "It's a poor madman who wandered in. He's quite harmless. We let him go where he wishes. Don't worry. He won't bother you at all."

Guinevere nodded. As she turned away, one of the balls rolled across the floor, stopping by her foot. She picked it up and held it out to the man with a polite smile. He looked up at her as he reached out to take it. Suddenly she felt as if her stomach had been rammed up into her throat and then dropped. She tried to speak, but all that came out were choking sounds.

"Guinevere!" Guenlian rushed to her, pounding her back. "Here, lean forward. Are you all right?"

Slowly Guinevere regained her breath. The man was staring at her in bewilderment. She met his eyes and instinctively turned away. Then she looked back. The look he gave her was dull and empty. There was no fire, no passion, no compulsion. There was no reason for her to fear this man. Why did she feel as if someone had just torn out her heart?

She took a step toward him and held out her hand. "Lancelot?" she whispered. There was no recognition.

Guenlian caught her hand. "Lancelot? It can't be! This man is nothing like him! You are mistaken, dear."

Guinevere paid her no attention. "Lancelot," she said a little louder. "Lancelot, please listen! It's Guinevere."

She knelt down so that her face was level with his. Guenlian watched her with a growing sense of alarm. Behind her, Rhianna and Letitia watched her with fascination.

Guinevere had forgotten about them all. Somewhere inside this creature who stared blankly at her was the Lancelot who had trod upon sharp steel for her sake, who had terrified her with the force of his love. She had to find him. Gently she reached out and touched his face, outlining the features hidden by the wild beard. He shrank at first from the caress, but then endured it with a puzzled expression. Guinevere cupped his chin in both her hands and forced him to look at her.

"Lancelot," she pleaded softly. "Lancelot, I'm sorry. I didn't mean to do this to you. Please forgive me! Come back! I'm not afraid anymore. Look at me! I won't ever deny it again. I promise. Lancelot?"

There was nothing, not a flicker of understanding. She let him go. He slipped away from her at once and began rolling the balls again. Guinevere looked to the others for help.

"He doesn't know me! We must help him! Mother? What can we do?"

"Guinevere, how can you be sure it is Lancelot? This man is so different. The coloring is similar, but that is all. He is so gaunt, his eyes so empty, his face—no, you've been brooding too much."

Guinevere stamped her foot in annoyance. "I know who this is! Why can't you see it? We can't leave him like this. Rhianna, Pincerna, don't you see?"

There was a pause as Guinevere challenged her family to help. Pincerna would not reply without guidance from Guenlian, but Rhianna slowly nodded her head.

"I think that it doesn't matter if this is Lancelot or not. We have assumed that this man cannot be cured, but we haven't tried. If we can find out what to do, I will help."

"Mother?" Guinevere made one more appeal.

"Rhianna is correct," Guenlian admitted. "It is our duty as Christians to try to restore this man, whoever he may be. But I have no experience with madness."

Pincerna coughed deferentially. "There are many books on medicine still in Tenuantius' room. We were going to give them to St. Docca, but no one has yet arrived to collect them."

Guinevere was relieved to find that there was something concrete for her to do. "Rhianna, Letitia, will you help me go through them?"

"We will all help, Guinevere," Guenlian interrupted. "But only after we eat."

No one ate very much, though. Their thoughts were all on the ragged man, contentedly playing in the corner.

Tenuantius, Guinevere's ancient tutor, had died during the winter. His large collection of books, many of which he had copied or edited himself, had been wrapped and left for the monks to collect. Rhianna sighed as they started to search them.

"There must be a hundred of them and some have four or five different treatises in them."

"There must be something here that can help us!" Guinevere stated firmly. "We can't give up before we start."

Letitia was sent to bed after a few hours, but, goaded by Guinevere, the others stayed up until after midnight, carefully unrolling ancient scrolls and opening more recent and heavier codices bound in wood. Finally Rhianna set one down on the floor with a plop.

"I can't do this anymore, Guinevere! My eyes are as dusty as my fingers and the letters keep dancing around. I must get some sleep. I'll help again tomorrow. Why don't you come, too?"

"No, we must find it. It must be here!" Guinevere was taut with exhaustion also, but she couldn't give up yet, even though she knew she had been staring at the same page for the past ten minutes without taking it in. She blinked hard and tried to concentrate.

" 'A translation from the Greek physician, Soranus, by the most learned Caelius Aurelianus, with a discussion on the causes and treatment of deranged minds. Scribed by me, Tenuantius, in the fortieth year from the departure of the Legions.' "

She mumbled it out loud and started to close the book. Tenuantius had certainly copied anything that had come his way. The treatment of. . .

"Mother!" she shrieked. Guenlian awoke with a start, knocking over the scroll she had been trying to read.

"I found it! Listen. It tells everything! Let me see. '. . . madness often caused by brooding or the imbalance of some passion, such as love or. . . .' Well, we don't need that. We want to know what to do now. Here it is. 'The patient should be put into a light room, with only soft colors in view. Nothing sharp should be allowed near him. He should wear light, padded clothes, so that he might not injure himself. Warm sponges should be applied to his eyes. He should be well fed but given no intoxicating drink or herbs which would further inflame his mind.' What else? Oh, music is supposed to help, too, and the afflicted should be 'reminded of his former occupation as much as possible through conversation.' That doesn't sound too difficult. We can try, can't we, Mother?"

Guenlian rubbed her eyes. "We can try anything you like, my dear, if it will wait until morning. We must get some sleep."

Guinevere allowed herself to be taken to her room, but how much she slept that night is not known.

Chapter Seventeen

"Guinevere, darling, you can't continue in this," Guenlian warned. "We have tried everything the book recommended and he is no better. You will do him no good if you go on and you will make yourself ill."

Guinevere refused to listen. "I must keep trying, Mother. How can I bring him back to Arthur like this? They will blame me even more."

She gestured toward the garden before them, where Lancelot, clean and shaven, was reclining. His eyes were open, staring, perhaps, at the clouds or, more likely, at nothing. Nearby, Letitia dutifully was humming as she hemmed a new robe. In the past three weeks, they had employed every art they knew, pampering Lancelot in a way which would have horrified him if he had known. But he didn't. He was docile and gentle, but gave no indication that he understood anything said to him or that someday he might recover. Guenlian's heart ached at Guinevere's discouragement. The poor child had never before encountered defeat. But remembering the way Lancelot had watched her, Guenlian was secretly grateful that the danger from him was now past. She chided herself for being more of a mother than a Christian, but the fact remained that she much preferred this Lancelot as a guest to the one who had visited before.

Guinevere had gone on speaking. "Letitia has been working there all morning. She has been such a help, considering she is barely ten. I'll tell her to go and play and I'll read him something. Ovid is cheerful enough, don't you think? I could read the part about Aeneas. That has battle in it."

Guenlian gave up. "I'm sure it doesn't matter, dear, for all he knows. Read what pleases you. I must see to dinner."

Letitia was willing enough to go, but promised she would be back at her post the next morning. Guinevere settled herself on a stool near Lancelot. Sunlight fell across the scroll, an old piece of vellum, commissioned by her grandfather from a scriptorium in Gaul. The poetry was accompanied by graphic illustrations which had always fascinated her. Even eighty years in damp Britain had not dulled the colors. She began reading in a drone, which faded as she forgot the man beside her and wandered again with Aeneas as he descended into Hell and out again on his way to founding Rome. When she emerged from the story, she discovered that Lancelot was sleeping.

The spring sunshine, not yet high overhead, shone upon his face and traced the contours and lines of it. Guinevere tried to remember if the wrinkles around his eyes had been there the year before. She wasn't sure. Until now she had feared to study him too closely. Without thinking, she ran her finger along the curve of his jaw to the cleft in his chin. Pincerna had complained at the impossibility of shaving it properly and vowed that any man with such a chin should remain bearded. Guinevere disagreed. Now that she saw it well, she found his face pleasing. It would be a pity to hide it. She brushed back a lock of his hair. The golden-brown curl was silky and warm. The texture surprised her. She had not thought that any part of him could be soft. She knelt beside the couch and leaned over him, bemused by all she was discovering. She held his head in both her hands and gently turned his face to hers.

"Guinevere!" Her mother's shocked tone so startled Guinevere that she sat down on her heels with a thump.

Guenlian tried to check herself. Anything she might say would only make matters worse. Guinevere might have been doing something innocent. She wished Leodegrance had not insisted that Arthur must have his support in trouncing the Saxons. She needed his advice. Guenlian cursed the Saxons, swallowed, and modulated her voice.

"Guinevere," she began again. "We have a visitor. He gave

his name as Torres. He says he is Lancelot's foster brother. Do you know him?"

Guinevere rose, brushing her hands across her skirts. "Yes, I sent a messenger for him. I thought he might help. Where is he?"

Guenlian led her to the main courtyard, where Torres stood leaning against a statue and contentedly eyeing the maids at work. He straightened up when they approached and greeted Guinevere without any of the coldness he had shown her all winter.

"I can't believe you have found him!" he exclaimed. "Is he all right? I sent word to the Lady at once. She should be here soon. Has he spoken yet?"

"The Lady of the Lake!" Guinevere had heard only that. "She can't come here!"

"Why not? She won't mind. This place is much nicer than Caerleon. She will feel much more at home here. But she won't stay long, in any case. If we have Lancelot ready when she gets here, she will probably take him and go."

"Mother!" Guinevere pleaded. "Say something. We can't let her do that!"

Guenlian was trying to take it all in. She did not believe in the irrational. Of course, Geraldus had always brought his singers with him, but she had never seen or heard them. And if the food left for them was gone in the morning, well, it was the same as when children leave a bowl of milk for the fairies. It was always empty by dawn, but who was to say that the cat hadn't drunk it? But how was she expected to play hostess to an unnatural thing, posing as a woman? Guenlian took a deep breath. This sort of thing did not happen in civilized society. She exhaled. Civilization did seem rather tenuous these days. It was better to prepare for the impossible.

"What does this Lady eat?" she asked Torres.

Pincerna, the old butler, had seen many strange and horrible things in his long life. He had survived the loss of his family and the death of two of Guinevere's brothers. He remembered the years of Vortigern and the slaughter of the kings. But during the past few years he had lulled himself into a comfortable, quiet routine. The last forces of magic, as far as he was concerned, had died with Flora, Guinevere's old nurse. It eased his final years to think that the inexplicable was vanishing from the earth. Therefore, he was outraged to witness the arrival of the Lady of the Lake, Adon, and Nimuë in a slow, shimmering manifestation in the center of the courtyard. It was with furious dignity that he announced them to Guenlian.

"Some people, my Lady, have arrived." He gave the statement every shade of doubt he could.

Guenlian smiled. "Thank you, Pincerna. They will wish to see Sir Lancelot at once. Conduct them to his room. If they wish to see me later, I shall be in my chambers."

The Lady did indeed want to see Lancelot immediately. Since word had come of his disappearance, she had been impossible to live with. Guilt and worry made her exceedingly intolerant of anything but finding him. She was furious with herself. How could she have let him go among such beings, poor innocent child? What had they done to him? What kind of beasts were they?

Lancelot was sleeping in his room when they arrived. The long afternoon had almost gone when they entered and only his outline could be made out.

"He seems the same," the Lady whispered. "Are you sure he knows nothing of himself at all?"

"So all my sources say," Adon replied. "He is like a child again, simple and unaware. Can you cure him?"

"Yes," she answered. "I'm not sure, though, that I should."

She knelt by the bed. "Lancelot," she called, "Lancelot! My precious."

His eyes opened, but no recognition brightened them.

The Lady sighed. "Not even me. I somehow hoped he would at least remember me. Nimuë! Fetch the herbs and some wine. Hurry, girl. Don't forget you're here on sufferance!"

She busied herself in the preparations. A brazier was brought and placed near Lancelot's head. The wine soon bubbled, sending out its alcohol. As the steam rose, the Lady threw herbs into the liquid, all the while chanting arcane rhyme. Lancelot coughed and shook his head, struggling to free himself from the fumes.

"No!" he cried. "I didn't mean that! Stop it! Don't laugh at me! No!" He clapped his hands over his ears.

The Lady covered his hands with hers. "Lancelot? Do you know me, dear?"

His head sank back onto the pillow. The muscles of his face tensed, as if he were straining against some great force. His eyes opened. He blinked several times, unable to focus. Then he saw the Lady.

"Lancelot?" Her voice was tremulous. "It's all right now. I never should have sent you away from me. I never will again. I've come to take you home."

His eyes filled. He closed them again. A long moment passed before he spoke. "Do you know all of it, Lady? I have failed in everything. I tried to be perfect and showed myself a pompous fool, instead. I could not make her like me. They all laughed at me, all but Arthur."

"They are not worth your regret," she snapped. "If I had remembered how wicked humans are, I would have kept you with me no matter how you begged. Forget them all. Torres is here, and Adon and Nimuë are with me. All of us will take you back home."

Lancelot took a deep breath and sat up. The Lady took his hand, smiling possessively. He swung his legs over the side of the bed and stood up. He glanced over her shoulder and his face lit up as though reflecting the dawn. At first the Lady thought the look was for her and her heart leaped. Then she twisted around to see what had caused him to react so.

There in the doorway stood Guinevere. She hesitated at the sight of the strange people. One look at Lancelot and she knew he had been cured.

"He will be angry with me," she thought. "But he has the right. I must face him before he goes."

When she saw him smile, she returned it without thinking. He didn't blame her! On an impulse, she reached her hands out to him. As if the Lady had vanished, he brushed past her and went to Guinevere. She took a step back, but he caught her hands and pulled her toward him. She had meant to apologize, to welcome him back, but all the speeches were washed away as she gripped his hands and gazed straight into his eyes.

"I'm not afraid anymore," she said.

"I'm glad," he answered.

They stood, smiling idiotically at each other, and they might have remained there indefinitely if the Lady had not interrupted. Outraged, she grabbed Guinevere's arm and yanked her away. Lancelot tried to restrain her.

"Lady, please! This is Guinevere. You mustn't treat her like that!"

"I know very well who she is," the Lady said angrily. "This is the spoiled, scheming little bitch who nearly sent you to your death. I've heard a lot more about her than she'd care to have known. Certainly her looks aren't what I'd expect from the tales, but age does mount up on a human. Don't waste your Christian claptrap forgiveness on her. She has no soul, nor heart, either. Send her back to her poor husband for him to deal with, and forget her. Come along!"

The moment she had completed her speech, the Lady realized that she had made the worst mistake of her limitless life. Guinevere and Lancelot were holding hands again and staring at her, mouths agape. Guinevere's cheeks were red and she was breathing quickly, but her demeanor was not of guilt, but rather dumbfounded confusion. The same emotion was on Lancelot's face.

"I never knew you could be so vitriolic, Lady." He spoke with sorrow. "Forgive her, Guinevere. She is not like us."

Us! In that one word, the Lady knew she had lost. How could she have blundered so! She had come so close. All the years of trouble and patience ruined! He was in love with that woman. How could she have been so stupid! It was Lancelot's capacity for loving that had endeared him to her and yet she had not even considered it in her plans for his sexual education. Oh, why could he not have been like Torres! She knew the answer to that. If he had not been what he was, she would not have wanted him so badly.

The Lady looked down. Lancelot still held Guinevere's

hand. When they saw how she was staring, they each dropped the other's hold and put both hands behind their backs, like guilty children. She clenched her teeth in exasperation. It was hopeless for now.

"Twice, Lancelot, I have given you life." She confronted him. "You will have only one more chance from me. That is three more than I have ever given anyone. When you see me again, it will be for the last time in your mortal existence. Don't forget."

She swept out of the room with an imperious gesture, followed by Adon and Nimuë. Guinevere stared after her.

"What in the world was she talking about? Why was she so angry? She didn't even give me a chance to thank her!"

Lancelot started to take her hand again and then thought better of it.

"I have hurt her," he tried to explain. "I wish I could be what she wants. I love her dearly. She is the only mother I ever knew."

Guinevere did not think that "mother" was a word anyone would use for a woman who managed constantly to look a sultry twenty-four. But she was oddly pleased that Lancelot thought of her that way.

Lancelot wanted to know what had happened to him, where he had been, and for how long. But there was no point in spoiling his reunion with Guinevere in unhappy discussion. Someone else would help him fill in the unaccounted-for time. His body felt good, stronger than before. Someone had taken care of him. He cringed at the thought of how helpless he must have been.

Guinevere smiled at him again, a trifle shyly. "Will you ever forgive me for the way I have treated you?" She stumbled over the words. She meant them and that made them harder to say.

Lancelot winced. He would rather not be reminded of his pride and how foolish he had been. Guinevere misinterpreted the movement.

"Of course not. I understand. I had hoped . . . but it is too much to ask. I have been very selfish and stupid. But please, don't abandon Arthur on account of what I've done to you. He needs you very much."

"Oh, no! I mean, I would never leave Arthur, as long as he wants me."

"That's good." She turned to go. "I would never want my childish behavior to hurt him."

"Wait." He caught her by the shoulder and spun her around. Tears made her eyes seem as gray as the winter sea. "I can't forgive you because there is nothing to forgive. It was my own stubbornness and idiocy that caused me to . . . to be hurt. I wanted to be a perfect man. That would drive anyone mad, I suppose. That's not the way to be human, is it?"

Guinevere knew as little about being human as he did, but she nodded agreement.

"We could try to forget the mistakes we made with each other," he continued. "We could try again and this time perhaps we can be friends?"

"Oh, yes," she agreed.

Anyone with an observing eye might have doubted then that friendship was the extent of their feelings. Fortunately, the only person who saw them was Torres.

"Lancelot! I passed the Lady thundering out to the courtyard. From her face, I assumed that she had failed to cure you. What did you say to her? Never mind. You can tell me about it later. It's good to have you back!" He stopped talking long enough to give Lancelot an exuberant slap on the back. "Anyway, we have to get the Lady to have Clades brought here at once. I gather we're going to fight with Arthur. She could probably transport us directly to him, but from the look on her face, I'd say we'd be safer on horseback. How are you feeling? You look all right. Well, come on. If we want to be in this, there's no time to waste."

He pulled Lancelot off with him, too bewildered to protest. As Guinevere was about to follow them, she was distracted by a hissing sound from behind the door.

"Psst! Here! Over here!"

Nimuë had not left with the Lady, after all, but had hidden behind the door to Lancelot's room. She had thought they would never stop talking. It had been her hope to catch Lancelot or Torres alone, but she would have to make do with this woman. The Lady would be looking for her soon.

"You, girl, ma'am, whatever you are, come here!" She beckoned frantically to Guinevere.

"What do you want?"

Nimuë drew her back into the room. Her voice lowered. "Do you know a man named Merlin? He is tall and beautiful with a brown and gray beard."

"Merlin?" Beautiful? Guinevere was afraid she had another lunatic on her hands.

"Yes, Merlin. You don't seem very bright. It's a pity and I'm sorry for you, but I don't have time and I must get help. Can you take a message to him?"

"To Merlin?"

"*Yes!* Why do you keep repeating what I say? Oh dear, there must be someone more intelligent around. It's not your fault, I'm sure, but can you direct me to Torres?"

"No, wait." Guinevere was more than annoyed at being called half-witted. "I know Merlin very well; he is my mother's cousin. I have no idea why you want to contact him, but I will see that he gets your message. What is it?"

Nimuë had no choice. She still doubted Guinevere's mental ability, but she would have to take the chance. Quickly she removed a large emerald ring from her hand and thrust it on Guinevere's middle finger.

"Give him this," she said carefully, trying to be as clear as possible. "Let no one else have it. Tell him . . . tell him that Nimuë has found a way. That's all. I have found a way. Can you remember that?"

"Of course," Guinevere retorted. "But a way to what? Don't you want to tell him more?"

Nimuë shook her head. "He'll know."

"Nimuë!" The call was piercingly clear and yet Guinevere seemed to hear it more with her mind than her ears. It was almost painful.

Nimuë thought so, too. She flinched as if struck and immediately began running toward the call.

"Don't forget!" she pleaded over her shoulder as she ran. "The ring! He must have it. It's our only chance!" She disappeared outside.

Guinevere looked at the ring. There was a flickering blue fire hiding in its green depths. She stood watching it a few moments. The last few hours had left her feeling rather storm-blown and she needed time to settle herself.

"Guinevere." Rhianna's voice was too soft to be intrusive. "Are you all right?"

"Yes." Guinevere drew herself back to reality and took her sister-in-law's arm. "Lancelot is well again. Have you seen him?"

"He and that Torres rushed by me a few minutes ago. I didn't speak to them. Your mother sent me to find you. Guinevere, who were all those people? Letitia will be talking about it for months. Did you see them appear? It was like a sudden mist that shaped itself into people. And when they vanished! On the spot where they stood there is now a huge white horse with silver trappings and a helmet decked with ostrich plumes across its saddle. You must come with me now. If you don't see it, you'll think I'm crazy."

Arthur laid his hands upon the Round Table, trying to draw strength from it before he spoke. Around it, in the smudged light from the torches, stood fifty men. Some of their names had already been recorded on the wood and some hoped for that honor. Two spaces remained empty; one was the strange SIEGE PERILLIEUX and the other said, SIR LANCE-LOT. Arthur looked at the men. They were all good fighters, he thought, or would be. Some had never been tried and some, like Ector and Leodegrance, had not wielded sword or spear for twenty years. He did not like to ask the old ones to force themselves the way they would have to during the next few days, but he knew they would not be left behind. He thought they would endure. Anger and grief would drive them.

Finally he addressed them. "This cannot be a battle as in the early days of the invasions. Then, when no king betrayed us, we could take them by surprise. They had no idea of how to fight a man on horseback. They know us better now and we can defeat them only if they are taken unawares, unable to choose the battle site. Therefore, we must catch them in the open, where they can take no shelter. Aelle is helping us in this. I had expected him to retreat at once to his hall and barricade himself. But our spies say that he is still on the move. The rumor is that his son, Ecgfrith, has been expelled and that Aelle is adopting his nephews, especially Cissa, as his heirs. That means he needs to show them everywhere."

The faces before him showed little interest. They did not care who led the Saxons or what strange customs they had. They were barbarians who had invaded and murdered and who must be destroyed. Arthur tried to work himself into that frame of mind, too. But sometimes he felt an odd sympathy for Aelle. How much did the old man control the rest of the Saxons? Did they doubt him or question him openly as some of Arthur's men did? Did Aelle worry about the future of his people? Did he ever imagine them settling down and farming or building towns or was his vision limited to an eternity of conquest? The prospect of spending the rest of his life countering the raids of the invaders made Arthur's heart sink. But about this battle, there was no choice. His only hope was that it would be over quickly and without too great a loss. The men were awaiting their orders. Arthur continued.

"Therefore, if we are to defeat Aelle, our strength will be in the speed and agility of the horses and in men who can keep their seats no matter what. I won't take a man who can't do this. Tomorrow we will set up a trial which everyone, including me, will run. My horsemaster, Briacu, has designed it. Briacu! Where is that man? I thought I made it clear that he was to be here."

"I am here, my Lord." A shadow detached itself from the wall and moved into the light.

Arthur beckoned him closer. "What were you hiding for? I

can never find you. Do the horsemasters in Armorica spend all their time in the stables?"

"No, sir. They are honored and sit at the Lord's table."

"Then why have I never seen you there?"

Caet had no answer. It had not occurred to him to take what he knew to be his right. What had he been waiting for? Some glorious moment, he supposed, that would never come.

Arthur had no time for a long explanation. When Caet did not answer, he went on.

"Unless the company of men is offensive to you, I will expect to find you sharing our food at Caerleon this winter. Now, every man here must be responsible for his own horse. If you are unseated, unless you can remount, we must consider you lost. Briacu will bring a few fresh horses for those who manage to get away on wounded animals. Remember, unless we can attack, sweep through them, and be away in a matter of minutes, we will have lost the edge."

"Sir?" Caet interrupted. "In Armorica, it is also the custom for the horsemaster to go into battle with his lord and not wait in the rear like a snot-nosed stableboy."

He glared at the men at the Table, expecting a rebuttal, but there was none. With a shock, Caet met the eyes of his old master, Leodegrance. He stiffened, expecting to be denounced as a runaway, a lowborn impostor. But the old man's face only showed amusement. Leodegrance smiled at him and nodded with pride. Arthur laughed and stated to the group at large, "It seems my horsemaster is finally getting enough oats to make him rear. It's about time. Very well. Will you ride with me or do you prefer to be in the lead?"

Shakily, Caet joined in the laughter. He felt as if he had been battering for years at a stone wall, only to find it turned to sand.

Arthur continued to outline the strategy. They would have to travel quickly in small groups and take little gear. Over and over he stressed the need for surprise.

"We will be inside Saxon territory and on the way you may be tempted to raid some of their holds. I will remind you all that this would be senseless, ungodly butchery. We want the men who burned Cador, no others. And, may I add, if you waste your time burning down peasant huts, Aelle and Cissa will be warned. They will certainly then escape. I will have no man with me who will not follow my orders completely. Is that understood?"

There was some muttering. Those who had left children at Cador, those who had been raised by Sidra there were not eager to spare Saxon villages. They wanted Aelle to feel the agony he had given them. Arthur waited.

There was a stir at the other side of the Table. Constantine, his face closed to emotion, had drawn his short sword. He held it aloft a moment, where it gleamed in the torchlight. Then he placed it on the Table, hilt to Arthur's hand.

"I will obey you, King Arthur. I would not have my mother's death turn us to the same depths of evil as those whom we fight."

Beside him, his father, Cador, also offered his sword. Arthur said nothing as, one by one, the others followed.

They were to leave at dusk on the following day. Gawain insisted on being taken with them. He promised Gareth that he could be one of those who guarded the extra horses if he would ride the night with him. Gareth, eager for a chance to prove his worth, was willing to do anything requested.

That night, there was none of the excitement and grand talk which usually preceded a fight. There was no anticipation of heroism or great deeds as there had been before Mons Badon. Most of the men were asleep early and the few who stayed awake sat in corners, talking quietly or cleaning their equipment, particularly the straps of the saddles. Arthur wandered among them, speaking with each group a moment, and then he ascended to the tower rooms that had been built especially for Guinevere. Without her and the rugs and hangings she used, they were barren and cold. He might as well sleep in the Great Hall, where there was a fire. It was chilly still, for spring. He went out onto the balcony. The moon was in the third quarter. He was glad to see it waning, since the darkness would help hide his warriors, but tonight it added to the gloom about Camelot. He resolved that, when this was over, he would see that lights shone there every night, whether he were there or not. Now it was all too dark. The place might have been as deserted as the Roman towns for all one could tell. No wonder the Saxons thought they were filled with ghosts.

Arthur's eyes were widening in the dark. He could make out shadows and spaces. Looking down, he could tell where the practice field met the woods beyond. The evening was starlit and still. He felt himself lulled into a sense of peace by the silence. So when the rider appeared from beneath the trees, silver glinting from his bridle and white plumes waving, he accepted it as part of the magic. Slowly he realized what he was seeing. He froze, wondering if Lancelot had died and come back to haunt him. The rider stopped and signalled to someone behind him. Torres rode out into the field and Arthur knew it was real. There was nothing ethereal about Torres.

"All the same," he breathed, "it must be a miracle."

Then, forgetting about the men slumbering below, Arthur cupped his hands and hollered at the top of his voice. "Lancelot! Lancelot!"

The plumes shook as the helmet was removed. Arthur waved with both arms and Lancelot swung the helmet around his head in delighted reply. A moment later he was galloping around to the entrance to the maze and Arthur was racing to unbolt the gates himself. They met forcefully, Lancelot almost knocking Arthur down as he leaped from Clades to greet the King. Arthur did not care. He needed solid reassurance that Lancelot was truly there.

"Where did you come from?" he panted. "Are you all right? Will you come with us tomorrow?"

Torres answered first. "Guinevere found him and sent for me. We'll tell you the whole story if you'll only find me a jug of wine."

Lancelot grinned. "I haven't missed it, then? Torres told me what happened. Tell me where you want me to ride. I'll do whatever you want."

"I want you at my left hand, my friend," Arthur assured him. "You haven't missed anything. The battle has not yet begun, but, now that you are with us, there is no doubt we will win."

Chapter Eighteen

More than a week had passed since Lancelot and Torres had left. No word of any kind had come back from the outside world. Guenlian followed the vernal rituals as usual, pausing occasionally in her work to instruct Letitia, always near her. Watching them, Guinevere realized how little she had ever learned of those necessary homely rites and, after the first day, she began to follow the lessons, too. It was comforting to know that some things were constant, even though somewhere men might be dying and killing. She noted that, instead of making the worn cloths into rags, Guenlian ordered that they be rolled into bandages.

They ate without ceremony in Guenlian's rooms, since Leodegrance was gone. Dinner was followed by sewing and the reading of devotional works. As she took her turn reading, Guinevere had to resist the urge to pause at an unfamiliar word and wait. Tenuantius had always explained them to her. Because he had been a holy man, Guinevere felt no grief for him, only for the change his going had made. He had always longed to ask the definitive question, to read from an uncorrupted text. She had no doubt that God would make him welcome. He had baffled her with his intelligence, but his piety had been simple and certain.

As she read, Guinevere also worried about her mother. She had never before seen Guenlian without Leodegrance nearby.

The days of fleeing and fighting in which her father had participated were over before her memories began. One by one, the people she loved were slipping away. What would Guenlian do if she were left here alone? What if Leodegrance did not come back?

"Darling," her mother's voice prompted her. "I believe you skipped a passage there. Perhaps St. Ambrose on the Holy Spirit is too philosophical before bed. Letitia has been memorizing some Vergil. Would you like to say it for us, dear?"

Guinevere rolled up the scroll with relief and tied it carefully. Tenuantius' marginal notes, precise and clear, reminded her of his passing all too vividly—someone else she had not appreciated enough to thank.

She was seized by a need to go to her mother and hug her and she obeyed it.

"Why, Guinevere!" Guenlian was surprised but delighted. As a child, Guinevere had not been demonstrative. Guenlian could say no more, as Letitia was still reciting, but she sat up on her couch and wrapped an arm about Guinevere's waist, to keep her near.

Letitia finished and Rhianna took her away to prepare for bed. Guenlian released her daughter, laughing.

"You must be missing Arthur, dear."

"No, Mother," Guinevere answered. "I mean, yes, of course. I miss him. But I was thinking of you. Won't you come to Camelot with us this summer? Arthur wants to have proper entertainment this year, not just tumblers and bawdy singers, but real drama and proper historians and poets to tell of the past and write the story of Britain. And there will be all sorts of people there. We get traders from as far as Marseilles now."

"You make it sound very appealing, dear. I don't mind tumblers and bawdy singers. It has been some time since I have been to an entertainment that made me laugh. Yes, I would enjoy that. But I cannot decide anything until your father comes home. He is busy here in the summer. There are only a few of us in the house now, but more people are coming back to the lands about here and they look to him for advice and judgment. It may not be possible for us to get away, but it is kind of you to ask."

"Mother, we have heard nothing all week." Guinevere bit her tongue.

"No, dear, we haven't and it is unlikely that a message will come tonight, so we may as well go to sleep. Don't worry. I learned years ago that there is no point in it. You may, however, pray."

"Yes, Mother. Good night."

Two days later the messenger arrived, almost breaking down the gate in his impatience. It was Aulan, one of the horsemen Leodegrance had taken with him.

"Hurry!" he cried to the guard. "They are just behind me!"

The guard let him in at once. Guenlian came running.

"Who is behind you? Are the Saxons upon us? Letitia, have someone fetch Aulan a cup of water so that he can tell us."

"Lord Leodegrance!" Aulan panted. "He was hurt in the fighting. He insisted on being brought home. He follows with Sir Gawain."

Aulan pointed down the road. There were two horses past the bend, pacing slowly, almost touching. One rider was slumped over and held up by the other. Guenlian did not wait to give orders. She raced down the hill, wading the stream without even lifting her skirts. Guinevere started to go after her, but was stopped by Rhianna.

"We must get bandages and potions and herbs from the cupboard. Help me, Guinevere. We must have it ready for him. Fiona!" she called to a maid. "Fetch warm water and cloths!"

Gawain and Guenlian eased Leodegrance to the ground and carried him to his bed.

"It is not as bad as it looks," Gawain reassured her. "He has a deep slash on his hip and leg and he is worn from too much exertion and loss of blood. The others have gone to Camelot, but he would go nowhere but home."

"Of course," Guenlian answered. "Where else should he be?"

She knelt over her husband. He seemed unconscious but his breathing was deep and even. She removed the bandages from his leg. The wound was long and ugly, but had bled freely, the blood taking any poison with it. He would survive.

"Gawain, help me undress him and then see to yourself. I know what to do. This is not the first scratch he has brought for me to tend."

Gawain hunted up Guinevere, who gave him a better welcome. She hugged him despite his coating of dust and gave him food and wine before she asked any questions. When he had eaten, she demanded that he tell her everything.

"Everything? Guinevere, for the first time in my life, I am tired before sundown. Do you know how many nights I have slept on horseback to be able to join this expedition? To tell you the truth, I'm not sure anyone knows all that happened, except maybe Arthur or Merlin. We were divided into groups, you see, and attacked Aelle from all sides at once. It was too thick to see what was going on elsewhere. We had to keep fending off the swords and axes, so we couldn't look much farther than our own horses. God! I hope never to have to do that again! It's no way for a man to fight. I could stand anything but the screams of those horses as their legs were chopped from under them."

He shuddered. So did Guinevere.

"I don't need to hear about that, Gawain. Is Arthur all right? Is . . . is Lancelot?"

"Them? Oh, yes!" Gawain grinned. "What a team! I wish I could have sat and watched them. No one will ever laugh at those feathers of Lancelot's again. He can wear the whole chicken on his head if he always fights like that! Amazing! We did well enough. Aelle got away somehow, though, and Cissa. I suspect they stole horses. Not all Saxons fear them. Ecgfrith is dead, and good riddance. Now, have I told you enough? May I go and play in your baths?"

"Yes, Gawain, but this time do it alone. Mother was terribly shocked by all the giggles she heard when you were here last."

"Guinevere, your mother has never been shocked in her life. But I'm far too tired to do anything more than soak. See that dinner is early tonight and very filling."

By evening Leodegrance was awake and more comfortable. Guenlian refused to leave him. He tried to laugh at her solicitude.

"You needn't hold on to me so, my love. I'm not going anywhere. You were good to let the old warrior have one more battle, but I assure you it is my last. That leg cut doesn't bother me half as much as the ache in my shoulder muscles. I had forgotten how wearying swinging a sword was. Didn't I once say we should find time for philosophy? It is a good hobby for an old man, since the ultimate answer will arrive soon."

"There is enough to keep you busy without retiring to your books yet," Guenlian retorted. "I won't be placed with the aged for some time and neither will you. But if you need mental stimulation, I'll let your granddaughter bring her studies to you. Now, get some sleep. If you want anything, I'll be here."

Leodegrance caressed her shoulder. "That offer, my dear, will keep me young forever."

Guinevere looked in an hour later to find Guenlian sound asleep, curled up on the floor, her hand still clasped in her husband's. She stared at them a long time, a queer jealous ache in her heart. Then she gently placed a blanket over her mother and tiptoed out.

The next morning, when she was sure Leodegrance would recover, Guinevere went to Gawain and asked him to take her back to Camelot with him.

"I know Arthur decreed there should be no women there this year, but that was before Lancelot was found. I want to go home, Gawain. When can we leave?"

"Whenever you like, Guinevere. I'll risk Arthur's wrath."

They decided not to send word that they were coming. When they arrived, the guard told them that Arthur and Lancelot were over at the chapel, checking on the building. Gawain went first and distracted them and then Guinevere ran up from behind and put her hands over Arthur's eyes, laughing.

He whipped around and caught her in his arms, kissing her over and over while she laughed.

"I'm staying here with you, Arthur, all summer and all winter, whether you like it or not," she stated.

Arthur held her against him so tightly that he nearly crushed her. He knew he should make some sort of banter, but all he could think of was that she was there willingly and that she wanted to stay. He didn't see her face change as she looked over his shoulder at Lancelot or see him quickly look away, but Gawain did and filed it in his mind as something he must ponder.

With Guinevere's arrival, all Arthur's and Merlin's carefully laid plans for the summer melted. If the Queen was there, other wives saw no reason why they should stay away and many of the richer lords decided that this time of victory was appropriate for them to gather up their households to pay their respects to the High King. There were so many that they had to put up tents between the buildings for the overflow. Flags and pennants fluttering from the tent poles added to the air of continual festivity. The confluence of so many wealthy people also drew an array of merchants, traders, magicians, and entertainers, some from as far away as Iberia. Every evening there was juggling or dancing or storytelling or sleight of hand. Some nights all were performed. Guinevere sparkled among such surroundings. She excelled at being beautiful and gracious. Many visitors left with only a vague idea of who Arthur was or what he was doing, but with a radiant, golden image of Guinevere as the central figure in a renascence of the good life.

Arthur found it easy to arrange his plans and to convince the lords and the leaders of the towns, who were beguiled by the gaiety of Camelot, to support him with tithes and men. He convinced them, too, to allow him to send emissaries back with them. One by one, the knights left to take up their duties across Britain. They were armed with authority from Camelot and primed by Arthur to serve the people they were among as well as to honor his orders. He had chosen them well, he believed, but this was the test. If the plan worked, he could truly say that there was again a central government in Britain and that it rested in him. It was the greatest step he had yet taken toward carving out a society that would endure long after he was gone.

Guinevere was not concerned about the future. She was free to enjoy the summer, to play in the courtyards, to watch the knights practice for her amusement. Lancelot and Arthur stopped to watch her one day before they went to meet a delegation of monks seeking royal protection. She was playing a game with Gawain in which a wooden ball was thrown and caught in woven baskets with long handles.

"Gawain is using less than a tenth of his strength," Arthur commented. "He always seems to know how much to use so that she isn't hurt."

"They have known each other a long time," Lancelot replied. His eyes were wistful.

"Almost since childhood. They were fostered together."

"I suppose that is why he can treat her so casually. He never appears to worry about looking like a fool before her."

Arthur nodded. They watched the game in silence for a few minutes. Then Arthur shook himself.

"Never mind," he said. "What we need to worry about now are those monks. Don't be put off by their robes, Lancelot. Their abbot is a shrewd man. He has four or five sons and is keen on amassing enough money to leave the abbotship to one of them and still have enough left over to start the others off well. We want him to support his family out of his own purse and not make the honest brothers sweat for him."

"I should not go with you, Arthur. I cannot see through a pretense of piety. How can this man have become an abbot if he is so full of worldly desires?"

"In this case, he inherited the office from his father. He'd have been better off becoming a merchant. He is a good administrator of the abbey, though, and leaves much of the religion to his prior. But don't worry. You need only to listen when the abbot gives his demands. You exude such forceful silent outrage at moral degeneracy that it might help discourage the man from insisting on too much for too little. Also, until Cei returns, I need someone to be with me and sit at my right when I hand out judgments."

"When is he coming back?" Lancelot was clearly nervous in the role of seneschal.

"Lydia wrote that her father had agreed to their marriage after the mourning for her mother is over. Now that he has won that battle, I expect him to be here soon. They would like to be married in the chapel as soon as it is finished. That seems an appropriate consecration, don't you think?"

Arthur was not sure if it was Lancelot who had changed since his return or if it was the attitude of others toward him that was different, but he was glad of it. While personally as devout and serious as before, Lancelot no longer made others uncomfortable about their own wayward lives. He was admired by all now, although he had few true friends. He seemed not to need them; it appeared that he had found some inner contentment. Arthur wondered, a bit wistfully, if it took madness to bring a man peace. Whatever the reason, Lancelot was now being treated as Arthur had always wished. And, as Merlin drew further away from him, it was necessary for Arthur to have a friend whom he felt to be his equal in all things, including respect. Even Guinevere had finally understood Lancelot's worth. She often asked him to join them to go riding or to sit with them in the evenings. He played chess with her, a game that was too rigidly structured for Arthur to tolerate.

Not many people noticed that Guinevere did not play well against Lancelot or that occasionally their hands would meet over a disputed piece and then tremble and recoil as if in panic at the touch. Risa did, but for once said nothing, even to Cheldric. And Gareth, who still served Lancelot with a steadfast worship, noticed. It frightened him and he went to Gawain for advice.

"The Queen is disturbing Sir Lancelot," was how he put it.

"You are overwatchful, brother," Gawain told him. "Guinevere is doing nothing to him."

"She may not mean to," Gareth was willing to allow, "but

she is. He does not sleep well and sometimes at dinner he will look at her and she will look at him and then he doesn't eat anymore. He leaves the table. I have followed him. He goes to the chapel site or some other place away from everyone. He becomes frightening then. Sometimes he pounds the earth or grips a piece of wood so hard that his hands come away filled with splinters. It is all her fault. She has no right to make him suffer."

Gawain grasped his little brother's arms tightly enough for Gareth to flinch.

"You have too great an imagination, Gareth. You see things that are not there. And what you are saying is vicious slander. If you repeat a word of your idiot's tale to anyone, I'll have you packed home to Mother and see to it that she sends you to spend the rest of your life mixing potions for Aunt Morgause. Do you understand me?"

"What's the matter with you, Gawain?" Gareth exhaled as he was set free. "I wanted help from you, not threats. I think someone should talk to Lancelot, warn him of what she's doing."

Gawain glared at him. "Gareth, I can't believe you grew up in the same home I did. Or maybe the problem is that you did. Do you think that every woman is like our sweet mother? All right, stop charging at me. I'll take away part of the reason for your worry. I had planned already to ask Lancelot to come to Tintagel with me this fall. The journey will give us a chance to talk and I can see what nonsense has started your panic. I'll sort it out. Until then, remember what I said. Not a word to anyone!"

Gareth rubbed his arms ruefully. "You never were a bully when we were little," he muttered.

As summer waned and Camelot was being closed for the winter, Lancelot and Gawain set out for a few weeks in Cornwall. Guinevere watched them go with a mixture of sadness and relief. It was harder, she had found, to be friends with Lancelot than to hate him. It made her angry at herself. What was wrong with her? She had always taken her friends for granted. If they were with her, that was nice; if they weren't, she would see them later. Why, then, did a room brighten and seem more welcoming if Lancelot were in it? Why did it matter if he liked what she wore, if he greeted her the moment he saw her? Why did it hurt her when he avoided her? Some instinct had warned her to keep her confusion to herself, but her hands were very cold as the two horsemen left the maze and she had to fight a terrible urge to run crying to her room. Arthur put his arm around her and she took his comfort gratefully. If she had bothered to look at him, the anguish on his face would have stopped her self-pity.

"Morgan!" Morgause interrupted her sister's work. "Put down those beastly accounts and pay attention. Gawain is bringing that Lancelot boy to Tintagel."

"Yes, I know. Agravaine told me yesterday." Morgan tried not to look at Morgause. She had no right to still be so beautiful. She was past fifty.

Morgause in turn wondered if her sister really enjoyed being such a frump. It didn't make her personality any more pleasant.

"Agravaine also mentioned that Gareth thinks Arthur's wife is trying to seduce him."

"Gareth! How ridiculous!"

"Not Gareth! Who would look twice at him? You really must have been bored the year he was conceived. Lancelot is the one! Agravaine thought it was all a lot of nonsense, but I put my spies on it."

"Since yesterday? What kind of spies are they?"

"My dear sister, you don't really want me to tell you. You're much too squeamish."

"All right, never mind. Have you had a report?"

"Yes, and I think there is something to it—at least, there might be. This may be our chance. Arthur is growing far too powerful, Morgan. We have to stop him soon. That fiasco with Meleagant didn't help matters."

"It was perfectly designed. How was I to know that Lancelot would be able to cross the sword bridge?"

"That wasn't nearly as bad as your neglecting to tell me that Gawain isn't bothered by ghosts. Your own son! Lord knows you have enough here to curdle anyone's blood."

Morgan bridled at that. "Did you ever try getting Gawain up at midnight? A legion of headless specters could wage a battle on his bed and he wouldn't stir."

"You see what your promiscuous procreation has brought us to? If you must traffic with the Devil, why can't you bargain for something more useful than children?"

"Morgause, we have had this argument a thousand times. We each have our own pleasures and our own ways. Now tell me what you have in mind. I want to go over these figures this afternoon."

"Now you're a clerk," Morgause sniffed. "Very well, it was actually the sword bridge that made me think of it. Only a man in love would attempt such a thing. I think it's time that our dear brother, Arthur, got a taste of what his father gave ours. Do you think that a cuckold's horns will sit any better on him?"

Morgan put down her papers. "I think he will look magnificent in them. But can you arrange it so that everyone knows? Do you think they are already sleeping together?"

"No, damn them, too moralistic and prim, I suppose. Also, this Lancelot is some sort of religious ascetic. They say the Lake woman is furious with him. He won't touch a woman."

Morgan smoothed her hair. "I, of course, have had some experience with that sort and—"

"Far too much, my dear. No, don't get your claws out. I'm not going to chase him, either. But there is a way. I have a fosterling. Lord knows how I got her. Pretty enough, but overromantic and not at all bright. Now, listen. She is staying with her father, not far from here. He owes me for several past favors. It will be very simple. First, give a dinner here for Gawain's good friend."

Lancelot did not care much for Tintagel. It was drafty and bleak, with wall hangings and floor coverings dusty or etched by mold. There was an air of impoverished decadence about the place. He was more intrigued by the tiny community of monks who survived in the caves in the rocks below the castle, enduring the full force of the restless ocean. He had climbed down to speak with them on his second day, but most of them only grunted and turned away. Visitors from "up there" were not welcomed, one finally told him with a scowl. So far, he had spent this third day admiring Modred's collection of knives and listening with polite boredom to Modred's tales of his feminine conquests.

Finally Gawain interrupted. "That's enough, little brother," he said firmly. "Lancelot doesn't care whom you've bedded or how often. I imagine he believes you even less than I do. One of mother's maids was looking for you a while ago. Why don't you go see what she wants?"

"Was it the dark one or the one with red curls?" Modred wanted to know.

"She had a cloth over her head, but I'd say she was rather fair," Gawain replied.

"In that case," Modred replied, "I will have to leave you. It would seem I am being called upon to prepare some more lies."

"I never did like Modred," Gawain confessed when he had gone. "It may be just that he's so blasted good-looking and can stay awake all night, too. Or maybe it's that he never cared about me. Look, Lancelot, I know how awful this place must seem to you. We're leaving tomorrow, but Mother and Aunt Morgause have planned some sort of dinner tonight in your honor. I can't be there, of course, but I'm afraid you'll have to go. Don't worry, just smile and be polite and don't let them make you angry. I told Mother that you don't drink anything but water and that you don't care for late nights. So you won't offend anyone if you leave early. Poor Agravaine will have to be there for most of it and he'll see to you. Ignore Modred. He enjoys making people uncomfortable and will do it if you let him."

The dinner was long. First, a poet recited an everlasting encomium to the glory of Cornwall, accompanied by an occasional harp twang. Then the meat was brought in. Both Morgan and Morgause did their best to be scintillating, coquettish, and charming. Lancelot did his best not to yawn in their faces.

"Tell me, Sir Lancelot," Morgan asked, "is it true that the Lady of the Lake sleeps with a different consort every night, and sometimes two?"

"I really couldn't say," Lancelot answered, alarmed by the closeness of his hostess.

"Really, Morgan!" Morgause snapped. "What a question! Sir Lancelot, they say that the lamps beneath the Lake are ringed in diamonds. How brilliant the light must be, far better than anything we can create here." She swept her arm out, dismissing the room they were in.

"The light here is very soothing." Lancelot smiled, wondering how long the dinner would last. He took another gulp of his water. It tasted brackish and metallic. He supposed the closeness to the sea caused the odd flavor. Morgause signalled a girl to refill the cup.

Morgan smiled at him. She wavered a bit in his eyesight; perhaps it was the light. The torches gave off a lot of smoke. The sweets were being brought in now and, with them, a group of girls who began to dance. At least, he supposed it was dancing. There were only the twanging harp and a small drum for accompaniment and none of the dancers was echoing the beat. Lancelot glanced at Agravaine, who gave him a tight, nervous smile in return. Modred, farther down the table, was leaning forward as the girls swept by, trying to catch at their thin robes. He was supported by a group of young men whom Lancelot had not met. The dancers seemed to know the pattern and came nearer to them with each circle until, finally, Modred snatched at a corner of one of the robes and caught it. The brooch holding the cloth together fell open and the robe unwound as the girl spun on until she was naked, still smiling and dancing.

Lancelot's eyes widened in horror and he looked around quickly for something to cover the poor dancer with. In the meantime the other men had succeeded in unwrapping more dancers. Morgan and Morgause went on sucking their sweetmeats and chatting, occasionally flicking a glance at Lancelot to see how he was responding.

He was angry, although he hid it. He realized what was going on now and wondered if it had been designed to shock him or to entice him. The thought crossed his mind that it might even be a normal entertainment for guests. The behavior of the dancers suggested that they were quite accustomed to the performance of the men. Lancelot moved closer to Agravaine and picked up a bunch of grapes from the table, turning so that he was facing his host and not the entertainment.

"I'm sorry, Lancelot," Agravaine muttered. "It's that filthy Modred. Mother gives him everything he wants, however disgusting. As the eldest son, I have to stay a while more, but you don't. Let me take you to your room; this is going to get worse."

Lancelot slowly finished his grapes. They were immensely soothing. He could not understand why his mouth was so dry; he had had several cups of water. Maybe it was the smoke. He waved the server to him.

"Another cup, please," he asked.

Morgan heard him and laughed. When Lancelot had finished drinking, he and Agravaine rose to go. Lancelot bowed to his hostesses. Morgause lifted an eyebrow at him.

"Leaving so soon, Sir Lancelot? Yes, I suppose if you live with Gawain. He can get one up impossibly early. Why don't you take the ewer with you? You may become thirsty in the night. You won't deprive us. No one here drinks water."

Lancelot did not try to decipher the reason for the delighted cackle Morgan made just then. Agravaine was urging him to go. The garments were gone from all of the dancers now and the men were beginning to move in among them. Agravaine all but pulled him away and into the corridor.

"I'm sorry, Lancelot," he kept repeating. "They don't know what it's like at Camelot. They think the nobility all act that way. It wouldn't have happened if my father had been home, but he prefers to remain in the north most of the year. Please, I would be grateful if you didn't tell Arthur about it. They are his sisters."

"I had forgotten that." Lancelot looked back through the archway at them, still laughing together as if oblivious to the scene before them. "He doesn't know them at all, does he?"

"No, but I would rather he never knew them like this." Agravaine waited.

"I won't say anything." It was unnerving, somehow, and sad to think that the same mother who had borne Arthur had also been responsible for those two.

Agravaine left Lancelot in the room he shared with Gawain. Lancelot took off his boots and settled into the warm sleeping furs and blankets provided. He had thought he was exhausted, but now that he was alone and lying down, he found that he couldn't sleep. The tension at the pit of his stomach was almost unbearable. His thoughts fixed on the image of the shining bodies of the dancers as they moved. To his mind, they were revolting, but tonight his body wouldn't listen. He reached for the ewer and poured more of the foul-tasting water. He set his teeth. He had often fought this battle before. It was simply another temptation, a test. He gripped the sides of the cot. He would not go back to the orgy, which must now be at its height. He would control his body. If the mind of man were not stronger than the shell God had set it in, then he was no better than the dumb, soulless beasts. His hands dug into the wood rails at his sides.

There was a knock at the door. Lancelot hardly noticed it for the pounding in his ears. Even when he realized what the sound was, he did not answer it. He suspected that Modred was the kind to send a woman to him. Then he heard Agravaine's voice, soft but insistent.

"Lancelot? Lancelot? Are you asleep?"

With an effort, Lancelot sat up and bade him come in. Two men entered.

"I'm sorry to wake you," Agravaine whispered, "but this messenger just came for you. He says he's come from the Queen."

"From Guinevere?" Lancelot tried to pull his thoughts together. "Who are you? I've never seen you at Camelot."

"I am a messenger for King Pellas," the man explained. "I was told to tell you that Queen Guinevere had arrived at his home tonight and begged to see you on a matter of great importance. That is all I know. I am to return with you at once."

Agravaine frowned. "Pellas has a home not far from here. I don't know why Guinevere would go there rather than to us. It's very strange, but there may be some trouble at Camelot. You had better go with him and find out."

Lancelot nodded. At the point he had reached, an hour of hard riding would be a blessing. He dressed himself hastily and followed the messenger to the stables. Agravaine went with them.

"In the morning I'll tell Gawain where you are. He can meet you then unless there is some emergency. If you need me, do you know where my rooms are?"

"Yes. I'll let you know if anything is wrong." And Lancelot swung up onto Clades and was gone.

"Odd," Agravaine thought. "What would Guinevere be doing in Cornwall? Oh, well. At least it gives Lancelot a reason not to return to Tintagel. I hope he doesn't hold it against us. God, what a family!"

He spat his aggravation upon the stone walls and went to bed.

Lancelot was met at the door by a maid. "The Queen says you are to go up to her at once. Here, you must be thirsty from your ride."

He gulped down the water without thinking as the woman led him to a closed door.

"In here, sir," she beckoned. She opened the door for him and then left, carrying the lamp.

It was completely dark in the room. Only the outline of a window could be made out. Lancelot entered carefully, fearing a trap. As his eyes adjusted to the dark, he realized that there was a large bed in the center of the room. Someone was rising from it, her arms outstretched to him. Guinevere!

Reason abandoned him. He could stand it no longer. In two strides he reached the bed and fell into her open arms.

The gray and dismal dawn slithered through the shutters

and alit on the bed. Lancelot moaned. His head was pounding and every muscle hurt as though he had been in heavy battle for weeks. He moved his hands to try to push himself into a sitting position. His left hand struck something soft and alive. His eyes flew open as he slowly turned his head.

Next to him, sound asleep, was a woman he had never before seen in his life.

"My God!" he cried, leaping up. "Who or what are you?"

He was too angry to care that he had no clothes on. He began to dress himself, not out of modesty, but to get away from there at once.

The woman opened her eyes lazily and smiled at him. "Oh, Lancelot," she breathed. "You are wonderful! When they told me about you, I was afraid, but now . . . now I don't mind at all."

She reached up to him.

"What are you talking about?" he shouted. "Who in hell are you and how did I get here?"

He stumbled backwards to avoid her and his foot hit something metallic. A water cup rolled across the floor. All at once he knew what they had done to him. He felt sick. He managed to make it to the window, threw open the shutters, leaned out, and retched his stomach empty. Then he returned to the bedside and stared at the woman as if she were some new and loathsome insect he had found.

"You have ruined me," he stated solemnly.

She gaped at him. "You! What about me? Until last night I was a virgin!"

"Oh? If that is true, which I doubt, I am sure it was not through your own vigilance. I admit that I must have sinned with you. But my sin was that of weakness and stupidity. You are far more evil; you are the serpent, with a malicious love for corrupting the pure. My penance will be long and hard. I fear God must see to yours."

He left her without a backward glance. In a fine white rage, he found his way through the halls to the stables. Gawain's horse was already there. As he finished saddling Clades, Gawain came rushing out of the main hall. He leaped on his horse and they galloped out without a word.

When they were far enough away for Gawain's peace of mind, he reined in.

"Lancelot, what happened back there? When I woke, there was a note from Agravaine saying Guinevere had summoned you here, which is impossible. I came straight over to ask Pellas about it. I routed him out of bed. He insisted that you had come to meet the Queen and, upon finding that she wasn't there, had forced yourself upon his daughter, Elaine, instead. He said you were too much for him or his men to stop. When I left, Elaine was up in her room screaming that you had seduced her and then run off." He paused. "I thought the matter might be better settled somewhere else."

Lancelot wiped his forehead. "Gawain, you must believe me. Before I even reached the age of reason, I vowed a life of frugality, temperance, and chastity. I have always kept that vow. I swear I did not take that woman to bed by force."

"But you did have sex with her?"

Lancelot shook his head, trying to clear it. "I must have. I don't remember." He closed his eyes. "Gawain, I could have resisted, I know it, even drugged, but they told me it was Guinevere!"

"Christ's teeth! Do you know what you just said? Good Lord, man, don't ever tell that to anyone else."

Chapter Nineteen

"Are you happy to be back at Caerleon?" Arthur asked, putting an arm about Guinevere's waist. Below them, the courtyard was noisy with the bustle of preparations for the winter. Guinevere smiled up at him and drew closer to his warmth.

"Yes," she said. "This is my favorite home. But Camelot is becoming very beautiful to me. That artist from Iberia draws very well. Don't you think we could let him do a mosaic in the small courtyard by the dining hall and maybe another on the floor of the chapel?"

"I have already sent traders to Gaul to find the tiles." Arthur was pleased with himself for anticipating her. "In the meantime he is going to work on a fresco on the west wall of the guest quarters. What do you think?"

It made him happy to know that she was learning to care enough about Camelot to be interested in the embellishing of it. Guinevere had indeed stayed near him all summer. She had sat beside him patiently, listening to the news and complaints brought to him, and often made suggestions for resolving them. She had helped to plan ceremonies and taken a kindly interest in the throng of hopeful applicants for knighthood. She had been busy and happy and the tight worry he had felt in the spring had relaxed. Guinevere had shown no signs of missing, well, anyone inordinately.

For Guinevere the summer had been peaceful and reassuring. There were no more sudden irritating jolts of her heart at the realization that he was watching her. She did not walk into any rooms with trembling anticipation, wondering if he would be there, waiting. No one upset her sense of balance. People were kind to her; they brought her gifts—silks, jeweled cups, stories. Even Merlin was more pleasant since she had given him that ring. It was not hard to keep her vow to pay more attention to Arthur's life. The affairs of Britain were more interesting than she had supposed. And it was little enough effort for the joy it seemed to give him. Now winter was creeping in again. She could retreat to her rooms during the cold weather and not arouse comment. How lovely that would be.

She noticed Cei arguing with a messenger just arrived at the gate. His voice could not be heard, but his stance was severe. It was apparent to everyone that the honor of being promised to Lydia had raised him far above common humanity.

Arthur was delighted. "You see him?" he pointed. "That man won't get up to me unless he has an earthshaking story to tell. Cei always had that authority, but he wouldn't take it before. I only hope his confidence lasts beyond the wedding."

"Lydia is her mother's daughter. She will see to it that he knows his own worth." Guinevere had caught a scent of regret in Arthur's words. She sighed. What did he want from her?

"It seems that the man has something to say, after all," Arthur decided as they watched Cei lead the man toward the small audience room Arthur sometimes used. "I suppose we should go down and find out what it is. Do you want to come with me?"

"Of course. I would freeze up here without you."

Cei met them at the bottom of the stairs, outrage making his face and voice taut.

"This man has been sent with the most insane tale! I don't believe a word of it, but he swears he came straight from King Pellas. He says that he took Lancelot there himself that night and that Sir Agravaine will attest to the truth of it. I thought you should deal with him yourself."

"All right, don't worry." Arthur tried to calm him. "I want to discover what you are talking about. Guinevere, would you rather wait in our rooms?"

"No, I'll come." Guinevere was furious with herself that the mere mention of his name could cause her throat to tighten.

The messenger was both puzzled and dismayed to meet Guinevere. "You weren't at Corbyne!" he blurted out.

Guinevere stared. "Of course not. What is it?"

"Never mind, dear." Arthur sat down and drew her next to him. The band of worry was beginning to tighten again. "Now, what is this story you bring?"

"But they told me . . . it wasn't her . . . ," the man muttered, looking at Guinevere and shaking his head. He pulled himself together.

"A week ago, sir, I was on duty at the gates of Corbyne, King Pellas' home. Early in the evening a woman rode in alone. She was veiled, but I could see that she was fair. Her clothes were fine and rich. They told me later that Queen

Guinevere had arrived and that I must go at once to Tintagel to fetch Sir Lancelot for her."

Guinevere started to expostulate, but Arthur stopped her. "Continue," he commanded the messenger.

"It was very late then, but I left and got Sir Lancelot out of bed. He seemed puzzled, but he came without any argument."

"But, Arthur, you know I was never—" Guinevere began.

"Let him finish," Arthur said quietly.

"We raced back to Corbyne. I could barely keep up with him. They let him in at the main house and I went to bed. The next morning he was gone."

"What of this woman you saw?" Arthur demanded.

"I don't know what happened to her," the man admitted. He studied Guinevere. "But it wasn't you, was it?"

"Of course not!" Guinevere was outraged.

"Well, then," Arthur relaxed. "Obviously someone was mistaken. Is that all?"

"No, sir." The man shifted feet and focused on a spot on the wall behind them. "About the time everyone had assembled in the main hall for the morning meal, the Lady Elaine came running in. Her hair was undone and she was still in her nightdress. She was screaming and wailing so that we couldn't understand what had happened. Finally she managed to tell her father that the night before, Sir Lancelot had forced his way into her room and . . . uh . . ."

"Go on," Guinevere snapped. "What did Lancelot do?"

"Well, sir—" The messenger fumbled for a term he could use in front of a woman. "He debauched her."

"What?" Arthur felt inclined to laugh. The whole story was obviously ridiculous. What angered him about it was that, for no apparent reason, Guinevere had been brought into it. He would not tolerate such slander.

Guinevere barely managed to keep her jaw from dropping. If he had accused Gawain or Torres, perhaps, she might have believed him. But not Lancelot. She composed herself. Of course it was merely a joke, or a mistake. Still, she felt her stomach knot.

Arthur had no doubts. "Is any of this recital of yours from

Pellas," he asked, trying to keep a straight face, "or did you manufacture it all on the way here? Who paid you to say all this?"

"Your Majesty, my Lord, sir! I swear I have spoken the truth! Lord Agravaine was with me when I saw Sir Lancelot. He will vouch for me. But I have not delivered King Pellas' message yet. He ordered me to say that he appeals to you for justice. Lady Elaine was a maid and now she is not, as her servants and her nurse will witness. He wishes you to either punish Sir Lancelot fully or, in view of his high birth, require him to marry the Lady Elaine."

"That is unspeakable!" Guinevere breathed in horror.

"I thought as much!" Arthur laughed in triumph. "Don't be so shocked, Guinevere, it was really very clever. Pellas has apparently not been very lucky in finding a suitor for Elaine. This is a rather crude method, but he may have been desperate.

"However," he added sternly, "it will not work. Go back and tell your master that I will not have my knights made fools of or tricked into marriage. Also, I am exceedingly angered by his use of my wife's name as a part of this deception. I will send a messenger of my own at once, to make the matter clear and to return with a complete apology, both to me and to the Queen. You may go!"

Guinevere managed to sit silent until they were alone. Then she could wait no longer.

"Arthur, what was all that about?"

Arthur chewed the corner of his lip and Guinevere knew he was more upset than he had pretended.

"I'm not certain, my dear. It may be just a wild scheme of Pellas, but I'm not sure. That king owes allegiance to my sister, Morgause. Merlin has warned me more than once that she is not to be trusted, but I never had any evidence to prove it. I don't know. But I am sure it did not happen as Pellas claims. We will have to wait until Lancelot returns to find the truth of it."

Guinevere did not want to wait patiently for Lancelot to arrive. The story was impossible; Lancelot would never do such a thing. Everyone knew that. Everyone. But Guinevere knew the energy that constantly pulsed through him and had felt the emotions which were kept so tightly reined. What if he had found someone else who could release those emotions in him? Guinevere choked at the thought, all the while reminding herself that it was nothing to do with her. Nothing at all. She ate hardly anything and drummed her fingers on the dinner table, waiting for Arthur to finish. She drove Risa distracted by unpacking her own clothes and leaving them all over the room. She could not sit still long enough to hear a new poem composed in her honor and offended the poet highly by requesting that he finish reciting it later. Cei suggested that she go riding more often to wear down her nervousness. Anything to get away from Caerleon for a while, where her mood was starting to affect everyone. Arthur agreed. He did not want to think about what was making her act so oddly. It was interfering with his work too much. So Guinevere went in search of Caet.

She found him in the small room he had been assigned, at one end of the living quarters near the stables. Because he had refused to be billeted with either the stableboys or the knights, he and Arthur had found this room as a compromise. Guinevere paid no attention to his new prestige.

"Caet," she announced. "I must go riding now. Come with me!"

Caet rose deliberately from his cot. "My Lady, my name is Briacu. Do you think it would be proper for you to go out with me alone?"

Guinevere stamped her foot. "Caet! Stop this now! I don't know why you go on pretending. Father recognized you at once. He told me about it. If you didn't like the name you were given, you were free to change it. I don't care. But I won't be treated as a stranger by you! I want to go riding. It never bothered you to come with me when we were children and I'm not going to let you start now."

Caet's jaw tightened. "When we were children, I was the slave boy who lived in the empty stall. I came along to hold the reins and carry the lunch. When you wanted me, I was there and when you didn't, I was invisible."

"That's not true!" Guinevere protested, hoping she was

right. "You were my friend then. You were the only one who had time to play with me when my brothers were gone. Do you remember all the times you hoisted me up into the apple trees so I could throw the good apples down? You were a servant—never a slave! No one in the house treated you like one. Matthew always brought you back something special. He taught you and Mark to ride and fight the same way. He cared about you just as he did his own brother."

Caet wasn't interested. "Matthew died. I would have fought with him, but no one thought to ask me to go. I was left behind to clean out the stables and mend harness. But I am just as good as any man here. I have been a hero in Armorica. I am Arthur's master of the horse. If you tell them about me, I will be nothing more to these people than another runaway."

"You are angry because no one would let you die with Matthew and John? Would you have been happy if you had gone into real slavery with Mark? I do not see why you could not have become a hero or whatever you wanted by staying here."

Caet longed to tell her why he had really left. The pearl he had sent her for her wedding still lay on her throat. He felt the urge to tell her what he had done to earn it and how every woman he had flattered and taken had been faceless because he could see only her. He wanted to shake her until she really saw him for once. But he stood silent, glaring at her with sullen, angry eyes.

Guinevere's lip trembled. "All right, be whomever you want to be. But you and Risa are the only people here from my childhood and sometimes I am very homesick. We could have helped each other and been friends again. But you do nothing here but hide. If you were such a hero in Armorica, why did you bother coming back?"

He took a step toward her, reaching out his arm, intending to twist the chain from her neck and smash it beneath his heel. She recoiled in panic.

"Never mind. I can go riding by myself. Don't worry. I will tell no one who you are."

Caet caught her wrist so tightly that her fingers grew

white. She stared at him as if he were the stranger he wanted to be. He opened his mouth to speak and then, swiftly, like a spring flood, all the rancor against her drained out of him. His hold upon her loosened, but she didn't run.

"Caet?" she pleaded. "What did I do to you? I don't want you to hate me. I'm sorry if I was cruel. I didn't mean to be. I never thought of you as a slave or even a servant. Please. I need you now to be my friend."

He cursed himself in three languages and then gave in. He knew it was hopeless. Even as a child he had been unable to resist her. He didn't remind her that he was the one who had been beaten for letting her climb the apple trees. She wouldn't remember or understand.

"All right, Guinevere. Put on your boots and I'll go with you. But this time, when I say the time has come to return, you listen to me!"

Guinevere flew at him and kissed his cheek. "Oh, Caet! Thank you! Thank you! It will be wonderful, just like the old days!" She ran off to get ready.

Caet walked slowly and unhappily to the stables to see that the horses were saddled, mentally kicking himself with each step. "Just like the old days," she had said. He had no doubt that it would be.

They came back several hours later, wind-blown and tired. Arthur drew Caet aside after dinner and thanked him for his trouble.

"I know you have more important work to do, Briacu, than entertaining my wife. So I'm doubly grateful. She has been very restless these last few days. Perhaps she misses Geraldus. This is the time he usually arrived. If you could take her out again tomorrow, I would be grateful. Maybe when Gawain and Lancelot return, they can keep her occupied."

Gawain was losing patience. They had been arguing for days about this.

"Lancelot, I know you're upset, but you shouldn't take it so seriously. No one is going to believe that you raped that girl. So what if you slept with her. You didn't want to, did you? You didn't enjoy it, obviously. How can you call it a sin when it wasn't any fun?"

"I should have been stronger," Lancelot reiterated. "I should have guessed what they were doing to me."

Gawain shrugged. "I don't see how. There isn't a man alive who ever outguessed my Aunt Morgause and you can bet it was her strange mind that planned this. It is only her idea of a joke, believe me. You should hear about some of the ones she played on me. You wouldn't believe the places and positions I've woken up in."

But Lancelot wasn't interested. He plodded along on Clades, weighted down with guilt, anger, and, most of all, fear of what Guinevere would say when she saw him. What Gawain could not understand was that the greatest sin he had committed was that he had believed the woman was Guinevere. He had given in to a desire he had refused to admit before. How could he face her now?

In spite of his reassurances to Lancelot, Gawain was worried. There was something wrong about this, something more complex than one of Aunt Morgause's practical jokes. If they had just wanted to drug Lancelot and throw him in bed with someone, why did they have to send him to Corbyne? And why drag Guinevere into it at all? It seemed unnecessarily complicated. He felt a clammy chill at the memory of the look of unholy glee his aunt and mother had exchanged before he went to bed that night. They were plotting something grandiose. He wished he could guess what it was before it was unleashed on Britain.

They reached Caerleon all too soon for Lancelot. He knew by the look the guard gave them that the tale had preceded their arrival. There was a feel of thick dust in his throat as he set out for Arthur's rooms. He hurried, dreading the interview but longing to have it done.

Arthur was alone except for Merlin when Lancelot entered. Arthur's face shone with delight at seeing him again. He jumped up to greet him and offer a chair.

"Lancelot! It's about time you got here. Briacu was telling me just this morning that the mare he bred to your Clades is due to foal soon. It's late in the year for a birth, but Briacu is sure that the colt will be strong. He'll want to get your permission to try again. Sit down. Are you hungry? Merlin, we can finish this later. How was your visit to Cornwall, Lancelot? We heard a rather bizarre story from King Pellas about you. I can't think what they've been putting in his wine."

Lancelot cringed. "I know all about it, Arthur. It wasn't *his* cup that was tampered with."

Merlin leaned back in his chair. He thought so. The whole story had been too improbable to be a complete fabrication. Pellas had neither the talent nor the imagination for such a thing.

"Where was that witch, Morgause, while you were being drugged?" he asked.

Lancelot gaped at him. He had heard the man could read minds. He wondered how much more he could discover. "She was at Tintagel, visiting Queen Morgan."

Arthur brought the ale jug from under the table, brushed some papers aside, and poured himself a cup. "Do you think that my sisters had something to do with this?" he asked.

Merlin threw him a look of disgust. "You know very well that they did and why. Don't deny it. I've warned you about them over and over, but you ignore me. The only question is, did they do this to hurt Lancelot, Elaine, or you?"

"Me!" Arthur thumped his cup on the table, spilling ale on the papers. He absently mopped it up with his sleeve. "What could any of this have to do with me?"

Merlin tipped his chair back again. He regarded Lancelot for a moment. "Look at him, Arthur. He is your model, isn't he? The prototypic knight. Think of what has happened to him in the last year. How many times do you think he can be made a fool of before it makes you seem foolish, too?"

Lancelot groaned and sat down, his face buried in his hands. Merlin went on remorselessly.

"Do you really think that Meleagant had the idea of kidnapping Guinevere all by himself? Have you ever wondered why your sister Morgause has never bothered to come here? Do you have any promise of allegiance from either sister? When are you going to understand that these women hate you—not just your father, you! You stole their mother away as much as he did. They would rejoice to see you mocked and destroyed as their father was. The only thing that puzzles me about them is that they could not pass on their hatred to your nephews."

"I'm sorry, Arthur." Lancelot raised his head. "I let them trick me. I should have suspected something immediately. Gawain tried to warn me. I should not have returned here. It's useless. I am only an embarrassment to you. Every time I try to behave like a proper knight, I end up looking like a clown."

"There was nothing amusing about the way you fought Aelle at the Fords." Arthur grabbed Lancelot's shoulder and shook it. "I need you, Lancelot. I need you here, with me, no matter what people say. I will not allow anyone to make my decisions for me or drive my best knight away. Now Pellas wants us to believe that you came into a house full of men-at-arms, guards, and fosterlings, all armed; greeted them pleasantly; and then dragged Elaine off to the bedroom while they all sat around, quietly drinking your health."

"But, Arthur, I never dragged—"

"I know that. Soon everyone else will, too. I've found out that, until a month ago, Elaine was living in the household of my sister, Morgause. Suddenly she was sent home to her father. I think she was seduced by a guard or potboy or someone Morgause would not wish to produce if Pellas found out. Just by chance, you happen to be at Tintagel with Gawain. Your pedigree and current station are both better than anything Pellas could arrange himself. They know you wouldn't be interested, but something might be arranged. So, you see, Merlin. They weren't trying to hurt anyone, they were trying to protect the girl. I'd be willing to bet that in about six or seven months Elaine just happens to have a premature, but very healthy, baby. Don't worry, Lancelot. You won't be the one who looks foolish then."

Lancelot started to explain further, but Merlin silenced him. Guinevere's name had not been mentioned. Without bothering to get a careful explanation, Arthur had devised his own. Arthur watched them now, daring them to add a word.

Poor Arthur! Merlin regretted fleetingly that he would be leaving so soon. Arthur would need someone to help ease the pain when it came. And it would. Even without a prophet's eyes, he could see that. But Arthur would have to face it alone. When Nimuë came for him, Merlin knew he must go.

Chapter Twenty

Arthur's prediction was not completely correct. It was not seven months, but nine, almost to the day, and the baby was small and sickly because Elaine had spent most of the pregnancy miserably longing for Lancelot to return and marry her. At least, that was what Morgause wrote to Arthur in a letter full of moral outrage. She insisted that Lancelot admit his actions, claim the child, and take on the responsibility of its support. Arthur snorted at that, in spite of Lancelot's obvious misery and confusion.

Gawain tried to reassure him. "Listen to me, Lancelot. No one here believes for a minute that you are that boy's father. It has nothing to do with you at all. Let my aunt rumble and fume as long as she likes. Then forget the whole thing."

There was a lot of humor about the matter, especially at meals. All of it was at Elaine's expense. The story had gone out that Lancelot had been drugged senseless and left in Elaine's bed for a practical joke. Although it embarrassed Lancelot, he found, to his surprise, that it made him much more popular with the other knights. Even the ladies laughed at Elaine, although more than one felt a sneaking sympathy with her tactics. Imagine anyone trying to dupe Lancelot into a marriage!

Arthur gave Guinevere his version of the story and no one contradicted him. It made her angry that anyone would play such a cruel trick, but she was satisfied that Lancelot was completely innocent. She did not discuss it with him, though. For most of that year she had little chance to discuss anything with him.

Camelot was glorious that summer. Everything should have been perfect. Even the weather seemed to behave better under Arthur's rule. The place was gaudy with all variety of dress and trappings. When people came to Camelot, they wanted to show off their best attire. Often, when they got there, their best looked drab. To remedy that problem, a flourishing trade had built up. There was now a ragtag village just outside the walls, made up almost totally of tailors, cloth merchants, hair stylists, and jewelry smiths. Two inns had also been built, and tents sprang up again to handle the overflow.

But what last year had been excitement and grandeur now grated on Guinevere's nerves. It was all wrong, too bright, too loud, too much in the way. In the way. . . . Lancelot was at Camelot, but he might as well have stayed in Cornwall and married Elaine for all she saw of him. He did not avoid her. He was at dinner every night. But if he asked her to go riding with him, twenty others decided to go with them. If she suggested a game of chess, Gawain or Gareth always wanted to watch and comment on the moves. If, for a miracle, they happened to meet in an empty hallway, they would no more than say hello before someone appeared. And that someone always wanted one of them. Lancelot was never anything but calm and polite, but sometimes she would see a hunger in his eyes and wonder if it were reflected in her own. On hot afternoons when the music and laughter swelled beneath her windows and the odor of roast meat and damp flesh permeated the courtyard, Guinevere wondered if she could last much longer. One morning she would wake up and commence screaming and she would not be able to stop.

In spite of Gawain's advice, Lancelot could not keep his mind off the child Elaine said was his. Gawain found him in the anteroom to Guinevere and Arthur's quarters one morning, sitting.

"Are you still brooding?" he asked. There was a world of scorn in his voice.

Lancelot bit his lip. "She has named the boy Galahad. How did she know it was one of my names?"

"Who knows? Maybe she didn't. She may just like it. Even if she named him after you, what difference would it make? He is still not your responsibility."

Lancelot shook his head. "How are you so sure?"

"Damn it! Lancelot, how many times do we have to go through it?"

Lancelot rose and glared at him. They were almost of a height and stood nose to nose as if preparing to fight. Lancelot shouted practically down Gawain's throat.

"You can go on yelling at me until you're hoarse, but it won't be settled until you can prove to me that there is no way that boy could be mine!"

"What?"

Both men jumped at the sound as if jabbed by hot pokers. Guinevere stood in the doorway, the flowers she had been carrying spilled around her. They crushed under her feet as she crossed the room and their perfume floated through the warm air. Gawain tried to smile at her as if nothing had happened.

"Hello, Guinevere! We were just leaving—going to check on those new colts. Coming, Lancelot?" He waited.

Lancelot closed his eyes, inhaled, and opened them again. "No, Gawain, you go. I know what you have tried to do all summer, but it's time I explained the truth to Guinevere. Alone."

"Don't be an ass!" Gawain muttered.

"I will meet you later, Gawain," Lancelot spoke firmly. "This is my affair."

"That's what I'm afraid of," Gawain hissed in his face. But he saw that there would be no more discussion. There was an authority about Lancelot at that moment that intimidated him. He laid a hand on Lancelot's shoulder.

"You are my friend," he pleaded. "But Arthur is my uncle and my King. Please don't make me choose between you!"

Lancelot gave him a twisted smile. "You will never have to do that, Gawain. Now go."

Guinevere had been watching them in a state of frozen anticipation. As Gawain left, he gave her a gentle kiss in passing.

"Lancelot?" She tried to keep her voice steady, but failed. "What did you mean? I thought . . . everyone says Elaine made up the story about you and her, didn't she?"

It was amazing how calm he felt. This moment had walked with him for almost a year. He had dreaded it awake and asleep. But when he was at last faced with telling her, it became simple. He had not wanted to hurt her, but he knew she would be hurt. He took a deep breath and set about doing it as carefully as possible.

"Most of what she said was a lie. I never saw her face until I woke that morning."

Guinevere stopped fidgeting with the tassels on her belt. "Then why are you so. . . ."

"Because I was there with her all night and I think that, in the condition I was in, I may have done what she said."

The corners of her mouth trembled. "Even so," she tried to speak. "Even so, Gawain is right. It was her doing; you were not responsible. Whatever happened, it was against your will."

He held up his hands. "That is it, Guinevere! Don't you see? Gawain will not understand it. You must! If I were sure that what happened was really against my will, that I could not have resisted, then I might not feel this guilt."

That was the blow. He watched her eyes widen and her hands clench as she absorbed it. If she knew it all and hated him for it, it was just as well. But if he could make her understand. . . . All that was rational in him said he should never try. It was like walking naked into a roaring bonfire. It would deny the principles he had based his life on: frugality, temperance, and chastity. His love for her was a profligate whirlwind that swept away altruism and self-abnegation. It cut through the image of Lancelot the savior and left only the man. Whether she knew it or not, he had damned himself in his own eyes for her sake. It was too late to repent. All he wanted to know was if she would be willing to accompany him to Hell.

"Guinevere, you heard that they got me to Corbyne by saying that you were there and needed me. There is no other way I would have entered that room. Do you think that any other woman on earth but you could have lured me into bed with her?"

She stiffened with fury. "You slept with her and then blame *me* for it? You are trying to tell me you thought this Elaine was me? I have heard that she is small and dark and rather plump! Do I look like that to you? And what ever gave you the idea I might want to lure you anywhere? Have I ever done anything that would suggest to you that I would ride three hundred miles alone and feed you love potions to get you into my bed?"

"No, Guinevere," he answered. "You would not have needed to." Suddenly he realized what her anger meant, and his face lit with joy. "But I wanted to believe it. Would you have?"

His smile undid her. All the fight and anger went out of her. She looked up at him, blinking away tears of bewilderment and shame. "Yes, if I had thought of it, yes, I would."

He stopped smiling as he took her in his arms. He held her tightly against his chest, his hand entwined in her hair. "Oh, Guinevere, I wish it had been you. If we had been together only that once, I might be able to endure this."

Her only answer was to lift her face to his. He bent his head, then jerked it up suddenly. There were voices at the bottom of the stairs. Arthur's seemed especially loud. Quickly he released Guinevere, who hurried to her room. At the doorway, she paused and turned back to him, trying to smile.

"Now we both must learn to endure," she whispered.

Arthur seemed unnaturally boisterous as he entered. Behind him were Cei, Cador, Constantine, and Lydia, who had just arrived. His eyes flitted from Lancelot to the closed door.

"Guinevere!" he called. "Bring out that wine from Marseilles that your father gave us. We have to toast Cei and Lydia. The chapel was finished today."

The door opened and Guinevere rushed out to embrace Lydia warmly. "You sent no word. How did you know the right day to be here? When will the wedding be?"

"As soon as the bishops get here," Cei said firmly, "and not a day later. The bishop of York will consecrate the chapel and ten minutes later the bishop of London will marry us."

Cador laughed. "I never thought I would see a man so eager to join my family. It must be your doing, Lydia."

Arthur joined in the teasing. "It is amazing how he has changed since he met her. I can remember when he was interested in nothing but horses and fighting. Now he is the only person in all of Britain I would trust to manage both Caerleon and Camelot and the only man who could. I certainly hope Lydia doesn't distract him too much from that work or I may have to forbid the marriage for the good of Britain."

Cei bowed to him in mock subservience. "You try it and you'll rule this country with a broken jaw." He smiled.

"None of that, darling," Lydia insisted. "I want to get along with your family and it won't help if you start by beating up your milk-brother on my account."

Cei sighed and ruefully opened his fist. "You see, we may as well have the ceremony soon. I'm a married man already."

Lancelot excused himself in the laughter that followed. Gawain was waiting for him at the bottom of the stairs. His relief in seeing him was clear.

"I tried to think of a way to warn you. I hoped you would hear them. Did you?"

"They were hard to ignore. From the way Arthur was shouting, I guess they must have started on the wine in the Hall and only later decided to move on to something better."

Gawain looked puzzled. "Really? He seemed sober enough to me. Well? What did you tell her?"

"Everything."

"Wonderful. You couldn't have forgotten anything, could you? What did she say?"

"She was angry at first, but I don't think she is anymore."

They were walking across the courtyard in the bright sunlight. Gawain whistled and hit his forehead with vexation. He recoiled quickly. In his annoyance he had forgotten his own strength.

"I don't want you to even hint to me how you convinced her. So. What are you going to do now?"

"Nothing."

"Nothing at all?" His skepticism was evident. "If that is true, Lancelot, and I hope it is, you've got more love of self-torture than any ascetic in Ireland."

"Look, Guinevere, my hands are shaking!" Lydia exclaimed. "Do you think I can get them steady enough for Cei to put the ring on?"

"I could give you a bit of mead to calm you down," Risa offered as she helped arrange the layers of silk in Lydia's wedding gown.

"Don't you dare!" Guinevere admonished. "A bit of mead on an empty stomach and she'll go to the chapel singing her own prothalamion. I don't know why you're so nervous, Lydia. It isn't as if you were marrying a stranger."

"I'm not nervous! Not about Cei, anyway. It's all this ceremony. Risa, does that have to be so long in the back? If I turn around, I'm going to get wound up in it and trip myself."

"Don't worry. I'll be right behind you to smooth it out before you enter the chapel."

"You're lucky, Lydia," Guinevere offered. "When Arthur and I were married, the procession went from where I was staying to the church, to the house where we spent our wedding night. It was the middle of winter and it seemed miles to walk in those thin silks. It didn't snow, but I was freezing. My teeth were chattering so, it's a wonder I could make the responses."

"You froze, but I may suffocate. That veil is so thick I can hardly breathe through it, let alone see."

Guinevere draped it over Lydia's head and fitted it in place with a circlet of gold. "Your father and brother won't let you fall. It's beautiful out today, just right for a wedding. It's a good omen. Everyone has worked hard to make it perfect for you. Even Merlin came out of his fog to do something. He was messing about with the windows of the chapel most of last night, but he won't tell anyone, even Arthur, why."

There was a knock at the door. "Lydia, are you ready?" It was her father.

Guinevere let him in. In honor of the day, he had put on the ancient Roman officer's armor and helmet. They had been polished until they blazed in the sunlight. Lancelot had lent him a plume to complete the picture.

"I have to go now, dear, and take my place at the chapel." Guinevere kissed her through the veil. "Don't worry. You are exquisite. Everything will go beautifully."

Lydia took her father's arm and he led her into the anteroom, where Constantine waited to escort her, too.

Cador carefully guided her down the stairs and out into the courtyard. As they stepped into the sun, he had a sudden qualm. He did not want to give her to Cei. He barely knew her, himself. It didn't seem fair that they should have spent almost her whole life apart and now, when she was finally back with him, he had to give her to another man. He wanted to hold her back so that he could share some time with his daughter before she belonged to someone else.

They were in the courtyard now and he knew it was too late to stop. Huge floral arches had been built and set up all along the pathway to the chapel and thousands of petals had been strewn beneath them so that the bride's feet need not touch the earth. The way was lined with people tossing more flowers and calling out blessings and good wishes. The flowers were soft and light where she trod, like walking through a cloud. By the time she reached the chapel door, she felt as if she had been drinking oceans of mead.

Nothing seemed real to her until she felt Cei take her hand and place the ring on it. She slipped her hand back beneath the veil and caressed the solid circle on her finger. That would not turn to moonshine at dusk. There was a long benediction and then Cei lifted the veil and kissed her. At that moment she didn't care if the whole world was watching. She wanted to shout and run and sing. But strict training prevailed and her only outward sign was a face so clearly joyful that her father had to rub his nose and eyes, muttering about the sawdust not being swept out from the building.

When they turned from the altar, Lydia gasped in amazement. Sunlight was pouring in through the window slots and, on every wall, across the people and dappling the floors, were a thousand tiny rainbows.

Arthur nudged Merlin. "You must have worked on that all night. Everyone will think it was magic."

Merlin dusted his fingers together. "It's not bad. I thought it might make a nice swan song."

Arthur did not hear him. The singers had started the epithalamium and the procession was leaving. Cei and Lydia were led to the room prepared for them. After the obligatory speeches and jokes, they were left alone. For everyone else, there was a feast, a riotous celebration in the courtyard that lasted until well past dawn the next day.

The sky was turning gray when Arthur and Guinevere finally staggered to their rooms.

"I'm glad Cei got her," Arthur observed as he undressed. "He's spent too many years always doing second best. Even when we were boys, people gave me more than they did him. And, apart from rubbing my face in the dirt occasionally, he never complained."

"That's nice," Guinevere mumbled from the pillows.

"It didn't seem to hurt them to wait a year," Arthur continued. "I sometimes think we might have been too quick to get married. You didn't really know me well, did you? I've always had to spend most of each year away from you. I won't be needing to do that anymore. We're young yet, Guinevere. Maybe we could—"

He was interrupted by a sonorous snore. Guinevere had succumbed to the alcohol and the hour and hadn't heard a thing. Arthur lay down beside her with a feeling of despair.

"No," he thought. "I don't suppose we could."

The next morning the packing began for the annual trek back to Caerleon. Arthur had volunteered Agravaine, Torres,

Cheldric, and Bedevere to do the work Cei usually did. It took all four of them to do it, plus Lancelot and Gawain helping Briacu. Guinevere had no more chances to discuss anything with Lancelot. She barely saw him in all the confusion. When they met, he treated her politely, spoke the same worn greetings. Yet it was different.

Those five minutes in the tower had altered her forever, but for a long time she refused to examine why. He loved her. She had always known that. To be loved was nothing new. Even knowing that he wanted her was nothing shocking. She had seen lust in men's eyes before. What was it in that flash of time that had changed everything?

It came to her one day as she sat alone in her empty room, waiting for Arthur to finish giving orders so they could leave. She was looking at her hands, idly thinking that she must get some cream from Risa to soften their sunburnt roughness. It would be terrible if Lancelot felt they were too harsh against his skin.

Lancelot.

It was like an unexpected brilliant flash of light, showing her all the shapes and corners once decently shadowed. She did not want to look. But it was etched there before her. She loved him. She wanted him with her now and forever. She needed him to be with her and touch her and to hold him as she had never needed anyone before.

Just as she was beginning to absorb this frightening revelation, came another one which caused her to blush from the soles of her feet to her hairline. This was not her private discovery. She covered her face, remembering.

"I told him," she whispered. "I never even thought to deny it. Oh my Lord, what must he think?"

"Guinevere." Arthur was worried and rushed. He did not notice her confusion. "Merlin is gone. I can't find him anywhere. Are you ready to go?"

"Yes, all the other bags have been sent down. Merlin probably decided to travel by himself again. Don't worry. He'll be waiting for you at Caerleon."

"No, he never leaves without telling me. And almost all of his things are here."

"Really?" She wasn't terribly interested. Merlin had never been one of her favorite people.

"Guinevere, something is wrong, I know it. He's been acting odd all year, telling me not to depend on him anymore, forcing me to make my own decisions. I think I should send out a search party."

"What for? They can't find Merlin if he doesn't want them to."

"But he may be ill. I should have paid more attention to him. Guinevere, I'm afraid he may have gone off somewhere to die."

"Someone like Merlin? Why would he want to do that?"

Arthur ran his hands through his hair. "Perhaps he had no choice. What other explanation could there be? He took no clothes nor coin, not even a cup. Everything of his is in his room, except his prisms."

"His what?"

"You know. Those pieces of glass he uses to make rainbows with."

Gawain and Torres had gone to the town below Camelot, asking for news of Merlin, but they reported that no one had seen him. Lancelot overheard and offered to try to track him.

"If he left this morning, there may still be some trace for me to follow. If I find him, Clades is strong enough to carry us both to you at Caerleon."

In his mind's eye, Arthur saw Merlin's face: worn, graying, tired beyond belief from juggling men's lives. Then he remembered it again, patterned by the rainbows in the chapel. It might have been a trick of the colors, but he seemed almost young again. He had watched the dancing bands of light with an expression of hope Arthur had never seen in him before. And the rainbows had gone with him.

"No, Lancelot. Thank you, but I don't think he wants us to find him." Arthur sighed. Now Merlin. They kept slipping away from him. Soon who would he have left that he could really talk to?

"Arthur?" Lancelot's hand was on his shoulder. "Are you all right?"

For a moment, Arthur was afraid to look into Lancelot's

face, fearing to uncover hidden deceit. But he saw only concern. Not yet.

"Yes, I'm all right. It's getting late. We must start out. Ride with me, Lancelot. We have a long journey before us and I need a friend beside me."

It had taken Merlin most of the year to discover the magic in the ring. He had found it almost by accident when, late one night, he had nearly fallen into a dark passage suddenly opening before him. The ring blazed in the cold vacuum and, gasping, he fell back. The light faded as the doorway vanished. His heart pounded in terror. Was that what they must step into? There had been nothing at all there. It was as if he had stood on the edge of the universe.

But Nimuë had sent him the ring.

It took some time before he discovered how to make the door appear. He made himself stand steadily before it as the searching winds of eternity billowed toward him, trying to pull him in. He peered into the blackness, begging for a speck, a spark of light. How could he force himself to leap blindly into the dark? He struggled with it, wrestling day and night until people were nothing but shadows in his path. He had spent his life in making dark visions clear, in weaving all the threads into patterns that would lead to Arthur. If only he could find the thread in this, only one place to see, to touch, to grasp in his human hand.

There was none. Slowly it came to Merlin that he must pass into that void on nothing but faith and love. He packed his rainbows and left to find his fate.

The rain was falling on the Lake in steady, individual spheres. When the ring brought Merlin to it, he sat on the edge of it, heedless of the wet, and waited for Nimuë.

After a long time, the waters separated as if cut by the prow of a ship. In the parting Nimuë appeared. She ran across the Lake's brindled surface to meet him.

"You found it," she wept as they embraced. "I could not make it work, but the Lady always said it was a key to other worlds. You have not come to tell me that you failed?"

He tried to ignore his own tears as he held her. She was clad in only a rough tunic of coarse wool. It did not repel the water as her other clothes had.

"I stole it from the house where Lancelot stayed," she admitted. "I cannot take anything with me that belongs to the Lady. I am already stealing myself and that may be more than she will allow. Do you still want me?"

"More than ever," he answered. "But before you decide, you must see where it is that we must go."

He stretched out his arm with the ring and the blackness rose before them. Nimuë clutched at him lest she fall.

"What is it?" she screamed.

"The borders of doom, for all I can tell," he shouted back above the wind's roar. "If we enter this, we may simply fall into infinity and never land. Or it may be an illusion or a passageway. There is only one way we will know. Would you prefer to return to the Lake?"

She stared into the emptiness with round, childlike eyes. Then she took his hands.

"If you will hold me as we fall, even eternity will be not long enough."

Merlin took a firmer grip on her hands and smiled. Then his face clouded.

"Nimuë! It's Arthur! I forgot to tell him. I should have warned him about Modred! . . . And Lancelot! How could I have forgotten? Nimuë, what can I do?"

She tightened her hold. "You can leave me now and go back. Or . . . you can let them go from you."

Duty and a sense of destiny had nipped at his heels all his life, never letting him rest. He shook his head. It was time to send them away to torment some other poor visionary.

"I imagine," he admitted, "that the stars will manage to rise and set without my help. And Arthur will manage, too. Shall we now find out what is at the end of the dark?"

Together they stood in the doorway and allowed the winds to pull them through and into the vortex. Merlin could see and hear nothing, not even the wind, and only the touch of Nimuë's hands kept him from screaming.

There was no time or place as they whirled down. They were hypnotized by motion and silence. Merlin was so lulled that he felt no sense of surprise when they finally stopped in their descent. The forces that tried to wrench him from Nimuë slowly abated, and she moved closer into his arms.

Was it the winds beginning again that he heard or was it . . . cheering? It sounded like a huge crowd of people, all laughing and talking at once and, over it, someone calling his name!

With no warning, the light returned.

Merlin choked. "I have gone totally mad. Nimuë, look around you, tell me where we are."

She gazed around. "It seems to be a large field near a forest. There are hills in the distance and a small stream running nearby. Beyond it there are so many people! Are we imagining them?"

"We must be. We can't be here. This is the road to my cousin Guenlian's home."

"Merlin! Over here!" the voice called again. "Welcome home!"

He knew who it was. He shaded his eyes and saw the speaker. "You died," he said. "I saw your body."

There stood Geraldus, ten years younger at least. Strangers dressed in a myriad of fashions were gathered around him, and a naked, brown child clung to his legs. Geraldus laughed.

"No, Merlin," he replied. "I finally began to live. Come. Join us."

He reached out his hands to them, and, like joyful children, Nimuë and Merlin crossed the water to begin their lives.

Chapter Twenty-one

There was nothing that Caerleon in winter loved more than a thick, meaty piece of gossip. It was a sure and certain cure for boredom and the nerves brought on by close quarters. At the end of November some news came that guaranteed excitement enough to keep tongues exercised until spring. Morgause, sister to the King, and, some said, a sorceress of rare talent, was coming to keep Christmas with Arthur. Even better, she was bringing with her that Elaine who claimed to have borne a child by Sir Lancelot. The final added spice was that Elaine was bringing the baby. Arthur had often said that he would like to clear out the theater at Verulamium, which had become a garbage midden, and stage the old plays. But until he got around to it, the arrival of Morgause and Elaine would do for drama.

The day of the great arrival, Guinevere woke up with a fever and chills. Her head felt swathed in linen and she could not stop shivering. Arthur was torn between frantic concern for her and the necessity of having everything ready for his sister. He sat on the edge of the bed, his hand clutching hers, and debated what to do.

Risa gently drew him away. "You mustn't worry, my Lord. I know how to care for her. This is a very mild case. I'll give her a posset and let her sleep. She'll be fine by tomorrow."

Still Arthur watched his wife, tossing and murmuring, unaware of him. "I've never seen her ill before. She has always been untouched by any weakness."

Risa was trying to hurry him. She was afraid of what Guinevere might say at this stage of the fever.

"You weren't with us those three years at Cador, my Lord. She spent most of each winter like this. It flares up from time to time. It's nothing for you to bother about. She won't like it, knowing you've seen her looking so."

Grudgingly, Arthur left. Risa sat down, her knees weak with relief. Twice already Guinevere had called out and it was not for Arthur.

Half of Arthur's mind was up in the tower that day, worrying. The other was waiting impatiently for Morgause. He gave a fleeting thought to Merlin, wondering where he had gone and wishing that he had stayed. Would he have known how to deal with that woman?

They arrived shortly after the midday meal. The tables had been cleared but not put away and most people had settled into the afternoon activities. When the guard called out that he saw her, Arthur decided not to go out to meet her. He waited for her to be brought to him and properly announced. He felt a strong need to remind her that he was not just her bastard brother but the King.

The room was silent with anticipation as she entered, as if the air had suddenly been drawn from it. Torres' jaw dropped when he saw her. He knew Morgause must be at least ten years older than Arthur, but she looked fifteen younger. Where was the powerful witch that Gawain, even Gawain, feared so? Morgause was tiny, almost frail, with big, dark, trusting eyes. Those eyes roved about the room, sliding over Torres as if he did not exist. He came to with a shock. God! To think he could have been taken in by a pose after being raised under the Lake! This was a woman he would not wish to cross! He mentally apologized to Gawain.

Morgause stood in the center of the room, her guards beside her, and Elaine, with Galahad in her arms, trailing behind. She waited in absolute stillness to be announced and for Arthur to rise and greet her. There were several men at the high table, but she knew him at once.

"Yes," she gloated. "He is Uther's scum, no one could doubt it. He has the same air, the same arrogant tilt to his head. Not quite as dissipated, but that will come. Perhaps I can hasten it a bit."

As Arthur stood, he felt her gaze riveted on him and a great weariness seized him. His hand grasped the back of his chair. His head spun.

"I must be catching Guinevere's ague," he thought in alarm. Involuntarily, he glanced up toward her rooms, as if his thoughts could pass through the walls to her. The dizziness passed.

"Welcome, sister." He held out his hands to her. "It is to my sorrow that we have lived so long unknown to each other. I welcome you to Caerleon with great gladness."

Morgause bowed. "It is I who am to blame for not coming to you sooner. If you are King of all Britain, then I am your subject and owe you my allegiance."

Arthur ignored her qualification as he came to her and led her to a place of honor at his side. The guards took their places at the table behind her and that left Elaine exposed to the eager inspection of the court. She clutched her child to her in a gesture that seemed to be more for her protection than his. She was small and dark and pretty in a garden-violet sort of way. More than one heart felt pity for her, so clearly lost and frightened. Morgause seated herself, accepted some wine, and then seemed to remember the girl.

"Oh, yes," she said as calmly as if continuing an older conversation, "I wrote to you about Elaine, but received no satisfactory answer. So, I brought her with me. We should settle this soon. Elaine, give Arthur the baby."

Holding the baby even more tightly, Elaine crept forward.

"He is not going to hurt it, my dear. Just show him," Morgause coaxed. She added to Arthur, "We want you to see how much he resembles his father. There really should be no doubt about it, especially under the circumstances. Poor Elaine has been much wronged. Look at them both. Then I want you to see that your Sir Lancelot legally recognizes his son."

Cups were set down carefully and whining children hushed as Arthur took the bundle into his arms. Before looking at it, he gestured for Lancelot to stand beside him.

Lancelot held out his arms. "I will hold him, Arthur, so that you may see us together and judge."

"It won't make any difference," Arthur muttered. "No child that age can name his sire." But he gave Lancelot the baby.

Gingerly Lancelot lifted the blanket from over Galahad's face. Being moved from arm to arm had caused him to stir and he yawned mightily and woke. He stared in solemn wisdom at Lancelot for a full minute while the hall held its collective breath and then Galahad opened his mouth and gave a resonant belch.

Lancelot broke into laughter and everyone else joined him. Her cheeks flaming, Elaine rushed to take him back.

"He fell asleep as I fed him," she explained, "and he usually needs to —"

Lancelot gave her a hard stare that stopped her chatter. He looked from her to the baby and back again. Then he shook his head.

"How could this wonder have come from such as you?" he said in disgust.

She recoiled as if struck and snatched Galahad away. Morgause's face had shown no emotion during the episode. She turned to Lancelot.

"Do you deny the child, sir?" she asked.

The laughter halted. Gawain leaned forward. Couldn't someone keep Lancelot from speaking? "Don't!" he pleaded silently.

Lancelot drew himself up. "I do not deny him, Lady." He spoke so firmly that even Morgause was astonished and somewhat daunted. "But I do deny that woman. You and she bewitched me and I will not acknowledge her. You say this is my son. Then give him to me. I will see that he is raised far away from your evil."

Morgause rose in her chair, ready to fly at Lancelot. Her nails seemed to grow longer as they reached for his face. Lancelot watched her without interest. As she lunged at him, he caught her and spun her around, into the arms of Agravaine and Gareth.

"There, Aunt Morgause," Agravaine soothed. "You're in

Arthur's court now. Please don't embarrass the family here. Gareth, perhaps our aunt would like to go to her room. The journey was a long one and she must be tired."

Gareth took her arm with a frightened smile. Morgause swore under her breath at them, but allowed herself to be escorted away. Elaine and the guards, who hadn't moved at all, went after them. Quickly the hall emptied as people decided to take their discussions of the matter elsewhere. When they had gone, Arthur exhaled in relief and motioned Lancelot to sit beside him. He poured himself some more wine.

"Do you really think the boy is yours?"

"Yes." Lancelot could not get over his amazement. "He has my chin, I think."

"The cleft is unmistakable. But that is not proof."

"There is more. I was afraid to look at him at first; I could not stand to see my features blended with that woman's. But, Arthur, he shows no sign of her. Do you think it could be possible? It might be her punishment. God would not let a child suffer for its mother's wickedness."

"I don't know, Lancelot. Theology is beyond me. You could ask the bishop when you see him again. It doesn't sound likely."

"I want to get him away from Morgause. How can I do that?"

"I could offer to take him on as a fosterling, but not for some time yet. He is not even weaned. I take it you will not marry Elaine."

Lancelot pounded his fist on the table. "Never. That's what they want. Would you foster him?"

"Gladly, if Guinevere doesn't object. Do you want me to ask her?"

Their eyes met for a moment and Lancelot's dropped.

"Thank you, Arthur. But Galahad is my son. I will have to ask her myself."

"Wait, then. She is not well now. You know how this will hurt her?"

"Arthur?" He could not read the King's face. "Yes, I know. I will be very careful of her."

"I expect you to be. She is my wife and I love her."

When Arthur had gone, Lancelot eased himself onto a bench. His knees were shaking. Had Arthur just told him to stay away from Guinevere or given him permission to be near her? What had he said? He pondered it all afternoon before he was forced to conclude that Arthur had simply told him that the decision was his own. He was not to hurt Guinevere, but how was he to keep from hurting Arthur?

Contrary to Risa's prediction, Guinevere did not recover at once. Her fever left soon, but she stayed in bed. Risa, who had to bring her meals and untangle her hair, soon grew tired of it.

"Are you going to keep Christmas from your bedroom?" she demanded one day. "You mean to hide in here until the woman and her baby are gone, don't you?"

"Don't be silly," Guinevere snapped. "Can't you see that I'm sick?"

Risa had long since abandoned any pretense of servile behavior with her mistress. They had been together too long for that.

"I see it very well and you won't get any better until you face up to it. Lancelot has claimed the child, not the mother. She means nothing to him. And it shouldn't matter to you in any case. How do you think Arthur feels? He's had to eat all of his meals with that awful sister of his. It's time for you to stop this moping and think about him for a change."

"Risa!" Guinevere screamed, throwing a cushion at her. "Get out of here! Leave me alone! Don't come back until I send for you!"

By herself, Guinevere wept into her pillow and admitted that Risa was right. She could not face Elaine, who had at least had Lancelot, however she had got him. But most of all, she did not want to see the child. They didn't understand. It was not just that Lancelot had fathered him—although that didn't make the situation any easier—but that he had done so without even trying, without even a modicum of love or caring. She could not bear it: the pity, the stares, the renewed whispers. She yanked the pillow over her head. She was being a coward. What must Arthur be feeling? Everyone, it seemed, had a son but them. What was wrong? If neither love nor perseverance nor honesty were needed to produce off-spring, why had this been denied them?

Finally, she got up and dressed. She had to be sure. Perhaps Arthur had been right the first time and this infant was the product of a liaison of Elaine's that had nothing to do with Lancelot. It was nothing but a hoax. The sun was almost gone for the day and everyone would be in the hall eating. Arthur had wanted to put Morgause and Elaine far from them, but the only rooms appropriate to their station were beneath hers. This was the only time she might get in unseen. She had to try.

At the top of the stairs she waited while the nurse spoke a minute with one of the serving women.

"He's sleeping at last, poor love. I must have walked that room for hours. Teething again, you know. He's quite worn out now. I'm going to get myself a bite. Coming along?"

Guinevere held her breath as the two women gossiped down the hall. Then she silently slipped into the room.

In the center, elevated like an altar, stood the crib. There was no sound from within it. Was the baby there at all? Guinevere panicked. Was he dead? She forgot her hesitation and rushed over to be sure that the child still breathed. The blanket had slipped over his face, so that only the tip of a finger and a wisp of golden hair shone in the lamplight. She stopped cold, both wanting and fearing to lift the cover. At last her hand inched toward him. Her fingers were hovering above his head when he suddenly jerked in his sleep, his arms flailing in powerless self-defense. His eyes opened wide and he stared at her in uncaring wonder. Guinevere fought the sob in her throat.

"Oh my Lord," she whispered. A terrible ache filled her soul. "He has Lancelot's own eyes, his chin! It must be; it is his son."

She wanted to hate this monster, this intrusion, this flaunt-ing of her emptiness. She wanted to throw him from her. She leaned above him. But he was beautiful, radiant, a golden star blazing at noon. Every irrational part of her begged her to take him in her arms. She bent closer and breathlessly stroked his cheek. It was silky and warm. She waited in fear. He would shriek at her, a stranger. They would hear him and find her there. They might accuse her of trying to hurt him or, even worse, divine her reason for being with him and pity her. But she could not stop herself. With infinite gentleness she gathered him up against her body and pressed her lips to the hollow of his neck. She startled him and he stiffened. She very softly kissed the tip of his tiny nose. A length of her hair fell across his face and he laughed and pulled at it in delight. His tugging reached to her heart as something inside her crumpled and she began to cry hopelessly and steadily.

"You are nothing of Elaine," she told him fiercely. "Nothing. She may have carried you, borne you. But there is no part of her in your soul. Her dark, weak, sallow body was a clay pot, unfit to hold you. You are my child, Lancelot's and mine. It was his love for me that conceived you. You have my hair, my skin, and I claim you for my own. However long that woman keeps you, she may never mark your sunlit spirit. Oh, Galahad! You must come to love me, for I am truly your mother!"

Her tears streamed down. Galahad loosed his hold on the tress and reached up to explore the drops falling from her face to his. He grimaced at the bitter taste and tried to brush them away. His fingernail scratched the skin beneath her eye and she flinched in pain. That frightened him. His face screwed up and his mouth opened wide as he began to wail.

Guinevere was terror-stricken. She had to get away before someone came. But what if something were wrong with him? Had she hurt him? He must never be hurt. With a convulsive wrench, she drew the baby from her and, holding him at arm's length, carefully set him back in the crib. His cries were reaching a crescendo as she fled from the room. She had barely reached her own door before she heard quick steps coming in answer to the cries.

She pressed her cheek against her door and waited until she heard the noise stop, to be replaced by the clucking inanities of the nurse. Then, shaken and numb, she collapsed onto her bed and sobbed until nothing remained in her but a parched, aching darkness.

She knew when Arthur came in, when Risa was called to bring cool, damp cloths to wipe her face and hands. But she didn't open her eyes. In the morning she would face it, think it out, make a decision. For tonight she wanted to lie close to Arthur, knowing that, with all the distance between them, this was one grief which only he could share.

Agravaine had been watching his aunt's behavior with increasing consternation. During Guinevere's illness, she had almost usurped her role at court. Morgause could be delightfully charming when it pleased her and there was no question that she was beautiful. She already had a cortege of knights who stumbled over each other to serve her. What was she trying to do? It worried him enough that, for the first time since they had joined Arthur's service, he called his brothers together for a family meeting. In the old days he and Gawain had made the decisions and then informed "the young ones," Gaheris, Gareth, and later Modred, of what they would do. It was hard for Agravaine to remember that the "young ones" were grown now and not obliged to listen to him. Well, he would have to find a way to make them listen. In this matter they had to present a united front.

When they had gathered, Gawain sitting on the windowsill and Gareth and Gaheris side by side on cushions on the floor, Agravaine rose, cleared his throat a few times and, at signs of impatience from his brothers, began.

"I have called you all here on a very serious matter which I feel we must discuss thoroughly."

Gareth shifted on his cushion. "Aunt Morgause is up to something and you think we should do something about it. Can't you get to the point? I have a lady waiting for me."

There was a burst of laughter from Gawain. "You! If you do, I'll bet it's only because she wants you to take a note to Modred."

"What would you know about it?" Gareth bristled. "The last time a woman sent you a note, you were too sleepy to read it!"

Gawain flushed angrily and started toward his brother. Gareth had been asking for a lesson lately. Agravaine intervened.

"Stop it, Gawain. We're not in the nursery anymore. Damn it, man! This is serious."

Gaheris had been leaning against the wall, eyes closed. Now he sat up.

"It is serious. Morgause has always hated Arthur. We all know that. Why is she staying so long and being so nice to him?"

They all stared at him. It was the longest speech they had ever heard him make.

"Right. That is the question." Agravaine was trying to regain control of the meeting. "May I presume that none of us shares her feelings?"

"Of course we don't, Agravaine," Gawain sighed. "Don't be so pompous."

"What about Modred?" Gareth interjected.

"He isn't here." Agravaine ground his teeth. "Does anyone want to send for him?"

No one did.

"All right, then. The question is, what do we do about Aunt Morgause? Someday we are going to be asked to take sides in this. I know we have all sworn loyalty to Arthur, but—"

"But what if we have to choose between hurting him or Mother?" Gaheris finished.

"I don't want to hurt either of them," Gareth said plaintively. "Can't we just stay neutral?"

Gawain pounded his hand into his fist carefully. "No, we can't, Gareth. We know too much of what might happen. We've all seen Aunt Morgause in action."

They shuddered in unison.

"I agree." Agravaine gave a curt nod. "We have to let Arthur know that we are on his side and we ought to prove it by finding out what our dear aunt's plans are before she unleashes them."

Gareth shook his head. "I suppose you are right. But I would just as soon Aunt Morgause never found out about us."

"You don't still think she can turn you into a toad, do you?" Gawain sneered.

Gareth shrugged. "I don't want to put it to the test, that's all."

Gawain turned to Agravaine. "I told you we shouldn't have included them in this. They're too young."

Gaheris spoke up again. "I wish you would stop referring to Gareth and me as 'them.' I have an opinion, too."

"Well, Gaheris," Agravaine asked, "what is it?"

"I think we have no choice but to stay with Arthur and fight for him if we must. Aunt Morgause and Mother want to do more than hurt Arthur. They mean to destroy him."

All four were silent then, trying to gauge how deep an ancient hatred might reach. In their hearts they were forced to admit that Gaheris spoke the truth. They had always known it.

Gawain spoke for them all. "If I must decide where my allegiance lies, even if it means thwarting Mother, I choose to stand with Arthur."

They made a pact to do so, swearing as they had done when children. No one hesitated, but Gareth took his oath quickly, glancing over his shoulder at the closed door behind them as if expecting to be discovered and punished.

Guinevere was able to come downstairs again for the Christmas observance and the midwinter festival that went with it. Arthur and Lancelot seemed to have an unspoken pact to protect her from Elaine, although neither one could have said why they thought she needed protection. If anything, Elaine was the one being attacked—not by Guinevere, who simply acted as if she did not exist, but by the court, a fickle audience at best. Guinevere's reputation for goodness was restored by her obviously wholehearted willingness to take the child Galahad as a fosterling. It was better than what Elaine deserved, they all agreed.

Elaine did not see it that way. When told of Arthur's generous offer, she cried and wailed and took to carrying Galahad with her everywhere, as if afraid he would be snatched away from her if she should put him down. She pleaded with Morgause to take her home.

"Haven't you any spine at all?" Morgause scolded. "Are you going to let them chase you away? I said we would stay until after Christmas and we shall. If you will stop sniffling and cooperate, I might think of a way to get Lancelot to come back with us."

Elaine's eyes lit up. "Oh, my Lady, are you sure? I will do anything you say. Do you hear that, Galahad? Your father is going to come home with us!"

At Caerleon, where there were dozens of tiny rooms created by the legions for some forgotten purpose, it was easy to have a place of one's own. Lancelot had a cubicle tucked against one of the long passageways from the council hall to the main living quarters. He enjoyed having the place, however small. Here he could continue his private devotions without embarrassing anyone. He could pace all night, wrangling with his conscience, and bother no one.

It was early Christmas morning when he came to bed, having fasted and watched until midnight. The long, quiet hours had left him calm and chastened, able to see his suffering in perspective. He felt more at peace with himself than he ever had. The hour was so late that he did not bother to light a candle in his room. He dropped off his long robe and unbelted his tunic. Then he sat down on the bed to pull off his boots.

There was a yelp and the bed moved under him. He was caught off balance and thudded to the floor, one boot half off.

"Oh, Lancelot, I'm so sorry! You sat on me! Here, let me help you. I have the bed all warm for you now."

He felt a hand under his elbow and started to get up when he realized whose it was. He wrenched the boot off, throwing Elaine back onto the bed at the same time.

"How dare you sneak into my room!" he roared in blind fury. "Get out of here! At once!"

"Lancelot, please!" she wept. "I will do anything for you. I love you!"

"Get out!"

A light shone in from the doorway.

"Lancelot?" Guinevere's voice called. "Are you all right? Arthur wants you. I thought I heard. . . ."

She looked from Lancelot standing, boot still in his hand, to Elaine lying on the bed, her arms open, waiting for him. The candle fell to the floor.

"Oh, excuse me. I thought . . . excuse me!"

"No, Guinevere." Lancelot reached out to her. "I didn't ask her here. I don't want any part of her."

"That's not true," Elaine cried hysterically. "He begged me to come. He doesn't need you! You can't have him. Lancelot! Tell her the truth."

Guinevere stood there, confused, betrayed. Lancelot could read the doubt in her eyes. He looked from her to Elaine, who was still swearing that he had brought her to his bed. In another few minutes everyone in Caerleon would be there. What could he tell them? His glance darted back and forth between them as he tried to gather his thoughts.

Guinevere was angry at him. He had lied to her, made a fool of her. She wanted to yell and scream like any fishwife who had been deceived. Why didn't he say something? He seemed to be losing contact with her, to be withdrawing from both of them.

"No!" she screamed. "You can't do that again! I won't let you go!"

She held his face still and forced him to look at her. "You mustn't leave me again, Lancelot. I believe you. I believe everything you say. You must stay sane. You can't love me if you're mad!"

His eyes focused on her. He smiled. "I have no intention of going mad, Guinevere. Not if you love me."

He took Guinevere's hands from his face and kissed them before letting go. She turned her eyes away from him.

"You are quite safe. I have never loved anyone in my life as I do you. But now you must go to Arthur."

The candle Guinevere had dropped in her haste had landed on the cold stone, flickered a few minutes, and gone out. By its last light Elaine saw Lancelot take Guinevere in his arms. She heard their whispers as they went from the room, but she no longer cared. While she thought he belonged to no one she could hope to bind him to her. Now there was nothing left but Galahad and they wanted to steal him too. She cried all night, with deep burning sobs of anguish. But no one came.

* * *

"How could you have been so clumsy!" Morgause berated Elaine. "If there had been anyone else I could have chosen for this, I never would have brought you."

"I wanted him to love me," Elaine whispered.

"That only confirms your stupidity," Morgause continued. "Never mind. You at least managed to distract them while I worked. I have found out what I wanted to know. Morgan will be very pleased with me. She never could have done it. All right, girl, stop that eternal weeping. Gather your things together. We leave today."

Arthur was relieved to hear she was departing, but he had to tell her that the snow which had fallen in the night made it almost impossible for anyone to leave.

"I really must go today," Morgause insisted. "Can't you command some of your men to clear the road for us? They have nothing better to do."

She was swathed in furs so that her face was almost completely hidden. Her arm appeared from between the pelts and gestured what she thought of Arthur's men. He fought the impulse to flatly deny her order.

"I will ask if any are willing to do it. I do not command people to do such work."

She pushed back her hood and pouted at him. "Ah, but which of your people would volunteer to help us? They have not been terribly hospitable."

Arthur thought everyone had treated her very well, some better than he would have liked. But it would still be hard to find men who would spend the day clearing snow for her benefit.

"If you must leave us today, then I will accompany you as far as Monlyth. We will see that you get that far by tonight."

Morgause thanked him profusely and went to prepare. Arthur wondered how she had managed to maneuver him into going with her, then gave up, deciding that it was worth it to be rid of her. He sent for Gawain.

"I will be taking your aunt on the first part of her journey to Cornwall," he explained. "I would like you and Lancelot to stay here with Guinevere. You both can sleep in the anteroom. Most of the other men will have to go with me to make a passage. What's the matter?"

Gawain was obviously upset. "I would rather go with you, Uncle. Gareth will stay here. Or Lancelot could come with you."

"No." Arthur was firm. "You can't work long enough in winter to be of use and Lancelot must be disassociated from Morgause and Elaine as much as possible. What's wrong? You never objected to staying with Guinevere before."

Gawain could think of no argument. He could not imagine why Arthur was doing this.

Pressing his fingers to his eyes, Arthur tried not to think of what might happen. He knew he could stand it no longer. He had to trust them now or spend the rest of his life watching them, afraid of catching them. Sometimes when he saw them together, he hurt more for their misery than for his own. "Let them have this one chance," he decided grimly. "It may be enough and then Guinevere will be mine again."

Gawain would have given anything to be able to keep watch that night. He wanted to have it out with Lancelot beforehand, but Guinevere ate with them and then suggested a game of chess with Lancelot in the anteroom. His last waking image was of the two of them on opposite sides of the board, sitting as stiff and taut as the carved pieces they moved.

They finished the game without speaking. Guinevere lost. She bade him good night and went to her room. Lancelot heard the bar drawn across the door with a mixture of relief and despair. He put out the lamp and lay down on his makeshift bed.

The room was heated only by a small brazier, but Lancelot was sweating. It was growing late. Gawain had been asleep for several hours and the rest of Caerleon seemed to have settled down for the night, too. There was only silence on the other side of the door. Guinevere was also asleep. She must be. He wanted her to be asleep. He told this to himself again. But he could not keep his eyes from the door.

The only sound was the soft sizzle as the coal burned itself to ash. Lancelot began to relax. Then he heard it, the scrape of the bar being lifted. He sat bolt upright as the door swung open. There stood Guinevere, draped in a blanket, holding a small oil lamp. The polished brass reflected the gold of her unbound hair.

Like a man in a dream that he is powerless to stop, Lancelot went to her. When the door had been barred again, she hesitated and then handed him the lamp.

"Hold it high, Lancelot. Don't blow it out."

She moved a few paces away from him, swallowed, and dropped the blanket to the floor.

"I know of your vows, Lancelot. I won't ask you to break them, but you must look at me now, because I never, never again want you to mistake another woman's body for mine."

His first reaction was one of exultation. He had known her body would not disgust him. The lamp shook in his hand.

When he made no move toward her, Guinevere's courage ebbed. She gathered up the blanket again and held out her hand for the light.

Instead of giving it to her, he set it carefully down on the table. To Guinevere, each separate movement was painfully slow. She had been so sure of him, now her breath stopped as she waited.

"Guinevere." His voice started an erratic beating in her throat. "There is no vow that could stand against my need for you now. May I stay with you the night?"

"Yes, Lancelot, oh yes!"

They touched each other, shyly at first and then more surely, with a growing sense of wonder and excitement. In the last moment before Guinevere forgot herself entirely, she felt a stab of regret for Arthur.

"This is what we never had. This is the difference—not love, but joy!"

Much later they lay together, close and warm, murmuring inarticulate sounds. Guinevere rested her head on his chest, lazily tracing the lines of his ribs with her fingers. She felt such contentment that not even the knowledge that it was almost dawn could disturb her. Suddenly Lancelot started laughing. With a shock, Guinevere realized she had never known him to laugh like that, with such effortless freedom.

"Guinevere!" he kissed her and laughed again. "I must have gone insane, after all. By all rights, I should be wallowing now in guilt and self-damnation. I should be hating myself for giving way to animal lust."

"I am not an animal," she teased.

"Oh, yes, you are," he said with triumph, "and so am I. And, God, am I glad of it. Tomorrow I may come to terms with myself, the fight may start once more. Tomorrow I will remember that I have a purpose, that I am the model for all the other knights. But now, this minute, I am only Lancelot and you are all the Heaven or earth I will ever need."

"Isn't it odd?" Guinevere mused. "I always felt somehow apart from everyone who loved me. However good they were to me, there was always something missing. They could never touch me. I will never feel that again. You are as much a part of me now as my soul. It is so good to know I will never be totally parted from you again."

He ran his hand through her hair and down her back and silently promised her that she never would.

Lancelot was in his bed by the time Gawain awoke, but he wasn't fooled. He knew that Lancelot was not asleep and probably hadn't been all night. He went over and shook him.

"So, you were going to do nothing? Arthur will be back this afternoon. If Guinevere's face glows anything like yours, he won't be able to ignore it any longer. I won't let you humiliate him in his own house."

"It's that obvious? I'm sorry, Gawain, but not for loving Guinevere. Nothing that could happen would make me sorry for that. But I will not shame Arthur. He gave us last night knowingly. Don't worry. I will not stay to hurt him further."

Gawain was skeptical. "She will let you go?"

Lancelot smiled. "Never. She will ride with me wherever I go. But I will find a way to leave Caerleon long enough for us to learn to hide what we share. Will you promise to stand by and help her?"

Gawain nodded. "Lancelot, don't think I'm judging you. I don't blame either of you for this. It's only that I'm afraid of where it might lead."

"I know, Gawain," Lancelot reassured him. "But you can rest your fears awhile. Right now it only seems to be leading me away from here. I will tell Guinevere as soon as she awakes. Give me some time. It will not be easy."

He waited until he heard her dressing and then knocked. She kissed him as if they had been separated a year. Gently he sat her down.

"You know that I can't stay here now," he told her bluntly.

"No, I don't!" She stood again, facing him. "Why not?"

"Because I love you too much."

"But you have always loved me. You never hid it. If you could stay all that time when I wouldn't even speak to you, why, by all the saints, must you go now, when I finally admit that I love you?"

Her face was nearly pressed to his. With a force greater than any he had used in battle, he wrenched his eyes away.

"What of Arthur?" he asked brokenly. "Do you not love him?"

Guinevere pulled back, puzzled. "Arthur? Of course I love him. He is my husband and my King. It is my duty to love him. But, Lancelot, it is my destiny to love you."

She did not try to touch him again, but her words seared him. "When I am with Arthur, I try to be good to him, to take care of him. It is not hard, for he is kind to me. But I feel nothing more. But when I stand beside you, I feel your heart beating out of time with mine and I long to change the rhythm of my body to make it one with yours. When you look at me, the whole earth might fall away and I would still be suspended in your eyes. You cannot go, for we have been joined in more than flesh. You would have to crack your soul asunder to tear me from you!"

"Guinevere!" he cried. "That is why I must go! Please, do not torture us any more than we can bear!"

He caught her hands roughly and pressed them to his face. She felt his tears slide between her fingers. She put her arms around him and he kissed her so fiercely that she was not sure if the salt on her lips were tears or blood.

"I must go. We would destroy ourselves, Arthur, and everything he loves. You must help me to take myself away from here!"

"I want you!" she pleaded. "I have always had what I wanted, however foolish. Why must I live without the first person who has ever had any meaning for me?"

He looked at her with those eyes that were so strangely familiar. She knew his pain to be as great as hers and the martyrdom she felt in him defeated her.

"Tell Arthur you are going, then," she said dully. "No!" She kept him away with a gesture. "If you touch me again, I will never let you go."

He went to gather his belongings. Slowly Guinevere went back to the bed. She smoothed her hand over the hollow he had left and then crawled into it, trying to hold his warmth a little longer.

That evening Lancelot told Arthur that he had decided to leave at once on a pilgrimage to Tours to pray at the shrine of St. Martin. Guinevere was able to smile and wish him a good journey. Arthur was harder to placate.

"But, Lancelot, I had counted on your wintering with us! We have so much to plan and do. You are not still worrying about Galahad, are you? I made arrangements with Morgause that he is to be sent to us on his fifth birthday. Guinevere, make him listen to reason!"

"I'm afraid that Lancelot will not listen to me if he will not obey you," Guinevere said. Her efforts to keep her voice steady made her sound cool and aloof. "But he knows that I join you in asking him to stay."

"My King . . . my friend," Lancelot began. "I would give anything to be able to remain with you, but I cannot rest here inactive. I am no good at winter games or fireside tales. And I have a great yearning to seek the answers to the mysteries of my life. Perhaps St. Martin can guide me."

Arthur agreed with a further show of regret, but he was surprised to feel a wave of relief. It would be a year or more before Lancelot returned. He would have time. They were giving him another chance.

"Go, then, may you find what you desire." He took Guinevere's hand. "We will always be ready to welcome you. It is a long journey. Try to send us word from time to time."

"Someone should go with you," Guinevere said. "Caet! He has crossed the channel before. Take him with you. Please! Then I won't worry so."

Arthur hunted mentally through his retainers. The name was familiar. "Caet? Wasn't that the boy at your father's house?"

Caet had been sitting in a corner, finishing his stew, when he heard his name mentioned. He knew it would happen one day. Guinevere could not be trusted to remember what should be kept secret. He got up, set down his bowl, and went to the King.

"You must go with him, Caet," Guinevere insisted before he had a chance to speak. "You are the only one I can trust."

"Caet?" Arthur studied him sharply. "It is. Briacu, why didn't you tell me who you were at once? He was with us, Guinevere, years ago, when I saw the vision of the Holy Mother in the forest. You saw her, too, didn't you? I don't understand. Why would you hide yourself from me?"

Caet had no answer. But he felt as if he had been stripped of his protection. He did not want to stay at Caerleon while Arthur sorted out his new self from the old. It crossed his mind that Guinevere might have intended it that way. She was still waiting for his answer.

"I am sorry to have deceived you, Arthur. I have no explanation that would make sense. If Sir Lancelot will allow me, I will be happy to go with him. I have never been to Tours, but the way is well marked. Perhaps St. Martin will also show me guidance."

"Thank you, Caet." Guinevere wanted to say more, but he would not let her.

"If you want to leave at once, Sir Lancelot, the snow has been cleared as far as Monlyth and I can be ready in half an hour."

"I am already packed. I will get the horses while you prepare, and meet you at the gate."

Guinevere steeled herself for their departure. She watched from the window as Arthur clasped both men's hands and wished them a safe journey. She would not say good-bye. He would be back, Caet would not let him be hurt. And if she grew tired of waiting, there was one night she could cling to. It was enough for now to know they had shared it.

As they prepared for bed that night, Arthur watched Guinevere pensively. He drew random shapes with his finger on the table, unable to bring himself to go to her.

Guinevere stopped braiding her hair to look at him, really look. She saw a tall, strong, handsome man who wielded immense power and yet was always gentle and loving to her. With a stab of guilt she also saw clearly, for the first time, a man bitterly tired and lonely who was too good to take what she would not offer first.

"Oh, Arthur," she wept to herself. "I didn't mean to hurt you. I didn't even know. I cannot share with you the joy Lancelot gives me, but I can at least try to give you comfort and, perhaps, a little understanding."

She left her hair undone and went to him.